Thomas Alfred Spalding

# A Life of Richard Badiley

Vice-admiral of the fleet

Thomas Alfred Spalding

**A Life of Richard Badiley**
*Vice-admiral of the fleet*

ISBN/EAN: 9783337412050

Printed in Europe, USA, Canada, Australia, Japan

Cover: Foto ©Raphael Reischuk / pixelio.de

More available books at **www.hansebooks.com**

# A LIFE OF RICHARD BADILEY

## VICE-ADMIRAL OF THE FLEET

### BY THOMAS ALFRED SPALDING

AUTHOR OF "ELIZABETHAN DEMONOLOGY," "FEDERATION AND EMPIRE," ETC.

"Admirals all, they said their say:
  The echoes are ringing still.
Admirals all, they went their way
  To the haven under the hill.
But they left us a kingdom none can take,
  The realm of the circling sea,
To be ruled by the rightful sons of Blake
  And the Rodneys yet to be."

*H. Newbolt*

WESTMINSTER
ARCHIBALD CONSTABLE AND CO
2 WHITEHALL GARDENS
1899

# Contents

# CONTENTS

# CONTENTS

Chapter I

## THE MAN AND HIS TIMES

RICHARD BADILEY makes no figure in history; his name has been forgotten. Only in manuscripts preserved amongst the State Papers, and in a few books, pamphlets, and documents in the British Museum, can any account of his doings be found. Yet in his own day he made some stir and won considerable reputation as a sea captain. The men of the Commonwealth and the Protectorate heard much of Richard Badiley. Giovanni Salvetti,[1] the Resident of the Grand Duke of Tuscany in London, who, as the story will show, had no reason to love the man, ranked him high in importance. "Admiral Badiley," he wrote, "died in London on the very day of the death of Admiral Blake at sea. Their deaths are greatly lamented by the Protector and the people, and with good reason, his Highness having in one day lost two such valiant captains."[2]

Robert Blake is a national hero; Richard Badiley is forgotten, although his name was associated with some of the triumphs of the greater commander.

[1] The son of Amerigo Salvetti. See *post*, p. 67.
[2] Despatch dated August 14/24, 1657, P. 237.

The reason for this forgetfulness may be that the enterprise in which Badiley held the chief command, and around which public interest at the time most centred, was not, in the event, successful. While Blake was establishing the naval supremacy of England in the war against the Dutch, Badiley was endeavouring to defend her interests in the Mediterranean Sea. In this attempt he was overpowered by superior force, and, after a gallant struggle, he was driven out of the Straits. The defeat was for the time so decisive that the peoples of the Mediterranean seaboard, both Christian and Turk, looked upon the English as "an undone nation."[1] The Dutch flag for a short time flew triumphantly in the Mediterranean.

The tendency of the patriotic historian is to magnify victories and to minimise defeats. Hence it is that the deeds of Richard Badiley are compressed into a paragraph or banished to a footnote.[2] The history of the Mediterranean episode of the Dutch war cannot compare in importance with that of the great duel in the Narrow Seas; but it does not deserve to be forgotten. Richard Badiley was one of the pioneers who helped to establish the naval influence of England in the Mediterranean Sea which has resulted in the making of so much

---

[1] Longland to Badiley, June 13, 1653. Cal. S.P.D., 1652–3, p. 409.

[2] Cf. Gardiner's History of the Commonwealth and Protectorate, vol. ii. pp. 140, 142, 192. There is a short sketch of Badiley's life by Professor Laughton in the Dictionary of National Biography, vol. ii. p. 388.

history.  If he had offered a less stubborn and less prolonged resistance to the overwhelming force of the enemy, the Dutch fleet would have been at liberty to return and take part in the conflict that raged along the English shores; in which case the issue of the war might have been different.

It is, therefore, worth while to rescue the story of Badiley's life from oblivion.  His doings have an historical interest; but even if this were not so, his indomitable courage and his devotion to his country deserve remembrance.

Of the early life of Richard Badiley but little can be discovered.  It is impossible to ascertain the year of his birth; but his handwriting, which is in the style of the men of Elizabeth's time, shows that he was no longer young when he entered the service of the Commonwealth.  He was appointed a captain in the Navy in February, 1648/9, not long after the execution of Charles I., and he remained in the service of the State until a few months before his death in 1657.

Before he entered the Navy he had been employed in the merchant service.  For many years—certainly between 1637 and 1645—he was captain of a small vessel called the *Advance*, with a crew of forty-four men, which traded to the Mediterranean Sea.  In those days the navigation of the Mediterranean was a perilous undertaking.  The captain who sailed thither must needs be a man of war, taking his life in his hands.  His ship was fully armed for self-defence; for even if the Spaniards or the French were not to be feared, the "Turk" was always ready to make it a prey. English sailors in those days called all the non-Christian peoples of the Mediterranean seaboard "Turks." They were the men of Barbary, Algiers, and Tunis : very formidable corsairs, whose hands were against every man. They issued from their African sea-ports and swooped down upon the shipping of all nations with rigorous impartiality. When they made a prize, they sold their unfortunate captives as slaves or held them to ransom. So daring were they that during the period of England's greatest maritime weakness, between the years 1630 and 1637, they infested our own shores and plundered the coasting vessels.

Thrice at least during his service as captain of a merchantman had Richard Badiley to measure his strength against the "Turks." In 1637, near Malta, the *Advance* encountered and beat off three of their warships. In 1640 Badiley defeated two great pirate vessels which attacked him off Cape Palos, near Cartagena; and again, in 1644, he successfully resisted the assault of three of these plunderers. These facts are gathered from the narrative of John Steele, who was mate on the *Advance* when these contests took place, and for many years after faithfully followed the fortunes of his old commander. Steele did not tell his story until 1653, and, although he may have coloured it somewhat highly, after the manner of sailors, the main incidents which he relates are doubtless true. He shall tell the story of the second encounter in his own quaint fashion :—

# THE MAN AND HIS TIMES

"In 1640 I was master's mate on the *Advance*, with Captain Richard Badiley. About Cape Paul we were laid aboard by two Turks' men-of-war, that were castles in comparison to us, and by report had at least 500 men to our 44, who, entering us, were beat back, where many were forced to leap overboard. And although many times we were fired, and burnt very much in several places, yet, God keeping up the resolution of both our commander and company, so it was (through God's assistance) that I believe never any could do more in a dispute of that nature. The commander, coming to encourage the men, would say, ' Come, gallants, let me know how it is with you now!' They would cry, fore and aft, ' We want nothing but a new place in the enemies' side, to make a new hole in.' In fine, how they[1] were baffled, that one's foremast and bowsprit were shot by the board, and the other torn so lamentably as I believe ever ship was, not being able to budge or stir, several men yet living well know, who saw many of their great platforms[2] of ordnance dismounted, and not above one man on all their middle deck with their guns, but the greatest part of their men run into the hold. And the Turks can best of all tell how they felt it."[3]

This story throws light upon Badiley's character. Cheery, robust, and resourceful, he inspired those under his command with a portion of his own

---

[1] *i.e.* the Turkish ships.

[2] *i.e.* gun-carriages.

[3] Badiley's Answer unto Captain Appleton's Remonstrance, p. 90.

vigour. A thing half done, or ill done, was hateful in his eyes. He never gave way to despair; the unforeseen difficulty only provoked greater energy of resistance. Even in his direst straits he was able to face misfortune with a quaint flash of humour which displayed his unconquerable spirit.

Badiley was a Puritan, and he served under the Commonwealth and the Protectorate; but there is no evidence that he took any active interest in the political and religious conflicts that followed the death of the King and the abolition of the Monarchy and of the House of Lords. He doubtless would have said, as Blake is reported to have said, "it is not for us (seamen) to mind State affairs, but to keep foreigners from fooling us." It was England that he served, loyally and with singleness of heart. If he suffered defeat, it was for the honour of England, not on account of his own reputation, that he bewailed it. Charles Longland, the English Agent at Leghorn, who knew Badiley well, described him as "that honest man Captain Badiley, who, like the silkworm, spun out his own bowels with the many cares and troubles that lay upon him day and night, yet ran through all with alacrity."[1] His subjection of his own interests to those of the State is apparent throughout his correspondence. At one time, when it seemed as if nothing but the speedy despatch of relief from England could save the English in the Mediterranean from utter destruction, his wife made bold to petition the Council

[1] Longland to Blackborne, Oct. 24, 1653. Cal. S.P.D., 1653-4, pp. 213, 214.

of State on his behalf. She could not understand why the Council kept so many stout ships in home waters while her husband stood in danger of his life, and she besought aid for him. Badiley, far away at Leghorn, heard from a friend of this pleading. "Although my wife, by her importunity, showed her affection," he wrote, "I wish she had left that to understanding gentlemen, as the honour of the nation was more concerned in despatching the fleet hither than a thousand particular concernments."[1]

It will be impossible to understand the character of Richard Badiley without some apprehension of the Puritan belief. The easy method of setting down the Puritan movement as the incarnation of cant will not serve, for here was a man who, hating hypocrisy, had phrases which to the modern ear sound like cant constantly upon his lips. To the Puritans God was the "Great Taskmaster," ever present and awful, who, through them, was working out His will on earth."[2] Every act of theirs, however trivial, formed part of His inscrutable plan. In victory they saw His hand, and they solemnly rejoiced. In defeat they recognised the signs of His anger, and as solemnly acquiesced. It was in many ways an invigorating creed; at any rate, to

[1] Badiley to Blackborne, Jan. 14, 1652/3. Cal. S.P.D., 1652–3, p. 105.

[2] "—That same lot, however mean or high,
    Toward which Time leads me, or the Will of Heaven;
    All is, if I have grace to use it so,
    As ever in the Great Task-Master's eye."
                —Milton, 7th Sonnet.

the vigorous mind.   It strung men up to courageous action, and it forbade them to be utterly cast down under reverses.   But, like all wholesome beliefs, it was liable to abuse.   To the sluggish man it afforded excuse for inaction.   It was so easy to say, " These calamities are the will of God, and therefore they must be borne."   It was also easy to adopt the phraseology of the creed without possessing the soul of it.   Captain Appleton, who will appear prominently in this story, was a type of the degenerate Puritan who was petrified by his profession of religion.

If, therefore, Richard Badiley is found constantly attributing events to the direct action of God, he must not on that account be set down as a hypocrite.   Such expressions are to be found frequently in the writings of the time, not only in public documents, but in private letters which were intended only for the eyes of the person to whom they were addressed.   After one of his battles, Badiley wrote thus to an acquaintance: "Thanks for your sympathy with your friends at such a distance, and praising God, by whom this squadron was miraculously preserved in our engagement with the Dutch.   He has many times been pleased to do great things by small means in our late war with the Royalists, yet I believe there was never more of God and less of man apparent in any disputes with the enemy."[1]

And that which he believed in the quiet of his cabin he believed also in the crisis of danger.   On

[1] Badiley to Blackborne, Nov. 5, 1652.   Cal. S.P.D., 1651–2, p. 477.   See the letter in full, *post*, p. 111.

the morning after the engagement to which he referred in the letter just quoted, his ships were sorely disabled, their crews were almost in revolt, and his gunpowder was nearly spent. The Dutch fleet lay to windward, preparing to renew the attack. The captains of the English merchant ships which he was commissioned to protect came to him in despair, advising him "to give up all," and fire or sink the fleet. That was not this brave sea-captain's idea of duty, while a plank of his ship remained to fight upon. "To this I replied, 'Now is God's time to work like Himself!'—and so it was. Although the sun did not stand still, yet the wind suddenly died and it fell stark calm, so that the enemy could not come near us all day."[1]

Cromwell, during the critical period before the battle of Dunbar, was enabled to effect certain defensive movements by a sudden clouding of the midnight sky. Of this good fortune he said that "the Lord, by His providence, put a cloud over the moon."[2] Badiley, in the Mediterranean, believed that the opportune dropping of the wind, which apparently saved him from capture by the enemy, was no less an intervention of the Almighty. In these days such an event would be termed a lucky accident; in the seventeenth century it was fraught with a far deeper significance.

At a subsequent date, when part of the squadron under Badiley's command was blockaded at Leghorn by the Dutch fleet, which was growing in

---

[1] See the letter in full, *post*, p. 112.

[2] Carlyle, Cromwell's Letters, No. cxl., Sept. 4, 1650.

9

number daily, and when hope of relief from England was slight, his faith never failed him. He wrote to the Navy Committee that the Dutch "give out that their State will outvie us and make their number always two to one. The arm of flesh and numbers is what most of them look to; but I hope that God will learn them another lesson ere long."[1]

There can be no doubt that Badiley's faith was sincere, and of that vivifying sort which urges to bold action. His career was adventurous and dramatic, and on that account alone it is worth recording. The story of it will display a quaint and attractive character, which, it is hoped, will justify this attempt to rescue it from the forgetfulness by which it has been hitherto shrouded.[2]

[1] Badiley to the Navy Committee, Nov. 5, 1652. Cal. S.P.D., 1651–2, p. 476.

[2] There is a pamphlet in the British Museum entitled, "Certain Queries to a printed paper intituled 'The Humble Tender and declaration of many well-affected Mariners and Seamen, Commanders of Ships and Members of the Trinity House to the Commissioners of the Navy,'" by R. Badiley, 1648 (Press Mark, E, 459 [22]). It has no historical or biographical value, and it is so dull that it gives rise to the suspicion that there must have been two Richard Badileys. M. Simmons, the printer, was also the printer of Badiley's Answer to Appleton.

## Chapter II

## THE REVOLTED SHIPS

AT the commencement of the Civil War the Parliament gained control of the fleet. Although it rendered them but little active service during the contest beyond provisioning coast towns that were besieged by the Royalists from the landward side, the fact that Charles possessed no navy was a great advantage to the Parliament. If Charles had been able to blockade the mouth of the Thames, and thus stop the trade of London, it is probable that the Civil War would not have resulted in his defeat.

Very few of these vessels had been built for the Royal Navy. In the reign of Charles I. it was deemed a considerable achievement if the dockyard at Chatham could launch one new man-of-war in every year. When danger arose, the fleet was recruited by requisitioning merchant vessels, which, being built for self-defence, were easily converted into war-ships.

The ship of those days presented a curious and somewhat ungainly appearance. It was designed for strength and resistance rather than for speed. It was consequently extremely short in proportion to its breadth of beam. The poop towered above the level of the main deck, and in front of most

men-of-war was a forecastle which afforded the last
vantage for defence if the vessel were boarded.
The masts were short and stout, and were furnished
at the cross-trees with "crow's-nests," capable of
containing six or eight men, to keep a look-out, or
to fire down upon the deck of the enemy.

A fleet of such vessels could not have kept the
seas for long had not the artillery of the period
been correspondingly ineffective. The range of
the cannon was exceedingly short, and in naval
engagements a vast amount of gunpowder was
burnt with surprisingly little result. Badiley said
that in the battle of Monte Cristo he fired from the
*Paragon*, his flagship, no less than 800 shot against
the enemy, but not a single Dutch ship was sunk.
The *Paragon* received fifty shot in her hull alone,
and yet Badiley was able to steer her safely to Porto
Longone, a distance of about forty miles.[1]

In 1647, at the end of the first Civil War, the
Parliamentary fleet numbered some thirty vessels,
under the command of Captain Batten, who was
a staunch Presbyterian. But in 1648, after the
troubled interval during which Charles was a
prisoner, and the Army and the Independents had
obtained the upper hand in Parliament, the allegiance of the fleet wavered. The second Civil War
was about to begin, in which the Presbyterians very
generally took the side of the King. The Scots,
under the Duke of Hamilton, were threatening invasion ; an insurrection had broken out in Wales,
and soon after a more formidable outbreak, under

[1] See *post*, p. 109-111.

the Earls of Norwich and Holland, flared up in Kent. At this crisis part of the fleet was riding in the Downs, commanded by Batten, whose Presbyterianism led him to sympathise with the leaders of the Kentish insurrection; the remainder was at Portsmouth. The Parliament suspected that Batten was in league with the Kentish insurgents. He was promptly relieved of his command, and Colonel Rainsborough, a strict Independent, who was trusted by the dominant party at Westminster, was appointed in his place. But the seamen were discontented, partly because they resented being placed under the command of a landsman, but more especially because their wages were in arrear. They listened willingly to the blandishments of their cashiered captain, and on May 27, taking advantage of the temporary absence of Rainsborough on shore, they revolted to Charles.

This defection was a heavy blow to the Parliament. Ten or eleven of their best ships had stolen away, leaving only about twenty at Portsmouth upon which they could rely. Batten believed that he could seduce these from their allegiance also.[1] If his plot proved successful, the Parliament would be rendered powerless at sea. Charles was to be released from Carisbrooke Castle and carried off to sea until his friends on shore had overthrown the forces of his rebellious subjects, and then he was to be restored in triumph to his throne.

[1] Historical Manuscripts Commission, 11th Report App. 6 (Hamilton Papers), p. 125. Batten's betrayer was probably the notorious Lady Carlisle.

The Parliament, having information of this design, appointed the Earl of Warwick to be Lord High Admiral, and despatched him in hot haste to Portsmouth. He succeeded in foiling Batten's attempt upon the remainder of the fleet, and the defeat of the insurgents at Maidstone rendered useless the continued presence of the revolted ships upon the coast of Kent. One or two of them, finding that the King's cause was by no means triumphing, deserted once more and returned to the service of the Parliament. The remainder, nine in number, sailed for Holland, and came to anchor off Goree.

Prince Charles left St. Germains to take command of the fleet which had so unexpectedly declared for the Royal cause. After a short delay the ships stood out to sea and cruised off the coast of Norfolk and Suffolk, endeavouring to stir up a Royalist rising in those counties, and thus to assist their friends who were making a last stand at Colchester against the Parliament's army under Fairfax. The attempt proved fruitless, and Charles sailed for the Downs.

He had already been joined by Batten, who was created a rear-admiral. After his failure at Portsmouth, Batten had lain in hiding in and about London. Great efforts had been made by the Government to arrest him, but he succeeded in eluding their emissaries. At last he managed to obtain possession of the *Constant Warwick*—a ship which will play a prominent part in Badiley's story—and he sailed with her to join the revolted ships.[1]

---

[1] Clarendon; History of the Rebellion, xi. 36.

The supplies of the revolters were running short, and Charles, seeing that his fleet was rendering no effective service to his friends on shore, desired to return to Holland. But this proposal found little favour with the sailors. Their one wish was to fight the Parliament ships; they were by no means eager to idle about the quays of a Dutch seaport. Charles was forced by their importunity to sail up the estuary of the Thames and bid defiance to the fleet of merchant ships which Warwick had hastily fitted out at London and was lying at the mouth of the Medway, before it could be reinforced by the Portsmouth squadron.

The situation was for the moment critical for the Parliament. Royalist ships, for the first time in the war, blockaded the port of London and paralysed trade. The few craft that ventured down the river were made prizes. No more effectual method of inducing the citizens of London to make terms with the King than the stoppage of trade could have been devised. On the other hand, the position of the Royalists was by no means encouraging. Their ships were victualled for a few days only, and the arrival of the fleet from Portsmouth, if perchance it was sailing for the Thames, would place them at the mercy of a superior force. In these circumstances it was decided to fight Warwick without delay. On August 30, 1648, the rival fleets were in sight of one another, and the decks of the revolted ships were cleared for action. It seemed inevitable that, for the first time in history, two English fleets would be engaged in death struggle. But before the

Royalist ships had weighed anchor the wind veered, and blew a gale which gave their opponents the weather gauge. The storm raged all the following day, and attack was impossible. The fear of starvation compelled them to hoist sail and make for Holland. On September 3, having passed the Portsmouth fleet in the night, they arrived safely at Helvoetsluys. They had achieved nothing by the expedition save the capture of a few merchant vessels.

All hope of success for the Royalist cause had at that time vanished. Cromwell had dashed the Welsh rebellion to pieces, and then, turning rapidly northward, had defeated the Scotch invaders at Preston. Three days before Charles had sailed out of the Thames, Colchester had surrendered to Fairfax. The struggle smouldered on hopelessly around isolated strongholds, under the command of a few brave men who preferred death to surrender, but there was no force in the field capable of operating effectually against the Parliamentary armies.

Not long after the departure of the revolted ships Warwick was enabled to take the offensive. On September 19, having effected a junction with the Portsmouth squadron, he lay off Helvoetsluys, blockading the Royalist fleet. Prince Charles had retired from the chief command, and had betaken himself to Jersey, busy with schemes for renewing the war against the Parliament in Ireland. Lord Willoughby of Parham, who had accompanied Charles upon his late expedition, acted as admiral for a short period, but he soon surrendered the post to Prince Rupert. Under Rupert's command the revolted ships were destined for a long time to prove a thorn in the side of the Commonwealth of England.

But the condition of that fleet was pitiful. The Royalists proved no better paymasters than the Parliament, and early in November the crews were in open mutiny. "Prince Rupert," says Clarendon, "had, with notable vigour and success, suppressed two or three mutinies, in one of which he had been compelled to throw two or three seamen overboard by the strength of his own arms."[1] The seamen were already regretting their defection from the Parliament. Three of the ships, one of them the *Constant Warwick*, "a frigate of the best account,"[2] slipped out of the harbour at Helvoetsluys and submitted to the English admiral. Batten no longer commanded the *Constant Warwick*. He had been knighted for his great services to the Royalist cause, but the man who had bombarded Queen Henrietta Maria at Bridlington could hardly be popular with the Cavaliers. It was hinted that his advice had prevented Prince Charles from destroying Warwick's fleet in the Medway. After a short and uneasy residence in Holland, he returned to England and was heard of no more.

If the Earl of Warwick had continued the blockade of Helvoetsluys, there can be but little doubt that the remainder of the revolted ships would have followed the example of the *Constant Warwick*.

[1] Clarendon ; History of the Rebellion, xi. 152.
[2] *Ib*. xi. 136.

But the Earl was either not so fully in command of the sea as to be able to secure continuous supplies, or he was only half-hearted in the task which had been entrusted to him. He abandoned the blockade, and retired with his fleet into the Downs.

Rupert was not slow to avail himself of this chance of escape. He sold or pawned the guns and fittings of certain of his ships, one of which was the *Antelope*, a vessel which not long after attracted the attention of Richard Badiley. With the money thus raised he prepared the remainder of his fleet for sea, and on January 11, 1648/9, he set sail with eight vessels. Passing the Earl of Warwick in the Downs, who, although he had received timely warning of the enemy's intention,[1] made no effort to intercept him, Rupert sailed along the south coast, and, making for Ireland, he reached the harbour of Kinsale in safety.

So far, although the revolted ships had not been able to inflict any signal defeat upon the Parliament, they had succeeded in showing its impotence. Affairs in England were in so unsettled a condition that the Parliament could not afford to be thus defied. It was necessary that the new Government should make more strenuous effort to prove to the world that it could crush its foes. On February 2[2] the House of Commons ordered that thirty ships and 2,000 men should be taken up for the service of the Navy.

The story of the revolted ships has been told in

[1] Cal. S. P. D., 1648–9, p. 337.
[2] Commons Journals, vol. vi. p. 129.

order to show the condition of naval affairs at the time when Badiley quitted the merchant service to enter the Parliament's fleet.[1]  On February 23, 1648/9, he was gazetted to the command of the *Happy Entrance*, an old ship which was certainly afloat in 1625.[2] There is no evidence to show whether he passed straight from the merchant service to the command of a man-of-war.   In one of his letters he speaks of events which happened when Warwick was before Helvoetsluys, as if he had been present when they took place.[3]   Possibly he served in Warwick's fleet in some subordinate capacity.   It must have been a hard task, when so large an addition was being made to the Navy, to find efficient captains for the ships, and Badiley's early experience of warfare, gained in his conflicts with the Turks, was a qualification which was not to be despised.   Be that as it may, from the date of his appointment to the *Happy Entrance* onward, his life was devoted, with scarce a moment's intermission, to the service of the State, until he returned home to his house in the village of Wapping, worn and spent, to die, " having spun out his bowels with the many cares and troubles that lay upon him, day and night."

[1] Cal. S.P.D., 1649–50, p. 13.

[2] Hist. Man. Comm., 12th Report, App. 1 (Coke MSS.), p. 223. Probably built in 1619.   Historical Review, x. 55.

[3] Badiley to Navy Committee, December 2, 1652.   Cal. S.P.D., 1652–3, p. 4.

# Chapter III

## PIRATES AND SEA-ROVERS

ON January 30, 1648/9, the great tragedy of the Civil War reached its catastrophe. The High Court of Justice had condemned Charles to death, and the "White King" laid his head upon the block in front of the palace at Whitehall. The Rump of the House of Commons, having abolished the Kingship and the House of Lords, addressed itself to the task of reconstructing the constitution and of saving England from the many dangers which threatened her at home and abroad.

The men who, as Badiley was fond of describing them, "sat at stern" had difficulties to face which might well have daunted the most courageous. Although all internal resistance to the Commonwealth had, for the moment, been crushed, England was begirt by enemies, open or secret. No foreign nation had as yet formally recognised the infant Republic, and the brightest hope of the exiled Royalist was that Europe would combine to restore the monarchy by force of arms.

But the possibility of invasion was not the most immediate danger with which the new Government had to cope. Although the Royalists were powerless on the mainland, they still retained their hold upon points of vantage round the coast whence they could harass and annoy their enemies. Scilly, Jersey, and the Isle of Man were all occupied by adherents of the defeated party, and nearly the whole of the south and east coasts of Ireland were in the power of the Commonwealth's foes. These places afforded havens whence privateers could swoop down upon the English merchant shipping, and whither they could retire in safety with their prey. The ships at the Scilly Islands more especially threatened the richly laden vessels returning from the Levant, and the unfortunate skipper found himself no more free from spoliation in home waters than he had been in regions dominated by the " Turk." Besides these dangers, privateers from Dunkirk pounced upon small coasting and fishing vessels and the French, although they were not openly at war with England, did not fail to snap up any small traders that chanced to fall in their way.

In order to realize the misery which this combination of foes was able to inflict, the methods by which the internal trade of England was carried on must be understood. There were in those days no canals by means of which goods could be transported from town to town, and very few of the rivers had been made navigable far inland. The roads were ill made and ill kept ; many of them were mere tracks, and most were almost impassable in the winter. The great bulk of the trade of the country was carried by small coasting vessels, which were liable to fall an easy prey to the privateer.  Every little ,seaport town, every creek and bay along the coast, was a place of traffic and commerce.

The eastern portion of England was the great grain-growing country, and the less fertile western side drew its supplies from thence.  The coal of Newcastle was carried to London by water.  There was a constant coming and going of merchant ships between Newcastle, Hull, Yarmouth, and London on the east, and Bristol, Chester, and Liverpool on the west.  The dangers which the coaster encountered were therefore manifold.  When she sailed out of her eastern port she was liable to be pounced· upon by a swift-sailing freebooter and carried off to Dunkirk.  If she escaped this fate, some prowling French or Jersey ship, bearing the King of England's letters of marque, might make a prize of her.  Further westward a swoop might be made upon her from the Scilly Islands, or she might fall into the clutches of Rupert the restless.[1]  If she survived all these perils, she might still fall into the hands of the adherents of the Earl of Derby, who, as King in Man, held sway for the King of England.[2]

The case of the fishermen was perhaps harder.  The fishing industry was in those times of great

---

[1] Rupert augmented his fleet with the prizes he took.  Salvetti : Despatch, April 2, 1649, M. 272.

[2] Cumberland was reported to be starving because Isle of Man pirates prevented the landing of provisions.  Council of State to the General at Sea, April 25, 1649.  Cal. S.P.D., 1649–50, p. 108.

importance. England exported a large amount of fish to France, Spain, and the States that bordered on the Mediterranean Sea. The fishermen plied their trade chiefly off the eastern and southern coasts, but at this period the Sea Rover was ubiquitous. The fishermen hardly dared to stir out of port, and their wives and children were clamouring for bread.[1]

These mischiefs had to be stopped if England was to continue to exist as a nation. The newly-constituted Council of State, which executed functions somewhat analogous to those of the King in Council, addressed themselves to the work with great vigour. In March, 1648/9, an order was issued to build five new frigates.[2] Such a demand upon the dockyard was unprecedented, and, moreover, the very evil which the new ships were designed to abate impeded their construction. England could not in those days produce all the materials needed for shipbuilding. The oak for the hulls was obtained by felling the grand old trees that adorned the King's forfeited estates, and sail-cloth was woven at home. But masts and spars had to be brought from Norway; tar, ropes and cordage from the Baltic; and much of the iron-work was imported from Sweden. Even the salt which was used to preserve the rations of the seamen was brought from Rochelle.[3] All the vessels which bore these precious

[1] See Cal. S.P.D., 1649–50, pp. 121, 138, 140, 165, 202, etc.

[2] Admiralty Committee to Navy Committee, April 12, 1649. Cal. S.P.D., 1649–50, p. 82.

[3] Council of State to Wybrantz, June 15, 1649. Cal. S.P.D., 1649–50, p. 186.

supplies had to run the gauntlet of the sleepless pirates and sea rovers before England could build a ship wherewith to defend herself.[1]

While these frigates were building, the Council of State was not languid in its endeavours to re-assert the power of England. It had three tasks to perform in regard to the affairs of the Navy. It was necessary to provide transports to convey Cromwell's army to Ireland ; to man a squadron powerful enough to shut up the devastating Rupert in Kinsale, and to equip ships to defend the fishermen and coasters from depredation. The Earl of Warwick, who had shown himself so little alert when Rupert dashed past him towards Ireland, was deposed from the office of Lord High Admiral, and three colonels of the Army—Popham, Blake, and Deane—were appointed "generals at sea." They held rank in the above order, but the transcendent ability of one of them soon altered the precedence. The preparations were pushed forward with great energy, but many delays occurred, which were caused chiefly by the lack of provisions and of seamen.[2] So great was the difficulty in manning the fleet, that the Council were fain to write to Dr. Hill, the Master of " Trinity House, Cambridge," asking " that such students of that Society as are willing to go in the summer fleet may not be prejudiced in their

---

[1] In April the Levant Company asked protection for their shipping in the Baltic. Salvetti: Despatch, April 16, 1649, M. 276.

[2] Cal. S.P.D., 1649–50, p. 23.

[3] Salvetti : Despatch, April 23, 1649, M. 282.

election to fellowships to be made about Michael-
mas."[1]

The convoys for the protection of coasters and
fishing-boats were speedily equipped. Four squadrons were sent to sea for this purpose. The first,
under the command of Captain Peacock, plied between Newcastle and London, keeping guard the
while over the North Sea fishery and the Hamburg
trade.[2] The second in command in this squadron
was Captain Owen Cox, subsequently Badiley's comrade in the Mediterranean troubles.

The second squadron, nominally under Popham,
but with Richard Badiley in active command, lay
in the Downs, to guard the London trade from
the south.[3] A third hovered about the Channel
Islands,[4] while a fourth kept the Scilly Islands in
check.[5] When the fleet which was preparing for
Kinsale had broken Rupert's power, it was hoped
that trade would cease to be paralysed by pirates
and sea rovers.[6]

When, in May, 1649, Popham sailed with Blake
to execute this latter project, Richard Badiley, of
the *Happy Entrance*, was appointed to the chief

---

[1] April 14, 1649. Cal. S.P.D., 1649–50, p. 86.

[2] Council of State to Capt. Owen Cox, May 28, 1649. Cal.
S.P.D., 1649–50, p. 160.

[3] Council of State to Capt. S. Howlett, May 28, 1649. *Ib.*

[4] Council of State to Capt. Reynolds, May 28, 1649. *Ib.*,
p. 161.

[5] Under Captain Hall in the *Leopard*. *Ib.*, p. 393.

[6] Council of State to Generals at Sea, May 19, 1649. *Ib.*,
p. 150.

command of the squadron in the Downs.[1] But before this date Badiley had performed some service which the records only scantily hint at. On April 21, 1649, the Council of State wrote to the generals at sea, desiring that "the persons mentioned by you as taken by Captain Bodiley[2] may be sent up hither, with examinations concerning them."[3] This entry may possibly refer to the capture of the *Guinea* frigate, on board of which Sir Hugh Windham was discovered in disguise;[4] but this cannot be verified.

It was a busy life that Badiley led during the ensuing months, sailing hither and thither to protect the coasting vessels from surprise by the enemy. A few samples of his instructions will illustrate, not only the nature of the work that he had to perform, but also the desperate condition of the trading vessels in the early days of the Commonwealth. On May 28 the Council of State wrote to Badiley: "As several vessels laden with corn, etc., bound for London, have lain seven weeks in Newhaven, Brighthelmstone, etc., in Sussex, attending a convoy, we require you to send some considerable vessel to these ports to

---

[1] Council of State to the Navy Commissioners, May 7, 1649. *Ib.*, p. 128. The first Commissioners for the Navy were John Holland, Thomas Smith, Peter Pett (the great ship-builder), Robert Thompson, and Col. W. Willoughby. *Hist.* Review, xi. 58.

[2] His name is variously spelt. I have adopted his own spelling.

[3] Council of State to the Generals at Sea, April 21, 1649. *Ib.*, p. 102.

[4] Same to same, May 7, 1649. *Ib.*, p. 129. Whitelocke heard of the capture of the Guinea frigate on May 1. *Memorials*, p. 399.

convoy them into the Thames."[1]  On June 2 he was informed that certain arms and ammunition were at Weymouth and Apsome, awaiting a convoy to London and on the same day he was ordered to provide protection for certain ships in the Thames, laden with corn, and bound for Chester, Liverpool, Wales, and Dublin.[2]

Sometimes his orders took him to a greater distance from home.  Occasionally he had to convoy as far as Rotterdam,[3] and once he was entrusted with important despatches for Walter Strickland, the English Resident with the States-General of Holland at the Hague.[4]

Before he commanded in chief in the Downs, it had fallen to his lot to convoy a vessel to Helvoetsluys.  Whilst in port he had seen the dismantled *Antelope*, which Rupert had left behind him when he made his dash for Kinsale.[5]  The sight of a Parliament ship in the hands of the enemy was grievous to Badiley, and it occurred to him that a few brave men might easily cut her out or destroy her.  He took counsel with Strickland, but that cautious politician by no means relished the project. While the Royalists in Holland were clamouring loudly for aid against the rebel Government, and the

---

[1] Council of State to Badiley, May 28, 1649.  Cal. S.P.D., 1649–50, p. 161.

[2] Council of State to Badiley, June 2, 1649.  *Ib.*, p. 171.

[3] Council of State to Peacock or Badiley, June 5, 1649.  *Ib.*, p. 175.

[4] Council of State to Badiley, May 19, 1649.  *Ib.*, p. 150.

[5] Warburton's Memoirs of Rupert, iii. 273, 281.

States-General were turning a not wholly inattentive ear to their demands, it was highly inexpedient to provoke the Dutch by any hostile act against one of their ports. Strickland had not yet obtained formal recognition of his office by the States-General, and the Parliament was about to send Dr. Isaac Dorislaus, a Dutchman born, to aid in bringing about a good understanding between the two Republics. The *Antelope*, and much more besides, might doubtless be obtained by skilful negotiation. It was the mere folly of a rash seaman to dream of imperilling such advantages for the sake of an old dismantled ship. Thus, no doubt, the "understanding gentleman" argued, and he eventually dissuaded Badiley from the attempt. Badiley returned to his post in the Downs unconvinced, and he communicated his design to the Council of State. The Council did not take Strickland's view of the case. To them the recovery or destruction of the revolted ships was a question of national honour. On April 23 they wrote as follows to the Generals at Sea : "As Captain Bodiley thinks that the *Antelope* might have been surprised or destroyed, had he not been dissuaded by Mr. Strickland, we desire you to order such as you think fit to try to seize upon and bring her away; or if that cannot be, then to burn or make her unserviceable."[1] The Generals at Sea, however, were too much preoccupied with preparations for their expedition against Kinsale to find time to execute this order, and it was not until after

[1] Council to Generals at Sea, April 23, 1649. Cal. S.P.D., 1649–50, p. 105.

they had sailed westward, and Badiley commanded in chief in the Downs, that it was obeyed.

Towards the end of June, 1649, the *Happy Entrance*, commanded by Badiley, and the *Dragon*, under Captain Young, sailed for Helvoetsluys. At dead of night, one of the ship's boats, manned by eleven sturdy seamen, under the guidance of Lieutenant Rose of the *Happy Entrance*, stole into the harbour and rowed towards the *Antelope*. Their instructions were to capture her if possible without the use of firearms, and with as little disturbance to the port as might be. Lights were shining from the port-holes of the *Antelope*, and it soon became apparent that she was being refitted and made ready for sea.[1] The assailants prepared for a struggle. They drew close to the ship's stern, clambered noiselessly up her sides, and gained the main deck. But there was no resistance; the men on board were civilians, and the *Antelope* was gained without bloodshed. Her occupants were made prisoners,[2] and then she was set on fire and destroyed.

The Council of State were not slow in recognising this service. On June 26 they instructed the Admiralty Committee " to consider what encourage-

---

[1] This is stated on the authority of Whitelocke. Memorials, p. 410. He gives the date of the assault as June 26, 1649. This is probably the day on which the news was received in London.

[2] One of them, Christopher Harris, a merchant, was subsequently discharged, " as he came accidentally " on board the *Antelope*. Warrant from Popham to Badiley, June 27, 1649. Cal. S.P.D., 1649–50, p. 214.

ment to give to Captains Badiley and Young and the men that destroyed the *Antelope*."[1] But the matter slumbered in the Admiralty Committee, and it was not until October that they reported. Then their recommendation was based, not upon the original reference, but upon a petition of Lieutenant Rose and the seamen of the *Happy Entrance*. They recommended that "for destroying the *Antelope*, Lieutenant Rose deserves a gratuity of £50, whereof forty shillings is to be in a gold medal; James Parker, a volunteer, and Thos. Tulley, corporal, £10, twenty shillings to be in a gold medal; and each of the mariners, £5."[2] Badiley and Young neither petitioned for nor received any reward for their services. In the previous May £1000 had been set apart for chains and medals to reward officers and seamen who should do eminent service at sea,[3] and this was the first occasion upon which the award was made. Moreover, the money grants were duly paid, a result which did not uniformly follow upon the generosity of the Commonwealth Government.[4]

Charles and the Royalists in Holland were loud in their complaints at the breach of neutrality which

[1] Council of State: Day's Proceedings, June 26. Cal. S.P.D., 1649–50, p. 206.

[2] Cal. S.P.D., 1649–50, p. 367. Oct. 27, 1649.

[3] Council of State: Day's Proceedings, May 8, 1649. *Ib.*, p. 130.

[4] *Ib.*, pp. 368, 590. Oct. 29, 1649. The names of the mariners who received the £5 grant were Thos. Young, Thos. Cowdery, Richard Knight, *Barthol. Ferdinando*, Jno. Mumford, Ed. Griffin, Thos. Sexton, and Robt. Bennett. Even in those days English ships were not entirely manned by Englishmen.

had been committed.   They told the States-General that it was infamous that the rebels should be permitted to destroy the King's ships in a friendly port. The Council of State evidently felt that the Dutch had just ground for dissatisfaction.   Immediately after the arrival of the news of the destruction of the *Antelope*, they sent a detailed account of the affair to Strickland, and they also informed the Dutch ambassador, laying stress on the care taken that no harm should be done to the town of Helvoetsluys.[1]   The Dutch were in no humour to risk further trouble with the English Parliament on the behalf of Charles.   On May 2 Dr. Dorislaus, who had been accredited ambassador to the States, was murdered by a party of Royalists at the Hague. The Dutch had enough to do to pacify England on this account, and they desired to avoid further complications.   So the States replied to Charles that he " had liberty to act the same upon any of the Parliament's ships in any harbour within their dominions."[2] The answer had all the appearance of the strictest impartiality, but it can hardly have proved gratifying to the Royalists, whose fleet was at that time blockaded at Kinsale.

The year wore on, and Badiley was still busily employed in convoy work, with the exception of one short period, during which the *Happy Entrance* was docked and careened.[3]   Meanwhile the western fleet

---

[1] Council of State : Day's Proceedings, June 26, 1649. *Ib.*, pp. 206, 208.

[2] Whitelocke, Memorials, p. 412.

[3] Popham to the Navy Commissioners, Oct. 28, 1649. Cal. S.P.D., 1649–50, p. 367.

was holding Rupert fast prisoner at Kinsale. The generals earnestly desired to draw him out of port and engage him, but for once Rupert was prudent, and he declined to adventure his small fleet against overwhelming odds. The Council of State were impatient at this delay. Again and again they wrote to Blake, beseeching him to do " something extraordinary" against the revolted ships. The expense of maintaining the fleet was crushing, but the loss of reputation while Rupert remained undefeated was infinitely more serious.[1] But Rupert remained snug in Kinsale harbour, and laughed at his enemies; for the power of the Parliament in Ireland had fallen very low. At that time, only Dublin and Londonderry were held by their scanty forces; the rest of the country was in the hands of their foes, and Rupert could draw unlimited supplies from the land.

But the man was travelling towards Ireland who was to change the face of affairs and break the Royalist power there, as he had already broken it in England. Cromwell, who with his stern Puritan horsemen had driven Rupert and his cavalry like

---

[1] Council of State to Generals at Sea, May 19, 1649: "We are of your opinion that it is of great concern to look to the breaking of Rupert's fleet; for though you keep the seas open for trade this summer while we have so great a fleet out, yet, if his fleet be not broken, our merchants will suffer most when they are here wind-bound in winter, besides our loss of reputation and their increase of it, that they have been able to subsist against all the endeavours of so great and powerful a fleet as we have not had at sea during all these troubles." Cal. S.P.D., 1649–50, p. 150.

chaff from the field of Marston Moor, was about to make the harbour of Kinsale untenable for him. But before Cromwell could reach Ireland, Michael Jones had, miraculously as it seemed, defeated and chased the great army with which the Duke of Ormond besieged Dublin. The battle of Rathmines was the turning-point of the fortunes of the Commonwealth in Ireland, and Cromwell, when he landed, was swift to press home the advantage which had been gained. The terrible story of Drogheda and of Wexford needs no re-telling. The rapidity and completeness of Cromwell's successes struck terror into the hearts of his foes, and garrisons began to surrender before his army approached them.

Rupert, at Kinsale, felt the heavy hand of Cromwell from afar. The area from which he could draw supplies was diminishing rapidly. He was compelled to disband seamen and dismantle some of his ships, but this expedient could not serve for long. With Cromwell on land and Blake at sea, he was between the upper and the nether millstone.

The day seemed to be fast approaching when Rupert would have to choose between surrender and a desperate dash for liberty. Happily for him, he was saved from making his election by one of those chances which all men in those days ascribed to the intervention of Providence. Early in November a furious gale arose from the north-west, which threatened to dash Blake's ships to pieces upon the rocky bluff called the Old Head of Kinsale. Blake was compelled to ply out to sea to avoid this disaster, and his ships were dispersed by the storm. Rupert seized the unexpected opportunity, and put to sea with six of his ships. Eluding Blake's scattered vessels, he sailed southward, favoured by the gale which had rendered his foe powerless to intercept him.[1]

[1] Warburton's Memoirs of Rupert, iii. 298, 299.

# Chapter IV

## CHASING RUPERT

WHEN the news of Rupert's unexpected escape reached London, the *Happy Entrance* was in dock at Chatham for repairs. Great efforts were made to send out ships to intercept or overtake, and if possible to destroy, the revolted ships. On November 14 Popham ordered Badiley to go on board the *Happy Entrance* and sail westward to join Captain Hall, of the *Leopard*, at Land's End.[1] On the same day Popham wrote to Hall that "hearing of Rupert's having come forth to sea from Kinsale with some ships of force, I have ordered Captain Badiley with the *Happy Entrance* to join you, and as soon as ships come in I will send you more force."[2] The overtasked Dockyard was unequal to the strain that had been put upon it, and the *Happy Entrance* was not ready to go to sea. But immediate action was essential if Rupert was to be overtaken. A week went by, and then the Admiralty Committee wrote to Peter Pett, the chief constructor, that "as the State receives prejudice by the delay in setting forth of the ships appointed

[1] Popham to Badiley, Nov. 14, 1649. Cal. S.P.D., 1649–50, p. 393.

[2] Popham to Hall, s.d. *Ib.*

for the winter guard, and particularly the *Happy Entrance*, we desire your care in speeding her forth, and have ordered Captain Badiley to come down to hasten her despatch." [1]  It may be imagined that the Dockyard authorities had an uneasy time of it while this restless, eager seaman was hourly urging them to speed ; but in spite of his efforts, he never sailed on that intended voyage, for, so late as December 17, he obtained a warrant to press twenty men for his ship,[2] and long before that date Rupert was safe in the Tagus.

Rupert not only broke through Blake's scattered line, but he eluded the squadron which was stationed off the Land's End.  He pressed eagerly southward, taking many prizes as he went, until he cast anchor off Lisbon.  John the Fourth, King of Portugal, who, only ten years before, had seen his country under the domination of Spain, felt a not unnatural sympathy for the adherent of a deposed monarch.  He permitted Rupert to refit as men-of-war the merchant vessels which he had captured, and Lisbon afforded a ready market for the prize-goods which had been taken in them.[3]

The outlook for the Commonwealth was gloomy. Rupert at large, and receiving the passive, if not the active support of France and Portugal, was a far more dangerous foe than Rupert blocked up in Kinsale.  The great sacrifices which had hitherto

---

[1] Admiralty Committee to Peter Pett, Nov. 20, 1649.  Cal. S.P.D., 1649–50, p. 400.

[2] Cal. S.P.D., 1649–50, p. 560.

[3] Warburton's Memoirs of Rupert, iii. 301.

been made had been made in vain. England's naval difficulties were only beginning. If she was to assert her control of the sea and to protect the trade of her merchants, it was inevitable that she should address herself to the contest with even greater vigour than heretofore.

The Council of State was not slow in coming to the decision that Rupert must be destroyed if possible. On December 1, 1649, they ordered a squadron of eight ships to assemble at Stokes Bay. Among these was the *Happy Entrance*, under the command of Captain Badiley.[1] The number was afterwards increased to seventeen men-of-war and two fire-ships. Blake was recalled from Ireland to take command of the expedition, and reinforcements were to follow under Popham so soon as the ships could be made ready for sea. It is reported that, while Blake was in Ireland, Cromwell urged him to quit the sea service and return to the Army, in which he had gained so much glory. Had that proposal been accepted, England would have lost one of the greatest of her admirals. It may well have proved tempting, for Blake had as yet achieved no renown as a commander of the fleet. Subsequently the fame of his naval victories eclipsed the memory of his magnificent defence of Taunton. Cromwell's offer was declined, and Blake sailed for Plymouth to await the Council's orders.[2]

---

[1] Admiralty Committee to Popham, Dec. 1, 1649. Cal. S.P.D., 1649–50, p. 420.

[2] Council of State: Day's Proceedings, Dec. 4, 1649. Cal. S.P.D., 1649–50, p. 424.

Many obstacles delayed the sailing of the fleet, the chief of which was the inability of the Dockyard to complete the fitting of the ships. The winter of 1649/50 was unusually severe, and until January 18, when the frost broke, the Thames was so blocked with ice-floes that the ships which had been ordered from Chatham to Stokes Bay were unable to sail.[1] Blake came to Portsmouth to hasten the preparations,[2] and by the end of February the final arrangements were completed. On March 2 the fleet sailed out of Stokes Bay, carrying with it Charles Vane, who had been accredited ambassador to the King of Portugal, and the ill-starred Ascham, who was so soon to share the fate of Dorislaus, to fill the same office at the Court of Madrid. A few days later Blake's fleet was anchored in the Bay of Cascaes, outside the mouth of the Tagus.

The estuary of the Tagus forms a magnificent natural harbour. Two tongues of land thrust themselves out into the sea on the north and the south, upon which, in Blake's day, stood castles guarding the entrance. Inside these natural bulwarks is an excellent anchorage, called the Bay of Oeiras, which, some few miles inland, broadens out into the sheet of water upon the northern bank of which stands the city of Lisbon. Outside the northern point of land, the coast, before turning north, trends with a curve westward, thus forming the Bay of Cascaes, which

---

[1] Admiralty Committee to Navy Commissioners, Jan. 13, 1649/50. *Ib.*, p. 486.

[2] Council of State: Day's Proceedings, Jan. 11, 1649/50. *Ib.*, p. 477.

is exposed to all the gales that blow from the south and west. Rupert's ships were lying in the inner harbour when, on March 10, 1649/50, Blake arrived in the Bay of Cascaes.

If there had been any doubt as to which side King John of Portugal would espouse, the question was speedily set at rest. When Blake approached the castles with the intention of lying in the safe anchorage afforded by the Bay of Oeiras, they promptly opened fire upon his ships. Blake's instructions were to avoid conflict with any foreign power unless its fleet joined Rupert in attacking the English.[1] He was therefore compelled to withdraw again to the dangerous Bay of Cascaes. He was, however, a few days later permitted to seek shelter from a heavy gale by lying in the Bay of Oeiras, he undertaking to quit it when the storm abated.

Prolonged negotiations ensued between Blake and the Portuguese Government. Blake wrote a letter in Latin to King John, in which he denounced Rupert as a robber and a pirate. He declared that Rupert's ships were the property of the Commonwealth, which had been stolen from it by rebels, and he demanded permission to enter the port and take or destroy them.[2] Rupert, not to be outdone, published a violent declaration, in which he asserted that he held a commission from the rightful King of England. He branded Blake and the Commonwealth Government as rebels and murderers, hinted

---

[1] Thurloe: State Papers, i. 134.

[2] Blake to the King of Portugal, March 10, 1649/50. Hist. MSS. Comm., 13th Rept., App. I. (Portland MSS.), p. 519.

that they were in alliance with Spain, the mortal foe of Portugal, and that Vane had been sent ambassador merely as a spy to hold correspondence with Spain. Finally, he urged the Portuguese to join him in an attack upon the common enemy.[1]

The hint of an alliance between England and Spain was a shrewd stroke of diplomacy. Although this alliance was not an accomplished fact, the mission of Ascham to Madrid seemed to lend colour to Rupert's insinuation. It was only ten years before that Portugal had freed herself from an eighty years' bondage to Spain, and the latter was still hankering after her lost province. John IV. would doubtless have rejoiced if he could have rid himself of both Blake and Rupert, more especially of the troublesome unbidden guest who seemed bent on permanently enjoying Portugal's hospitality. But he dared not disoblige Rupert, lest France should take offence, and cease to support Portugal against the pretensions of Spain. On the other hand, Blake's fleet afforded a more present possibility of evil. After much negotiation a compromise was effected. Blake was permitted to enter the Bay of Oeiras when stress of weather rendered Cascaes Bay unsafe, on condition that he withdrew again when the weather moderated, and that he observed strict neutrality while he lay within the harbour. He was also allowed to obtain provisions and water on shore.[2]

[1] Declaration of Prince Rupert to the Kingdom of Portugal. Cal. S.P.D., 1650, p. 115.

[2] Articles of Agreement between John Mendez de Vasconcellos

This latter permission gave rise to the first skirmish between the hostile forces. On April 15 a boat was sent ashore from the English fleet to obtain water. Whilst the sailors were landing their barrels they were set upon by a party of Rupert's men. In the scuffle which ensued one of the boat's crew was killed and several others were either wounded or taken prisoners.[1] The rest regained their boat and rowed back to the fleet with tidings of their misadventure.

Rupert alleged that the English party had landed with the intention of assassinating him and his brother Maurice while they were hunting[2] and on this ground he excused, not only this attack on the boat's crew, but a somewhat dastardly attempt which was made later in the day to blow up the *Leopard*, the flag-ship of Vice-Admiral Moulton. Since permission had been given to the English to obtain supplies from shore many small craft had come out to the fleet with victuals, and consequently the commander of the *Leopard* would take no especial notice of a boat which came alongside that afternoon. Its crew professed to have a barrel of oil to sell, and the purser, suspecting nothing and tempted perhaps by a cheap offer, struck a bargain and ordered the barrel to be hoisted aboard. While

on the part of the King of Portugal and Charles Vane on the part of Admiral Blake, March 28, 1650. Hist. MSS. Comm., 13th Report, App. I. (Portland MSS.), p. 520.

[1] Vane to the King of Portugal. Thurloe : State Papers, i. 141.

[2] Warburton's Memoirs of Rupert, iii. 304.

this was being done, one of the occupants of the
boat, who was holding a guiding rope to steady
the barrel, let fall an expression which sounded
curiously familiar to English ears, and certainly was
not Portuguese.  Suspicion was aroused ; the barrel
was lowered into the boat again and the would-be
vendors were placed under arrest.  They proved,
upon examination, to be two negroes and an
Englishman from Rupert's fleet, the latter disguised
as a Portuguese.  When the barrel was opened,
it was found to contain "fireworks" and an ingenious contrivance for exploding them by means
of the rope which was held by the man whose
exclamation ruined the plot.[1]  It was intended that
the explosion should not take place until the barrel
was safely on board, and it was hoped that the
*Leopard* would be seriously damaged, if not destroyed.  Rupert's excuse for this attack was a
mere subterfuge.  Even if he believed that the
landing party in the morning had been told off to
murder him, this curious infernal machine, which
was probably invented by Rupert himself, could
not have been constructed in the few hours that
elapsed between the two events.  Charles Vane
protested loudly at Lisbon against the outrage, but
he was unable to obtain redress.[2]

Blake resolved to take his own redress at the first

---

[1] " A bombshell in a double-headed barrel, with a lock in the
bowels to give fire to a quick-match."  Warburton's Memoirs of
Rupert, iii. 305.

[2] Vane to the King of Portugal.  Thurloe : State Papers, i.
145.

opportunity, and the chance was not long delayed. In the middle of May the merchant fleet which traded yearly from Lisbon to Brazil sailed out of the Tagus. Nine of the ships chartered for this voyage were English built and English manned. Although Blake had been forbidden to meddle with Portuguese property unless the Portuguese attacked him, he had been authorized to press for the service of the State any English ships or men that might come under his power.[1] So he seized these nine ships and added them to his fleet, the crews joining him not unwillingly. Upon this King John declared openly for Rupert. He cast into prison the English merchants in Lisbon who adhered to the Commonwealth and confiscated their goods. This was tantamount to a declaration of war, and it was fortunate for Blake that, ten days after the taking of the merchant ships, Popham arrived from England with eight men-of-war, and, what was quite as important, with instructions that, if King John continued to protect Rupert, the Portuguese shipping might be attacked.[2]

This definite rupture with Portugal placed Blake in a very difficult position. He could no longer obtain supplies upon the Portuguese coast. Fortunately for him, as Portugal grew more hostile, Spain became more friendly. Spain was the more anxious to do good offices for England because Ascham had recently been murdered at Madrid by

---

[1] Thurloe: State Papers, i. 135.

[2] Instruction for Col. Edward Popham. Thurloe: State Papers, i. 144.

a party of Royalists.[1] The assassins took sanctuary; the priests refused to allow them to be dragged forth to justice and his Catholic Majesty dared not insist upon it. To prove that he had no sympathy with the murderers, he gave Blake permission to obtain supplies and water at Cadiz. But it was a long way to send for water; the casks ought to have been replenished daily, and the convoys that fetched the supply needed to be numerous, lest they should be assailed and overwhelmed by the enemy.

Badiley was selected to command the expedition to Cadiz. On his way thither he was attacked by six French men-of-war. He sunk one of them; the rest, not liking their entertainment, sheered off. Badiley, who was under orders for Cadiz, was prevented from giving chase.[2] Blake, with the remainder of the fleet in Cascaes Bay, continued the weary and apparently endless task of blockading Lisbon. " It hath pleased God," he wrote at this time, " to exercise us with various and mixed providences, sustaining us with apparent evidences of His good will in our extreme straits and yet withholding from us the fruit of the desire of our souls in our greatest hopes."[3]

[1] See Clarendon; History, xiii. 10. Clarendon and Cottington were representing Charles II. at Madrid at the time. As one of their servants was present at the murder, they were unjustly suspected of being privy to the plot.

[2] Blake and Popham to the Council of State, Aug. 15, 1650. Hist. MSS. Comm., 13th Rept., Appendix (Portland MSS.) p. 531.

[3] Blake and Popham to the Council of State, Aug. 15, 1650. *Ib.*, p. 531.

Hope deferred was making Blake's heart sick. On July 26, while Badiley was away at Cadiz, Rupert sailed out of Oeiras Bay with a large fleet, composed chiefly of Portuguese and French ships. Blake thought that at last he was to have the chance of measuring himself with his enemy. But the combined fleet, when it found itself in Cascaes Bay, showed no stomach for fight. Its commanders contented themselves with the execution of some admirable manœuvres, designed to keep a respectable distance between themselves and their foe, and Blake was unable to bring them to close quarters. Only a few long shots were exchanged, and when evening came, Rupert withdrew under shelter of the guns of the castles.

The next morning was calm; little wind was stirring and the enemy hugged the shore, declining action. On the following day they were still in the same position. The breeze had freshened and Blake stood in towards them, hoping to tempt them out into the open sea; but the guns of the castles beat him off. The next day Badiley's squadron rejoined the fleet with the water that they so much needed. This reinforcement made Rupert more chary than ever of risking an engagement, and on the following morning it was found that he had retreated into the security of the Bay of Oeiras.

Soon after this futile demonstration Blake sent home the nine English ships which he had taken from the Portuguese merchant fleet. On September 3 Badiley was again despatched to Cadiz with eight ships to obtain water, leaving Blake with the remainder of the fleet to ply outside the harbour. Blake had given up all hope that Rupert would engage him, and he was making his plans for the coming winter, when it would be almost impossible for the fleet to outride the storms which swept the Bay of Cascaes.

The morning of September 7 was foggy; so thick indeed that the English ships could not keep touch with one another. Suddenly the fog lifted, and Blake found himself with only two other ships —the *Phœnix* and the *Expedition*—face to face with the enemy's fleet, consisting of thirty-six sail. Fortunately Rupert was to leeward, and despite the great odds, Blake bore down upon him, singling out for attack the *Reformation*, Rupert's flagship, which led the line. The three English frigates poured their broadsides into the *Reformation*, and her fore-topmast came crashing down upon her deck. At that moment, when it seemed that the long-desired trial of strength was about to take place, the fog enveloped the combatants again, and they were hidden from one another. Rupert re-tired once more within the harbour.[1]

Well might Blake complain that these "pro-vidences" were "mixed." The season was wear-ing on, and as Rupert would not come out to fight, it seemed wiser to let him escape from Lisbon if he so desired, and then to chase and destroy him. Ships belonging to the Portuguese were near at hand which could not decline battle, and if con-

[1] Blake to the Council of State, Oct. 14, 1650. Hist. MSS. Comm., 13th Rept., App. I. (Portland MSS.), p. 536.

quered, would yield rich plunder. The fleet from Brazil was approaching the harbour of Lisbon, twenty-three sail, laden with sugar and other valuable produce. A week after the engagement in the fog the Brazil fleet was sighted, making for the land. A wild gale was blowing, and the sea ran furiously. Blake bore down upon the Portuguese Admiral, but the latter was "too nimble" and declined the encounter. So Blake was forced to content himself with falling upon the Rear-Admiral, "a ship of no less force." The rest of the fleet grappled with the enemy when and where they could get at them. For three hours they fought, the rough Atlantic boiling and surging beneath them so fiercely that they could not use their lower tiers of guns. The Portuguese Vice-Admiral was boarded and burnt, and the Rear-Admiral, battered and torn, yielded to Blake. Seven merchantmen were captured; the rest made their way to Lisbon to tell their tale of woe.[1]

After this victory Blake sailed for Cadiz to repair the damage which his ships had suffered in the encounter and to lie in wait for Rupert, if he should be tempted to make a dash for the open sea. He decided to send his prizes home, but three of them were so battered that it was necessary to transfer their cargoes to the other four. In this overladen condition they set sail, convoyed by four men-of-war, under the command of Captain Badiley in the *Happy Entrance*. Badiley, on his arrival in England, wrote an account of his homeward voyage.

[1] Blake to Council of State, Oct. 14, 1650, *ut ante*.

"On board the *Happy Entrance* in the Downs. It pleased Colonel Blake . . . to send me from Cadiz the 14th of October with order to ply my voyage for England, having assigned a squadron of ships to accompany me, viz., the *George*, the *Assurance* frigate, belonging to the State of England, and the *Hercules* and *Merchant*, ships employed in the service, that so I might be the better enabled to take into my charge and be a safe convoy unto four prizes—to say, the *Peter*, *Anthony*, *Lady Remidia*, and *Good Shepherd*—that were lately taken from the Portugal in their homeward way from Brazil, laden with sugars and other commodities. For an invoice whereof, as also what sugars is [1] upon the rest of our fleets, I humbly refer you to the enclosed packet from Colonel Blake. There came also under this convoy twelve other merchant ships that laded at Leghorn and Malaga, and in their homeward way stopped at Cadiz for the aforesaid end. Now, therefore, to advise your honours that, after many hazards by stormy weather, which of late we have often met withal, through God's great mercy all the aforementioned ships are safely arrived in this Road, the *Anthony* prize excepted, which, having broken some of her yards and split some of her sails in a storm near Portland, she went away for a harbour in the night, and that we judge was Weymouth or the Isle of Wight. The 28th of October, forty

---

[1] In this and other quotations I have modernized the spelling and used my discretion in the matter of punctuation ; but I have never tampered with grammatical construction.

leagues off the Land's End of England, I seized upon a Frenchman that came from St. Christopher's, laden with such goods as are specified in the inventory I send your honours herewith enclosed; but the ship being so leaky that the men I put aboard her could hardly keep her above water, two days since, in a storm, I bid them shift for themselves and their lives, and so venture for the shore, although very thick weather, to find a harbour, and I do not in the least doubt but she is well arrived either in the Isle of Wight or the adjacent places; and the next fair weather and opportunity of winds I shall endeavour with the above-said ships to hasten into the river Thames." [1]

After a very short interval Badiley was at sea again. On December 17 he was appointed commander of a squadron sailing north with supplies for the Army in Scotland.[2] On the same day a warrant for £50 was issued on the collectors of prize goods in Badiley's favour as a reward for good service. This sum was subsequently increased to £100.[3]

While Badiley was upon his homeward voyage from Spain, Blake lay at Cadiz ready to spring upon Rupert if he should venture out of Lisbon harbour.

---

[1] Badiley to the Council of State. Hist. MSS. Comm., 13th Rept., App. I. (Portland MSS.), p. 541. This letter is dated Nov. 9, but it was reported to the Council of State on Nov. 4 (Cal. S.P.D., 1650, p. 412) and read in Parliament on Nov. 8 (C.J., vi. 491). The Journals give the date as Nov. 2, and this is no doubt correct.

[2] Cal. S.P.D., 1650, p. 472.

[3] *Ib.*, pp. 605, 607.

The Portuguese were growing tired of Rupert's presence, and the loss of their seven merchantmen increased their anxiety to be rid of him. Towards the end of October Rupert left Lisbon and sailed for the Straits.[1] Blake thus had him in a net, and pursued him. One of Rupert's ships mutinied and surrendered; another was captured, and five more, seeking to avoid battle, were cast ashore near Cartagena in a gale, and were adjudged by the friendly Government of Spain to be the property of the English Commonwealth.[2] Rupert and Maurice, with only three ships, escaped to Toulon. Rupert was not destined any longer to be a danger to England. Eventually he sailed the Atlantic as a mere pirate, doing great destruction to merchant shipping, but of no account as an enemy whom the Commonwealth need fear.

[1] " Poverty and Despair being our companions and Revenge our guide." Warburton : Memoirs of Rupert, iii. 313.

[2] A Relation of what hath passed in Velez Malaga, and Cartagena between the Ships of Prince Rupert and those of the Parliament of England, Dec. 26, 1650. Hist. MSS. Comm., 13th Report, App. I. (Portland MSS.), p. 547.

Chapter V

CONVOY WORK

THE year 1651 opened more brightly for the
Commonwealth of England. Rupert was
reduced to impotence. Ireland, although not yet
quite subdued, was so far under the control of the
Parliamentary forces that her seaports no longer
afforded shelter to the enemies who preyed upon
English commerce. The anxiety that had been
felt during the previous summer as to the fate of
Cromwell's army in Scotland had passed away.
On the morning of September 3, the day on which
Badiley sailed for the second time for Cadiz to fetch
water for the fleet, Cromwell in an hour routed and
crushed the overwhelming force of Scots which had
driven him to bay at Dunbar. England was in possession of the whole of Scotland south of the Forth,
and the adherents of Charles II. were disunited and
disheartened. Although the Scilly Islands, Jersey,
and the Isle of Man were not yet reduced, it was not
difficult to keep their piracies in check, and before
the year was ended they had all fallen under the
dominion of the Commonwealth.[1]

[1] The Scilly Islands were surrendered on May 23, the Isle of
Man on Oct. 31, and Elizabeth Castle, Jersey, on Dec. 12.

After the battle of Dunbar, Parliament found leisure to take steps for the protection of the trade of English merchants outside the Narrow Seas, and more especially in the Mediterranean. The trade with Turkey was the monopoly of a rich Company called the Levant Company, which maintained an ambassador at Constantinople, and agents at all the larger Mediterranean ports. During the late troubles this trade had sadly decayed. The Company told Parliament that it was " now near quite lost to the nation," and was rapidly passing into the hands of the Dutch and the French. A report was presented to the House of Commons which showed that since the proclamation of the Commonwealth in February, 1648/9, the French had captured 5,000 tons of English shipping, 400 cannon, goods to the value of £500,000, and 1,000 sailors.[1] Parliament was anxious to content the London merchants, who would be quiet under any form of government so long as trade prospered. On the last day of October, 1650, an Act was passed authorizing the provision of armed convoys for ships trading to the Mediterranean. The cost of the convoys was to be paid by the State, and the commanders were forbidden to take any fee from the merchantmen for the services rendered.[2] This was the first attempt which England made to establish herself permanently as a naval power outside the Narrow Seas, and as such it merits more attention than it has hitherto received.

[1] C.J., vol. vi. p. 489.  Oct. 31, 1650.
[2] Statutes of 1650, Cap. 32.  Scobell, pt. ii. p. 143.

It was in this convoy work that Badiley was destined to be engaged. He commanded a convoy which left England early in 1651, and once again he found himself in waters which were made memorable to him by his former encounters with the " Turk," and were to become more memorable by the dramatic exploits which were so soon to be enacted there under his command. But no record of this voyage has been preserved. The fact that Badiley was engaged in it is known only by a chance reference in a letter from Captain Appleton, the commander of the first convoy, which sailed in November, 1650, who was then bound upon his second voyage.[1]

By the end of July, 1651, Badiley was in England once more. The times had again grown troublous, and he was detained at home for more urgent service than the guarding of the Mediterranean trade. The news had just arrived in London that Charles II., finding his position in Scotland untenable, had made a sudden dash upon England, hoping that, in the absence of so considerable a part of the Parliament's forces as that which had been concentrated in Scotland, he might rally the disheartened Royalists and gain some striking success. The Council of State feared that the invasion had been undertaken in concert with some foreign power, and that, while every available man who could handle a musket,

---

[1] Capt. H. Appleton [to Navy Commissioners] June 1, 1651. From Naples. "This is a copy of the two letters I sent to you, one from Zante, left with Captain Badiley there," etc. Cal. S.P.D., 1651, p. 228.

or trail a pike, was being drafted towards the point of danger, foreign troops would be landed upon the undefended seaboard. Blake, who was in command of the fleet in the Downs, was ordered to be on the alert against any such attack. Badiley, on board the *James*, was acting temporarily as Blake's Vice-Admiral.[1] On August 27, 1651, the Council of State wrote to Badiley, warning him of the danger which they feared.

" The Scotch army having now come into England," they wrote, "all endeavours will be used to give them assistance from foreign parts, and that we may have timely notice of it, send some ketches to the coast of Flanders and France to observe what store of shipping is in any of those parts that may serve for transportation of forces, if any be prepared there for that purpose. Use all diligence both in sending them out, and informing us of the discovery they make. We have appointed several ships to come into the Downs and receive orders from you in the absence of General Blake. When these ships come to you, make the best use of them for preventing the landing of any forces, if there be any such design."[2]

No foreign levies essayed to come to the assistance of the doomed Scotch army, and on Sep-

[1] Council of State to Capt. Cuttance, Aug. 27, 1651. "You are forthwith to repair to the Downs with the ship under your command, and there receive orders from General Blake or Captain Badiley." Cal. S.P.D., 1651, p. 377.

[2] *Ib.*, p. 378. A similar letter was sent to Blake, instructing him to hurry back to the Downs.

tember 3 Cromwell won his last great victory, his "crowning mercy," at Worcester. The Council of State was free once more to devote itself to fostering England's foreign trade. On October 30 they appointed Charles Longland, a merchant at Leghorn, to look after the interests of English shipping in that port.[1] Longland had spent most of his life in the countries bordering the Mediterranean Sea. In 1637 he was living at Aleppo, where Badiley had made his acquaintance. Badiley says that he "then showed himself as grave, sober, discreet, and religious a merchant as ever I met withal."[2] At the time of his appointment he was a man of considerable wealth and credit, and he proved himself such in the troublous days which followed, for it fell to his lot to find money to supply the needs of the English ships when none could be had from home, and the effort nearly ruined him.[3]

Not long after the destruction of the Scots army at Worcester a convoy set forth from London for the Levant, which played an important part in the struggle with the Dutch in the Mediterranean that was so soon to commence. The commander of the squadron was Captain Henry Appleton, and his ship was the *Leopard*, which Rupert had vainly endeavoured to destroy off Lisbon with his "fire-

[1] Cal. S.P.D., 1651, p. 505. Longland had lent Penn £1,000 for the use of the fleet when that commander was cruising in the Mediterranean during the summer. *Ib.*, p. 342.

[2] Badiley's Answer, p. 12.

[3] See *post*, p. 276.

works." Of Appleton's earlier history nothing is known save that he was a native of Hull,[1] and that he had previously done convoy work in the Mediterranean. Like Badiley, he had probably been a captain in the merchant service, but with this all points of resemblance between the two men cease. His religious belief was that common to the Puritans, but, if it was anything more than lip-service, it never prompted him to energetic conduct. He was a halting, hesitating man, not to be relied upon in any crisis which demanded a cool head and a steady hand. The necessity for decisive action in an emergency either paralysed him into inactivity or provoked him into rashness. He possessed, moreover, the fatal fault of seeing events, not as they were, but as he desired that they should be— a shortcoming that inevitably leads to discrepancies of statement which, if they do not amount to conscious falsehood, have all the appearance and all the inconvenience of that vice. Appleton was not a man upon whom implicit reliance could be placed in times of difficulty.

Under Appleton's command sailed also the *Constant Warwick*, in which Captain Batten had escaped to Prince Charles in 1648, and the *Bonadventure*. The *Constant Warwick* was commanded by Captain Owen Cox, who had done good service in "convoy" work when the English coast was infested by pirates and sea-rovers.[2] Cox was a bold, dashing officer, always eager for a fight, and well to be trusted to do his work

1 See *post*, p. 220.    2 See *ante*, p. 25.

thoroughly. A tendency to mistake himself for the commander-in-chief was the worst fault that could be imputed to him. Service under a captain such as Appleton was hardly likely to prove congenial to this brave sailor.

The captain of the *Bonadventure* was named Witheridge. He served, so far as can be ascertained, with honesty and zeal, but he died at Leghorn just when the troubles with the Dutch were commencing, so he played no part in the most important incidents in the career of Richard Badiley.

It is necessary to follow the fortunes of this convoy, because its earlier adventures, in themselves unimportant, wind themselves into the thread of Badiley's history. It sailed from London early in October, 1651, and reached Genoa without mishap. Its subsequent doings are told in Appleton's despatches.

"Our abode at Genoa," he wrote, "was longer than you ordered by reason of the extraordinary foul weather, insomuch that the merchant ships could not discharge their goods, and being unwilling to leave them, hearing that many French men-of-war were upon the coast, I was forced to endure the torment of a very bad Road.

"Being at anchor with the *Bonadventure* in Genoa Road in a great storm of wind, there came in a French vessel with her colours on the bowsprit-end, at whom I made some shot, but by reason our ship rolled so much I could not exercise my desires. The Genoese, perceiving I shot at her, sent a boat aboard of her and caused the French colours to be taken in.    The Signors were somewhat displeased with me, but I forthwith salved the cure and gave them content in full.

"On the 27th [1] ult. Jonas Poole, commander of the *Mary Rose*, arrived safe at Genoa, and having but little goods for that port, was ready with the first of the fleet to proceed for Leghorn.    On the 6th, the wind presenting fair, in the morning we saw a ship under the shore, three leagues westward of Genoa, whereupon I ordered Captain Cox in the *Constant Warwick* to make all sail to her in company with myself in the *Leopard*.    He endeavoured to get from us, but the *Constant Warwick* coming near, discharged a piece of ordnance at him.    The chase not answering again, being very near the shore and knowing that he could not escape from us, he blew up his ship, and the men took to their boats and got on shore.    It was a French vessel, laden with Backahlews,[2] and had some twenty-six guns, which we heard the report of as she burnt.    Seeing her in that condition, we proceeded with our merchant shipping for Leghorn, and arrived in this Road on the 11th [3] with the rest of the convoys, where we found the *Benjamin* from Smyrna with news of the death of many of our English nation this summer.

"The *Constant Warwick* sailed so very heavy that we are having her careened and tallowed, which we will effect in five or six days, as many French merchant ships are expected from Alexandria and Con-

---

[1] Of October, 1651.                    [2] Cod.
[3] Of November, 1651.

stantinople, some of whom, no doubt, we shall meet."[1]

Appleton lingered at Leghorn for some time, partly because he was in want of money, which he could not obtain. "I showed your bill of credit to the merchants here," he wrote to the Navy Committee, "but they have not any money, and promise to supply me at Smyrna. Had it been directed to any particular merchant, I might have procured the money." He went on to lament that the rate of exchange was only five shillings and twopence for the dollar in Leghorn, whereas it would run as high as six and sixpence in Smyrna.[2] A week later, however, he was able to report that Longland and Morgan Read, the representative of the Levant Company, had been prevailed upon to advance 3,000 dollars at the rate of five and fivepence a dollar.[3]

Soon after the despatch of this letter an event occurred which subsequently became the subject of considerable negotiation. Appleton gave two accounts of the transaction ; one immediately after it had taken place, when he hoped to raise his reputation with the Government as a bold and able commander ; the other, about two years later, when it would have been very convenient if he could have shifted the responsibility to other shoulders. As the question whether Appleton was a truthful

---

[1] Appleton to Navy Commissioners, Nov. 14, 1651. Cal. S.P.D., 1651–2, p. 17.

[2] Appleton to Navy Committee, Nov. 28, 1651. *Ib.*, p. 40.

[3] Appleton to Navy Commissioners, Dec. 5, 1651. *Ib.*, p. 51.

witness subsequently became important, it will be well to test his credibility by comparing these two statements.

On December 30 he wrote thus from Naples: " Having notice of some small French merchant ships that were expected from the Levant for Leghorn, I ordered the *Constant Warwick* to ply out to sea, when she discovered a French sattee, which she chased and took, laden with Provence wine, linen, etc., which I intend to sell here. Morgan Read, counsellor for our nation, much dislikes the taking of the vessel so near the port of the Grand Duke, and used all possible means for her re-delivery, and wrote me that I had much affronted the Grand Duke's port.[1] But I could not much perceive, by the well affected merchants of our nation, that the Grand Duke was so much displeased as the popish affected counsellor."[2] A fortnight afterwards he wrote : " I advised you of our surprising the French sattee near the Malora, which I have sold to George Baker, a merchant at Naples, and left twelve pieces of skamity with him to be sold for the State. The remainder of her goods I have kept, and will give an account of."[3] These two letters contain a series of statements which were either true or false. Appleton said that he ordered the *Constant Warwick* to chase French ships while the

[1] Leghorn. The sattee was taken close to Leghorn harbour.

[2] Appleton to Navy Commissioners. Cal. S.P.D., 1651-2, p. 84.

[3] Appleton to Navy Committee, Jan. 13, 1651/2. From Naples. Cal. S.P.D., 1651-2, p. 100.

convoy was at Leghorn. A French sattee was captured. Certain persons urged that the ship and cargo should be given up, but Appleton refused. His decision was applauded by the well affected, and the Grand Duke was not particularly offended. He sold the ship and part of the goods, retaining the remainder.

His subsequent account of this affair, when responsibility for the taking of the sattee would have been inconvenient, ran thus : "Arriving at Leghorn, the *Warwick* discovered a sail, weighs anchor without my order, and takes a French sattee coming into the Road. The Great Duke demands restitution of this sattee as being taken in port. I called a consultation hereupon, but Captain Witheridge and Captain Cox would by no means agree to it, giving me under their hands that they would answer to your honours. I then returned this answer to his Highness, 'that as the vessel was not taken by my order, so I could not restore it of myself.'[1] Amongst other wine the sattee had in her several chests of Frontignac and other presents for his Highness, of which Captain Cox sent me a couple, but I immediately sent them ashore to Mr. Longland for the governor, advising Captain Cox that he should on no terms keep away anything that belonged to the Great Duke. He said that there was all, and so I answered the messenger. The Duke, finding himself affronted in his port, and thus abused in the detaining of his goods, falls into

---

[1] It must be remembered that Appleton was commander-in-chief.

choler with me for the same, and charges his Resident in England [1] to lament of me to your honours. And I found afterwards that he had reason to be angry, though not with me, for Captain Cox kept several of those presents which were sent to the Great Duke, and did dispose of them, as he confessed to Colonel Thompson here in London." [2]

When this was written, Witheridge was dead; Cox was away with the fleet, and Appleton was anxious to discredit him. In every particular the second story contradicts the first. There can be no doubt that the earlier account gives the correct version of the affair of the sattee, and it is confirmed by numerous references to the subject in Salvetti's despatches. The Grand Duke relished so little the loss of his Frontignac that he sent a remonstrance to Parliament against the taking of the sattee, and the capture of that vessel became a State question between England and Florence for many a day.[3] Longland only alluded to the subject slightly at the time, but the little that he said corroborates Appleton's earlier account. "I hear the State is pleased to honour me with their commands here to see to their naval affairs," he wrote. "Until I have my instructions, I can say no more than that I shall faithfully serve them. A month since a letter was sent by the Great Duke to Parliament, complaining against Captain Appleton for taking a

[1] Salvetti.

[2] Appleton : "Remonstrance of a Fight in Leghorn Road," etc., p. 1.

[3] Salvetti : Despatches, N. 360–392.

French sattee coming into port, and the concurrence of this factory[1] was required. They accompanied the same with a remonstrance to Parliament, and my signature was earnestly demanded, but I answered it did not become me nor any of our nation to accuse the Parliament captains for what they had commission to do. Let me know how this business is relished at home for my government in future."[2]

When Appleton returned to Leghorn in June, 1652, he found that the taking of the sattee was causing difficulties between England and Florence. He therefore endeavoured to mislead the Council of State in regard to the date of her capture. He took occasion to send home one of his despatches by a sailor named Edward Domelow,[3] who had served on the *Leopard.* Appleton doubtless foresaw that this man would be examined by the naval authorities upon the question in dispute between the two countries, and there can be little doubt that he instructed his emissary in the evidence that he should give. The plan adopted was a barefaced attempt to throw the whole blame for the capture of the French sattee upon Captain Cox. As Appleton had anticipated, Domelow was examined, and a copy of his deposition is preserved in Salvetti's despatches.

---

[1] *i.e.,* the English merchants at Leghorn.

[2] Longland to Blackborne, March 1, 1651/2. Cal. S.P.D., 1651–2, p. 165.

[3] Appleton to the Navy Commissioners, July 2, 1652. Cal. S.P.D., 1651–2, p. 315.

Domelow had the effrontery to swear that the vessel about which the dispute arose had been taken by Cox when convoying a vessel from Leghorn to Genoa while Appleton and the rest of the ships were in the Road of Leghorn.[1] This perjury resulted in confusing the issue for a long time because Domelow refrained from giving any date to the encounter which he professed to describe, and it was assumed that he referred to Appleton's visit to Leghorn upon his outward voyage; but it was exposed at last, because the Tuscans were able to point out that Cox never sailed to Genoa on that occasion, and that the only time he convoyed a ship to Genoa was in June, 1652, when Appleton reached Leghorn on his return journey.[2]

After the capture of the sattee, which brought the English into ill odour at Leghorn, Appleton sailed with his convoy for Naples and Messina. Thence he plied eastward for the Levant, whence little or nothing was heard of him.

As Leghorn was destined to be the scene of the incidents which have soon to be related, it is necessary to give some account of that port and its surroundings. The town stands on a point of land protruding seaward, which is formed by a spur of the Tuscan mountains where they slope down on the north to the flat and marshy estuary of the Arno. It was fortified by strong ramparts, and, fronting the sea, stood a castle for the defence of

---

[1] Salvetti : Despatches, N. 413.

[2] See Appleton to the Navy Commissioners, July 2, 1652.   Cal. S.P.D., 1652, p. 315.

the harbours. Of these there were two—the inner harbour, an artificial basin cut into the heart of the town, which was reserved for the Grand Duke's galleys, and the outer harbour. The latter was used for commerce, which of late years had, through the energy of the English and the Dutch, grown very rapidly. It was formed by a stone pier, or, as it was then called, a mole or mould, built out into the sea upon the south. This harbour was so shallow that a moderate-sized ship under cargo could not enter it. She was obliged to lie in the Road outside and unlade by means of small boats. At the landward end of the Mould stood the Lazaretto, where travellers who could not show a clean bill of health were detained to undergo quarantine. Just south of the centre of the Mould stood the " Lanthorn," or lighthouse. Three or four miles out at sea, to the north-west, lay a long low sandbank, hardly visible above the water, which was a serious danger to shipping. This was called the Malora,[1] and it was the place near which the French sattee was taken. The Tuscans contended that the roadstead inside the Malora was part of the port of Leghorn ; so if the sattee was captured between the Malora and the mainland, the taking of the Grand Duke's wine was not the only offence committed by the English on that occasion.

[1] " Isoletta, o piuttosto banco del mar Tirreno. Ha una lunghezza de nove chilometri circa ed una larghezza di due, e porta sulla sua parte meridionale una torre esistentevi fino dall' epoca della Repubblica Pisana, e situata proprio dirimpetto all' antico Porto Pisano (Leghorn)." Amati : Dizionario Corografico, v. 28.

The Grand Duke Ferdinand II. of Tuscany, who will figure so largely in Badiley's story, was the son of Duke Cosimo II., who died in 1621, when Ferdinand was only eleven years old. During his minority the regency was in the hands of his grandmother, Christina of Lorraine, and his mother, the Grand Duchess Maria Maddalena of Austria. The Regents were weak, bigoted women, slaves of the priesthood, and by women and priests young Ferdinand was educated. Under the unenlightened rule of the Duchesses the trade of the country decayed, and the commerce of the port of Leghorn fell very largely into the hands of the English and the Dutch. When Ferdinand assumed the reins of government he was quite unfitted to rule. He has been described as " a badly educated and naturally weak and irresolute prince, the pupil of bigoted women and the captain of bravos." [1] The tendency of his policy was to oppose France and to ally himself with Spain. In 1647 Tuscany was attacked by France, and Piombino and Porto Longone, a Spanish possession upon the Island of Elba,[2] were captured by the French fleet, assisted by the Portuguese. The two towns were re-taken by the Spaniards under Don John of Austria in 1650, not many months before the adventures of the English convoys in Tuscan waters commenced. Ferdinand's weak, irresolute character and his preference for a

---

[1] Napier : Florentine History, v. 465.

[2] Part of Elba belonged partly to Tuscany and partly to Spain. Porto Ferrajo was acquired by the Grand Duke Cosimo I. from Charles V. in 1548. Amati : Dizionario Corografico, iii. 509.

Spanish alliance throw light upon much that is otherwise inexplicable in his conduct towards the English during their war with the Dutch. He died in 1670, and was succeeded by his son, Cosimo III.

Amerigo Salvetti, Ferdinand's Resident in London, whose despatches contain so much information concerning Badiley, was not a Florentine by birth. He was a native of Lucca; his real name was Alessandro Antelminelli. He was born in 1572, and, when little more than a boy, he was engaged in business at Antwerp. In 1596 his father and his three brothers were executed for high treason against the Republic of Lucca, and he was also condemned to death in his absence. As he declined to return home to undergo this sentence, assassins were hired to put it in force, and for years he travelled hither and thither, under the name of Amerigo Salvetti, to avoid destruction. He was appointed Resident in London for the Grand Duke of Tuscany in 1616, and he remained in that office until his death on July 2, 1657, Richard Badiley, of whom he had so low an opinion, surviving him little more than a month.[1]

---

[1] Hist. MSS. Commission, 11th Report, App. I. (MSS. of H. D. Skrine), p. 1. This report contains a translation of Salvetti's Despatches from 1625 to 1628. As to the attempts to assassinate Salvetti, see pp. 174–84. The remainder of the despatches may be found, transcribed from the Italian originals, in the British Museum. Addl. MSS., 27,962.

## Chapter VI

## THE QUARREL WITH THE DUTCH

WHILE Appleton was at Naples on his outward voyage, Badiley, commanding the *Paragon*, lay in the Downs waiting for the ships that were to sail with his convoy. His orders were to sail on December 10, 1651; but on the 8th, few of the merchantmen for whose safety he was to be responsible had joined him. On that day he wrote to the Navy Commissioners stating the causes of the delay. "We arrived here yesterday," he wrote, "with the *Nightingale*, where we found only five ships bound with red herrings for the Straits; the other seven herringmen bound that way are not yet come down, neither are the three rich ships bound for Turkey got over the Flats. As the 10th is drawing near, say whether I shall proceed according to the strict letter of my instructions, and, if the wind be fair, sail on that day with such ships as are bound southward, although I leave the Turkey ships behind, or whether I shall linger until they come down."[1]

The reply was an order to wait for the "rich ships." Meanwhile, the herringmen, impatient at the delay, took advantage of a favourable wind, and

[1] Badiley to Navy Commissioners. Cal. S.P.D., 1651–2, p. 53.

sailed without the convoy. Their captains held in light esteem the dangers which might befall them from Frenchmen and Turks compared with the advantage of a speedy voyage and a quick return of profits. But Badiley, who knew the Mediterranean, foresaw mischief. " I do not desire to aggravate any man's failings," he wrote, giving an account of the matter ; " but if these or any of the others be lost to a foreign enemy, the nation will lose a part of its strength. You will consider of a way for its prevention in future." [1]

The wind continued to blow from the south-east, preventing the laggard merchant ships from coming down the Thames. So Badiley resolved to sail for Plymouth, and thence to Falmouth, there to await the completion of his convoy. The three men-of-war appointed to sail with him were the *Phœnix*,[2] commanded by Captain Wadsworth, who was to prove himself a not altogether reliable subaltern ; the *Elizabeth*, under Captain Reeves ; and the *Nightingale*, a small vessel of twenty-four guns. But there was delay in provisioning the *Elizabeth*,[3] and after thirteen days' useless lingering at Falmouth, Badiley sent the *Nightingale* in search of her. She did not reach Falmouth until December 31, having passed the *Nightingale* without recognising her. Meanwhile, the merchant ships for which Badiley had been waiting had sailed by

---

[1] Badiley to Navy Committee, Dec. 13, 1651. *Ib.*, p. 62.
[2] Built in 1647. Thirty-eight guns. Historical Review, ix. 95.
[3] Badiley to the Navy Commissioners, Dec. 31, 1651. Cal. S.P.D., 1651–2, p. 86.

Falmouth in the night without troubling to inquire after the convoy.[1] On December 31, Badiley started in pursuit of them, leaving orders for the *Nightingale* to follow; but the ships encountered foul weather in the Bay of Biscay, and the little *Nightingale* was unable to overtake them, so it did not sail upon that expedition. "I have inserted the passage about the Straits ships passing by Falmouth," Badiley wrote from Cadiz, "that you may see that several merchantmen do not think your chargeable convoy for the Mediterranean Sea worth the stay of half a day. The five ships bound for the Straits [2] even went out of the Downs without coming on board to know whether we could convoy them, but I wish they may all come safe to their ports.

"The day after we left Plymouth,[3] our frigates seized a small Frenchman which I sent back for England, and sank another that would not yield in time, with sixteen pieces of ordnance. On 25th January I sent off the *Phœnix*, which seized the *Charity* or *Love* of Amsterdam from Marseilles and Toulon bound for Newhaven in France, 350 tons, and fully laden with goods, money,[4] etc.; the goods belong to French merchants. I . . . have desired Captain Penn to take care that the prize is convoyed to England by some of his fleet."[5]

[1] Badiley to the Navy Commissioners, Bay of Cadiz, Feb. 4, 1651/2. Cal. S.P.D., 1651–2, p. 133.

[2] The herringmen.

[3] He meant Falmouth.

[4] Silks, spices, seeds, drugs, fruit, boxwood, dollars, etc., according to the inventory enclosed with this letter.

[5] Badiley to Navy Commissioners, Feb. 4, 1651/2. Cal. S.P.D.,

After a short stay at Cadiz, Badiley sailed along the Spanish coast for Genoa, and from that harbour he forwarded his next despatch. "Since my last of February 4th, I have been on my passage from Cadiz," he reported : "stopped at Alicant six days for the merchantman's business, and left the 21st ult. A little before that the Vice-Admiral of France with his ship of fifty pieces of ordnance met the *William and Thomas* and the *Lewis*,[1] and having passed a broadside or two together, the Frenchmen left our ships, which went into Iversey,[2] and sent to desire that I would call for them, which I did, and took the *William and Thomas* under convoy ; but the other, having fish on board, put it to the venture and went alone.

"We chased and came up with several Hollanders, but could not meet with any Frenchmen. They heard that we were coming along that coast, and so plucked in their horn and got into Toulon, where they were in a panic lest our six ships were coming in there to land men and endeavour their destruction. They have put themselves in a defensive posture, and got their ships into the Mould. I suppose a guilty conscience dictated to them they deserved no better at our hands and thus made that stir. As affairs stand, they cannot set forth such a

1651–2, p. 133. Penn was returning from the Mediterranean. He met Badiley at Cadiz on Jan. 26. Diary of W. Penn, Hist. MSS. Comm., 13th Report, App. II. (Portland MSS.), p. 81.

[1] Two of the ships that ran past Falmouth in the night without inquiry after the convoy. The captain of the *Lewis* was named Ell. He proved a troublesome person throughout the voyage.

[2] Ivica (?).

strength but that eight or ten of our best frigates may master them and keep them in. . . . When near Majorca on the 14th ult., our frigates fetched up an Algiers man-of-war, out of which I took the English captives by virtue of the article in my general instructions, giving me command to take all Englishmen out of any shipping belonging to foreign States or princes." [1]

Whether the appearance of Badiley's fleet in the Mediterranean produced so great a panic among the French as he attributed to it may perhaps be doubted, but his view of its effect illustrates the cheery confidence with which he faced the duties which were laid upon him.

From Genoa Badiley sailed for Leghorn, where he met his old friend, Charles Longland. Longland had succeeded, though not without difficulty, in appeasing the Grand Duke's anger on account of the captured Frontignac wine, and he had been able to secure very advantageous concessions for English ships trading to the port of Leghorn. In his letter conveying the terms of these concessions to the Navy Committee, he warned the home authorities against permitting any repetition of Appleton's escapade. "In requital," he wrote, "let instructions be given to the States' ships intended hither that they neither affront nor disturb the port, and that frigates do not lie before the town and in sight thereof, tacking to and again, to hinder the coming in or going out of shipping; and when they once

[1] Badiley to Navy Commissioners, March 16, 1651/2. Cal. S.P.D., 1651–2, p. 183.

come to anchor in this Road, that they do not weigh anchor and go out again upon sight of any sail coming in, as these people take it to be a kind of besieging the town, or at best a great obstruction to trade."

The continuation of this letter illustrates the dangers which had to be encountered by ships entering the port of Leghorn, and the conditions under which the convoy work had to be performed.

" At the instance of some of our nation, Captain Badiley suffered the *Elizabeth* frigate to take in thirty bales of silk and carry them to Arrassia,[1] and lade them on board the *Society*, which was then lading oils for England ; but the frigate, in coming back, ran upon the sands [2] before this Road during the night, and it has cost me fifty-two dollars in ballast and boats to get her off, which I shall demand of Captain Badiley.   The cause of this accident, which might have been the loss of the Frigate, is the want of mates acquainted with this port.   The Captain (Reeves) has only been here once before, and it was worse with Captain Witheridge aboard the *Bonadventure*, late gone from Zante to Smyrna.[3]   He had no officer in his ship that had ever been here before, and at Zante he would have hired a Greek for a pilot, but could not find one. Such dangers should be prevented by those that have the shipping of the men.   There should be

---

[1] Arassi (?).
[2] *i.e.* The Malora.
[3] In Appleton's squadron.

two mates well acquainted with the parts to which the ships are designed."[1]

Soon after the *Elizabeth* had been brought off the Malora, Badiley and his convoy sailed southward for the Levant. In those seas he passed Appleton at Zante, the latter being then upon his homeward voyage. At about this time a small cloud appeared upon the horizon, which was soon to spread and cause disaster to the English ships in the Mediterranean Sea. Longland reported that fourteen Dutch sail had appeared off Toulon, giving out that they had come to claim reparation from the French for injuries done to Dutch trade and shipping.[2] The purpose for which this Dutch fleet was afterwards used was far different.

To understand the danger which was threatening the English convoys, it is necessary to glance at the events which had been taking place in England. The Parliament had for long been endeavouring in vain to bring about a good understanding with the States of Holland. In the spring of 1651 they had sent Oliver St. John, the Chief Justice of the Common Pleas, and a member of the Council of State, to aid Walter Strickland in the negotiation of a treaty. St. John travelled with a great retinue, and took elaborate precautions against assassination. The English plenipotentiaries pro-

---

[1] Longland to Navy Committee, April 19, 1652. Cal. S.P.D., 1651-2, p. 224.

[2] Longland to Navy Committee, May 10, 1652. Cal. S.P.D., 1651-2, p. 237. Longland subsequently reported the number of Dutch ships to be eighteen. *Ib.* p. 293.

posed a strict offensive and defensive alliance between the two nations, and that each should refuse asylum to the enemies of the other. Prolonged negotiations ensued which led to no result, and on June 20, St. John and Strickland left Holland.

The Parliament thereupon resolved that, as the Dutch declined alliance, they should be treated with disguised hostility. Early in August a Bill was brought forward which ultimately became the Navigation Act. This Act forbade, with a few unimportant exceptions, the importation of any goods into England, Ireland, or the English plantations in ships that were not English built, and to a large extent English manned.[1] Holland was not specifically mentioned in the Act, but it was aimed against her alone. It destroyed the Dutch carrying trade, and threatened ruin to the flourishing merchants of the States.

The Dutch upon this sent ambassadors to England, with instructions to endeavour to renew the negotiations for a treaty. Since the departure of St. John and Strickland from Holland, the battle of Worcester had been won, and all men could see that the Commonwealth of England was, for the time, firmly established. England claimed, and always had claimed, two rights which were galling to the Dutch. She demanded that all foreign ships should recognise her sovereignty of the Narrow Seas by dipping their flags when they passed her men-of-war. She also claimed a toll, either in fish

---

[1] Acts of 1651, Cap. 22. Passed Oct. 9; Scobell, Pt. II. p. 176.

er money, from all foreign fishermen who plied their calling in these seas. It was perhaps to advertise that the Commonwealth meant to abate no jot of these pretensions that, at the moment when the Dutch ambassadors were setting sail for England, ships were sent to demand this toll, known as "the tenth herring," from the Dutch fishing fleet in the North Sea. The Dutch refused to pay, and fired upon the English. A fight ensued, in which one of the Dutch vessels was sunk.

Negotiations that led to no result dragged on through the winter. Both countries saw that war was hardly to be avoided, yet neither desired to take the step which would cause it to break out. Each was rapidly augmenting its fleet in order to be ready for the struggle when it should at last commence. Charles II, who was then at Paris, was delighted at the prospect of a rupture between England and Holland. He sent the Earl of Norwich to the States to represent the advantages which must accrue to them from a war with England, reminding all the time of the advantages that might accrue to himself. On March 19, 1652, when Badiley was at Leghorn, the States gave orders that all English vessels then in Dutch ports should be stopped.[1] A few days before, Cromwell had hurried down to Chatham to hasten the setting out of the reserve ships.[2] Every one in England regarded the action of the States in laying an

[1] Jan. 3, 1652 ¿ Cal. S.P.D. 1651-2, p. 114.
[2] Ib. p. 112. Whitelock Memorials p. 529.
March 19. Cal. S.P.D. 1651-2 p. 114.

embargo on English shipping as the prelude to a declaration of war.

At the beginning of May, 1652, the main English fleet, commanded by Blake, was lying in and about Dover harbour, under the protection of the guns of the castle. Blake, with eight ships, had plied out to sea southward, and was riding in Rye Bay, leaving the vessels off Dover under the command of Major Bourne. During his absence, on May 18, the people of Dover discovered a large fleet approaching from the east, which, when it drew nearer, proved to be forty-two Dutch men-of-war. This fleet, which was commanded by Van Tromp, came to anchor off the South Foreland. Bourne, not knowing what to make of it, sent out a swift cutter to inquire the cause of its coming. The reply was that the Dutchmen had been driven thither by stress of foul weather. This answer was perplexing, because the storm which had forced the Dutch fleet upon the English coast had not made itself felt at Dover. It was probably intended as a defiance; but the English, in the absence of Blake, were too weak to resent it, even if they had been empowered to do so. So the Dutch were politely informed that "the reality of what they said would be best proved by their speedily drawing off that coast." But that course did not meet with the approval of Van Tromp. He evidently designed to provoke the English to fire the first shot in a war that could be no longer avoided. He stood in towards Dover and anchored within shot of the castle, hemming in the English fleet about the harbour. He proudly ignored England's claim that his ships should dip their flags to her men-of-war. He was reminded of his oversight by three shot from the castle, but he refused to take the hint. Until noon on May 19, he lay outside the harbour, defying the English fleet. Then he hoisted sail and made towards Calais; a ruse, possibly, to draw the English into the open. Soon after, Blake's fleet hove in sight, so Van Tromp put about and bore down upon it without the accustomed salute. Blake fired three shot in succession at Van Tromp's ensign. The latter, in reply, fired once at the scarlet flag, emblazoned with the arms of England and Ireland, which floated above the English Admiral's ship. Then he ran up a red ensign and followed the single shot with a broadside. From five o'clock in the afternoon until nine, the two fleets were locked in deadly encounter. When night fell and the battered ships drew off, it was found that one Dutch vessel had been sunk and another captured. On the following day Van Tromp was far away on his return to Holland.

When news of the fight reached London, a not unrighteous anger inflamed the hearts of the citizens. It was not doubted that Van Tromp intended to provoke attack. Such action, pending negotiations for a settlement of the questions in dispute between the two nations, seemed inexcusable. An order was at once made to stay all Dutch shipping in English ports.[1] The London

[1] Council of State: Day's Proceedings, May 20, 1652. Cal. S.P.D., 1651–2, p. 249.

mob found vent for their rage in threatening the Dutch ambassadors, and the Council of State were compelled to place a strong guard before the house in the quiet village of Chelsea to which the Dutchmen had retired to escape the turmoil of the city.[1] Cromwell rode post-haste to Dover to inquire into the circumstances of the fight, and the preparations for war were redoubled.

The States-General perceived that a great mistake had been made. The Pensionary Pauw was at once despatched to London to offer apologies and explanations. The Council of State were stern and unbending. They demanded reparation for the unprovoked attack upon the English ships, the recognition of the English claim to salute at sea, and of their right to the tenth herring. Pauw was not authorized to assent to such terms, and he, with the rest of the ambassadors, departed from Gravesend on June 30.[2] The Council of State, with somewhat cruel politeness, ordered that the ambassadors' belongings should be transported to Holland in one of the ships which had been taken from the Dutch.[3] With the departure of the ambassadors, all hope of a peaceful solution of the differences between the two countries was at an end. England and Holland were at war, and the cause of the conflict was the question of trade supremacy.

---

[1] *Ib.*, pp. 250, 252.

[2] Council of State to Blake, June 30, 1652. *Ib.*, p. 307.

[3] Council of State : Day's Proceedings, June 30, 1652. *Ib.*, p. 306.

The significance of those Dutch men-of-war lying off Toulon was becoming more and more apparent to Longland. Early in June he wrote : " The twelve [1] Holland men-of-war are still at Toulon and have been at Marseilles, and have been treated well at both places. The French here report that they came to see their (*i.e.* the French) King about the relief of Barcelona,[2] and the Dutch here affirm their order was to take or sink any French men-of-war. But seeing they have not done one hostile act makes our nation jealous that they lie there to watch how the treaty takes in England, and will make use of the first opportunity to fall upon our Turkey ships ;[3] but they shall be fore-warned." [4] It was well for the English ships that they had secured so watchful a friend at Leghorn. Had it not been for Longland, both of the convoys in the Levant, as they returned homewards in ignorance that war had been declared, would in all probability have fallen a prey to the Dutch.

[1] Fourteen in his previous letter. See *ante*, p. 74.

[2] Barcelona had revolted against Spain, and was closely besieged. The French, at war with Spain, were endeavouring to assist the insurgents.

[3] *i.e.* Appleton's and Badiley's convoys.

[4] Longland to Navy Committee, June 3, 1652. Cal. S.P.D., 1651–2, p. 276.

## Chapter VII

## THE ENGLISH AT LEGHORN

WHILE the fight between Blake and Van Tromp was raging off Dover, Appleton was at Messina on his return voyage, and Badiley was in the Levant. Neither of them had any knowledge of the storm that was brewing, or any anticipation of the perils which would beset them before they set foot once more upon the shores of England. Longland feared that the French fleet, destined for the relief of Barcelona, if it succeeded in its attempt, would then act in concert with the Dutch and fall upon the English ships in the Mediterranean. "Their ordinary way of payment," he said, "is to catch what merchant ships they can." The Holland fleet off Toulon had increased to eighteen ships, and Longland expressed a hope that England would send out a fleet to reinforce her squadrons.[1]

There can be little doubt that the Dutch did not send their fleet into the Mediterranean to attack the French, but to attempt the total destruction of English trade in the event of war breaking out.

[1] Longland to Navy Committee, June 14, 1652. Cal. S.P.D., 1651-2, p. 293.

The war was to be a trade war, and the annihilation of the nascent influence of England in the Mediterranean would prove a sore blow, not only to her commerce, but to her prestige. In this respect the Dutch showed themselves wiser than the Council of State, who, although they were implored by Longland to send adequate relief, delayed to do so until relief was useless.

The news of the battle of Dover did not reach Leghorn until the end of May. A month later Captain Appleton with his convoy anchored in the Road, having despatched the *Constant Warwick* to escort a ship to Genoa. Badiley's safe arrival at Smyrna had been reported. Appleton for the present was secure in a friendly port, but Badiley's position was precarious. The ever-zealous Longland took what steps he could to forewarn Badiley of his danger. "I sent a felucca with letters to Captain Badiley," he wrote, "advising him what passed between us and the Hollanders, that they may be more vigilant for their own safety. I have also written to him by way of Venice, Naples, etc., so that some of my letters must find him."[1]

The Dutch fleet was not long in closing round the prey for which it had been waiting so patiently. Before the *Constant Warwick* had returned from Genoa, the ships which Longland had watched with such suspicion sailed into the Road and came to anchor. The eight English ships, of which only two, the *Leopard* and the *Bonadventure*, were men-

---

[1] Longland to Navy Committee, June 28, 1652. Cal. S.P.D., 1651–2, p. 305.

of-war, lay at their mercy should they choose to attack them. The Dutch also had heard of the battle of Dover, but as yet they had received no orders to assault the English ships. Tidings of the declaration of war had not yet reached them.

Captain Appleton on July 2 sent home an account of his position at Leghorn. Later on he issued a revised edition of the facts. Once more it will be well to compare two statements made by him, in order to take the measure of his trustworthiness.

"Fourteen Holland men-of-war," he wrote, "arrived in Leghorn Road under Captain Katcs, and wearing his colours on the foretop as vice-admiral of Holland. Each ship has from forty-six to thirty-four pieces of ordnance. The *Constant Warwick* is yet at Genoa, as, being very foul and eaten by worms, I ordered Captain Cox to have her careened. The Hollanders often call their council of war, and the commander-in-chief went yesterday to the governor of Leghorn,[1] and told him that if our merchant ships discharged any of their English goods in this port he would either sink or burn them. Whereupon I caused them to go as near to the Mould-head as they could, and I, with the *Leopard* and the *Bonadventure*, went to seaboard of them. The governor has promised our nation that he will secure them to the utmost of his power, and has ordered the guns of all his castles and forts to be in readiness to fire on the ships that begin or attempt a disturbance. Yesterday the English merchants and factors and the

---

[1] Col. Miniati: Salvetti, Despatches, N. 404.

commanders of each ship came on board the *Leopard*, when it was thought fit to land all fine goods into the Lazaretto. We guard the barks ashore with our boats." [1]

These precautions seem to be those which a prudent commander, whose first duty it was to protect the goods in the merchant ships, would naturally take. But afterwards, in England, Appleton gave a very different version of his conduct. "So soon as I espied the Dutch fleet," he said, "I put to sea with the *Bonadventure* and four merchant ships, *and towed the Leopard through their fleet, there being no wind at all*, expecting the engaging. But seeing they came to anchor in a friendly manner, I towed a second time among them and anchored betwixt them and the shore, our merchant ships lying betwixt me and the shore. While they [the Dutch] were under sail and I close by, their admiral fired nine guns without shot. Being persuaded by my officers that it was a salute to me, I answered him with nine shotted, not having any drawn. But afterwards he [Kates] made that pass as a salute to the port." [2]

It is somewhat remarkable that Appleton's contemporary account of his meeting with the Dutch fleet contained no mention of these astonishing circumstances. The fact that he twice tempted the Dutch to attack the ships that it was his duty to protect, and that when there was "no wind at all,"

[1] Appleton to Navy Commissioners, July 2, 1652. Cal. S.P.D., 1651–2, p. 315.

[2] Appleton : Remonstrance, p. 3.

the *Leopard* was towed through the Dutch lines, could hardly have failed to impress the most unimaginative of men. Badiley, when he read this later account, thought that it must have been written for the entertainment of landsmen. "We need not say to all seamen 'pray laugh,'" he wrote, "for all such men know that a land commander might have been as soon believed in saying 'a mouse with a string in my nose led me and my troop through a regiment of Dutch, and so valorous it made us that it pulled us through them again.'"[1] Appleton's later version must be set down as apocryphal; the marvel is that he should have thought it worth while to tell so preposterous a story for purposes of self-laudation.

Appleton received orders from England that he was to confer with Longland before taking action in the difficult circumstances in which he was placed. Longland prudently advised that nothing should be done until the result of the negotiations with Pauw were known, but that for greater safety, in the event of an attack by the Dutch, the more valuable part of the merchantmen's cargoes should be landed and stored in the Lazaretto. While the rowing boats were busily plying between the ships and the Mould in this service, the Dutch commander sent to the governor of Leghorn a threat that if the unlading were continued he would sink the English ships. The English ships, "they say, are besieged by them, and consequently the goods are theirs."[2]

[1] Badiley : Answer, p. 33.
[2] Longland to Navy Committee, July 12, 1652. Cal. S.P.D., 1651–2, p. 329.

This seemed strange doctrine, and Longland was anxious to ascertain whether the Grand Duke assented to it. A messenger was despatched to Florence to beg protection, and Ferdinand, irritated at the insolent conduct of the Dutch, at once granted it. He ordered " all the succour the town can afford us either by castle, galley, or armed boats." [1] So on the following day the removal of the cargoes was completed, and the ships withdrew into the shelter of the harbour, where the Dutch did not dare to molest them. For this protection the Grand Duke received the thanks of the Council of State. [2] So far, the English had obtained the first advantage, thanks to the overhastiness of their enemies.

But the English could not hope to secure the permanent friendship of the Grand Duke if their ships should be the cause of a prolonged blockade of the port of Leghorn. Apart from the annoyance and injury which this would inflict upon the trade of Tuscany, there were other forces antagonistic to the English which would be in constant operation. The Dutch merchants were powerful at Leghorn, and they would assuredly complain of the favour shown to their enemies. The English merchants were unfortunately divided in opinion. Some of them were Royalists, who would not keenly regret a blow inflicted upon the Commonwealth, even if it should result in some temporary loss to themselves. The Dutch took an ingenious

---

[1] Longland to Navy Committee, July 12, 1652. Cal. S.P.D., 1651-2, p. 329.
[2] Salvetti : Despatches, N. 410.

advantage of this division. They refrained from enforcing the blockade against ships belonging to Royalist merchants, while they fired upon and chased such as were the property of friends to the Commonwealth.[1] Thus, not only the Tuscans and the Dutch, but also a considerable number of the English at Leghorn, were either open or covert enemies of Appleton's convoy, and would gladly have seen it captured or destroyed.

A vast amount of intrigue was carried on amongst the disaffected for the purpose of paralysing the English ships. However diverse the objects of the various parties might have been, all were anxious that terms should be arranged which would prevent any disturbance of the trade of the port. If Appleton could be induced to enter into an agreement binding himself not to engage with the Dutch in the Road-stead, such an arrangement would be the next best thing to the departure or destruction of the English ships. No difficulty was to be feared on Appleton's part, but it would not be an easy matter to persuade Longland to agree to such a surrender. It was not probable that the representative of England would submit to terms which would prevent the imprisoned ships from striking a blow for freedom if the chance offered. But if Longland could not be persuaded he might be circumvented, and this was the course which the intriguers eventually adopted.

Whilst these schemes were afoot, the position of the English ships was growing more perilous every

---

[1] Appleton to Navy Committee, Sept. 17, 1652. Cal. S.P.D., 1651-2, p. 407.

day. War was known to be declared, and the Dutch Government had issued peremptory orders that all Dutch merchantmen in the Mediterranean should be impressed as men-of-war. "Consider the condition of our ships here," urged Longland, when he reported this fact to the Navy Committee, "bound up by so strong an enemy, their provisions nearly consumed in a dear country, and money scarcely to be found by exchange."[1] Before long Katcs' fleet would be strongly reinforced; but the Parliament delayed issuing any similar order, although the Levant Company was constantly urging that the ships at Leghorn should be relieved.[2] The English merchantmen in Appleton's convoy absolutely declined to undertake the State's service unless they were impressed and payment from the State was guaranteed.

Appleton described the situation on August 5 thus: "You know the condition of this squadron. Though the *Constant Warwick* could not have made us equal to our enemies, yet its absence makes us considerably weaker, and the protection of this port will scarcely poise the disservice we shall receive from the most unnaturally disaffected here on shore. . . . Should I take up the merchant ships, who would willingly go could I assure them satisfaction from you and such pay as the rest of the ships in your service have, I would then defy their

---

[1] Longland to Navy Committee, July 31, 1652. Cal. S.P.D., 1651-2, p. 352.

[2] Levant Company to Morgan Read, Aug. 2, 1652. *Ib.*, p. 353.

fleet, nor question meeting with Captain Badiley. But where is my order? I believe with two or three months' pay I could entice most of the two hundred English and Scotch [1] from the service of these Dutch ships, who owe them about fifteen months' pay and feed them very hardly. This would much weaken them and make our merchantmen good men-of-war. There is no way for that design but this, or endeavouring to have men from Venice upon some such terms." [2] On July 17, the Dutch fleet stood out to sea, hoping perhaps to lure Appleton out of harbour. While it was away the *Constant Warwick* returned from Genoa, and was at once despatched to meet Badiley and inform him how matters stood at Leghorn. The next day the Dutch fleet sailed into the Road again. [3]

The Dutch at this time began pressing the Grand Duke to withdraw his protection from Appleton. They asserted, not without reason, that his sheltering the English ships was a breach of neutrality. They pointed out that, according to the Law of Nations, no belligerent men-of-war ought to be permitted to remain in a neutral port indefinitely, and that it was the duty of the neutral Government to put a period to their stay. They proposed, therefore, that Appleton should be allowed a reasonable time to relade his ships and depart, and they undertook not to give chase until five days after he had

[1] Royalists, no doubt.
[2] Appleton to the Navy Committee, Aug. 5, 1652. Cal. S.P.D., 1651–2, p. 357.
[3] Appleton to the Navy Committee, July 23, 1652. *Ib.*, p. 346.

sailed. These terms sounded generous, but neither English nor Dutch had forgotten that fourteen Dutch men-of-war lay off Cadiz, ready at any moment to block the Straits of Gibraltar against the English fleet.[1] It would be small comfort to escape from Katcs only to fall into the clutches of this squadron. The Grand Duke was not yet ready to risk a quarrel with England, so he refused the Dutch demand.

It was therefore thought wise that the English in Leghorn should show their gratitude to Ferdinand for the protection that he had afforded them. It was agreed that a deputation should be sent to Florence to express thanks for past favours, and to secure the best terms possible for the future. The conspiracy for paralysing the English squadron now began to disclose itself. Among the many contradictory accounts of the doings of this deputation it is difficult to arrive at the truth, but Appleton's character for veracity has been sufficiently displayed to justify the rejection of any unsupported evidence which may be found in his account of the embassy. It was agreed that Longland, together with a merchant named Boneile, Captain Roope of the *Mary*, Captain Wood of the *Peregrine*, Captain Seaman of the *Sampson*, and a certain Nathaniel Reading should constitute the deputation.[2] Reading was a

---

[1] Appleton to the Navy Committee, July 9, 1652. *Ib.*, p. 325.

[2] Seaman's Declaration: Appleton's Remonstrance, p. 14. The evidence is tainted at its source, but the names are no doubt correct. He says that Reading was appointed to represent "the nation," and the rest to represent the merchants of Leghorn. This

merchant at Leghorn, an unscrupulous, glib, smooth-spoken man, who had a great opinion of his own abilities. In early life he had been made prisoner by the Turks, and had worked in their galleys. Subsequently he had lived in Naples, and a cloud of suspicion hung about him, on account of the murder of a child, which had never been satisfactorily cleared away. And now he was starting for Florence, ostensibly a member of a deputation to secure advantages for the blockaded fleet, but in reality the advocate of the malcontents at Leghorn, charged, if possible, to effect an arrangement which would render it unserviceable.

For this purpose it was necessary that he should carry with him some authority to speak on behalf of the embassy, because Longland, as the representative of England, would naturally undertake that duty. To this end he obtained a secret commission from Appleton, the commander of the English squadron.[1] The promise which Appleton authorized Reading to make will appear clearly in the sequel.

When, after a four days' journey, the envoys arrived at Florence, they took counsel how they should conduct themselves at the audience with the Grand Duke. At this meeting Reading produced his commission from Appleton, and claimed to act

is most improbable. Reading was almost certainly the representative of the disaffected merchants.

[1] Appleton : Remonstrance, p. 4. Appleton says : " Longland and I with the merchants desired Mr. Nath. Reading to undertake this ; " but the statement is clearly false. See Longland's Defence. Cal. S.P.D., 1653–4, p. 243.

as spokesman. Reading afterwards asserted that Longland had declared that he had no authority to speak on behalf of the State, " and that beside, his education had not been to understand how to treat with princes, and that he did not know how to speak unto a duke." [1] This is probably a fabrication ; in any case, Reading admitted that " Mr. Longland, while altering his clothes, changed his mind," and declared that Appleton had no authority to issue a commission, adding that he would protest against it both at Florence and at home. That the rest of the embassy were not privy to Appleton's action is proved by the fact, admitted by Reading, that they all followed Longland to the audience, leaving Reading to his own devices.

Reading at once sought out Sir Bernard Gascoigne,[2] the unofficial representative of Charles II. at Florence. This fact sufficiently indicates the origin of the plot to which Appleton had consented to become a party. Gascoigne promised that Reading should have an interview with the Duke after Longland and his friends had taken their departure. Accordingly, when the English envoys had made their orations of thanks and had bowed themselves out, Reading was ushered into the presence. He made a fine speech to the Duke, of which he afterwards gave a detailed account, and producing

[1] Reading to Council of State (undated), but probably not written until it was required for Appleton's Remonstrance, where it is printed on p. 25.

[2] Bernardo Guasconi, an Italian who had fought for Charles I. during the Civil War. He narrowly escaped execution after the taking of Colchester, when Lucas and Lisle were shot.

Appleton's commission, he represented himself as the authorized agent of the English.

The Grand Duke was bewildered. It was clearly impossible to deal with two accredited representatives of the same party. He sent for Longland again, and asked Reading to return the next morning. Longland endeavoured to persuade his Highness, that the commission of an English captain could not be construed to over-ride the commission of the Parliament of England. But the Duke was not to be convinced, especially as Longland had not supposed it necessary that he should bring his credentials with him. The Tuscan courtiers thought the affair suspicious. "If you were what you pretended," they urged, "Captain Appleton, who is a commander of theirs [*i.e.* the English], would not thus slight you, but acknowledge you for such, and not commission another for that service."[1] As Badiley afterwards declared, Longland was treated as an impostor. He was forced to send a messenger post-haste to Leghorn to fetch his disputed commission. When Appleton heard from this messenger the story of what had occurred at Florence, his courage failed him. With Longland's commission came a formal revocation by Appleton of Reading's appointment, but it came too late. The journey to and from Leghorn consumed eight days. Long before the messenger arrived in Florence, Reading had received his second audience from the Grand Duke, and had taken his departure. Reading had entered into an agreement with the Duke in

[1] Cal. S.P.D., 1653-4, p. 248.

Appleton's behalf, pledging the English ships to
inaction. When Longland presented his commission, together with the revocation of Reading's
authority, the Grand Duke was by no means satisfied. He laughed heartily, and said, "What will
you say if Reading returns in three days with
another commission to revoke this revocation?"[1]

Ferdinand's object was now to get rid of Longland and his company with all speed. He had
obtained from Reading an undertaking which he
could never have extorted from Longland—an
undertaking which would pacify the Royalists, the
Dutch, and the Tuscans. Appleton dared not dis-
avow his envoy, and was forced to confirm the
promise which had been made in his behalf. On
August 26, 1652, he wrote a letter to the Grand
Duke, in which he adopted Reading's undertaking.
The contents of this letter he revealed to no one.
Its exact terms would never have been known if
an Italian translation of it had not been forwarded
to Salvetti some time afterwards. It is so characteristic of the man, and it exercised so important
an influence upon subsequent events, that it must
be given in full.

"*26th August*, 1652.[2]

"MOST SERENE GRAND DUKE,—

"The favours which I have received from your
Highness' most gracious hands demand from me all
possible recognition and service, and it causes me
great regret, most gracious prince, that my present

[1] Cal. S.P.D., 1653–4, p. 248.
[2] 1653 in the copy, which is clearly an error.

ability to serve is not better proportioned to the debt which I owe you.  Nevertheless, I offer it to your Highness with all my heart, in the hope that the displeasure you have felt against me on account of the French ship (which, however, was not taken by my order, and being taken, it was not in my power to restore her) will no longer continue.  And I promise, on my return to England, to serve your Highness to the extent of my power in that matter as well as in the recovery of the rice that was taken by Captain Hall.[1]  I have given a detailed account to my masters the State of England of the great care your Highness has been pleased to take for the protection of their ships, and I kiss your Highness' hands in recognition of the great courtesy shown to me and to Mr. Reading, who went to your Highness in my behalf, and I endorse all he then did for me.  *I now bind myself to your Highness not to disturb the Dutch in any way within sight of the lighthouse of Leghorn, and to keep this promise with all exactness, unless I am commanded to the contrary.*  And wishing you all the happiness due to so glorious a monarch as your Highness, etc., etc."[2]

There was no condition attached to this undertaking that the Dutch should not attack the English,

---

[1] This was another question of capture at sea, which was agitated almost as long as that of the French sattee.  Captain Hall had appropriated some rice belonging to one Cardi, a Florentine, that was in a French ship which he had taken.  Longland to Council of State, Sept. 6, 1652.  Cal. S.P.D., 1651-2, p. 392.

[2] Salvetti : Despatch, dated Jan. 3, 1652/3.  N. 498.

although the Duke afterwards alleged that he obtained a similar promise from them.  Appleton, to ensure the privilege of remaining in Leghorn harbour, which was not then threatened, surrendered his right to attack the Dutch fleet so long as the lighthouse of Leghorn was visible.  This concession was only one degree better than a surrender of the fleet.  Under such conditions a couple of Dutch men-of-war would be able to maintain the blockade of Leghorn, and the rest of the fleet would be freed to attack English commerce in other directions.  It is not wonderful that Appleton concealed this agreement from his friends until it was wrenched from him.  The undertaking that Longland had given was that the English ships should not " in any way offend or disturb the port," [1] and this was the promise by which every Englishman except Appleton and Reading conceived himself to be bound.

The undertaking that Reading had given was communicated to the Dutch before Appleton's confirmation of it arrived at Florence.  Katcs had just been superseded by Jan Van Galen.  Van Galen had passed through Florence on his way to Leghorn, and he had been well received by the Grand Duke, who doubtless then informed him of the happy issue of the recent negotiations.  So Van Galen assumed his command in a fortunate hour.  As the English were firmly bound not to fight, he was free to engage in other enterprises.  On August 26, the day on which Appleton wrote his letter to the

---

[1] Longland to Council of State, Aug. 22, 1652.  Cal. S.P.D., 1651–2, p. 378.

duke, he sailed westward with ten ships, leaving only five to guard Leghorn harbour.[1]  Longland sent out a swift felucca to watch Van Galen's movements, for he knew that Badiley's squadron could not be far off.  Even if the *Constant Warwick* had found Badiley, he would only have four men-of-war with which to encounter the ten that had sailed under Van Galen.  But Longland, ignorant of the fatal undertaking that Appleton had given, consoled himself with the thought that if Badiley were hard pressed, Appleton could easily break through the weak force that held the ships at Leghorn in check and sail to his relief.  Appleton, knowing what he had promised, consoled himself with prayers for Badiley's safety.

Late on the evening of August 27 a felucca sped swiftly into Leghorn harbour.  It bore a message from Captain Cox, imploring the English ships to sail southward at all hazards, because Badiley's convoy was attacked by ten Dutch men-of-war off the island of Monte Cristo, and was hard beset.

[1] Appleton to Navy Committee, Aug. 27, 1652.  Cal. S.P.D., 1651–2, p. 384.  Written the day after he sent his undertaking to the Grand Duke.  No mention is made of it in this or any other letter home.

# Chapter VIII

## THE BATTLE OF MONTE CRISTO

WHILE English freedom of action was thus being bartered away at Leghorn, Badiley was returning with his convoy from the Levant. Longland was in constant anxiety for the safety of this convoy, and he watched keenly the movements of all Dutch ships in the Mediterranean. At one time he concluded that the Dutch squadron at Cadiz was appointed to cut off Badiley's convoy, but this was not the case.

It is doubtful whether any of the warning letters which Longland addressed to Badiley ever reached him, but Captain Cox was more successful. The *Constant Warwick*, plying towards the Levant in search of the threatened convoy, found it at Zante. Cox told Badiley of the breach with Holland and of the perils which threatened the English ships in the Mediterranean. Both Appleton and Longland surmised that Badiley would put in at Messina or some other friendly Spanish port, and there abide until these troubles had blown over. If Captain Cox tendered this advice to Badiley, it was rejected. Badiley was not the man to hang back when danger was ahead. He called a council of war, at which it was resolved that the squadron should make for

Leghorn with all possible speed, without touching either at Messina or Naples, as was the custom. His prime object was to go to Appleton's relief, but the plan might also baffle the Dutch. If a hostile squadron were on the outlook for the convoy, it would keep a strict watch upon the ports at which ships were accustomed to call. The resolution of the council of war was founded on the assumption that when the Dutch fleet sailed westward from Leghorn on July 17, the object was to intercept Badiley. This departure westward, therefore, was probably a feint to throw the English off their guard.[1] The Dutch would doubtless sweep southward down the western coasts of Corsica and Sardinia and waylay the convoy off Cape Spartivento. If these were the Dutch tactics, Badiley determined to outstrip his foe and endeavour to reach Leghorn and relieve Appleton before Katcs could overtake him.[2]

With this intention the convoy pressed onward under all the sail that it could carry, in no great fear of any foe that it might encounter. It consisted of four men-of-war, gallantly armed and manned, and four well-found merchantmen, who, at a pinch,

[1] Badiley could not know of Katcs' return to Leghorn after the departure of *Constant Warwick*. He says that the course described in the text " was thought the best, the rather as we were advised that those fourteen sail of Flemings were gone to the westward, and if they wheeled about as was suspected, to seek after us, it would be about Cape Spartivento [South of Sardinia] and not near Leghorn."

[2] Badiley to the Navy Committee, Aug. 31, 1652. Cal. S.P.D., 1651–2, p. 402.

could offer stout resistance to a foe. The odds were not so very unequal, even if they did fall in with Van Galen and his ten ships.

They passed the Straits of Messina and sailed northward along the coast of Italy, keeping a careful outlook westward for the expected enemy. But none appeared, so it became evident that if the Dutch intended to wheel in upon the convoy from the south of Sardinia, he had miscalculated. All went well till they sighted the little island of Monte Cristo, south of Elba and not more than twenty-five leagues from Leghorn. There, on the afternoon of August 27, the enemy hove in sight. The decks were cleared for action while the two fleets approached one another. The merchantmen, whose assistance was essential if the Dutch were to be defeated, began to slacken sail and fall behind the men-of-war. When the fleets, at about four o'clock, arrived within gun-shot, there was a pause. Possibly the Dutch expected a chase rather than a battle, and their only fear had been lest their prey should escape them and find refuge in some neutral port. A shot or two was fired at intervals in challenge or defiance, but both commanders knew that it was too late in the day to close upon one another in the death struggle. The swiftly coming night of those southern seas would envelop the fleets before victory could declare itself for either party. So, during the waning hours of that August afternoon, the rival fleets lay within shot of one another, while now and again a puff of smoke issued from a porthole, the boom of the cannon was heard, and a ball crashed into a hull, or more frequently sped wide of its mark and splashed along the blue waters, raising fountains of white foam as it sped. When the sun sank and the desultory firing ceased, little damage had been done on either side, and most of the ships' guns had not been brought into action.

When the Dutch fleet was first sighted, Captain Cox had hailed a passing felucca, and by it had sent a message to Appleton, urging him at all hazards to break out of port without delay and sail to the relief of the convoy. There was some cheer in knowing that this message was speeding on its way to Leghorn, for if the convoy could make good its defence during the following day, Appleton might arrive before nightfall, and, taking the enemy in the rear, would in all probability defeat if not destroy him. The comfort to be derived from the thought would have been considerably diminished if the English commanders had known that at the same moment another messenger was posting to Florence, bearing Appleton's undertaking not to engage with the Dutch within sight of Leghorn lighthouse.

At sunrise on the morning of Saturday, August 28, there was activity and eagerness on both fleets. Guns were trained, the seamen were stripped to the waist, hangers were loosened, and pikes were placed conveniently to hand in case the enemy should attempt to board. Badiley gave orders that the ships were to keep close and follow his lead, so that none of them should be cut off from the fleet and exposed to overwhelming attack. The Dutchmen bore down upon the English, who got under way to engage them.  But from the first moment of the encounter Badiley's orders were neglected.  The three men-of-war followed his lead, but the merchantmen, having but little stomach for fighting, fell astern, and during the whole of that day kept out of the battle, only dropping in an occasional shot when the chance offered and suffering but little damage.  So the brunt of the encounter fell upon the four men-of-war, who endeavoured to hold their own against ten ships.  It was too late for appeal or remonstrance, and they had to make the best of the perilous work before them.

When the ships came to close quarters a fierce cannonade commenced, and it was continued within pistol range with deadly ferocity until a thick pall of smoke hung above and around the contending ships. The *Constant Warwick* and the *Elizabeth* obeyed Badiley's command to the letter, and with the *Paragon* maintained the unequal struggle.  But early in the action, Wadsworth, of the *Phœnix*, either through carelessness or rashness, left the line.  He speedily found himself cut off from the rest of the fleet and exposed to the onset of superior force.

The Dutch trusted to their overwhelming strength to carry the English ships by boarding, and four of their largest men-of-war attacked the *Paragon*. That vessel was assailed on both sides, and on one side she was quite unsupported.  On the other, the *Elizabeth* and *Constant Warwick* kept the enemy somewhat in check, but the isolation of the *Phœnix* and the inaction of the merchantmen precluded all hope of relief on the unsupported side. It was at this point, therefore, that Badiley had to concentrate his resistance. One of the enemy grappled and boarded him, but his "gallants" resisted the attack so stubbornly that the Dutchmen were driven back in confusion. At that moment the cry arose that the Dutch ship had caught fire; her crew were seized with panic and cried quarter. Some of them desperately leapt into the sea and, swimming to the *Paragon's* boat, which was riding astern, they clambered into her in such numbers that she capsized, and many of the unfortunate men were drowned.

The cry for quarter was, according to the custom of war, a surrender of the Dutch ship; but Badiley was not in a position to possess her. Three of the enemy were still harassing him, and he was fully occupied in repelling their persistent attacks. The fleets had been engaged for some hours, and their plight was pitiful. The ships were torn through and through with shot; their sails and shrouds were hanging in ribbons and a great number of their crews were killed or wounded. Captain Wadsworth at length perceived the mistake which he had made in not obeying orders, and he tried to force his way back to the *Paragon*. But his ship had been so mauled as to be unmanageable, and he was overtaken and boarded by a big Dutchman. Fifty of the *Phœnix's* men had been slain, and twenty lay upon the deck wounded. The wearied residue, seeing the Dutch leap on board, lost heart. Thirty of them rushed madly astern, jumped into the ship's boat and rowed for dear life towards the *Paragon*, which they reached in safety.  Those who remained on board the *Phœnix* sought refuge in the round-house, and, clapping to the doors, made a last desperate defence.  The crew of another Dutch ship had by this time boarded the *Phœnix*, and the odds against the defenders of the roundhouse were heavy.  They continued to fire upon their assailants so long as their powder lasted.  When it was giving out, one of their number went down through the lower deck into the hold to fetch a further supply.  But the lower deck was already in the enemy's possession, and the man was shot.  Then the Dutch, eager to complete their victory, thrust cutlasses between the beams of the door to sever the leathern thongs that fastened it.  A hasty retreat was made to the lower deck, where the brave fellows only fell into the hands of another body of the enemy and were forced to surrender.  The *Phœnix* was captured and taken off as a prize by the victors.[1]

At last night closed upon the scene of blood and destruction, and the wearied survivors of the crews drew the battered ships out of action.  Except for the loss of the *Phœnix*, which was a sore blow to the English, the fight had been maintained with no small success, considering the odds against the convoy.  The Dutch ships were not a little damaged, and two of them had been dismasted.  But the English ships were in a still more battered condition, and the crews were perilously reduced in

[1] Certificate of Chr. Bovey, Wadsworth's clerk.  Badiley's Answer, p. 94.

number. But the English had not succumbed, and Appleton, they hoped, was by this time on his way to relieve them.

But the long day's task was not yet over. The tired seamen must needs labour to remove the horrid signs of carnage and to restore their torn ships to as good condition as might be to resist further attack. The gruesome work was performed amidst subdued mutterings of discontent. "What is to be our fate to-morrow?" the sailors murmured, while the corpses of their comrades shot with a sullen plunge into the dark water. "Have we not done enough? The State has better ships, but we have no more lives."[1]

When the dreadful task was done, the wearied, battle-stained seamen on board the *Paragon* crowded round their captain. They told him that they had made up their minds, if the Dutch resumed the attack in the morning, that they would cry quarter and surrender the ship.

Badiley was resolved that the *Paragon* should never be surrendered while he could stand up to defend her, but his heart went out in sympathy for these poor men who had fought so gallantly and to whom the future looked so dark. But Badiley's faith did not fail him, and he saw it to be his clear duty, while he could lift a hand and strike a blow, to protect the ships entrusted to his charge. So he spoke his thoughts to his men in rough, stirring words. The hearts of the brave, weary sailors were cheered by his courage, and, when he ceased, they

[1] Affidavit of John Steele. Badiley's Answer, p. 91.

swore that they would live and die with their commander.

But in the cabin their enthusiasm waned. The men who had escaped from the *Phœnix*, to excuse their cowardice, told grim stories of the Dutch, what "giants" they were, and how they refused quarter to men who attempted to defend untenable ships. The courage with which Badiley's words had inspired his crew died out of their breasts, and they were re-possessed by the spirit of mutiny.[1]

Sunday morning dawned fair, and a fresh breeze was blowing, which gave the Dutch the weather gauge. The enemy lay not far off, but on all the northern horizon no sign was to be seen of Appleton's ships. The crew came on deck surly and discontented. The succour which their captain had foretold was not approaching. They were deserted by God and man. They were no longer stripped for action ; each man had donned his best clothes as a sign that he had definitely resolved to fight no more. Around the guns they had collected such lumber and rubbish as they could lay hands on, to clog them and make them unserviceable. They threatened that they would damage the rudder of the *Paragon*, and some were even heard to mutter that a bullet in the obstinate brain of their commander might prove the easiest method of settling the difference between them and him. As if to confirm their fears, the shattered main-mast of the *Paragon* crashed down upon the deck, rendering her for a time unmanageable.

[1] Badiley : Answer to Appleton, p. 25.

But Badiley did not lose heart, even in face of this relapse. " I made a speech among them," he said afterwards, "to encourage them what in me lay, although now so spent that it was a very great pain to me to speak so as to be heard twice or thrice my length."[1]  But his influence with his crew was waning.  This time only a few hands were held up in response to his appeal to know who would stand by him.  The rest of the men stood aloof, sulky and silent.  Still Badiley was nothing daunted.  Even with this small remnant of adherents he would fight to the last.  With his own hands he began to cast overboard the rubbish which the sailors had collected for choking the guns, and not a man stirred to prevent him.

While these things were being done on board the *Paragon*, boats were seen approaching her from the merchant ships.  They brought the captains of those vessels, who were anxious to tender their advice.  When they came on board the crew crowded round them.  If the merchant captains would declare that they deemed further resistance useless, the men-of-war need fight no longer.  And this was precisely what these brave captains, who had stood aloof from the battle all the previous day, had found it in their hearts to advise.  Their counsel was that the merchant ships should be burnt to prevent their cargoes falling into the hands of the Dutch, that the half-wrecked *Paragon* should be sunk, and that commanders and crews should escape on the least damaged frigate to the nearest port.  The men who

[1] *Ib.*

had just held up their hands for fighting, they declared, had altered their minds. Every man in the fleet was resolved to cry quarter if the Dutch renewed the attack.

So Badiley stood alone on the deck of his shattered ship, with nothing save his own indomitable spirit and his unwavering faith in God's providence to support him in his hour of need. All men had deserted him : Appleton, who should have come to his relief; the captains of the merchant ships which he had so long protected, and even his own crew. "'I will not give you such leave as you desire,' he said; 'but if you will begin upon your own account, do it. I can fire our ship when the enemy comes within musket shot; be but patient, and wait upon God a little, and I am persuaded that God will save this part of England's strength and wealth, whether men will or no.' And so it fell out, through God's mercy, in causing it to fall flat calm."[1]

The wind had suddenly dropped; the renewal of the Dutch attack was impossible, and the men for very shame were compelled to resume work. In reality, if they could have known it, they were in no danger of a renewal of the assault. The Dutch, as they afterwards confessed, were as much disabled as the English. They had set forth to catch a gnat and they found themselves handling a hornet. They had already resolved to wait for reinforce-

---

[1] Badiley: Answer to Appleton, p. 25. This is Badiley's latest account of what took place. It does not vary from, although it is less dramatic than, the story which he told at the time. See *post*, p. 112.

ments and in the meantime attend the motions of the English fleet, so that it should not elude their grasp. In these circumstances Badiley met with no resistance while he slowly worked his way to Porto Longone, a Spanish port on the eastern side of Elba, where he was received with friendliness.

This story of the battle of Monte Cristo has been compiled from various narratives. Badiley wrote two accounts of the fight soon after it had taken place. The first was a formal report to the Navy Committee, which was transmitted to London by Longland. It is dated August 31, 1652, from Porto Longone.

"On the 27th instant, eleven [1] of the best Flemish men-of-war came up with this ship (the *Paragon*) and the *Elizabeth, Phœnix* and *Constant Warwick*, between Lilboa (Elba) and Corsica, I having the *Mary Rose, Thomas Bonadventure*, and the *Richard and William* from Scanderoon and the *William and Thomas* from Smyrna under convoy, and at 4 p.m. they began an engagement with us; but at the close of the day there was not above four in five hundred pieces of ordnance spent on both sides, and we had suffered but little. Next morning they began afresh and we replied until evening, when they seemed out of breath, and, by my gunners' account, we discharged from this ship eight hundred pieces of great ordnance that day, which must have done no small execution, having sometimes two of the enemy's best men-of-war aboard, and their Admiral, Vice-admiral, and Rear-admiral,

[1] Most accounts give this as the number.

with all the rest sometimes within pistol and musket shot of us. One of them that boarded us found it so hot that many of that ship's company leapt out of their ports and called to us for quarter, but so many of them hanging at our boat astern, they sank her and were forced to address to their ship and bear her off with our help because she was on fire (although afterwards quenched), but we were not then in a condition to possess her, other ships being so ready to enter this. Yet had some other commanders[1] performed their words to me, or come within musketshot of them, this ship might have been relieved, on which lay all the heat of the service, and to all outward appearance, we had ruined their great strength and gained reputation to our nation, two of their main-masts being shot down.

" The *Phœnix* frigate was lost in a most sudden and strange manner, and there must have been great carelessness, to say the least, for had order been complied with, and the frigate fallen astern to my assistance as the *Constant Warwick* did, for which her commander and company deserve great reputation, the enemy had been repulsed and tired out sooner than they were, but while there were four on board and surrounding us in this ship we could not stir. They suffered themselves to be run aboard by a heavy ship of the enemy's that overcame the men and possessed the ship for want of a forecastle. We had not much assistance from the merchant ships, some of them not receiving a shot. Considering we lost twenty-six men slain and fifty-

---

[1] *i.e.* the merchant captains and Wadsworth of the *Phœnix*.

seven wounded, amongst which were all our leading officers, so as to be useless to us in the midst of the work, and withal considering this ship received fifty shot between wind and water and elsewhere in the hull, and in all her masts, yards and rigging impossible to number, so that none of our stays, shrouds, or other rigging were free, by the thousands of great shot that were discharged upon her; also considering that she had been fired in many places, yet preserved, and with her so much wealth of the nation upon the four merchant ships, as must in all likelihood have perished with her, and that we are brought safe to this place of security, I believe you will not esteem it among the meanest of the Lord's mercies."[1]

The above was Badiley's official account of the battle, and it is worth noting how little blame he cast upon any of his subordinates for failure of duty. The misconduct of his crew is not even mentioned. But in a subsequent letter to a private friend he became more communicative.

"Thanks for sympathising with your friends at such a distance," he wrote, "and praising God by whom this squadron was miraculously preserved in our engagement with the Dutch. He has many times been pleased to do great things by small means in our late war with the Royalists, yet I believe there was never more of God and less of man apparent in any disputes with the enemy. After this ship had been engaged with all the Dutch fleet single-handed for almost half a day,

[1] Badiley to Navy Committee. Cal. S.P.D., 1651–2, p. 402.

they, on the night of 28th August, strove to get from us, except the one that surprised the *Phœnix* and towed away with their boats; and the mariners of our ship being then called together, individually promised that if the enemy had any stomach to meddle with us next morning, they would stand by me to their death. But when the time came our mainmast broke down, the Flemings following afar off to see what we would do, having, as they have confessed, no intention to meddle with us again. Yet the mariners' resolutions were changed, and one and all would have left the ship and fled away on the frigates. And to such a height was this their humour that although, after a speech I made amongst them, twenty or thirty held up their hands to stand by me, no sooner did I turn from them than some of the commanders of the merchant ships told me I strove in vain to keep the ship; that those men who held up their hands had changed their minds, that there were none to stand by me, and that I had better resolve to give up all, and, before this ship was fired, theirs should be either burnt or sunk.

"To this I replied, 'Now is God's time to work like Himself!'—and so it was. Although the sun did not stand still, yet the wind suddenly died and it fell stark calm, so that the enemy could not come near us all day and the men could not for shame but rally again to their business, their distemper being caused chiefly by this :—thirty of the *Phœnix's* men ran away with their boat, and, having lost many men, I thought good to entertain them here; but those wicked fellows—as if it had not been enough by their cowardice to lose so good a frigate—raised a report among our men what giants the Flemings were and how they would give no quarter if we stood out any longer, and so caused that lowness of spirits in them. But some of them will be trussed up if ever God sends us home! Finally, it is worth observation that the Almighty saved the English ships at Porto Longone, whether the men would or not. Those who sit at stern take well their servant's endeavours in this dispute, which is an encouragement, although it was but my duty."[1]

[1] Badiley to Blackborne, Nov. 5, 1652. Cal. S.P.D., 1651-2, p. 477.

# Chapter IX

## BLOCKADED

THERE was anxiety and excitement among the English residents at Leghorn when, late on the night of August 27, it became known that Badiley's convoy was engaged with the Dutch men-of-war which had so recently sailed out of the Road. Longland was at that time in Pisa, but Morgan Read, the agent of the Levant Company, with the foremost English merchants, hastened down to the quay and urged Appleton to put to sea at once and attempt Badiley's relief. The captains of the merchant ships were called into council, and two of them—Wood of the *Peregrine*, and Marsh of the *Levant Merchant*—professed their readiness to sail in the service. The captains of two smaller vessels, the *Hunter* and the *Merchant's Relief*, were also ready to go out; but Seaman and Roope, commanding the *Sampson* and the *Mary*, the most powerful of the merchantmen, utterly refused to stir. It was not their business, they said, to convoy men-of-war, and they would not budge in the service of the State unless they had the orders of their owners to enlist. Nevertheless, the four merchantmen which were willing to undertake the enterprise, together with the *Leopard* and the

*Bonadventure*, would have proved more than a match for the five Dutch vessels lying outside the port, one of which was only a small merchantman lately taken up for the service. The two English frigates, in weight of metal and the number of their crews, were fully equal to the four Dutch men-of-war.[1] Morgan Read and the English merchants were unanimous that Appleton ought to attempt to break the blockade at once. Under cover of the night he might have succeeded in eluding the enemy's ships in the Road, and so would have reached Badiley in good fighting trim. If not, there could be no doubt that he would be able to give a good account of them when they tried to intercept him.

Appleton's behaviour was a mystery to his English advisers, because they did not possess the key to it. At one moment he seemed eager to set sail at once, the next he hesitated and saw difficulties. Now he would talk loudly about compelling Seaman and Roope to do their duty ; then he would fall into despondency and declare that the ships were not ready for action. Morgan Read wrote to Badiley not long after : " I found in Captain Appleton courage and resolution ; I am sorry it was not put in execution. . . . Time gives the enemy opportunity to recruit. They are

---

[1] Longland to G. Thompson, Sept. 20 (10, o.s.), 1652. " While the ten Dutch sail went out to fight Captain Badiley they left but four sail here to keep in all these ships, and it was a great shame that two such ships of the State (the *Leopard* and the *Bonadventure*) should be kept in by four Dutch, that had not so many men as our two." Longland did not take the small merchantman into account. Cal. S.P.D. 1651–2, p. 410.

diligent and vigilant: I wish we were, or had been so, from hence!"[1]   The reason for this lack of diligence was that Appleton had just bound himself not to engage with the Dutch within sight of the lighthouse of Leghorn.

Later on, when Appleton was seeking to justify his inaction, he gave two reasons for his failure to sail to Badiley's relief, neither of which was alleged at the time.   One was that "the Lord" had "at that time visited" him "with a violent and tedious sickness, so that" he "could not write." The other was that Captain Witheridge, of the *Bonadventure*, was dead.[2]   Captain Witheridge died suddenly on September 3, after an illness which lasted only four days.[3]   He was not, therefore, on the sick list on the night of August 27.   Even if he had been, the *Bonadventure* could have sailed under the command of her lieutenant, Lyme, whom Appleton afterwards promoted to be her captain. It is true that Appleton had been unwell, but on August 23 he had reported to the Navy Committee that he was "on the mend after his long and tedious fever."[4]   Neither Morgan Read nor any of the merchants who expressed regret at Apple-

---

[1] Read to Badiley.   Dated Oct. 18, but clearly written Sept. 8.   He wrote four letters to Badiley on the subject—all full of distrust of Appleton and regret for his neglect.   Badiley: Answer to Appleton, p. 53.

[2] Remonstrance, p. 4.

[3] Wood to Badiley, Sept. 3, 1652.   Answer to Appleton, p. 50, *bis*.   Appleton at the time gave the date as Sept. 2. Appleton to Navy Committee.   Cal. S.P.D., 1651–2, p. 391.

[4] Appleton to Navy Committee.   Cal. S.P.D., 1651–2, p. 380.

ton's inactivity attributed the fact to his illness. Captain Wood wrote thus to Badiley on September 3 : " Captain Witheridge this day departed this life, and Captain Appleton not very well, consequently the squadron is not in a good posture, which I am sorry to see, wishing that we had good resolutions to do a little work before us. Not above four sail of ships do keep us all here, and I suppose at last it will be put to you to contrive our work for us, and the Lord direct you in it." [1]

Appleton himself wrote four letters to Badiley between August 28 and September 3, and in none of them did he mention his indisposition. The man who on August 27 was so ill as to be unable to write succeeded in sending his comrade a long letter on the following day. It is not surprising, therefore, that Badiley afterwards called the alleged distemper " a feigned sickness." [2]

The first letter which Appleton sent to Badiley is undated, but its contents clearly show that it was written on Saturday, August 28, the day of the battle of Monte Cristo, while the English were urging Appleton to go out to Badiley's relief, and when his letter to the Grand Duke was half-way on the road to Florence.

" By the vessel Captain Cox found at sea," he wrote, "which arrived late here yester-night, we perceive that the ten sail of Hollanders have met with you and were in fight. We have sent two feluccas on purpose to see how it is with you, of which we

[1] Wood to Badiley.  Answer to Appleton, p. 50, *bis.*
[2] Answer to Appleton, p. 2.

hope well. If you go in for any port I pray you give me notice, that I, with the rest of our ships here, may give you our best assistance. We are hauling out of the Mould with the *Leopard* and the *Bonadventure*. The ships *Mary, Peregrine, Levant Merchant*, and one *M. Edge*, of eighteen guns,[1] will be all ready to depart this place in the morning, and shall watch the motions of these five ships that are here. I am minded to take in 100 barrels of powder more, in case you should want, and intend to bring two feluccas along with me, to go to and again upon occasion, in having correspondence and taking advice with you. I have not else but my prayers to God for you and the ships under convoy, and that our meeting may be safe and successful."[2]

It is doubtful whether Appleton ever went so far as to "haul out of the Mould," but he may have endeavoured to create some such appearance of activity on board the fleet in order to lull suspicions. On September 2 Longland wrote to Badiley : " As well the men-of-war as the merchantmen lie very safe in this port, for I see no inclination in the first to stir without the latter."[3] Morgan Read, in his last letter to Badiley, when he had apparently given up all hope of spurring Appleton to action, said : " God knoweth the vexation of spirit I have had hereabouts, and the more for that unto me it appeared facil to have at the first destroyed or beaten out of the way the small force of the enemy

---

[1] The *Merchant's Relief.* Edge was her captain.
[2] Answer to Appleton, p. 53, *bis*.
[3] *Ib.*, p. 46.

then lying before this port. . . . My opinion at first was embraced with a seeming forwardness in Captain Appleton and some others, and voted requisite by most of the nation at that time, but how dulled and not put in execution I leave it to them it concerns to answer."[1]

Captain Wood had written truly. It was "put" to Badiley to contrive the salvation of both fleets. For many months he was engaged in the task, with but poor results when all was done. His first duty was to secure his position at Porto Longone, where he was blockaded by Van Galen's fleet, and to repair his shattered ships. The governor of the town gave him a friendly reception, and when the Dutch, reinforced by fresh vessels, attempted to enter the harbour and attack the English, he ordered the guns of the fort to play upon them, and so made them keep their distance.[2] Thus foiled, the Dutch tried another plan. They offered the governor a bribe if he would permit them to destroy the English ships,[3] but he, virtuous above his kind in those days, declined the money. He showed his friendliness to the English by giving them the use of a house for their wounded men,

[1] Read to Badiley, Oct. 16 (o.s.), 1652. Answer to Appleton, p. 48.

[2] Longland to Navy Committee, Sept. 3 (o.s.), 1652. Cal. S.P.D., 1651–2, p. 401.

[3] Longland to Navy Committee, Oct. 1 (o.s.), 1652. "He told me, with much disdain, that the Dutch agent here brought 8,000 pistoles to tempt him to betray our ships into their hands by giving them liberty to fall upon them." Cal. S.P.D., 1651–2, p. 435.

the number of whom was increased, the Dutch having sent ashore the wounded from the *Phœnix*.[1] The sound men they retained, and compelled them to serve in their own fleet. Longland felt doubtful whether this courtesy would be of long continuance so he obtained from the Viceroy of Naples an order for the protection of the English ships;[2] and to gratify the governor of Porto Longone, he presented him with a gold chain, "which he accepted gratefully and with much modesty."[3]

Not content with merely repairing his ships, Badiley set himself to strengthen them. He thought that the loss of the *Phœnix*, although it was mainly due to neglect of orders, was also partly accounted for by its lack of a properly constructed forecastle. He therefore added forecastles to the *Elizabeth* and the *Paragon*.[4] Within a month from the date of the battle of Monte Cristo, Longland reported that "Captain Badiley has so repaired his ships that it is hardly discernible that they have been in fight."[5]

Badiley held his vessels in readiness to sail at an hour's warning, always expecting the appearance of Appleton and his convoy. During the month

[1] Longland to Navy Committee, Sept. 3 (o.s.), 1652. Cal. S.P.D., 1651-2, p. 391.

[2] Same to same, Sept. 10 (o.s.), 1652. Cal. S.P.D., 1651-2, p. 409.

[3] Same to same, Oct. 1 (o.s.), 1652. *Ib.*, p. 435.

[4] Badiley to Navy Committee, Nov. 11, 1652. Cal. S.P.D., 1652-3, p. 488.

[5] Longland to Navy Committee, Oct. 11 (o.s.), 1652. Cal. S.P.D., 1651-2, p. 436.

that had passed he had been too much engaged in repairing his ships to be able to examine the state of affairs at Leghorn, although the accounts which he was continually receiving from Longland and Read must have convinced him that much was amiss in that port. If he did not then suspect that Appleton was playing a double part, he knew that his fellow-commander had been guilty of negligence that was almost culpable. But it was no part of his policy to aggravate difficulties by coming to a breach with Appleton. He was compelled to work with him for the redemption of the English ships; so, as he afterwards said, " I did, as it were, take a mantle and cover his failings and miscarriages," it being his fixed policy " to mix sincerity with authority and cover mistakes." [1] But he was determined that he would not be placed in the position of being compelled to rely solely on Appleton's word or judgment in relation to the management of the ships, so he sent Captain Cox to Leghorn to act as eyes and ears for him. Appleton had at this time given up all idea of attempting to break the blockade, and had gone away, first to Lucca and then to Pisa.[2] Captain Cox's report fully bore out the suspicions of Read and Longland. That there had not been any serious intention to break out of port was proved by the fact that the ships had never been in trim for undertaking a voyage. The *Leopard* was dismasted, and the sailors' rations

---

[1] Badiley's Answer to Appleton, pp. 2, 11.
[2] Longland to Badiley (undated). *Ib.*, p. 48.

had only been provided from day to day.[1]   A two months' supply would have been needed if a voyage for England had been seriously contemplated.

At about this time the Dutch brought the *Phœnix* into Leghorn harbour for repairs, with the Dutch flag flying above the English "George" at her masthead, and Captain Wadsworth a prisoner on board.   The anger of the English sailors when they saw the good ship being strengthened for the purpose of fighting against them was intense. Longland pointed out to Cox how easy it would be to set her on fire some dark night,[2] and Cox was eager to undertake the enterprise; but Appleton strongly protested against the design.   Afterwards, when the *Phœnix* was repaired and was riding in the Road, Captain Cox renewed his proposal, but Appleton still remained inexorable.   Cox's description of what took place shows the low esteem in which he held his superior officer.   " I wrote you in my last the hopes I had of reducing the *Phœnix*. The business was brought to a head.   I then received a command from Captain Appleton not to persist any further in it, which hath been a great trouble to my spirit, yet resolved to proceed in it. But to cross me in my resolution the Flemings were made acquainted with it, and set a strong guard aboard the frigate.   I had fitted two barques, with forty men a-piece, to board her, which I did not

---

[1] Affidavit of John Butt, carpenter of the *Peregrine*.   Badiley's Answer, p. 85.

[2] Longland to Navy Committee, Sept. 17 (o.s.), 1652.   Cal. S.P.D., 1651-2, p. 421.

question in the least but to have carried her, but was betrayed by him whom it doth so much concern." [1]

While the *Phœnix* was still in harbour Captain Wadsworth effected his escape.  He plunged from the side of the ship and swam to the *Leopard*. While he was a prisoner he had written several letters to Badiley and others, endeavouring to explain away the loss of the *Phœnix*.  He asserted that the fault lay with the captains of the *Constant Warwick* and the *Elizabeth* because they did not come to his relief. [2]  He had succeeded in persuading himself that he and Badiley had borne the brunt of the conflict with the Dutch, while Cox and Reeves had shirked it.  The following letter to Badiley shows how quickly the fiction developed in his mind :—

" Sir, I kindly salute you : these being to acquaint you of the intents of my proceedings in the time of the fight, by reason I hear so many false tales and such reproachful speeches come from those you sent, of which I conceive you might be an eyewitness of their unworthy carriage before our coming to fight, in making no more haste to us, and in the latter part of the fight in not coming to rescue *yourself and me*.  When I saw you laid on board of both sides and the other ready to clap

---

[1] Cox to Badiley, Oct. 9, 1652.  Badiley's Answer, p. 52, *bis.*  See also Longland to Badiley, Oct. 9 (o.s.), 1652. *Ib.*, p. 56.

[2] Wadsworth to Longland ; same to Boneile ; same to Badiley, Sept. 2, 1652.  Badiley's Answer, pp. 94–98.

you thwart the hawse, and one coming on your bow, I thought the rest would be as forward as myself, being in better capacity, but finding it contrary to my expectation and their unworthy promises, *I have suffered, but the fleet is preserved by it.*" He went on to complain that Cox had declared that he ought to be hanged, and to express the hope that Badiley would call both Cox and Reeves to account for their cowardice. He threatened, if this were not done, that he would undertake the task himself if he ever returned to England. Badiley was not the man to be moved either by bluster or menace, and Wadsworth's fiction was not likely to deceive him. He replied : " I have received yours of yesterday's date, and take notice of what you say. But, by the way, I must needs tell you that if you had followed order, I suppose this trouble of yours had been prevented. However, I shall not make it my business to add affliction to the afflicted, but sending such things as you stand in need of, I remain, etc." [1]

Wadsworth escaped to the *Leopard* on Sunday, October 17. He clambered up the side of the ship while the chaplain, the Reverend Edward Spradborough, was delivering his morning exhortation. The sudden appearance of the dripping man on deck put an untimely end to the sermon. To the astonishment of both minister and congregation the captain lifted up his voice and held forth. " He made a speech among all the people there then present, tending to the vindication of himself from

[1] Answer to Appleton, p. 98.

those aspersions that were cast upon him because of his losing the said frigate, in which speech he seemed to asperse others. But being demanded whether Captain Badiley could do any more than he did, his answer was 'No'; to which he added this reason, ' because his ship was so much battered and torn that he could not come to his (Wadsworth's) assistance, but had work enough on board his own ship. He added, moreover, that he spake concerning the commanders of the other two frigates.' " [1]

This captain, who thought it seemly to proclaim his grievances before the common sailors, was no fit person to remain in the fleet, even if his fiction had been fact. On the morrow he was sent away to England overland, harbouring bitter thoughts against his old commander, who, he deemed, had refused to do him justice.

While these events were taking place the Dutch fleet was growing daily stronger. Soon after the Monte Cristo fight it numbered twenty sail, and it gradually increased, as time went on, to thirty-two, and then to forty vessels, twenty-five of which were men-of-war and the remainder merchantmen. [2] The Dutch also took up more sailors to man their ships, enlisting them at Toulon and the Italian ports hard by Leghorn. Most of these ships maintained the

---

[1] Certificate by Reynold Newnham, master ; Ed. Spradborough, minister; and Geo. Wrightington, master's mate (of the *Leopard*). Answer to Appleton, p. 98.

[2] Badiley to the Navy Committee, Sept. 23, 1652. Cal. S.P.D., 1651–2, p. 414. Same to same, Oct. 17, 1652. *Ib.*, p. 443. Longland to Blackborne, Oct. 21, 1652. *Ib.*, p. 451.

blockade of Leghorn and Porto Longone; the remainder plied between those towns to prevent communication between the two portions of the English fleet, and to cut off supplies. Badiley became convinced that, whatever might have been done by courage and resourceful energy before these reinforcements arrived, it was then too late to attempt to break the blockade with any chance of success. It was necessary to wait until either aid from England should arrive or an order should be received compelling the merchantmen to enter the State's service. Longland and Badiley did not cease to implore the Council of State to adopt one of these courses, but the attention of the English Government was so pre-occupied with the war in the Narrow Seas that they failed to imitate the vigour with which the Dutch asserted their interests in the Mediterranean.

The cost of the fleets at Leghorn and Porto Longone was heavy and money was hard to obtain. The Council of State sent no remittances, and trade with England was so dead that scarcely a merchant could be found who was willing to advance cash upon English bills of exchange. The few who were ready to do so would only take the risk at a heavy rate of interest. But the sailors had to be fed, and the cost of repairing the ships had to be defrayed. Before many weeks had elapsed Longland had advanced £3,000[1] for these purposes, and Badiley had found £1,000. But it passed the

---

[1] Longland to Col. Geo. Thompson, Sept. 10 (o.s.), 1652. Cal. S.P.D., 1651–2, p. 410.

power of these men to continue to support the fleet, and Longland wrote home urgently for remittances. If the fleet failed to pay ready money for its supplies, it would soon be ordered out of the ports, and left to the tender mercies of the Dutch. One financial plan which Longland propounded sounds strange to modern ears. "Some years since,"[1] he wrote, "the King of Portugal sent a squadron of ships into these seas to join with the French in taking of Porto Longone, for supply of which squadron he sent 2,000 bags of pepper to make money of, and this, or some such way, I represent to you, for your ships must be served."[2]

When Captain Witheridge died it became necessary to appoint a new commander to the *Bonadventure*. Appleton wrote to Badiley asking that Captain Cox might be allowed to take the post.[3] He said that the ship had not been well governed hitherto. The appointment was eventually made; but the reason for Appleton's selection of Cox, who, according to Appleton's later story, had disobeyed him so disgracefully in the matter of the French sattee, is inexplicable, if that story were true. If Appleton thought that Cox would submit to his policy of inactivity, he was strangely mistaken. Cox was not the man to sit idle on his quarter-deck and strike no blow for the liberation of the ships. It

---

[1] In 1647. See Ante, p. 66.

[2] Longland to Navy Committee, Sept. 10 (o.s.), 1652. Cal. S.P.D., 1651–2, p. 409.

[3] Appleton to Badiley, Sept. 3, 1652. Answer to Appleton, p. 54, *bis*.

was soon after his appointment to the *Bonadventure* that Appleton frustrated Cox's second design against the *Phœnix*, and after that there was no chance of harmony between the two men. Cox suspected Appleton as a traitor; Appleton saw in Cox the germs of insubordination, and became as anxious to be rid of him as he had previously been eager to secure his services. " Upon the death of Captain Witheridge," he wrote to the Navy Committee, " I placed Captain Cox in the *Bonadventure*, but finding his carriage intolerably proud, never owning me in anything he did, but daily acting to the prejudice of this port, and having also, without my order, placed his purser in the frigate, I ordered him, Cox, to quit the ship and return to the *Constant Warwick*, but he replied that he would not stir. Thereupon I sent for him, and acquainted him that I could not any longer endure his contempt for authority. I gave Lieutenant Lyme a commission to be commander until further order, and directed Cox to return to Porto Longone; but he said he would stay in despite of me, and so will force me to keep him a prisoner on board until I bring him to give me a writing to carry himself better for the future." [1]

Appleton went on to assert that Cox called together the crew of the *Bonadventure* and incited them to mutiny. If there was any truth in the statement the probability is that Cox declared that he would not relinquish the attempt to recapture the *Phœnix*; a grave breach of discipline, but by

[1] Appleton to Navy Committee, Nov. 1, 1652   Cal. S.P.D., 1651–2, p. 465.

this time Cox was weary of Appleton's inexplicable inaction.

The convoy at Leghorn was clearly in a bad way, and its condition was likely to grow worse unless a strong hand was ready to control it and to restore discipline.   Fortunately, just at this time an order arrived from England empowering Badiley to take supreme command of the ships in the Mediterranean; Appleton was, for the future, to serve under his orders.

Badiley's instructions ran thus : " In case you arrive at Leghorn, you are to consult with Charles Longland concerning all affairs relating to the ships under your command, as well for their preservation as for the security of trade, and to take special care that neither you, nor any of the ships under your command, give disturbance *to the said port.*" [1]

On receipt of this order Badiley at once sailed for Leghorn in a felucca, and succeeded in entering the harbour.   After hearing the difference between Appleton and Cox, he decided to confirm the latter in his command of the *Bonadventure.*   " I cannot interpret his pretended fault," he wrote, " to any other cause than his zeal to do the State service in regaining the *Phœnix* by a stratagem, and that beyond the range of the Grand Duke's ordnance.   I suppose it could not be accounted such an affront to the Great Duke and his port as to incur his dis-

[1] Instructions by Navy Committee to Captain Badiley, Sept. 17, 1652.   Cal. S.P.D., 1651–2, p. 407.   Badiley did not receive these instructions until November.

                                        K

pleasure, but rather he would have commended the diligence of the English to come by their own again, although in such a way."[1]

This letter seems to indicate that Appleton's defence of his conduct in forbidding Cox to attack the *Phœnix* was his fear of offending the Grand Duke; and it shows clearly that he still kept his undertaking with the duke a secret, and permitted Badiley to believe that the English fleet was free to engage with the Dutch so long as, in accordance with the instructions of the Navy Committee, the port of Leghorn was not disturbed.

Appleton could not take his deposition like a man. "I told you in my last what passed between Captain Cox and myself," he wrote home, "and find now that he had some pretence for what he did. Knowing I should not long be his commander, he thought he was not obliged to own me; whilst I, little thinking so soon to lose that power, resolved to make him do it."[2]

This surmise was quite groundless; neither Badiley nor Cox had any knowledge of the order until it came to hand. But it served to insinuate that these two commanders had been in league against him, and thus to show him in the light of an injured man. "As nothing made me undertake your service," he concluded, " but the great affection I bear to my nation, so all the undervaluing I can receive, with other disadvantages I have met with,

---

[1] Badiley to Navy Committee, Nov. 5, 1652. Cal. S.P.D., 1651–2, p. 476.

[2] Appleton to Navy Committee, Nov. 5, 1652. *Ib.*, p. 478.

shall neither make me repent nor neglect the same."

Thus Captain Appleton sank to the position of captain of the *Leopard*, under Badiley; but, unfortunately for him, he was not destined in that lowlier office to escape undervaluing and disadvantages.

# Chapter X

## THE RE-CAPTURE OF THE "PHŒNIX"

WHEN Badiley assumed the chief command of the Mediterranean fleets, a great change was rapidly wrought in the aspect of affairs at Leghorn. Hitherto the ships had only been victualled from day to day. They were at once provisioned for two months, in order that they might be ready for sea at any moment.[1] An order from England empowering Badiley and Longland to take up merchant ships for the service having tardily arrived, inquiries were set on foot at Venice, Genoa, Naples, and Alicant for ships suitable for that employment. The *Peregrine*, at Leghorn, willingly joined, and Seaman of the *Sampson* and 'Roope of the *Mary* were compelled to do so.[2]

Soon after this the more welcome news arrived that a relief fleet was preparing to sail from England. On September 28, Blake had obtained a considerable victory over the Dutch fleet, under the command of De Witt, off the Kentish Knock, a sandbank lying outside the estuary of the Thames.

[1] Badiley to Navy Committee, Nov. 5, 1652. Cal. S.P.D., 1651–2, p. 476. Longland to Navy Committee, Nov. 5 (o.s.). *Ib.*, p. 493.

[2] Cal. S.P.D., 1651–2, pp. 501, 514.

The Council of State, assuming too hastily that the Dutch would make no effort to retrieve this disaster until the spring, turned their thoughts to the condition of the ships in the Mediterranean. On November 12, 1652, they decided to write to Blake, apprising him of their intention to send twenty ships to the Straits. Blake was asked to advise the Council as to which ships ought to be sent on that service, and the selected vessels were ordered to rendezvous at Stokes Bay to be fitted out on December 1.[1] On November 18th, Captain Peacock, who had done good service in convoy work during the troublous times when the shores of England were infested by pirates, was appointed to command the squadron, with instructions that Badiley was to command in chief when the fleets met.[2]

The hope thus raised in the breasts of the English at Leghorn was doomed to disappointment. The squadron was not destined to sail to their relief. Within a week of Captain Peacock's appointment, the Council of State heard the astonishing news that the Dutch were preparing to put to sea, in spite of the lateness of the season, with a more powerful fleet than that which Blake had overcome off the Kentish Knock. England was quite unprepared for a winter campaign. Many ships were in dock, undergoing repairs. When all the vessels that could be mustered to meet this emergency had sailed into the Downs, Blake found himself in command of only forty sail, while the Dutch fleet was

---

[1] Council of State : Day's Proceedings. Cal. S.P.D., 1652, p. 489.  [2] *Ib.*, p. 498.

reported to number about one hundred and twenty ships. On November 30 the two fleets engaged off Dungeness. Blake, in spite of the most gallant efforts, was outnumbered and defeated. He retired into the Thames with his broken fleet, leaving the Dutch in command of the Narrow Seas.

Until England was able once more to assert her naval supremacy, all thought of relieving Badiley had to be abandoned. The most that could be done was to send him authority to press more merchantmen, and to advise him to force his way home if he was able.[1] If he lacked men, he might obtain them by ransoming English prisoners from the Turk. This counsel was somewhat vain, in face of the emptiness of the exchequer at Leghorn.

The lingering of the English ships at Leghorn was doing much mischief. The trade of the town was injured, and the Grand Duke and his subjects were growing heartily weary of their presence. This feeling was increased by rumours which reached them from time to time, mainly through Dutch channels, of reverses which the English had suffered in the Narrow Seas. The report of Blake's victory off the Kentish Knock was metamorphosed into a decisive defeat, which had resulted in the destruction of fourteen English men-of-war, and the flight of the remainder of the fleet to seek shelter in the harbour of Brest.[2] The Duke was not unnaturally anxious to court the favour of the winning

---

[1] Council of State : Day's Proceedings, Dec. 10, 1652. Cal. S.P.D., 1652–3, p. 21.

[2] Longland to Badiley, Oct. 19, 1652. Badiley's Answer, p. 56.

side.  If he showed marked favour to the English, and the Dutch were eventually triumphant, the consequences might prove unpleasant.  The Dutch report soon proved to be unfounded; but it became evident that if it were known that England had really suffered a reverse at sea, the friendship of the Tuscans would grow exceedingly cold.

The crews also had suffered from their enforced idleness, especially during the period of Appleton's command.  Some time afterwards Badiley hinted that the conduct of the sailors hardly suited with the strict Puritanism professed by many of them. He mentioned a story of a certain Turk who, having turned Christian, reverted to Mahomedanism because he was so shocked at the excesses committed by the English seamen.[1]  He told it in the heat of just wrath, and he probably had it only on hearsay.  But idle sailors were sure to get into mischief, and to offend the inhabitants of Leghorn. Even Appleton had begged the Navy Committee not to send pay for the men.  "They should have clothes," he said, "as winter is coming on : money is less necessary, in case they should disorder themselves."[2]  And Badiley complained, no doubt with justice, that inaction was rendering the sailors cowardly.

Badiley resolved that the crews should no longer rust for lack of active service, and his vigorous preparations to fit the ships for sea kept them con-

---

[1] Badiley's Answer, p. 40.

[2] Appleton to Navy Committee, Aug. 27, 1652.  Cal. S.P.D., 1651–2, p. 384.

stantly employed.    But something more than this was needed ; some enterprise to put heart into the men, the success of which would prove to them that the Dutch were not entirely their masters.

No exploit could be better suited for this purpose than the attempt to recapture the *Phœnix*, upon which the heart of Captain Cox had so long been set.    Success in such an enterprise would serve the double purpose of encouraging the sailors, and of removing a source of danger to the few English traders who still dared to sail those dangerous seas. The Dutch used the *Phœnix* as a decoy.    Whenever an English sail appeared in sight, the Dutch ships drew off to a discreet distance, leaving the *Phœnix* riding alone, with the "George" flying at her masthead.    The trader, sighting only a vessel of the well-known clumsy English build, and flying the national flag, came on in fancied security until she was under the guns of the *Phœnix*.    Then, without warning, a cannon ball crashed through her hull, and she had no alternative but to fight, sink, or surrender.

In November, when the plan for surprising the *Phœnix* was being matured, this trick was played upon a small merchantman called the *Samuel Bonadventure*, a ship of twenty guns, laden with salt fish and lead.    The little vessel showed some fight, but she was speedily overpowered.    The Dutch brought her in triumph into the port of Leghorn, dragging her English colours in derision through the water at her stern.[1]    The captive crew

---

[1] Badiley to Navy Committee, Dec. 2, 1652. Cal. S.P.D., 1652-3, p. 4.

were taken to man the Dutch ships ; but one sailor, who had been wounded, and the surgeon, were sent ashore to Longland.[1]

This insult to the flag acted as a strong tonic to the appetite for fighting of the English sailors, and they clamoured to revenge the affront. Not a man among them, except Appleton, dreamt that the Grand Duke would resent an attack on the *Phœnix*, which was lying at anchor in the Road, beyond range of the castle guns. Appleton held his peace about his promise to the Duke, and even encouraged the enterprise.[2] He knew that he had a ready excuse for himself if the Grand Duke attempted to call him to account for such an exploit. His undertaking had been limited by the saving clause, "unless I am commanded to the contrary." If Badiley ordered the attack on the *Phœnix*, the condition would be fulfilled, and Badiley would have to bear the blame. So neither Badiley nor Longland had any warning that the project would give rise to complications. They were even incited to it from home. Robert Blackborne, the secretary to the Navy Committee, wrote, in a letter which came to hand at about this time : " I long to hear of the regaining or destruction of the *Phœnix*, as it cannot but be a very great eyesore to you and Captain Badiley so long as she remains in the Mould."[3]

Appleton therefore kept his secret, while Badiley

---

[1] Appleton to Navy Committee, Nov. 19, 1652. Cal. S.P.D., 1651–2, p. 500.   [2] *Ib.*

[3] Blackborne to Longland, Oct. 22, 1652. Cal. S.P.D., 1651–2, p. 453.

and Cox pressed forward their preparations for the attack upon the *Phœnix*, quite unconscious of the trouble that would ensue from their enterprise. Events appeared to combine to favour their plans. Van Galen, with his flagship and another vessel, had gone cruising, either on the outlook for the succour which the English then expected, or to snap up any merchantmen that might be endeavouring to avoid the dangerous neighbourhood of Leghorn. He met with little success, for Badiley reported that he did not meet "with anything but a good appetite, his men being like to starve at sea, having been beaten back many times by contrary winds."[1] The Dutch had been lulled into a false security by the inactivity of the English, coupled with the Duke's assurance that Appleton had undertaken not to attack them. Many of their sailors had been invited to a feast at Leghorn to be held on St. Andrew's Day, November 20 (old style), and those who were left behind to guard the fleet were to hold revel on their own account. In such circumstances it was probable that a lax watch would be kept, and this would favour a sudden and determined attack.

By the night of November 20 the preparations for the assault upon the *Phœnix* were completed. In order that no shadow of excuse should be furnished for complaint of any disturbance of the port, the attacking party were strictly enjoined not to use firearms except in the last resort. The work was

---

[1] Badiley to Blackborne, Jan. 14, 1652/3. Cal. S.P.D., 1652–3, p. 105.

to be done, if possible, with pike and hanger.[1]  If the assault proved successful, the *Phœnix* was not to be brought into Leghorn harbour.  Her captors were ordered to stand out to sea, and steer for Spanish waters, where the Grand Duke could claim no jurisdiction.

It was a moonless night, and dark clouds hung murky over land and sea, obscuring even the dim light of the stars.  Silently, with muffled oars, three boats drew up alongside the *Leopard*.  The first was the *Elizabeth's* shallop, which was entered by Captain Cox, who commanded the attacking party, and fourteen sailors.  When she was manned, she shot out into the darkness, and was lost to sight.  She was followed by Lieutenant Young of the *Leopard* and Lieutenant Lyme of the *Bonadventure*, each in a pinnace containing thirty-four men.  Badiley and Appleton watched the embarkation and departure from the deck of the *Leopard*.  When the boats were lost to sight, Badiley, too anxious to be able to sleep, went up into the hills behind Leghorn and waited for the first streak of daylight to reveal whether the *Phœnix* still rode outside the harbour or not.[2]

The inky darkness of the night proved a hindrance rather than an aid to the adventurers.  It concealed them from the Dutch, but it also hid the boats from their comrades.  Cox had disappeared into the gloom with the light shallop, and the

[1] Badiley to Navy Committee, Dec. 2, 1652.  Cal. S.P.D., 1652–3, p. 3.
[2] Badiley's Answer, p. 13.

heavier-going pinnaces were unable to overtake him or to discover his whereabouts. For a long time they rowed hither and thither upon the dark oily water, seeking in vain for their commander. They dared not shout, lest their voices, travelling far over the silent sea, should give warning to the enemy of approaching danger. The night was waning, and the search for Cox seemed fruitless. Young and Lyme came to the conclusion that the expedition must be abandoned for that night, and they unwillingly turned their boats' heads towards port.

When they came alongside the *Leopard*, Appleton and the other officers strongly urged them to pull out into the Road once more, and make a last effort to find Captain Cox. Daylight was not far off, but the clouds still lowered over the sea, and it would be long before another St. Andrew's feast afforded so prosperous an opportunity of executing their design. So they rowed out again, and they had not pulled very far before they fell in with Cox's shallop. Cox was eager to pursue the enterprise upon which his heart had been so long set, and the three boats quietly and cautiously resumed their course towards the *Phœnix*. As they went a slight breeze sprang up before the coming day, the sea ruffled, the clouds parted here and there, the morning stars gleamed down upon the silent waters, and straight before them loomed the dark hull of the *Phœnix*. Not far off lay two Dutch frigates,[1] dimly

---

[1] *The Butter-pot* and *The Red-hair*, according to the English. Appleton to the Navy Committee, Nov. 22, 1652. Cal. S.P.D., 1651-2, p. 503.

visible in the grey half light between night and
dawn.

Lights flashed pale from the ports of the *Phœnix*,
and now and again a shout or the scrap of a song
became audible, which showed that the votaries of
St. Andrew were still doing homage to their patron
saint.   On the upper deck all was silent.   If watch
was being kept, it was with no alertness.   Cornelius
Van Tromp, the son of brave old Martin, commanded the *Phœnix*.   He was sitting at wine with
his officers, little dreaming of the danger that was
so near.

The two pinnaces lay to under the stern of the
*Phœnix*, while Cox shot forward in his shallop to
cut the cable.   Lyme and his men scrambled up
one side of the ship, while Young with his party
scaled the other.   Before they were well aboard,
they were followed by Cox and the rest of the
sailors, and the upper deck was gained.

Then followed the cry of alarm, the flash of
swords, and the hasty rush of the surprised watch
against a foe whose numbers they were not able to
estimate.   These were soon overpowered, and
young Van Tromp, hearing the alarm, hurried on
deck with one other officer to ascertain the cause of
it.   He found his ship swarming with the enemy.
Many of them were already aloft, unfurling the
sails, which began to catch the freshening breeze.
A few minutes later the water was hissing about the
prow of the *Phœnix* as she felt the wind.   Resistance was useless ; capture was disgrace.   Van
Tromp and his companion sprang upon the bul-

warks and then plunged, but not before the cutlass of an English sailor had slashed Van Tromp where a brave man is never proud of a scar. " Take that," cried the fellow, " for dragging our George astern your ships!" The grim symbolism was more painful than serious. The fugitives were able by swimming to gain the boat of the *Phœnix*, and to row off with their ill tidings to the nearest Dutch man-of-war.

The alarm was now given, and the two Dutch vessels cut cable and gave chase. But the *Phœnix* was by this time well under way, handled by sailors who knew every rope of her. She was swifter than her pursuers, and, the wind freshening with the growing day, she dashed gaily onward, the distance between her and the Dutchmen growing greater every minute. Now and again the few cannon that could be brought to bear upon her by her pursuers boomed forth across the water, but with little effect; and when the sun rose, chasing away the landward mists that hung about the hills, Captain Badiley might have descried the *Phœnix* in the dim distance, ploughing her way southward and leaving her enemies far astern. The success was, as he afterwards said, " to the joy of his heart." [1]

The *Phœnix* had been captured, but, though her Dutch commander had deserted her, her crew, who were superior in number to their assailants, were by no means subdued. For two hours after the *Phœnix* had got under sail, these brave men maintained a stubborn resistance upon the main deck

---

[1] Badiley's Answer, p. 13.

with hanger and pistol. But at last they were compelled to surrender. Eight had been slain and thirteen wounded, some mortally. The English only lost three of their party, one of whom was Lieutenant Young, who was shot down early in the struggle. The recovered *Phœnix* sailed triumphantly for Naples with near a hundred prisoners on board, and the English George flying once more at her masthead.[1]

This was evil news for the Dutch when they returned to their fleet from the banquet at Leghorn. Badiley somewhat gleefully told a story about that feast. "It is worth noting," he wrote to Blackborne, "that on St. Andrew's Day the Dutch used to make a feast in Leghorn, but to ingratiate themselves with the Italians, they would show their friendship to the religion of this country, and therefore now a friar must preach to all their captains and merchants before dinner. His text was, 'Follow me, and I will make you fishers of men.' As a just judgment, near a hundred of their men were fished from them that night in the *Phœnix*."[2]

It is improbable that the Dutch, who were stanch Protestants, would thus bend the knee before the Scarlet Woman, to curry favour with the Catholic Tuscans. Their ships had been recruited with

---

[1] For various accounts of the retaking of the *Phœnix* see Cox to Navy Commissioners. Cal. S.P.D., 1651–2, p. 515. Badiley to same. *Ib.*, 1652–3, p. 3. Longland to Navy Committee. *Ib.*, p. 44. Badiley to Blackborne. *Ib.*, p. 105. Appleton to Navy Committee, Nov. 22, 1652. *Ib.*, 1651–2, p. 503.

[2] Badiley to Blackborne, Jan. 14, 1652/3. Cal. S.P.D. 1652–3, p. 105.

Frenchmen and Italians, and some of the English and Scotch sailors in their fleet were probably Catholics. These men would willingly attend the friar's discourse, which was no doubt pointed with a political as well as a theological application. Badiley, who, like most men of his time, saw "judgments and mercies" in every event, would not doubt that the friar's sermon had received an unexpected illustration in the sudden capture of the *Phœnix*.

A few hours later Van Galen returned from his cruise after a good appetite, and Badiley reported that "he stormed like a madman to hear the frigate was lost, and when he went to the Great Duke at Court, he told him he knows young Tromp will lose his head for his neglect when he comes home, except his father does some notable exploit."[1] Cornelius Van Tromp's head was redeemed not many days later, when Martin Van Tromp won his first and last victory over Blake off Dungeness.

It is not difficult to surmise the nature of the complaint which the Dutch admiral lodged at the Court of Florence. In his opinion the attack upon the *Phœnix* was an unpardonable breach of faith. He believed, and he had good reason for believing, that the contending parties had come to an agreement, through the mediation of the Grand Duke, that the English should not attack the Dutch within sight of Leghorn lighthouse. Van Galen, relying upon this promise, had not kept the vigilant outlook which would have been necessary

[1] Badiley to Blackborne, Jan. 14, 1652/3. Cal. S.P.D., 1652-3, p. 105.

had no such promise been given. The Duke was bound in honour, he declared, to see that instant satisfaction was given for the outrage. The terms which he demanded did not err upon the side of moderation. He asked that all the English ships in the port of Leghorn should surrender their sails and rudders until the *Phœnix* was restored to him. Such satisfaction was easier to demand than to obtain, even if the Grand Duke was willing to demand it. Ferdinand's position was difficult. As the negotiator of the agreement which had been violated, he was manifestly the proper person to complain of any breach of it. But he knew that the English had been victorious over the Dutch at the Kentish Knock, and the battle of Dungeness had not yet been fought. He was therefore anxious not to offend the English in any way. The report went that he failed to treat the capture of the *Phœnix* seriously. He told the Dutch that he thought the Turks must have been among them, not the English, and he rallied them on the excellent watch that they had kept upon the night of the feast of St. Andrew.[1] It is hard to say whether the affair, if it had stood alone, would have affected adversely the relations between the English and the Tuscans. Probably very little notice would have been taken of it had it not been for the fact that just at that moment Appleton took upon himself to commit a folly which was a personal affront to the Grand Duke, and that hard upon the com-

[1] Badiley to Navy Committee, Dec. 2, 1652. Cal. S.P.D., 1652-3, p. 3.

mission of that folly arrived the news of Blake's defeat off Dungeness.

The capture of the *Phœnix* produced the good effect upon the sailors which Badiley had anticipated. He said that it had "put a new face on business" at Leghorn.[1]  The English recovered courage, for they had been made to feel that they were no longer hemmed in by an enemy whom it was useless to assault, and they grew eager for some more determined effort to free themselves from bondage.  The Dutch, on the other hand, were cast down.  They saw that the policy of waiting until the English should surrender out of sheer weariness was not likely to be crowned with success. They would rather have lost six ships, they said, than the *Phœnix*, which they had captured from the English in fair fight.[2]

[1] Badiley to Blackborne, Jan. 14, 1652/3.  Cal. S.P.D., 1652–3, p. 105.
[2] Longland to Navy Committee, Dec. 13, 1652.  *Ib.*, p. 24.

## Chapter XI

## THE ATTACK ON THE SENTINEL

APPLETON'S foolish act, which brought disgrace upon himself and trouble upon the English fleet, was on this wise. On November 21, the *Phœnix* having been re-captured on the previous night, a young Dutch sailor named Bergh was discovered on board the *Leopard*. What his purpose might be no man knew, but his intentions could hardly be other than hostile. The English, who had good reason to surmise that the Dutch would attempt some signal revenge for the loss of the *Phœnix*, suspected danger. Badiley, when he had assured himself of the success of his design, had returned to Porto Longone; so Appleton, after consultation with Longland, placed Bergh in confinement. The young sailor did not long remain a close prisoner, for on November 23, he obtained leave, upon some plausible excuse, to go to the ship's head. He then made a sudden plunge into the water and struck out for the Mould. Appleton, who was on deck at the time, shouted to two of the *Leopard's* men, who were standing on the pier-head, to secure the Dutchman, and then, jumping into a boat, with such of his crew as he could muster, he gave chase.

A Tuscan sentry, one of the guard which the Grand Duke had ordered for the protection of the English merchants' goods when they were landed and stored in the Lazaretto, was pacing to and fro upon his beat at the point where Bergh scrambled up the pier. The two English sailors attempted to stop the fugitive, but he succeeded in eluding them, and he took refuge in the sentry box.

At that moment Appleton, enraged at the escape of his prisoner, landed with his crew. He drew his sword and rushed upon the sentinel, followed by his men. The soldier, surprised by this unexpected attack, began to handle his musket as if he were about to use it. Appleton caught hold of the weapon, while his men, with shouts and imprecations, forced the cowering youth out of the sentry-box, and began dragging him towards their boat.

The uproar of the sailors, and the cries of their captive, speedily drew a crowd of loiterers to the scene of the disturbance. Among them were a Tuscan officer and two soldiers, who, having seen the sentinel struggling with the English, presented their pieces. By this time Appleton and his followers had secured their prisoner in the boat, and were endeavouring to push off, but the threatening attitude of the Tuscans brought them to a standstill. Appleton, who had quite lost self-control, shouted to the men on board the *Leopard* to fire upon the soldiers, but they, wiser than their commander, forbore. The boat was secured by the Tuscans, the prisoner was taken on shore again, and Appleton was forced to return to the *Leopard*, defeated and furious.[1]

Nothing more unfortunate could have happened for the English at a time when they needed all the tact and forbearance at their command to prevent difficulties arising out of the capture of the *Phœnix*. The latter exploit, although it was a breach of the understanding between Appleton and the Duke, was an affront only to the Dutch. The attack upon the sentinel was an affront to the Grand Duke himself, and one which every Tuscan was sure to resent. Appleton's offence, if it had been committed by a native, would have amounted to high treason.[2] It was intolerable that a man who had for months received protection and succour at Leghorn should thus outrage the port. Many Englishmen feared that although Ferdinand had been inclined to treat the taking of the *Phœnix* lightly, he would not deal with this offence in the same manner, and that the affair of the sentinel would make him much more willing to turn a ready ear to the complaints of the Dutch.

The Dutch made the most of the incident in their

---

[1] The story is compiled from various contradictory accounts. See Badiley to Navy Committee, Dec. 2, 1652. (Enclosing correspondence with Grand Duke.) Cal. S.P.D., 1652–3, p. 3. Appleton's Relation, Nov. 23, 1652–3. *Ib.*, p. 31. Appleton to Council of State, Dec. 18, 1652. *Ib.*, 1652–3, p. 40. Grand Duke to Salvetti. Despatches, N. 477–480. Longland to Council of State (copy in Italian). *Ib.*, N. 495.

[2] "E facil cosa conoscere quanto importi quest' atto, che arriva ad esser punibile come delitto di Lesa Maesta." Grand Duke to Salvetti. Despatches, N. 479.

own interests. They urged the Duke either to order the English ships to quit the port at once, or to compel them to comply with the demand for the delivery of their sails and rudders. No doubt the Grand Duke would willingly have brought the trouble to an end in some such fashion, if he could have been sure that an end would have been made of it. But at that time the only news which had reached Florence about the progress of the war in the Narrow Seas showed that the Dutch had been worsted. The wily Italian politicians were unwilling to offend the English, so long as a chance remained that England might take vengeance for the injury.

The Grand Duke played his game not unskilfully. The governor of Leghorn was ordered to request Appleton to attend the Court, which was then at Pisa. This request was in fact a command, and might not be disobeyed. So Appleton, accompanied by Longland and some of the merchant captains, set forth upon his journey. They knew that a storm was brewing, but they were not able to ascertain whether the cause of it was the *Phœnix* or the sentry. To these rough seamen a row in the harbour did not appear a matter to cause such a stir, and it seemed unreasonable that Appleton should be taken to task for the capture of the *Phœnix*. But Longland knew from experience "how unlimited a thing an absolute prince is,"[1] and that it would be well to be prepared with a defence upon both charges. On the road he asked Appleton

[1] Longland to Badiley, Dec. 24, 1652. Badiley's Answer, p. 59.

what he was going to say for himself if Ferdinand should raise the question of the *Phœnix*. Appleton replied that he could easily clear himself of his promise to the Grand Duke, "for it was conditioned," he said, " if I were not commanded to the contrary, as here I was, by Captain Badiley, who positively did command to retake or destroy the frigate." But he still left Longland under the impression that his promise to the Duke had been limited to the Port of Leghorn.

When the travellers arrived at Pisa, Appleton was arrested and cast into prison, much to the astonishment and anger of his companions, who were forbidden to hold any communication with him.[1] Longland went at once to Court and begged an audience, which was granted. He spoke in Appleton's defence, but he laboured under the disadvantage of not knowing the precise charge against the culprit. He enlarged upon the indignity which the Commonwealth of England had sustained in the imprisonment of one of its officers, and he threatened retaliation. This menace, on behalf of a nation which had left its ships in the Mediterranean for months without succour, did not greatly terrify the Tuscans. The Dutch were at Court also, clamouring for justice on account of the loss of the *Phœnix*. Their ships were in the Road, while the fleet which

---

[1] It should be noticed that this is Appleton's contemporary account of the affair. He says: "Upon my arrival I had no audience, but was committed prisoner to the castle, with orders that no one should speak with me." Appleton to Council of State, Dec. 18, 1652. Cal. S.P.D., 1652-3, p. 40.

was to vindicate the honour of England was still lying at Stokes Bay. Longland found it necessary to lower his tone. He pleaded that Appleton might be set at liberty, and be tried by his own countrymen for any offence that he had committed against the Grand Duke. Ferdinand seemed more inclined to listen to this proposal. He replied that he would consider the question of Appleton's release, when he had received from Captain Badiley an answer to a letter of complaint, which had been addressed to him as commander-in-chief.

On the following day, Longland learned for the first time the true nature of the undertaking that Appleton had given to the Grand Duke. Pandolfini, the Secretary at War, sent for him and showed him Appleton's letter of August 26, 1652.[1] Pandolfini told him that his master had communicated the contents of that letter to Van Galen, and upon the strength of it the Dutch now demanded satisfaction for the loss of the *Phœnix*. He concluded by hinting that unless Longland could persuade his Government to grant some satisfaction it would be difficult for the Grand Duke to protect the English ships any longer.

Longland now understood many things that before had been dark to him : why Appleton had been so unwilling to sail to Badiley's relief at the time of the battle of Monte Cristo; why the ships at Leghorn had never been ready for sea ; why Cox had been hindered in his scheme for recovering the *Phœnix*, and why Appleton became so eager to

[1] See *ante*, p. 94.

attack her, when the command of the fleet had passed out of his hands. He at once wrote home an account of what had happened.[1] The courier who carried his letter took also a long despatch from the Grand Duke to Salvetti, complaining of both the loss of the *Phœnix* and of the capture of the sentinel,[2] and a formal letter of protest addressed to the Parliament of England.[3]

All the Grand Duke's letters told practically the same story as regarded the attack on the sentinel, and purported to be founded upon the sworn evidence of witnesses of the transactions which they professed to describe. The following is his letter to Badiley, translated probably by the Captain himself, who did not pretend to an intimate knowledge of the Italian language.[4]

" Signor Appleton has been uncivil, not remembering the courtesies which the English ships have received in Leghorn. His unreasonable proceedings run against all conventions established, and he has also laid hands upon the arms under the faithful trust of our sentinel of the Mould, and taken a person away with violence from such a man who was in his house there appointed. This has obliged me to premeditate upon sincere satisfaction, and

[1] Longland to the Council of State, Nov. 27 (o.s.), 1652. Salvetti : Despatches, N. 496.

[2] Grand Duke to Salvetti. *Ib.*, 477–480.

[3] Hist. MSS. Comm., 13th Report, App. I. (Portland MSS.), p. 662. Reported to the House, Jan. 7, 1652/3. C.J. vii. 244, and referred to Council of State to hear Salvetti and report.

[4] " I profess not to understand every word that shall be spoken in Italian." Answer to Appleton, p. 44.

doubting he might draw himself out of chastisement by flying, I have arrested him and put him in custody in this castle of Pisa, that he may have such chastisement as he merits. I would not do it without informing you by express, being assured you will be displeased with things so ill acted, concurring in this my understanding, which always shall be within the limits of that observance which I profess to the Parliament and Republic of England, and shall always demonstrate my sincere estimation; and in order therefor, have renewed the commissions to my officers in Leghorn to be vigilant in defending the English ships which are there as they did at first, and with greater attention in regard to Appleton's and your absence."[1]

It is to be noticed that this letter, which was the first complaint written by the Grand Duke, contains no specific remonstrance against the capture of the *Phœnix*. In the later correspondence it takes its place with the attack on the sentinel in the general indictment of Appleton's conduct. This seems to support the opinion of both Longland and Badiley, that little would have been heard of that exploit if it had not been for Appleton's foolish behaviour on the quay at Leghorn.

This was the first news that Badiley received of the affair of the sentinel, and he found himself unexpectedly plunged into a difficulty that was none of his making. The capture of the *Phœnix* he was ready to avow, but he could offer no defence for the

---

[1] Enclosure with Badiley to Navy Committee, Dec. 2, 1652. Cal. S.P.D., 1652-3, p. 5. Dated Pisa, Nov. 25/Dec. 7, 1652.

assault upon the Grand Duke's officer. His main duty, however, was to get the English ships safely home, and he did not want to be hindered in the attainment of that object by any unnecessary complications. The following was his politic reply to Ferdinand :—

"I am greatly troubled at your displeasure, well knowing your favour to our nation, especially in protecting our ships and our merchants' great estates from the rapine of the Dutch. Were it not from your hands, whose words are of unquestionable verity, I could not believe that Captain Appleton, who is commanded by the Council of State to give all due respect to you within your ports and dominions, would willingly suffer his subordinates to commit so inexcuseable an affront as the gainsaying, much less the detention or constraining, of any that had the trust of arms as sentinel at the guard upon the Mould of Leghorn. As I heard nothing of this business before, I hope it will prove only the incivility of such as are under him. In case your pleasure be that the person or persons have their chastisement referred to me and a council of war that I shall call about that business, their punishment shall be severe according to their demerit ; but if you think fit that they be judged according to the laws of your dominions, the offenders shall be resigned to you. Only I beg that Capt. Appleton, having been one of our admirals in these seas, may not longer be under such a disgrace as imprisonment in your castle, lest our enemies, that made such a sign of victory in taking a fish-ship, trailing our English colours at their stern, should triumph more at this than any other act of hostility or treachery they have done upon us, which the Parliament of England could not but lay to heart.

"If Appleton has done any unworthy act willingly in your port, I know both himself and all others that do not consider that it's bad dallying with princes in such kind of actions, will be called to a strict account for the same in England, and therefore I again pray you will reckon his lying in prison so long a sufficient punishment. I do not doubt of your continued care in securing our shipping from the rage of our enemies until our redemption comes, which I hope is not far off." [1]

If Badiley had been a professed diplomatist, he could not have written a more tactful letter. But the main point to notice is the care which he took to excuse Appleton from blame as far as possible—a care which was afterwards to be most ungenerously rewarded. Badiley's letter had the desired effect. Appleton, after being detained in prison for four days, was released towards nightfall, and sent under a strong escort to St. Vicenzio. He was taken by a roundabout way, along unfrequented roads, possibly because it was feared that the Tuscans might attempt to execute summary justice upon him. From St. Vicenzio he was sent by boat to Porto Ferrajo, a town in the island of Elba which belonged to Tuscany, six miles from Porto Longone, whence Badiley was to fetch him at his leisure.

[1] Enclosure with Badiley to Navy Committee, Dec. 2, 1652. *Ib.* Dated Nov. 27, 1652.

A Council of War was called and Appleton was arraigned. There could be no doubt that an offence had been committed, although Appleton tried to extenuate his fault. He declared that he had behaved with great forbearance in his altercation with the sentinel, and that his arrest was really due to a conspiracy between the French and the Dutch to get him out of the way.[1] Appleton had not proved so formidable an opponent that his enemies should need to contrive against him in that manner. The Council of War decided that Appleton should " forbear executing his command upon the *Leopard* for the present," and Captain Jonas Poole, commander of the *Mary Rose*, was appointed in his place.[2]

Appleton was in a miserable state of alarm when he found himself at Porto Longone, without a command, and practically a cashiered man. He knew that when he returned home he would have to make answer to three charges which would inevitably be brought against him. First, his conduct in regard to the French sattee, then his concealed agreement with the Grand Duke, and lastly his assault upon the sentinel. He, and some of his companions, thought that it might prove a hanging matter. Brooding over his misfortunes, he gradually came to view them as a series of injustices, and it is not improbable that, during this period of idleness, the idea first occurred to him that Badiley and Longland were really to blame for all that had hap-

---

[1] Appleton's Relation, Cal. S.P.D., 1652–3, p. 31.
[2] Badiley to the Navy Committee, Dec. 15, 1652. Cal. S.P.D., 1652–3, p. 29.

pened—an idea which he afterwards elaborated with some ingenuity.

Badiley had no conception that he was making an enemy. Like most brave men, he was generous to a fault. He was sorry for Appleton, against whom so many offences could be alleged, and he was anxious to give the man a chance of redeeming his good name before he returned to England. He therefore "threw a mantle" once more over Appleton's misdoings. "Although none can excuse him of blame in the business," he reported to the Navy Committee, "it is not so bad as was declared to the Great Duke, and therefore, by your favour, he shall be re-established in his command as soon as we are clear of the coast of Italy, or sooner, if his Highness desire it." [1]

To the Grand Duke, Badiley was more explicit. "I have examined Captain Appleton," he wrote, "and though he pleads innocency of intention to give you any distaste in his action against your sentinel, yet I cannot excuse him, as he should have known that when a prisoner escaping puts foot in the dominions of an allied [2] prince, he is a free man, and it was both imbecility and incivility to take him from your men in arms. Therefore, upon mature deliberation with other of the State's servants, I have dismissed him from his command . . .

"About the *Phœnix*: I would add to what I have already written, that, not having heard of the

---

[1] Badiley to Navy Committee, Dec. 15, 1652. Cal. S.P.D., 1653-3, p. 29.

[2] He meant "neutral."

reciprocal obligations you name between the English and Dutch, I supposed I had not failed in respect to you in ordering the recovery of the frigate. If two persons, with their men in arms, meet in the chamber of a mutual friend, on pledge not to fight or make an uproar, and if one quietly and secretly takes part of his adversary's arms, this other would be justified in seeking restitution by stratagem, and the loser has no right to claim satisfaction. I leave the application to you, apologising for my presumption." [1]

The Grand Duke was pacified, but he was hardly contented with the mildness of the sentence. He would have preferred that the culprit should be dealt with more stringently. "I have seen what you have understood from Captain Appleton about the insult to the sentinel," he replied, "and, however it was related by him differently, nevertheless you see that I have not done anything against him without knowledge of the fact and without reason. Though he deserves more rigorous chastisement, nevertheless, having remitted myself to your judgment, I am satisfied with your removing him from the command of the ships in Leghorn." [2]

Concerning the *Phœnix* the Grand Duke said that he would prefer to discuss the question with Badiley at Pisa, whither he invited him to come, assuring him that he might do so "without any doubt of being molested." Badiley not long after accepted this invitation. The Duke evidently

[1] Enclosure with Badiley's letter of Dec. 15, 1652. *Ubi sup.*
[2] Dec. 11, 1652. *Ib.*

respected this straightforward man. Badiley was lodged at the Palace, and was treated as a person of great consequence.[1] Unfortunately no record remains of what passed between Ferdinand and Badiley. Badiley merely reported that the Duke " was very civil, and discoursed much with me, but did not mention a word about the *Phœnix*." The latter fact appears somewhat surprising, because the affair of the *Phœnix* was the avowed object of the interview. It affords further proof that the capture of the frigate had not been the real cause of the Duke's anger with the English.

When the Grand Duke's letter to Salvetti, complaining of Appleton's conduct, reached England, the Tuscan Resident lost no time in laying it before the Council of State. The Council on January 7, 1652/3, instructed the [2] Committee for Foreign Affairs to give Salvetti an audience. On January 10 the Committee recommended " that Captain Appleton should be summoned to attend Parliament or Council, to answer complaints of his carriage in his command, that the matter of fact may appear, and he is to come speedily overland." [3]

This recommendation was adopted, and Appleton was peremptorily summoned home to answer for his

---

[1] Longland to the Navy Committee, Jan. 3, 1652–3. " I went to kiss the Great Duke's hand, and thank him for favours to Captain Badiley, whom he entertained and lodged in his own palace like a general, and sent him back to Leghorn in one of his coaches with six horses." Cal. S.P.D., 1652–3, p. 78.

[2] Cal. S.P.D., 1652–3, p. 88.

[3] *Ib.*, p. 91.

attack on the sentinel.[1]   The Parliament sent also a letter to the Grand Duke, full of profuse apologies for Appleton's outrage, informing him of the steps which had been taken.   In regard to the capture of the *Phœnix* they were more reticent.   They merely promised to inquire into the matter when Appleton returned to England, and to send a further reply.[2]

Thus Appleton was not only deprived of his command, but ordered, in terms which portended disgrace, to come home and take his trial for his offence.   But while the correspondence relating to his conduct was travelling from and to Leghorn events had taken place which resulted in Badiley's arrival in England before Appleton.

[1] Council of State to Appleton, Jan. 14, 1562/3.  Salvetti Despatches, N. 510.
[2] Parliament to the Grand Duke, Jan. 14, 1652/3.  *Ib.*, O. 1.

# Chapter XII

## "PERVERSENESS AND OBSTINACY"

THE news of Blake's defeat by Van Tromp reached Leghorn early in January, 1652/3. Badiley knew well that, unless better tidings should speedily arrive from England, the Grand Duke would, sooner or later, give ear to the importunity of the Dutch and force him to quit Leghorn harbour. His aim was to postpone the evil day as long as possible in order to gain time to prepare for the inevitable conflict. Badiley's difficulties were increasing daily, for not only was the Grand Duke's friendship cooling, but the Viceroy of Naples was beginning to show signs of hostility. This was probably due to the fact that the French were endeavouring to effect an alliance with England, and the friends of France were of necessity the enemies of Spain. The first symptom of this unfriendliness was the refusal of the governor of Porto Longone to allow the ships which Badiley had taken up for the service of the State to land their merchandise. Badiley was therefore compelled to take them to the neighbouring harbour, Porto Ferrajo which was part of the dominions of the Grand Duke of Tuscany. Fortune favoured him in this enterprise, for the Dutch ships, which had hitherto closely blockaded Porto Longone, at about this time stood out to sea. The merchantmen quitted the harbour unmolested, and two of the frigates, the *Elizabeth* and the *Constant Warwick*, were ordered to sail for Naples to meet and return northwards with the *Phœnix* and the *Harry Bonadventure*, a merchantman which been impressed in that harbour.[1]

The attempt to hire ships at Venice having proved abortive, Captain Jonas Poole, Appleton's successor in the command of the *Leopard*, was sent thither to press that business forward.[2] Badiley's scheme was that if any merchantmen at Venice could be made ready for sea in time, they should effect a junction with the four vessels at Naples, sail for Leghorn, and, together with his own squadron, endeavour to engage the Dutch and release the English ships.[3] Captain Poole encountered many difficulties in the performance of his mission. When he arrived in Venice he was cast into the Lazaretto at the instance of the Dutch, upon the pretence that he could not show a clean bill of health. When he was released, every obstacle was placed in his way to prevent his

[1] Longland to the Navy Committee, Dec. 20, 1652. Cal. S.P.D., 1652–3, p. 44. Badiley to same, Dec. 15, 1652. *Ib.*, p. 29. Same to same, Jan. 30, 1652/3. *Ib.*, p. 133.

[2] Longland to Navy Committee, Jan. 3, 1652/3. Cal. S.P.D., 1652–3, p. 77.

[3] Badiley to Navy Committee, Dec. 15, 1652. Cal. S.P.D., 1652–3, p. 30.

engaging ships.[1]   At last he succeeded in persuading the captains of six merchantmen to undertake the service.   While the ships were being fitted
for sea, the news of Blake's defeat off Dungeness
came to hand.

The account of that defeat was, as usual,
exaggerated.   It was reported that the English
fleet had been annihilated.   The unvarnished truth
was bad enough without fictitious colouring.   For
several weeks the Dutch dominated the Narrow
Seas and all communication between England and
Italy was intercepted.[2]   Salvetti sent home gloomy
accounts of the condition of the Commonwealth.

A report was spread about that the Dutch were
going to aid the Royalists in an attempt to restore
Charles II. to the throne of England.   This rumour
was rendered more probable by the fact that the
Dutch bragged loudly that Prince Rupert, who had
just returned from his piracies in the Atlantic, was
coming to take command of the Dutch ships at
Leghorn.   "If he comes before your intended
fleet," wrote Longland, "he would do much mischief, and easily inveigle away many of the men,
who are apt to take any new impression, being
weary of so long an idle life." [3]

The Royalists endeavoured to foster the belief
that the Dutch had taken up their cause.   In the

---

[1] Poole to the Secretary of the Navy Committee, Feb. 28,
1652–3.  Cal. S.P.D., 1652–3, p. 192.

[2] Salvetti : Despatches, N. 489.

[3] Longland to Navy Committee, Jan. 3, 1652/3.  Cal. S.P.D.,
1652–3, p. 77.

month of January a letter had arrived for the Grand Duke from "the person called Charles II."[1] asking him to surrender the two ships which he had taken from the English rebels, and Sir Bernard Gascoigne was directed to make arrangements for their delivery. The ships referred to were the *Leopard* and the *Bonadventure*. The assumption that Ferdinand had seized them was a diplomatic fiction. Charles and his advisers knew well enough that Ferdinand had protected the English ships, but it was politic to pretend ignorance of the fact that a fellow-sovereign had sheltered and comforted Charles' rebellious subjects.

These events all tended to convince the Italians that England would be defeated in the war with the Dutch, and that any friendliness shown to them would not only be wasted, but would provoke the hostility of the victors. Badiley discovered that nations, like men, are averse from being found upon the losing side, and that his weakness gave England's enemies " advantage to offer many affronts " ; for " these people, like the fashion of the world, give most reason to the strongest."

One of these affronts was offered by the Viceroy of Naples. The *Elizabeth* and the *Constant Warwick*, when they were nearing Naples, fell in with a small Dutch ship carrying twenty-six guns, called the *Red Cross of Horne*, and after a short dispute

---

[1] Badiley to Navy Committee, Jan. 30, 1652/3. Cal. S.P.D., 1652–3, p. 133. Charles II. to Ferdinand II., Dec. 27, 1652. Clarendon State Papers, 1649–54; No. 914. Hyde to Sir Bernard Gascoigne, s.d. *Ib.*, No. 915.

they captured her.[1]   Even so inconsiderable an addition to the English fleet would have been acceptable, but there were no mariners to man her, so she was ordered to be sold at Naples.   There was no doubt that the prize was a Dutch ship ; her master did not dispute the fact.   Nevertheless, the Viceroy forbade the sale and ordered the question of nationality to be tried in his Court of Admiralty. Captain Cox, who commanded in chief at Naples, refused to obey this order, and he, with Captain Reeves, was cast into prison.[2]   Although both Badiley and Longland resented this unfriendly act, they thought Cox had acted foolishly in provoking hostility about such a trifle as the value of a small vessel.   But Cox was stiff-necked and preferred jail to compliance.[3]

At this juncture, when four of the English ships were rendered unserviceable by the imprisonment of their commander, the Grand Duke began to show himself more openly favourable to the Dutch.   He had come to Leghorn with his Court early in January, and Badiley soon perceived " that accord-

---

[1] Badiley to Navy Committee, Jan. 26, 1652/3.  Cal. S.P.D., 1652-3, p. 84.   Longland to Blackborne, Jan. 17, 1652-3.  *Ib.*, p. 107.

[2] Badiley to Navy Committee, Jan. 29, 1652/3.  *Ib.*, p. 132.

[3] Longland to Badiley, Feb. 3, 1652/3.  " I wish Captain Cox had condescended to the [Vice-] King's motion rather than have gone to prison, which brings disgrace and contempt upon the Parliament's commanders, and except the Parliament at home resents it in some high manner, it will grow customary among the Italian princes, and consequently make every man fly their service."  *Ib.*, p. 145.

to England's success, such are our friends among these foreign princes."[1] The Duke had by this time resolved to be quit of his troublesome visitors without coming to an actual breach with them. After hearing of Blake's defeat by Van Tromp, he espoused the Dutch complaint concerning the capture of the *Phœnix* with unexpected warmth. He directed one of his secretaries, Desiderio Montemagni, to see the rival commanders and endeavour to arrange terms. Montemagni first visited Van Galen, who would not abate one jot of his former demand for the surrender of the rudders and sails of the English ships. When this proposal was rejected by Badiley, Van Galen lowered his terms. " He said it would suffice if two of the men-of-war should resign their rudders and their sails into his Highness' hands until the *Phœnix* was restored." " Hereupon," Montemagni said, " I acquainted Captain Badiley with what had passed, laying before him the necessity of finding out some way for to adjust this business ; but it was all in vain, for he denied to yield to anything, saying that rather than he would yield the least unto his Highness or the Dutch, in case he might have time to fit himself, he would go out to sea with all his fleet. After my having waited for a better answer, giving him time to think of the badness of the consequences of such a resolution, I told him in case he would deliver one of his ships into my master's hand, I would endeavour that should pass for satisfaction, but this he slighted too.

[1] Badiley to Navy Committee, Jan. 6, 1652/3. *Ib.*, p. 84.

"At last I told him that if he would give it under his hand that he would return the frigate,[1] that that should pass for satisfaction, and that his Highness would continue still his best protection to him.  But such was the perverseness and obstinacy of Captain Badiley that he refused to hearken to any of these reasonable monitions."[2]

This account was written some time after the event, for the purpose of exculpating Appleton and bringing Badiley into discredit.  Such "perverseness and obstinacy" would hardly operate to Badiley's prejudice with the Council of State.  He saw clearly enough that, sooner or later, he would have to fight for his life and the lives of the men under his command, and, above all, for the honour of England.  Not a spar, not a rope's end, would he surrender to conciliate any Grand Duke in Christendom.

Badiley's position was the more difficult because he was not certain that he was receiving the moral support of the Parliament.  The Council of State, in their reply to the Grand Duke's remonstrance, had neither adopted nor repudiated Badiley's action in regard to the *Phœnix*, and this ambiguity placed him at a disadvantage.  "I hear that the regaining of the *Phœnix* frigate is not publicly owned in the letter to the Great Duke," he wrote, "but I hope it is owned in the hearts of those who sent the letter. I may have been rash, but I did not then know any-

---

[1] *i.e.* the *Phœnix*.

[2] A relation of Signor Montemagni. Appleton's Remonstrance, p. 19.

thing of Captain Appleton's obligement to the Great Duke, nor had I heard that the Great Duke had passed his word to the Dutch that the English should not molest them in his road or chamber. It seems unreasonable that the besiegers, being four to one, should desire the Prince to pass his word that the besieged should not come out and assault them. I was commanded to render the Great Duke all fair respect *within his ports*, yet none of your servants in consultation in these parts could judge it was intended to divert us from regaining their frigate, which might prove so very prejudicial to us while in their hands, especially since the Dutch would not at all be bound to render his Highness any of that civil respect which ought to have been, but would commit acts of hostility upon English merchantmen close to the Mould-head." [1]

Although the Grand Duke professed to have bound the Dutch, as well as the English, not to commit hostilities within the Road of Leghorn, the undertaking was not enforced against the former. On one occasion the Dutch seized a Tuscan vessel, called the *Tartan*, laden with food for the English sailors at Porto Longone. It might have been expected that Ferdinand would have resented this affront to his flag no less than he had resented the assault on the sentinel, but he passed it over in silence. Soon after, Longland was the victim of the enemy's depredations. His trade had been ruined by the blockade, and he was, as he said, " at

<hr>

[1] Badiley to Navy Committee, Feb. 11, 1652/3. Cal. S.P.D., 1652–3, p. 161.

his wit's end for money,"[1] not only for his own needs but for those of the State. He had shipped a cargo of tin, to the value of £4,000, on a French merchantman bound for Smyrna. The vessel was riding outside the harbour, ready to sail, when two Dutch men-of-war bore down upon her. They sent off four boats, filled with armed men, who boarded the ship and carried off the tin. When complaint was made to Ferdinand about this breach of the agreement, he replied "that it must go upon account of the frigate."[2] Longland, notwithstanding his loss, was not altogether dissatisfied with the result of this appeal to the Grand Duke. It had forced Ferdinand to show his colours. "At least we now clearly see by this action," he wrote to Badiley, after giving an account of the taking of the tin, " that when we have a power, we need not be scrupulous in what place we fall upon the enemy, and although the unhappy loss falls upon me, yet it may prove advantageous to the general business."[3]

Badiley received a further warning that Leghorn was no longer a safe refuge for the vessels under his command. The Duke ordered cannon to be placed upon the Mould, and their muzzles pointed threateningly towards the English ships.[4] " The Italians,"

[1] Longland to Badiley, Feb. 3, 1652/3. Cal. S.P.D., 1652–3, p. 145.

[2] Badiley to Navy Committee, Feb. 4, 1652/3. Cal. S.P.D., 1652–3, p. 148. Longland to the same, Feb. 14, 1652/3. *Ib.*, p. 165.

[3] Longland to Badiley, Feb. 8, 1652/3. Badiley's Answer, p. 61.

[4] Badiley to the Navy Committee, Jan. 30, 1652/3. Cal. S.P.D., 1652–3, p. 134.

Badiley said, "like politicians, took the strongest side."[1]    But it was of the last importance that he should not be forced to quit Leghorn before the ships which had been chartered at Venice, and those under Cox at Naples, could come to his assistance. So he left Montemagni to make the best he could of his failure to bring about an agreement, and he carried his perverseness and obstinacy straight to the throne of the Grand Duke.   On February 4/14 1652/3, he wrote to Ferdinand thus :—

"Whereas it hath been your pleasure to honour me with a credential letter bearing date the 8th instant,[2] four days since I received it by the hands of that right worthy and honourable person, your Secretary of State,[3] from whom I was informed of what was his message from your Highness, and unto whom I returned such a modest and humble answer as I hope hath been satisfactory.

"Among other commands, the Council of State (appointed by authority from the Parliament of England) hath required me, as well out of respect of what I obliged myself unto your Highness for in my former letters or humble addresses, as for other ends, in no case, nor upon any pretence, to assault the Dutch in the ports and chambers of your Highness, except they first began with us, the English ; which commands or orders of theirs, according to my duty, I shall readily render obedience unto.

"But may it please your Highness, since our enemies, the Dutch, do continually persist and go

---

[1] Badiley's Answer, p. 24.          [2] *i.e.* Jan. 29, 1652 (o.s.).
[3] Montemagni.

on, without rendering that respect which is due unto your Highness within your ports and chambers,
and lording it over all men of sundry nations, do
undertake to search their vessels, and, being dex-
terous at the trade of plundering, in hopes of such
lucre, chase barques and vessels passing about the
Mould head, and that as well of the subjects of your
Highness as elsehow.

"I do therefore humbly disoblige myself from
what I have been formerly, by letter or otherwise
engaged unto, and being, it's judged, they [who]
have given the first assault, since the receipt of the
commands before mentioned, I do hope it will not
be taken amiss by[1] your Highness, although, whenever the power is in the hands of us the English, we
may take advantage upon them in a reciprocal
manner. And so, wishing your Highness all increase of splendour and happiness, I shall subscribe
myself, as I am,

"Your Highness' very humble servant,

"R. BADILEY."[2]

This letter fell like a bomb into the enemies
camp. The Dutch and the Tuscans thought, as
Badiley intended them to think, that nothing save
the knowledge of approaching relief could prompt
the English commander to adopt so defiant a tone.
The Grand Duke and his counsellors meditated
over the situation for nearly a fortnight. At the
end of that time news arrived from Salvetti which
showed that the English were not in a position to

---

[1] "From" in orig.
[2] Badiley to the Grand Duke. Badiley's Answer, p. 104.

send reinforcements into the Mediterranean, and the Tuscans grew bold again.

On February 18 Montemagni was despatched to Badiley with another letter from the Grand Duke.[1] This letter contained a threat, couched in courteous language, that unless Badiley acceded to the Duke's terms, Montemagni would declare his ultimatum. Montemagni demanded the delivery of one of the English ships into the Duke's hands as security for the surrender of the *Phœnix*. " It is not in my power," Badiley replied, " willingly to deliver up one of the State's ships to the Duke or any other Prince or State, without special order from my masters in England."

"Well, then," said Montemagni, "his Highness' pleasure is you shall depart his port. What say you to that ? "

" Rather than I would willingly give consent that any of my limbs should be cut off, I would fight for the whole body as long as I could," was Badiley's answer; to which, he said, Montemagni rejoined that, " It was the Grand Duke's order that I must depart his port or mould with the English ships of war that were there once in [2] ten days." " To which I made this modest reply, in effect, as I said before," he continued, "'The Grand Duke is patron;[3] he may do what seemeth him good, although he knoweth best what he hath to do; yet, in my opinion, to require us to go out into the mouth of our enemies whenas they shall be three to one would be an

---

[1] Dated Feb. 18/28, 1652/3.          [2] *i.e.* within.
[3] *i.e.* autocrat.

eclipse to his honour among all the Princes in Europe.'"[1]   He instanced the case of the King of Portugal, who refused to turn Prince Rupert out of Lisbon, although the English constantly pressed the king to fix a date for his departure.

Montemagni was not to be moved.   The irrevocable verdict had gone forth that the English ships must depart in ten days.   Badiley offered him a bribe, " as much money as the *Phœnix* was worth to do what he liked with,"[2] if he would extend the time to thirty or forty days, to enable the ships to come in from Venice and Naples.   All the favour that he could obtain was that the following day should not count as one of the ten.   So, finding bribery as well as cajolery useless, the old sea-captain, calling to mind " how vain a thing it was ever counted to lie in a ditch and not stir to get out,"[3] hastened away to Porto Ferrajo to make his ships ready for prompt and decisive action.

The delay which had been caused by Badiley's defiant letter to the Grand Duke had enabled Cox with the *Phœnix* and two other vessels to return to Porto Ferrajo.   Had Cox obeyed orders, he would have rejoined Badiley sooner.   He had been compelled to purchase his freedom at Naples by giving up his claim to the *Red Cross of Horne*.[4]   Upon his release, instead of sailing northward, he made for Messina with the three frigates and the *Harry*

[1] Badiley's Answer, pp. 107–8.        [2] *Ib.*, p. 108.
[3] *Ib.*, p. 109.
[4] Longland to the Navy Committee, Feb. 14, 1652/3.   Cal. S.P.D., 1652–3, p. 165.

*Bonadventure.* He excused himself for this breach of orders on the ground that the wind had been contrary, but nothing could palliate his conduct when he reached the coast of Sicily. His clear duty was to preserve his ships for the relief of the vessels blockaded at Leghorn. Instead of doing this, he chased and fought a Dutch convoy consisting of six merchant ships and two men-of-war. The contest lasted for twelve hours ; then the Dutchmen, taking advantage of the wind, sheered off, and Cox's squadron was so crippled that it could not give chase. The English had the better of the fight, but their ships were pitifully torn, and many precious lives had been uselessly sacrificed at a time when the fleet was badly undermanned. Cox had to put in to Messina for repairs, and it was only a few days before Badiley was bound to go out to sea that he returned to Porto Ferrajo, having been compelled to leave the *Harry Bonadventure* at Messina.[1]

Badiley knew that he would have to encounter many dangers in the attempt to free the ships at Leghorn. In order to enter that shallow harbour, the merchantmen had been obliged to unlade. If they were compelled to sail without ballast, they would run great risk of heeling over in a gale. If they were to take up ballast, they must needs ride for twenty-four hours in the Road, where, unless a

[1] Cox to Navy Commissioners, Feb. 14, 1652/3. Cal. S.P.D., 1652-3, p. 165. Same to Badiley, Feb. 17, 1652/3. Badiley's Answer, p. 63. Longland to Navy Committee, Feb. 14, 1652/3. Cal. S.P.D., 1652-3, p. 165.

temporary truce could be arranged, they would lie helpless at the mercy of their enemies.  Even if the ships had been in fighting trim, they could not hope to get out of harbour and form into line of battle before the Dutch assaulted them, unless the Road were declared to be neutral water.  The long, low bank of the Malora, lying ahead of the emerging fleet, would prove an insurmountable hindrance to manœuvring, or to escape.

To fight the Dutch with any hope of success, it was essential that the two English squadrons should be able to join outside the Malora without molestation.  Badiley thought that he might secure this advantage if the Duke were sincere in his desire to prohibit all fighting in the Road.  For a time it appeared as if this were the case.  Van Galen, presuming upon his growing influence with the Tuscan Court, had threatened to assault the English ships within the harbour of Leghorn, unless they were ordered to put to sea at once.  The Grand Duke was not prepared to brook such an insult, and he showed his displeasure by ordering the arrest of all the Dutch sailors and officers who chanced to be on shore.  These, to the number of about a hundred, were cast into prison.[1]

While Badiley was hastening the fitting of his ships at Porto Ferrajo, he wrote another letter to the Grand Duke, in which he made certain proposals which he deemed the Duke could hardly

---

[1] Longland to Badiley, March 2 (o.s.), 1652/3.  Badiley's Answer, p. 65.

refuse without declaring himself openly upon the side of the Dutch.

" On Saturday last," he wrote, " I received those lines with which your Highness was pleased to favour me, bearing date the 28th[1] of the last month, and although that I desired with all my heart that this dispute about the *Phœnix* frigate might be finished at this treaty, nevertheless, having recovered the vessel by so notable a stratagem, I rest not in any way satisfied how I can answer it to them that employ me, if I should deprive myself voluntarily of her again, or of any other vessel in her place. And lastly, when I shall intend your Highness' will about that time limited for my going out I shall immediately apply myself to comply therewith, and that most joyfully, hoping it will succeed. I only beg that in case our vessels are not gone out of the Mould at Leghorn before the last day, and that the wind should be contrary, this should be interpreted (as it really is) a just impediment. I only fear that being we cannot stay one day in the Road for the providing of ballast without being molested, lest that some of our vessels should perish in case that any strong wind should arise before the dispute were ended.

" Your Highness pleaseth also to remember that since by my former letter I released myself of my engagement which I had first made concerning the

---

[1] New style. He refers to the letter brought by Montemagni. See *ante*, p. 173. Badiley, unusually for him, is using the new style. This letter is dated March 6, but it was written on Feb. 24, old style.

Hollanders and their confederates, I assure your Highness upon my honour that this was occasioned by the insolency of our enemies, to the end that when they knew it, they might rest mortified, and, in some measure, humbled, and consequently, reduced by the treaty to accept that which should be judged reasonable ; because, being there was no other means probable to prevail, I did believe that by this they would be seized upon by some fear, thinking that we were provided with a greater strength than they knew of.

" I was always of opinion that if a body entered into another man's house to refresh himself, although a private person, he should carry himself humbly, and much more in the chamber of a Prince ; and therefore, according to the commands I have received from my lords and masters in England,[1] I shall render your Highness all due respect, and shall not molest your[2] ports, particularly the Road of Leghorn, while the Hollanders shall do the same. And supposing all within the Malora to be the port and chamber of your Highness, so neither shall I directly nor indirectly molest the enemies of our nation, or any that belong to them ; and moreover neither myself nor any under me shall weigh anchor to chase any one coming in or going out, and shall be obedient unto any just commands your Highness shall give us, as well in our going away with all our fleet within three or four days, more or less, or to anything else. And I really believe that the Parlia-

---

[1] English in original.
[2] " His " in original.

ment of England will order the same respect to your Highness from all others that shall succeed me in these parts, to the end the most flourishing trade of Leghorn, which hath been eminent for so many years, should not meet with any impediment from the English.

" The Dutch now will not give the same respect, because they believe themselves strong enough to ruin us, but indeed they may be deceived for all that. We have eight men-of-war in this place (Porto Ferrajo) and Porto Longone, and six in Leghorn, which is not much disproportionable to the strength which they had yesterday in Leghorn, and if your Highness shall please to send once more another messenger to the Dutch admiral to know if they will render to his Highness' port the same respect as was promised by the English,[1] and to the end your Highness should be no longer troubled with us, I have made certain propositions, which shall be by me punctually observed, as also all that is contained in this letter; and for the execution thereof I believe that Mr. Longland, the public minister of the Commonwealth of England, will oblige himself together with me, as on the other side I do desire that Van der Staten[2] will oblige himself, together with Van Galen, in the presence of some public minister of your Highness'. So leaving all this to the consideration and discretion of your Highness, I say no more."

[1] The words " to give them encouragement for the better encouragement of the Dutch " occur here in the text.

[2] The Dutch Resident at Leghorn.

The following were the "propositions" which Badiley forwarded with this letter :—

"I. If the Dutch admiral will oblige himself that, without being molested, I shall come into the Road of Leghorn with my eight ships and flyboat which are here, and shall within forty-eight hours be ready to set sail, and that we may stay without fighting till the other ships can come out of the Mould and provide themselves with ballast; then on the other side will I oblige myself not to molest the Dutch while they are there, and that I will go without the Malora when he shall appoint; and, being without the Malora, I shall there freely wait until his ships come within musket-shot, there to dispute it, fighting like men, and not to molest and dishonour the port of that Prince who hath refreshed both of us with the fruit of his country.

"II. Having understood that the Dutch the other day bragged that they would fight with the English seven to seven, to the end that they should not make this [1] objection, I say that I shall grant them for every seven ships of ours, one, so that if we are fourteen in number, they shall be sixteen, and to the end they could not say that our vessels are bigger than theirs, I shall give them, when I make a list of the men, in every seven, one.

"III. When the fight shall be over, in case the English prove conquerors and return into the Road with all their fleet, and there find four or five merchantmen, or perhaps some of their [2] men-of-war,

---

[1] *i.e.* the objection which he at once proceeds to meet.

[2] *i.e.* the Dutch.

which may be soundly torn, I do promise not to shoot or fight with them within the Malora, provided the Dutch will do the same with us." [1]

Badiley well knew that he was proposing terms which the Dutch admiral would never accept. It was not to be supposed that Van Galen, who had about forty ships within call, would voluntarily reduce his fighting strength to less than half that number. The proposals were made to test the sincerity of the Grand Duke. If he really desired the continued friendship of the Parliament of England, he could easily ensure the safe departure of the English ships from Leghorn harbour and the neutrality of the Road by threatening to turn the guns of the castle upon the aggressor. If he re-

---

[1] Badiley to the Grand Duke. Appleton's Remonstrance, p. 21. The same letter is given in Badiley's Answer, in different phraseology, on p. 110, *et seq.* I have taken Appleton's version because the Remonstrance was compiled with the assistance of the Tuscan authorities, and he was probably furnished with a copy of the original. Badiley's version may have been printed from a rough draft or reconstructed from notes. There is evidently some copyist's or printer's error in Appleton's version of the second proposition. In Badiley's Answer it runs thus : "Whereas the Dutch did lately give out that they would fight the English when they were seven to seven, *lest it should now be objected that if this squadron and that at Leghorn meets, we shall be too hard for the Dutch, then thus :* if it pleaseth them to accept of the proportion, there will be granted to them to advance one in every seven ships, so that if we be fourteen, they may be sixteen ; and lest they should say some of our ships are bigger than theirs, there will be allowed to them to advance (when the men are polled) one man in every seven, so that there may be nothing to object against such endeavours as hath (*sic*) been used to preserve the great Duke's port from violation." Badiley's Answer, p. 112.

fused to do this after having insisted so long and so strongly upon the neutrality of the Road, he would by that fact declare himself the ally of the Dutch, and the Parliament would take note of it.

The Grand Duke did not even forward the proposals to Van Galen. It was enough for him that he was at last about to rid his port of the intruders who had so long disturbed its peace. He did not care greatly whether the battle which had to be fought took place within the Malora or outside it. He replied to Badiley as follows :—

"In answer to your letter received to-day,[1] I cannot but tell you that although the times are so disturbant, I see your resolution and diligence is that those ships may depart which are under your command at Livorno; and I, being desirous to pleasure the Parliament and Republic of England, am contented to prolong your time for the departure of your above mentioned ships till the 18th day of this present month,[2] that they may have a considerable time for their getting out, not dissenting from what you in yours advise that if wind and weather do not present [opportunity], and your ships cannot depart out of my Mould of the port of Livorno, [they] shall suspend till some other day.

" Now unto the propositions which you imparted unto me, that I might take notice of, concerning the ships which are under your command, for engaging with those of the States-General, it is not a thing convenient for me to meddle in.

[1] Feb. 28, 1652/3.
[2] *i.e.* March 8, 1652/3 (o.s.).

" I do accept of what you mention not to offend my ports with your ships against the Hollanders, which promises I do expect from you to be fulfilled, and doubt not but to have the like from the Hollanders, in such manner, to the content of both parties ; and for time to come all quietness and liberty shall be had in ports ; and the Almighty prosper you.

" I hope that this favourable weather will cause the departure of your ships out of my Mould of Livorno, so that you need [be under] no obligation for the regaining the frigate." [1]

It must be noted that the Grand Duke at this time insisted that there should be no fighting within the harbour, but he did not prohibit fighting in the Road. The English ships were to depart on or before March 8, unless the weather rendered departure a physical impossibility. The letter ended with a hint that the weather was at the time of writing favourable for setting sail, and the guns of Leghorn Castle, trained upon the English ships, gave significance to that comment.

There was nothing for it, therefore, but to bring the ships at Porto Ferrajo as near to Leghorn as might be, and to order the vessels in the latter harbour to be ready to sail with the first favourable wind. Before leaving Porto Ferrajo, Badiley found time to think of Appleton's hard case. He had always wished to give the man a chance of redeem-

---

[1] Grand Duke to Badiley, Feb. 28, 1652/3 (o.s.). Badiley's Answer, p. 114. This letter, which afterwards proved of vital importance, Badiley had in his possession.

ing his reputation before he returned to England.
To this end he took upon himself the responsibility
of setting aside the order of the Council of State,
which required Appleton to return home by land.
He called a Council of War, at which it was agreed
that, if the Grand Duke would consent, Appleton
should be restored to the command of the *Leopard*
in place of Captain Poole, who was still at Venice.[1]
The Duke, caring little who commanded the ships
so long as they departed out of Leghorn harbour,
offered no opposition, and Appleton found himself
once more captain of the *Leopard*. Badiley soon
had bitter reason to repent his generous indis-
cretion.

[1] Badiley's Answer, p. 4.

# Chapter XIII

## PREPARING FOR THE FIGHT

WHEN Badiley elected to force his way out of Leghorn harbour rather than submit to the terms which the Grand Duke had attempted to impose upon him, he was aware of the enormous difficulties which he would have to encounter. He had to face overwhelming odds, for the enemy possessed more than three ships for every one that he could bring out against them. The Dutch would begin the fight with the advantage of position. Their line cut the English fleet in two, so that they could easily fall upon and destroy one squadron before the other could be brought into action. If the wind blew from the sea it would be difficult for the ships in Leghorn harbour to come out and get into fighting order before the Dutch bore down upon them. If it blew off the land, it would impede Badiley in coming to their rescue if they were attacked at the harbour mouth. It was impossible to lay down any precise plan of action for the two squadrons when success or failure depended upon conditions that might change from hour to hour.

On night of February 28, Badiley sailed from Porto

Ferrajo with eight ships, four of which were men-of-war, and a fire-ship.[1]  The weather was then favourable for his exploit, and he was resolved, if it continued to hold fair, that the attempt to free the ships at Leghorn should be made at once.  At six o'clock on the morning of March 1 he was off Piombino, a town situated on the point of the Italian mainland nearest to Elba.  Thence he sent a letter to Appleton containing his instructions, so far as it was possible to give them.

" I am glad," he wrote, " that the Grand Duke, is so far pacified with you, and is willing you should continue your command until this dispute is over, and then, upon a consultation with some friends I shall do for you what I can, and hope we shall reach your desires.  I request that all the ships may be of your squadron for the present except the *Bonadventure*, and that is to be of mine.  I came from Porto Ferrajo last night with eight ships and a fire-ship, in good equipage, having got the fly-boats, men, and guns, and all the crew seem to be gallantly resolved.  I suppose we may be almost a third of the way over, and, ere this reaches you, we may be in sight.

" Consult with Mr. Longland and the commanders whether it were not best to warp the

---

| [1] MEN OF WAR. | CAPTAIN. | MERCHANTMEN. | CAPTAIN. |
|---|---|---|---|
| *Paragon* . . | Badiley. | *Lewis* . . . | Ell. |
| *Phœnix* . . | Cox. | *William & Thomas* | Godolphin. |
| *Elizabeth* . . | Reeves. | *Mary Rose* . . | Turtle. |
| *Constant Warwick* | Upshott. | *Thomas Bonadventure* | Hughes. |
| FIRE-SHIP . . . | Whyting. | | |

ships without the Mould-head, as I think it would be best this fine weather. If I see the ships[1] plying out to meet me, I intend plying to windward of them until I see you under sail and plying after us, and when it's a gale, I shall endeavour to break through them so that I may join you. If the wind be off shore, and you see them coming out to me, haste as for your life to follow with all the sail you can, *that we may not be too much oppressed before you come.* Desire Mr. Longland to supply you with powder and shot for me.

" P.S.—Tell Captain Lyme[2] if he sees me boarded, I expect he will board them that board me. I suppose you and the Dutch vice-admiral will try a pluck for it, and although he is a great Boar, yet he is but a boar, and, who knoweth, being the game of this country, he may be hunted as well as others."[3]

The meaning of these instructions is made clearer by the resolutions of a Council of War which was held just before the letter was written, and sent in writing with it. They ran thus: " Upon the question whether we shall stand into Leghorn Road with the wind westerly [*i.e.* on shore] so that we judge our ship(s) [*i.e.* Appleton's squadron] can-

---

[1] *i.e.* the Dutch.

[2] Of the *Bonadventure*, which was to be of Badiley's squadron.

[3] Badiley to Appleton, March 1, 1652/3. Cal. S.P.D., 1652–3, p. 195. The letter also appears in Badiley's Answer, with certain verbal alterations. This confirms the surmise mentioned *ante*, p. 181, note 1. It also suggests that Badiley, when he was preparing his Answer, was not allowed access to the documents in the possession of the Council of State.

not come out of the Mould, it was resolved in the negative ; but rather that we shall keep the wind of our enemy and not wilfully engage them without hope of help from our other squadron.

" Upon the question, in case the wind be easterly when we come near Leghorn Road, whether it were not best to tack and stand off to the southward a little while, thereby to endeavour the drawing or touling of our enemy out, that our dispute might be where we may have sea-room enough, it's resolved in the affirmative." [1]

These two documents reveal Badiley's plan of action. The wind, when he was writing, blew from the west. If it continued in that quarter, he intended to keep to windward in the hope that the Dutch would tack out to fight him. Appleton was then to draw out of harbour as best he could, and, when he was free, Badiley would bear down upon the Dutch ships before the wind and endeavour to break through them. If, however, the wind changed, and blew off shore, Badiley meant to run before it and try to decoy the Dutch into open water. If he were successful, Appleton would be free to come out of port and bear down upon the Dutch. But, remembering how little inclined Appleton had been to come out of port at the time of the battle of Monte Cristo, he added the warning to " haste as for your life," lest his own squadron should be overpowered before the Leghorn ships came into action. [2]

[1] Badiley's Answer, p. 69.   There was a third resolution of no importance.                    [2] Badiley's Answer, p. 28.

# PREPARING FOR THE FIGHT

The postscript to Badiley's letter is characteristic of the man. The *Great Boar* was Van Galen's flagship. According to the courtesies of naval warfare in those days, it was Badiley's privilege to assault the enemy's admiral. He magnanimously offered the post of honour to Appleton, so that the latter, in the event of victory, might return home with credit, and thus retrieve his lost reputation.

Badiley's letter was despatched to Leghorn by a felucca, and it reached its destination at sunset on March 1. The Dutch had received notice of the Duke's order for the departure of the English ships. Their fleet lay in a half-moon round the mouth of the harbour, and they had already despatched messengers summoning to their aid all their vessels which were cruising in neighbouring waters. While the wind continued to blow on shore, it seemed impossible that the Leghorn squadron could escape the clutches of the Dutch. Twice had Longland and two of the captains, Seaman, of the *Sampson*, and Wood, of the *Peregrine*, implored Montemagni to persuade the Duke, who was forcing the English ships out of the Mould, to take order that they should not be destroyed before they were in readiness to defend themselves. Montemagni made a half-hearted attempt to persuade Van Galen to allow the ships to pass the Malora unmolested ; but the news of Badiley's approach reached the Dutch Admiral during the conference, and it broke up without any agreement.[1]

[1] Longland to Badiley, March 2, 1652/3. Badiley's Answer, p. 66.

Badiley and his squadron arrived off the Malora early on the morning of March 2, and, as the wind was still westerly, he plied up and down outside in the hope that the Dutch would tack out to engage him. But the day wore on, and the Dutch fleet remained in a motionless crescent around the harbour mouth. Van Galen no doubt desired to postpone fighting until the ships which he had re-called were nearer to the scene of action.

At 4 o'clock on the morning of March 3 the wind still blew from the west. Badiley, finding that no enticements would draw the Dutch out to fight him, determined to change his plan. So he wrote a letter to Appleton, of which the following is the substance :—

"CAPTAIN APPLETON,—I perceive the Dutch have no mind to come out to me, but remain in the Road with hope to ruin you at your coming forth. And the squadron with you[1] being somewhat the less, whatever I suffer myself, I would not have it hazarded. Wherefore be very cautious what you do as to coming forth if you have not opportunity in the night. I would have you remain at the Mould-head while I come near to that place to re-

---

[1] The ships in Leghorn harbour were :—

MEN-OF-WAR.

| | |
|---|---|
| *Leopard* . . . . . | Appleton. |
| *Bonadventure* . . . . | Lyme. |

MERCHANTMEN.

| | |
|---|---|
| *Levant Merchant* . . . | Marsh. |
| *Peregrine*. . . . . | Wood. |
| *Mary* . . . . . | Fisher. |
| *Sampson* . . . . . | Seaman. |

ceive you, unless you see me engaged. And in that case pray take Mr. Longland's opinion what to do, who is a discreet gentleman, and one that will not only give you the best counsel he can, but, I am confident, is as loath to hazard you as myself."[1]

Badiley, having failed in his design for drawing the Dutch fleet outside the Malora, meditated incurring the risk of an engagement in the Road. He offered Appleton two alternatives : either that the ships at Leghorn should, on the following night, attempt to escape under cover of the darkness, or that, on the next day, Badiley should sail in and endeavour to engage the Dutch while Appleton's ships got free of the Mould and came to his relief.

It was difficult to pass letters through the Dutch lines in daylight, and Appleton's reply was not written until four o'clock in the afternoon. Before that time the wind had shifted and blew a light gale off shore. He therefore suggested another course. " I received yours bearing date 4 o'clock this present morning," he wrote, " and do acknowledge your great care in advancing the public [weal] and of not hazarding this squadron. I sent for all the commanders and showed them not only your letter, but the results of your council of war, which were all with a unanimous consent very well approved of, together with your intentions for managing the fight squadron to squadron.[2] I shall to my

---

[1] Badiley to Appleton, March 3, 1652/3. Badiley's Answer, p. 67. Badiley only professed to give the letter as he remembered it.
[2] Referring to the third resolution, which has not been quoted.

utmost endeavour to execute what you please to order, we being at present in a very good posture, all men exceeding willing. If you can draw near in the night within the Malora, the wind being off the shore, we shall, by God his assistance and your approbation, break through the enemy, which by a general consent is referred to you. Our eyes are towards Him who by the breath of His nostrils can make these vaunters fly before us, for which I continually pray."[1]

Appleton had made a proposal which combined both of the alternatives which Badiley had suggested. He elected to come out in the night, and he asked Badiley to sail in to his support. Badiley was by no means averse from any plan that savoured of prompt action, and he was anxious to encourage Appleton in his apparent forwardness to come out of port. At the same time he heard from Longland that the Grand Duke had released all the Dutch sailors whom he had arrested a few days before, and that there was no doubt [that the Tuscans would remain neutral if the Dutch fell upon the English ships as they quitted the harbour. " The Colonel[2] told me," Longland wrote, "his opinion was, as soon as our ships had their sterns to the Mould, the Dutch would assault them. He likewise asked me if you intended to assault them in the Road. These are symptoms that the Road is theirs that win it. As I cannot get so much from them in plain terms, neither will I persuade you to

---

[1] Appleton to Badiley, March 3, 1652/3. Badiley's Answer, p. 67.　　[2] Miniati, the Governor of Leghorn.

begin any hostility in the Road, for I believe you will not want provocation, or at least the ships now here, before you come in. Yet I should not wish you to desist from any notable advantage upon niceties when no assurance or certainty can be got from any of these great officers. The ships are all ready to undertake anything that is within the compass of possibility, but except part of the Dutch go out to you, or at least your fleet come in to our succour, it is impossible for these ships to get away without great loss and hazard." [1]

This information probably caused Badiley to decide in favour of Appleton's scheme for an escape by night. In the evening his squadron tacked in stealthily towards the land, taking a long sweep to avoid the southern horn of the Dutch crescent, and he came to anchor hard by the lighthouse without attracting the notice of the enemy. A felucca was brought alongside the *Paragon*, and Thomas Hughes, Badiley's lieutenant, dropped overboard into her. He crept into the harbour, bearing a message to Appleton that his desire to escape from Leghorn that night was to be fulfilled.

As he approached the English ships, he was surprised to note the absence of any evidence of impending departure. Hardly a light was to be seen aboard, and the only sign of life upon the decks was the usual night watch. When he clam-

---

[1] Longland to Badiley, Sept. 3 (o.s.), 1652/3. "At 22 hours," *i.e.* four o'clock. Badiley's Answer, p. 68. The Italians counted their day of 24 hours from sunset. On March 4, therefore, 22 hours would be about 4 p.m.

bered up the side of the *Leopard*, it was evident that everything had been made snug for the night. This was a strange posture for a fleet whose captain had so recently expressed his wish to make an immediate dash for liberty.  Hughes had expected to find Appleton and his subordinates alert to take advantage of the first chance of escape that might offer, but Appleton's energies had evaporated in his prayers.  He and the rest of the captains had to be roused from their peaceful slumbers, and they came slowly and unwillingly to that night council.  It was an hour before Fisher, of the *Mary*, could be induced to come aboard the *Leopard*.  Captain Seaman sprawled on Appleton's couch "like a lordaine" during the consultation, and Badiley's earnest advice that the ships should sail at once was heard with discontent and apathy.  The time for action had come, and Appleton's fatal hesitancy seized upon him.  He and the rest of the captains went on debating and doubting while the precious hours of darkness were passing away.  "First they would, and then they would not," as Hughes afterwards reported.  At last, when the night was far spent, they decided that they would not.  The attempt to break out was deferred until the morning, and Hughes was forced to return to the *Paragon* with this unwelcome intelligence.

The seamen were more eager to go out than their commanders.  The men of the *Leopard*, guessing that somewhat smacking of action was toward, had gathered on deck, and were waiting impatiently for the order to haul out their ship.  While Hughes was returning to the felucca he heard their growls of muttered discontent. Wrightington, the master's mate, was stamping up and down the deck in a rage. " These cursed men," he cried, " are so bewitched or besotted to this Mould that they care not for going hence ! Why cannot we go, having such a gallant gale of wind, now that the Admiral hath sent for us ? "[1]  It boded ill for the morrow's work that the men had thus lost faith in their commanders.

There is no report of what Badiley said when his lieutenant brought back the ill news.  His thoughts were doubtless the thoughts of Wrightington, expressed in words more strictly within the bounds of Puritan propriety.  But hard words were of no avail.  Badiley could not force the ships out of harbour against the will of their captains. Dawn was at hand, and with it would come discovery and a hopeless struggle with the Dutch without the aid of the ships inside the Mould. There was nothing for it but to draw out beyond the Malora again, running before that "gallant gale of wind" which an hour or two earlier might have proved the salvation of the whole fleet, and there await Appleton's good pleasure.

It had been an anxious, sleepless night for the men of Badiley's squadron, but the morning found them alert and eager for action.  A gale still blew from the east, and therefore the plan held good according to which Badiley was to endeavour to lure the Dutch to chase his squadron before the

---

[1] Affidavit of Thomas Hughes.  Badiley's Answer, p. 73.

wind, and then, if the bait took, Appleton was to watch his time and sail forth to Badiley's assistance before he was overwhelmed by superior force.

When the sun rose over the Tuscan hills, brightening the crests of the waves that danced and broke upon the Malora under stress of the fresh easterly breeze, Badiley's squadron tacked in towards the Dutch fleet that still lay crescent-wise round the entrance to Leghorn harbour. When this movement was perceived by the Dutch, there was a sudden stir on board their vessels. One by one their sails ran up to take the wind, and ere long the whole fleet was under way and standing seawards. Everything had fallen out as Badiley desired, and when from the poop of the *Paragon* he gave the order to put about and run before the wind, while the stern guns were brought to bear upon the enemy, ready to make play with him and provoke him to engage so soon as he should draw nearer, the old seaman felt the presage of coming victory within his breast. He was clear of the Malora : soon he would give the order to slacken sail and allow the Dutchmen to draw up to him. There, in the open sea, they would "fight it out like men," until Appleton's squadron came to his relief. The only question was, Would Appleton come out in time to save him ? Would he seize the opportune moment, or would he, at this crisis, hesitate and delay, as he had done before ? However that might be, the die was cast. Even if Appleton lingered, the fight must be fought, nevertheless; and the man who with only four frigates had made stand against ten Dutchmen throughout a long August day off Monte Cristo would not greatly fear that with nine ships he would be able to offer a prolonged resistance to the twenty-five vessels that were bearing down upon him with all their canvas spread.

But before the time for slackening sail had arrived, and while the Dutch were as yet hardly out of cannon-shot of the Mould, Badiley's keen eyes beheld a sight which dashed his hopes. In the ever-lessening port of Leghorn he espied a movement of ships. A vessel was clearing the Mould-head, and it was followed by another and another. In a few minutes all the six ships were out of harbour, as if, as Longland said afterwards, "they were greedy of their ruin." The Dutch had perceived this movement also. They at once put about, and the whole of their twenty-five sail were tacking down upon the six doomed English ships.

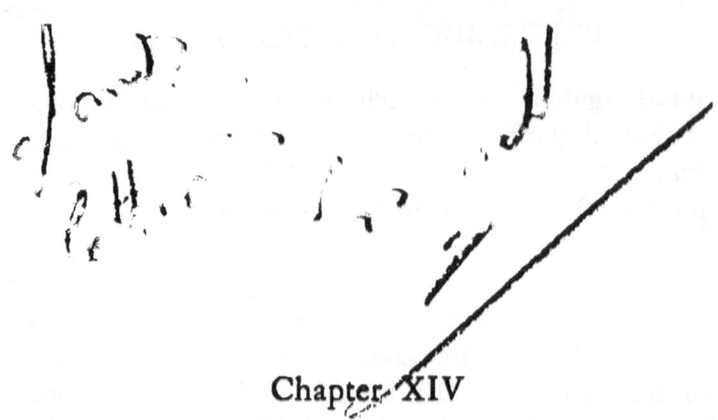

# Chapter XIV

## THE BATTLE OF LEGHORN

IT is impossible to account for the premature departure of the English ships from Leghorn except upon the supposition that Appleton lost his head. Longland has placed on record what took place on board Appleton's squadron on the eventful morning of March 4, 1652/3. He went down to the ships before daybreak, and he was present at a Council of War which was held on the *Leopard*. Appleton declared afterwards that he then informed Longland of his refusal to sail on the previous night, and that Longland approved of the decision;[1] but this Longland denied, declaring, on the contrary, that it was "inexcusable" that Appleton did not obey, "having such an authentic warrant as the call of his chief commander."[2]

The plans for the day were fully discussed at this Council of War, and it was agreed that, in case the Dutch chased Badiley's squadron, the ships should not go out until the two fleets were actually engaged, or in the alternative, if the Dutch should remain within the Road, the English ships should

[1] Appleton's Remonstrance, p. 8.
[2] Longland to Cromwell, Nov. 14, 1653. Cal. S.P.D., 1653–4, p. 245.

lie in harbour until Badiley, if he sailed in on the Dutch, should be within musket-shot of the enemy.

When the Council broke up the dawn was already brightening the water, and Longland paced the deck of the *Leopard* with Appleton, discussing for the last time the plan of action. Away in the distance they could see Badiley's squadron standing in towards shore, the sails pink under the rising sun. Then they perceived the stir on board the Dutch ships, the sailors busy in the cross-trees; and the shouted orders of the commanders came clear to them across the blue water of the Road. In a few minutes the Dutch fleet was under way, running out to sea after Badiley's ships, which, having at the same time put about, were becoming less and less in the distance. Longland rejoiced, as Badiley was rejoicing upon the poop of the *Paragon*, for he saw that the plan which offered the best chance of salvation for the imprisoned ships was about to prove successful.

At that moment he was startled by a cry from the deck of the *Bonadventure*, which lay nearest the mouth of the harbour, the *Leopard* being the next. It was the voice of her captain, Lyme, who shouted to Appleton, asking if he should haul out of harbour. Longland was astounded. It seemed impossible that any member of the late Council of War could be so reckless, or so forgetful, as to set at naught the decision which had been arrived at not an hour before. Badiley was miles to leeward of the Dutch fleet, which was still within cannon-shot of the shore. Longland implored

Appleton "to remember what they had all agreed to"; namely, "not to stir out of the Mould until the enemy had engaged Captain Badiley."[1] Appleton promised that he would observe the resolution faithfully, and then Longland, as he could be of no further service, took his departure, after wishing the captains "God-speed" in their dangerous exploit. He sprang ashore, leaving the English ships, which he had so long befriended, for the last time, and he walked slowly down the Mould, hoping that "God would appear for the English nation in His wonted mercy."

When he reached the town he turned to cast a parting glance at the ships which were soon to be engaged in such deadly strife. To his amazement he saw the *Bonadventure* standing out of port, followed by the *Leopard* and the rest of the English ships. He ran back along the Mould, shouting to them to stop, but it was too late. The squadron was already free of the harbour, and the foremost ships were running free before the breeze. The Dutch had perceived the mistake, and were putting about. Soon after the stern of the last ship had cleared the port the cannon of the Dutch were playing upon the doomed vessels.

None of the conflicting accounts of the events of the morning of March 4 attempt to explain how this folly came to be committed. It is not unreasonable to suppose that the error was due, in the first instance, to the action of Captain Lyme of

[1] Longland to Cromwell, Nov. 14, 1653, Cal. S.P.D., 1653-4, pp. 243-250.

the *Bonadventure*.  Lyme was a brave man, as his conduct in the assault upon the *Phœnix* proved. But the hardy fighter is not always the prudent leader, who can bide his time.  He had been eager to go out of port the moment that the Dutch had hoisted sail.  Perhaps he held Appleton, whom he must have known to be half-hearted and hesitating, in some contempt.  Such an one is precisely the kind of man under whose influence Appleton would be liable to fall in the supreme moment of difficulty. A harsh word or even a contemptuous gesture from Lyme would at such a crisis be enough to induce Appleton to take the rash and ruinous course, because, for the moment, it was the easiest.

One man in the fleet saw the deadly danger of this precipitancy.  Captain Wood, of the *Peregrine*, the fifth ship in the English line,[1] knew that they were rushing upon their ruin.  He shouted to Fisher, of the *Mary*, to pass the word to Seaman, of the *Sampson*, to implore Appleton not to go out until the Dutch were engaged with Badiley.  Seaman was rough-tongued, and he was hated by his comrades. " You know what manner of man Captain Seaman is, that a man cannot speak to him!" was Fisher's reply.  So this warning from a brave sailor, who was soon to pay with his life for his commander's folly, never reached Appleton's ears.[2]

---

[1] The order in which the ships sailed was : (1) *Bonadventure*, (2) *Leopard*, (3) *Sampson*, (4) *Mary*, (5) *Peregrine*, (6) *Levant Merchant*.

[2] Longland to Cromwell, *ut ante*.  Longland had this statement from Wood just before he died.

While Badiley, far away from the scene of action, was straining every sail and timber to come back in the teeth of the wind to the rescue of his comrades, the deadly and unequal struggle was raging between Appleton's six ships and the overwhelming force of the Dutch. The Leghorn squadron ran before the wind, hoping, with that advantage, to be able to break the Dutch line and join Badiley. But they soon found themselves begirt by a ring of fire and smoke. In the first moments of the action a disaster befell them which threw them into confusion. Hardly had twenty rounds of shot been fired when a cannon-ball pierced the *Bonadventure's* powder magazine, and she blew up with a thunderous report.[1] Captain Lyme, with most of his brave crew, paid for his rashness with his life in that fearful explosion. The *Bonadventure* was the first ship of the English line; the *Leopard* was coming up behind her at a distance of about three ships' lengths. She sailed straight into the descending storm of wreckage, and her deck was bestrewn with broken timbers, tangled cordage, and the corpses and limbs of men.[2]

This disaster checked the progress of the English ships,[3] and the Dutch took swift advantage of their evil plight. Before the *Leopard* had freed herself from the cumber of the destroyed *Bonadventure*, two large Dutchmen, the *Julius Cæsar* and the *Sun*, grappled her on the port side. The

---

[1] Appleton's Remonstrance, p. 9.

[2] *Ib.*

[3] Fisher's Declaration. Appleton's Remonstrance, p. 17.

*Sampson* was boarded by another man-of-war, commanded by young Van Tromp. The *Levant Merchant* and the *Peregrine* were similarly attacked by the *Pilgrim* and the *Madonna della Vigna*, ships of superior force. Only Captain Fisher, in the *Mary*, succeeding in eluding the grip of the enemy, and, instead of endeavouring to help his distressed comrades, sailed off to join Badiley's squadron,[1] which was still struggling against the wind towards the scene of the dispute. The rest of the Dutch ships, which on account of their numbers could not be brought into such close action, sailed round and round the chief combatants, pouring their broadsides into the English vessels whenever they could do so without injury to their comrades.

The fate of Appleton's squadron was sealed when the *Bonadventure* blew up. Even if Badiley had been within fighting distance at that moment, it is doubtful whether he could have saved it from destruction. But before he could come up against the wind other misfortunes had befallen the English. Seaman held his own well for a time against Van Tromp's assault, and indeed had somewhat the better of the encounter, when he was boarded on the other side by a fire-ship. The *Sampson* was not well enough manned to resist this double attack and cut the fire-ship adrift. The latter was ignited, and her men put off in boats. The flames soon roared up and caught hold of the *Sampson*, which, being no longer defensible, surrendered.[2] Seaman

---

[1] Appleton's Remonstrance, p. 9.
[2] *Ib.*, pp. 12, 16.

and a few of his men got on board Van Tromp's ship. In a few minutes the flames would reach the powder-magazine, so Van Tromp was compelled to leave the rest of the crew and the wounded to their horrible fate. He had hardly time to receive his prisoners on board and get clear of the burning vessel before the explosion took place, and the *Sampson* disappeared in a towering column of smoke and flame. Only one man of those who had been left on board escaped. Captain Hall was commander of the *Dove of Bristol*, a small merchantman which had been captured by the Dutch off Leghorn. He and his two sons were prisoners on board the *Sun* at the battle of Monte Cristo. Later on they were exchanged, and " being very passionate to serve the State against their enemies," they took service on board the *Sampson*. During the fight with Van Tromp one of the sons was slain, and the other was wounded. When the *Sampson* was fired, Hall was one of those who, in the wild rush for safety, succeeded in gaining the deck of Van Tromp's ship. The wounded youth was perforce left to his fate. When the ship blew up he was hurled into the air. He fell into the sea, blinded by the explosion. He happened to fall near some fragments of wreckage, by the aid of which he succeeded in keeping himself afloat until the battle was over, when he was rescued.

Only three ships of the Leghorn squadron remained to continue the unequal contest. The *Levant Merchant* and the *Peregrine* were small trading vessels, quite unfit to fight unaided against well-equipped men-of-war. The *Peregrine* did not hold out against such odds for long. Her main- and mizzen-masts had both been shot away; Captain Wood had been mortally wounded, and most of her crew were either slain or injured, so she surrendered. Captain Marsh defended himself a little longer. He succeeded in sinking the *Madonna della Vigna*, but he was immediately assaulted by *The Maid of Enchuisen*.[1] The *Levant Merchant* was maimed, and most of her crew were disabled: she was powerless to resist this fresh onset, so she lowered her colours. The *Leopard* was therefore at this juncture the only ship of the Leghorn squadron that was capable of showing fight.

But just before Marsh surrendered, Badiley had arrived within striking distance of the enemy. When he saw that Appleton had sailed out of Leghorn harbour prematurely, he did all that man could to return to his relief. His ships crowded on so much sail that the masts groaned under the press of canvas, and the sailors were in fear lest they should come crashing down upon the decks.[2] It was difficult to sail the clumsy frigates close to the wind. They were built for strength rather than for speed, and were, moreover, foul from long service at sea.[3] The nimbler merchantmen outstripped them, and thus the line of advance became broken. Badiley found it impossible to keep these ships in hand, for their commanders, little accustomed to

[1] Declaration by Longland, Oct. 16, 1654. Cal. S.P.D., 1654, p. 376. [2] Badiley's Answer, p. 30.
[3] Affidavit of James Thomas, master's mate in the *Mary Rose. Ib.*, p. 76.

obey orders, were too ready to act according to their own inclinations.

While the ships were thus tacking back upon the enemy, the wind veered a point or two southward, then abated somewhat, and blew in puffs. This increased their difficulties, because the lee-way that they made was taking them towards the dreaded Malora. Captain Cox, sailing too close to this fatal reef, ran the *Phœnix* aground, and he did not get her afloat again for half an hour.[1]

Badiley, before the merchantmen had sailed out of earshot, shouted an order that they were to go to the relief of the *Leopard*. For himself he proposed to "try a pluck" with the *Great Boar*, Van Galen's flag-ship, the honour which he had intended for Appleton. The *Great Boar* had been riding outside the main fight, watching the destruction of the English ships. Getting to windward of her, Badiley ordered Whyting, who commanded his only fire-ship, to endeavour to grapple her. Then he sailed past her, giving her the benefit of one broadside, while he bestowed the other upon the *Julius Cæsar* and the *Sun*, which were engaged in destroying the *Leopard*. When this manœuvre had been effected, Badiley observed that the merchantmen had disobeyed orders. Instead of going to relieve the *Leopard*, they had sailed "after their own inventions." Captain Fisher had broken through the Dutch line once more, thus placing himself in extreme peril. Captain Ell, with the *Lewis*, "was out of call, doing I know not what." Only the

---

[1] Seaman's Declaration. Appleton's Remonstrance, p. 15.

small, ill-manned *Mary Rose* was within hail of the *Paragon*. The relief of the *Leopard* was at this juncture the sole object of the fight. If she could be freed from her tormentors in any condition for sailing, no end could be served by continuing the unequal struggle. So Badiley determined to put about, rake the *Great Boar* once again, then drive the *Paragon* between the *Sun* and the *Julius Cæsar*, and try to make them loosen their grip upon the *Leopard*. But at this moment the wind dropped, or as Badiley expressed it, "it pleased God the wind dullard all of a sudden," and the *Paragon* refused to answer to her helm. She lay upon the water like a log, and all that she could do was to annoy the enemy as much as possible with her guns.

Meanwhile, the attack of the fire-ship upon the *Great Boar* had failed. The Dutch flagship, when Badiley was disabled from raking her a second time, had been left free to turn her undivided attention to Whyting's assault. All the guns that could be brought to bear upon the fire-ship riddled her as she approached, and she sank at the stern of the *Great Boar* before the crew could grapple the enemy and set her ablaze. Whyting and most of his men[1] escaped to the *Paragon*.

Badiley stood upon the poop of his motionless ship, fuming at his enforced inaction and exchanging a dropping fire with the *Great Boar*, which did not attempt any closer encounter, possibly because she, like the *Paragon*, was wind-bound. He looked

[1] Among them was John Steele. See *ante*, p. 4.

around for aid.  The rest of the frigates—the *Elizabeth*, the *Constant Warwick*, and the *Phœnix*, the latter of which, after heaving four of her guns overboard, had by this time freed herself from the Malora—were all heavy sailers, and were as little able to go to the relief of the *Leopard* as the *Paragon*.  They were lying upon the water, with sails drooping, firing upon the enemy at intervals.  The position of the English ships was growing desperate.  The drift of the tide and the puffs of wind which occasionally made themselves felt, were carrying the contending fleets slowly towards the Malora.  The *Leopard* was lying helpless in the cruel embrace of her foes.  Her fire had slackened, and no man was visible upon her upper deck.  But the George of England still hung, scarcely stirring, at her mast-head, and Badiley resolved to make a last forlorn effort to save her.

He signalled to the *Mary Rose* to attempt the relief of the *Leopard*, but Captain Turtle pleaded his lack of men and prayed to be excused.  Badiley knew that he would be sending the small ship and her crew to certain destruction if he persisted in the order, so he allowed the plea.  Then he looked round for one of the larger and better manned merchant vessels, the *Lewis* or the *Mary*, but they were still out of hail, skirmishing aimlessly with the enemy, but rendering no effective service.[1]

Badiley afterwards confessed that, while he stood thus at bay, deserted by the captains of those nimble ships, who alone could relieve the *Leopard*

[1] Badiley's Answer, p. 31.

at this crisis, he was "almost distracted with passion."
He had a low opinion of the captains of the
merchantmen. "When such vapouring blades are
in a gentlewoman's chamber," he thought, "oh,
then, they are mighty men of valour! But now
here is service to be done, they turn shifters above
all any commander-in-chief was troubled withal
before me!"[1] He concluded, from the condition
of the *Leopard*, that her captain and chief officers
had been disabled, and he conceived the desperate
design of going to her in his own pinnace, and
attempting to board and command her. He ordered
the boat to be lowered; but when his officers perceived his intention, they strongly dissuaded him
from the attempt.[2] They knew it was impossible
that he should ever reach the *Leopard* alive, but
that was not the argument which they used. They
pointed out that the wind was freshening again,
and that the two fleets had already drifted into the
shallows of the Malora.[3] In a short time the
English ships, which were deeper in the keel than
those of the Dutch, would run aground and become
an easy prey to the enemy. They directed his
attention to the plight of the *Leopard*, which for
some time had not fired a gun. To all appearances
she had already grounded. In addition to this, it
was well known on the English fleet that another
squadron of the enemy was approaching Leghorn,

[1] Badiley's Answer, p. 35.
[2] *Ib.*, pp. 32, 34.
[3] Affidavit of Thos. Hughes. *Ib.*, p. 74. Affidavit of Ant.
Watts, master of the *Paragon*. *Ib.*, p. 80.

which at any time might command the exit from the Road, and render impossible the escape of the remainder of the fleet.   Was it wise, in such circumstances, to risk the sacrifice of all the English strength in the Mediterranean Sea for the sake of one ship, which manifestly they were not strong enough to rescue from the hands of the enemy?

The most distasteful duty that can be imposed upon a brave man is that of being compelled to desert a friend in his hour of need, when it is impossible to render him effectual aid.   Perhaps it is even easier, in the wild passion of battle, to rush upon certain death than to take the calmer and more prudent course which minimises the evils of defeat.   Every fighting man who does the latter knows that his conduct will be criticised by those who have never seen a sword flash or heard a bullet sing, and will confidently declare, " you should have done this, or you should have done that; or, at any rate, you should have done more."   The problem presented to Badiley was whether he should attempt further the relief of the *Leopard*, knowing that, if he did so, he would almost certainly lose the nine ships which he still commanded, or whether, by retiring while a way of retreat was still open, he should save what remained of the English squadron.   He decided that his duty was to retire, and, taking advantage of the rising wind, he set sail seaward, chased by eight Dutch men-of-war, which, after about an hour's pursuit, put about, and returned to Leghorn.[1]

<hr>

[1] Appleton's Remonstrance, p. 10.

Only one ship which had left Leghorn harbour that morning, the *Mary*, commanded by Captain Fisher, had escaped with the flying fleet. Of the remainder, the *Bonadventure* and the *Sampson* had been destroyed; and the *Peregrine*, the *Levant Merchant*, and the *Leopard* had been captured by the Dutch, who only lost one vessel, the *Madonna della Vigna*. There is no account extant, save Appleton's, of what took place on board the *Leopard* during the fight, and that, bearing in mind Appleton's somewhat flexible notions of accuracy when his own interests were concerned, can hardly be accepted as authentic, even if it were coherent. He declared that he fought single-handed with the Dutch for two hours after Badiley had sailed away. This cannot be true, for many eye-witnesses of the fight testified that the *Leopard* was aground or sunk in the shallows at the time of or soon after Badiley's departure, and that for at least half an hour previously she had not fired a gun.[1] Appleton went on to say that when his crew saw that their friends had forsaken them, they declared that they would fight no longer. It is improbable that they failed to notice the desertion, and the consequent departure of eight Dutch ships in chase, until two hours had passed. He also said that the *Leopard's* stern was beaten in, her tiller shot to pieces, fourteen guns rendered unserviceable, and the ship very pitifully torn. He asserted that nearly half his men were disabled out of a crew of about two

---

[1] Affidavit of T. Hughes, John Butt, etc. Badiley's Answer, pp. 7392.

hundred sailors ; but when Longland came to count up the losses of the fleet, only ten of the *Leopard's* crew were reported missing.[1] This does not suggest that the ship had fought very desperately. At last, he said, a cry arose that the enemy was upon the poop, and he ordered the master gunner to blow it up. At this, the crew broke into open mutiny, and in the scuffle which ensued Appleton's shoulder was put out of joint. While he was thus disabled, the crew surrendered the ship.[2]

This account of what took place upon the *Leopard* has probably some truth in it, but Appleton post-dated the events in order to bring Badiley into disgrace. The mutiny of the crew had doubtless taken place before Badiley's departure. The fact that the cry went round that the enemy had gained possession of the poop proves that neither Appleton nor any of his men were upon the upper deck. This confirms the evidence of Badiley and many other eye-witnesses that, for some time before the *Leopard* was left to her fate, not a man was to be seen upon her. The report that the enemy had boarded her was evidently false, for Appleton admitted that the *Leopard* was surrendered, not captured.

[1] Deposition of Jonathan Parker, Nov. 14, 1653. Cal S.P.D., 1653-4, p. 249.

[2] Appleton's Remonstrance, p. 10.

# Chapter XV

# THE FATE OF THE PRISONERS

WHEN Longland, standing on the Mould-head at Leghorn, found that Appleton and his ships were past recall, he turned and, seeking his chamber, shut himself up in it while the battle was raging. Overborne with shame and grief, he had no heart to witness, amongst the crowd which surged down to the harbour at the sound of the first cannon, the inevitable defeat and dishonour of England.[1] Later in the day, when the result of the fight was known, he wrote a short letter home announcing the fact. "Captain Badiley," he said, "with the ships and frigates, came before Leghorn this morning to help out those ships that have lain here so long besieged; but the remedy has proved worse than the disease, as of six, only one has escaped to him, and the rest have been taken or [2] burnt."[3]

Longland soon found fresh labours imposed upon him. On the day after the battle a line of boats, crowded with men, was seen approaching the harbour from the Dutch fleet. The Dutch were cum-

[1] Longland to Badiley, April 25, 1653. Badiley's Answer, p. 71.

[2] "And" in original.

[3] Longland to Navy Committee, March 4 (o.s.), 1652/3. Cal. S.P.D., 1652-3, p. 214.

bered with their prisoners, and, after stripping them of everything valuable that they possessed, even to their shoes and hose, they determined to turn them adrift in Leghorn to shift for themselves. Two hundred and eighty sound men, and ninety wounded, were landed on Leghorn Mould that day.[1] Longland was quite unprepared for such an incursion. The sufferings of the wounded, whose injuries had received little or no attention, while they lay upon the Mould, must have been terrible. Twelve of them died soon after landing, and as many more were expected not to survive.

Longland set about the work thus thrust upon him with energy. He hired a house, which he quickly turned into a hospital, purchasing beds and other necessaries to furnish it. Then he bespoke the services of all the best surgeons in the town, and contracted with a resident Englishman to provide the sufferers with proper food at the rate of half a dollar a day for each man. Once in every day he went the round of this improvised hospital, to see that the patients wanted for nothing, and listening, doubtless, to many a woeful tale.[2] Among the sufferers was Captain Wood, of the *Peregrine*. He was mortally wounded, and the Dutch, out of humanity and respect for a brave foe, would fain have kept him on board the *Pilgrim*, which had taken him, until his end came. But he besought so

---

[1] Longland to Navy Commissioners, March 11 (o.s.), 1652/3. Cal. S.P.D., 1652-3, p. 223.

[2] Longland to Cromwell, Nov. 14, 1653. Cal. S.P.D., 1653-4, p. 243.

earnestly that he might be taken on shore to die amongst friends, that his wish was granted. " He was a pious and discreet man," Longland said, "and very forward to serve his country." During his last hours he was haunted by the memory of the mistake which Appleton had made in going out of Leghorn harbour before Badiley was engaged with the Dutch, a mistake which he had tried in vain to remedy. " Master Longland," he would moan, " our destruction is of ourselves—our destruction is of ourselves. We cannot blame Captain Badiley or anybody else, since we went not out in the night whenas we were sent for. I saw we went out too soon in the morning. If we had stayed while the Admiral had been engaged, all might have been well enough."[1] Longland could only listen pityingly to the dying man's groans, and when at last they ceased, he laid him to rest in his forgotten Italian grave.

It would appear that the sound men caused Longland more trouble than the sick. He had no authority from the State to do anything for these, but he could not see them starve, so day by day he made shift to find means for their support. And this burden was placed upon his shoulders when he was already " at his wits' end for money." Do what he might, he could hardly hope to satisfy these castaways, who were not too reasonable in their demands. " I used my discretion," he said, " and entertained them all at the State's charge, lest they

[1] Badiley's Answer, p. 28. See also affidavit of John Butt, carpenter of the *Peregrine. Ib.*, p. 84. Butt heard Wood's statement.

should put themselves into the enemy's service for want of a livelihood. To common men I gave a dollar and a seventh a day for five, and to officers a dollar a day for three."

" I will not speak," he went on, " of the many troubles these occasions brought upon me, to the neglect of my own affairs, for my house was constantly blocked up with these poor men, and when they found me abroad they followed me by droves. I much pitied them, yet such people are commonly unreasonable. Some would have money to carry them home overland : some wanted clothes, and some would have one thing and some another." [1]

Longland was quite unable to maintain these men at free quarters indefinitely, so he arranged to send some of them to Venice, to man the ships which Captain Poole had chartered for the State's service, and others to Messina, to complete the crew of the *Harry Bonadventure*, which had been left there by Captain Cox after his fight with the Dutch. Even this was no easy task. Sailors are usually great spendthrifts. There was grave fear that they would exhaust their journey-money before they arrived at their destination, and find themselves adrift in a foreign land, penniless. To prevent this, he despatched them in gangs of about twenty at a time, and he entrusted their money to " a sober man whom the men themselves approved of." To each he gave a new shirt, shoes and hose. [2]

The mariners who went to Venice found their

---

[1] Longland to Cromwell. Cal. S.P.D., 1653-4, p. 243.
[2] Longland to Navy Committee, April 18, 1653. He sent

way home in safety some months afterwards without much adventure, but those who joined the *Harry Bonadventure* were not so fortunate. That ship, after the departure of Cox for Porto Ferrajo, cruised about the coast of Sicily for some time under the command of Captain Swanley, and she took one or two prizes. Swanley had been ordered to join the Venice squadron, but he liked an independent, roving life so well that he failed to obey. He seems, indeed, to have set up as privateer on his own account, for he sold at least one prize, and neglected to account for the purchase money. In June, 1653, he captured a rich Dutch merchantman, the *St. Peter*, sailing from Venice for Holland, laden with quicksilver, glass, and other goods, to the value of £20,000.[1] The Dutch determined to put an end to Swanley's piratical enterprises. They sent a small squadron, under the command of Cornelius Van Tromp, to intercept the *Harry Bonadventure* and her prize, which were making for Messina. Van Tromp came up with the two ships off Trapani in Sicily, and he chased them into that harbour. Swanley imagined that the Spanish governor would afford him protection, but he was deceived. Van Tromp followed him into the port, captured his

160 men to Venice. "Not half of those sent to Venice," he said, "went there, but to Genoa and other places; but I shall have a list of those who have given me the slip, and will forward it. Those of the *Leopard* may have the impudence to ask for their wages, and then you will deal with them as you see fit." Cal. S.P.D., 1652–3, p. 284.

[1] Longland to Admiralty Committee, June 27, 1653. Cal. S.P.D., 1652–3, p. 442.

ships without difficulty, and brought them back in triumph to Leghorn. Thus the unfortunate seamen who had enlisted on the *Harry Bonadventure* found themselves once more prisoners on board the Dutch fleet.[1] Twenty of these men succeeded in escaping to Leghorn, and looked again to Longland for sustenance.[2]

Appleton, Seaman, and Marsh were the only prisoners whom the Dutch detained on board their fleet after the victory in the Road of Leghorn. Marsh was on the *Maid of Enchuisen*; Seaman was on Van Tromp's ship, and Appleton was prisoner to Van Galen, on the *Great Boar*. Thence Appleton sent home two letters, in explanation of his conduct, which illustrate the evolution of a myth. One was addressed to the Council of State, and ran as follows :—

" I wrote you by Charles Longland of our great loss here at Leghorn, and to satisfy you of my disobedience to your summons for appearance. That I may not seem voluntarily to have lost my ship, which much troubles me, I send you a copy of my Admiral's letter for my going out of the Mould,[3] to which on 4/14 March Mr. Longland and all the commanders on consultation consented.

" I am loth to stir in troubled waters, but if Captain Cox had obeyed Captain Badiley's order we should not have suffered so. Captain Badiley said to me,

---

[1] Longland to Admiralty Committee, July 18, 1653. Cal. S.P.D., 1653-4, p. 35.

[2] Longland to Admiralty Committee, July 25, 1653. *Ib.*, p. 48.          [3] See *ante*, p. 186.

'The State of England had better have given Captain Cox £20,000 than that he should have disobeyed order'; but Cox thought to slight him, as he did me.

"Pray examine the whole company of the *Leopard* and of all other ships at their arrival as to my deportment, both before and in the late engagement, and you will receive the truth in time. I think some captains under my Admiral, who were willing to come to my relief, but were called off, will testify for me. Pray use means for my enlargement, that I may give you an account of my actions. The Dutch use me very uncivilly; but if I had had my will, I should not have to complain of this, for I should have blown up the ship."[1]

It is plain from this letter that Appleton had resolved to cast the blame for his mishap upon somebody, but he hesitated to affix it upon Badiley in a communication which would become a public document. He selected Cox as an alternative scapegoat, possibly because he knew that Cox was liable to be called to account for disobedience to orders in sailing from Naples to Messina. So he dragged that story into his letter, alleging it as one of the circumstances which contributed to the disaster at Leghorn. How he proposed to show that Cox's expedition contributed to the defeat, it is impossible to surmise. The only result of it was a delay in the sailing of the fleet; but Appleton's

---

[1] Appleton to ——, March 25, 1653. Cal. S.P.D., 1652–3 p. 233. This next letter shows that this was addressed to the Council of State.

subsequent contention, when his accusation was fully developed, was that Badiley had forced the ships out of Leghorn harbour too soon.

In his second letter, which was almost certainly addressed to Sir Harry Vane, he made no mention of the charge against Cox, and elaborated that against Badiley. " The disaster befallen the Commonwealth in these southern parts," he wrote, " will be rung in your ears long before the receipt of this, but that the truth may appear, I have written it to the Council of State, and fearing lest it should miscarry, I enclose a copy to you, as burgess for the town of Hull, of which I am a member, and desire you will see it delivered. I am loth to burden any man, but I am sure that *if Captain Badiley, with his squadron, had come to my relief,* we should have gone away victors, notwithstanding the blowing up of the *Bonadventure* by her own powder, and the firing of the *Sampson* by the Dutch fire-ship. If I could have had my will, the *Leopard* would never have been surrendered to the Dutch, although no hope of saving her was left, for I would have blown her up, but was restrained by my own company, in doing which they put my shoulder out of joint. As divers members of Parliament can testify to my readiness and former good service for the State, I beseech you to move for my enlargement, that I may appear to give an account of my actions." [1]

Appleton no doubt imagined that Badiley, immediately upon his return to England, would charge

---

[1] Appleton to ——, M.P. for Hull, March 25, 1652/3. Cal. S.P.D., 1652–3, p. 234.

him with disobedience to orders before the naval authorities, and he wished to enter a caveat and countercharge as early as possible. Appleton did not know his man. It was not in Badiley's nature to rake up past offences against any one unless he were provoked to it. In this letter is apparent the first germ of the extraordinary assertion that Badiley's squadron never attempted to come to the rescue of the Leghorn ships, a charge which was afterwards to be developed in a most wonderful fashion.

Appleton, Seaman, and Marsh had doubtless a bad time of it during their imprisonment. Appleton complained that the Dutch used him "very uncivilly." Prisoners of war do not usually find that their lot is cast in pleasant places. The Dutch found it difficult to supply their own wants, and it was not to be expected that the prisoners would fare better than their captors. But Longland had not forgotten them. On the day after the battle, when he was overwhelmed with the work of caring for the wants of the English sailors whom the Dutch had sent on shore, he despatched his kinsman, Jonathan Parker, to visit the captives, with supplies of bread, meat, and wine, and with instructions to inquire what else could be done to ameliorate their lot. Appleton replied that he wanted nothing but his liberty, and he prayed Parker to obtain it for him. So Longland instructed his kinsman to negotiate with Van Galen for the release of the prisoners. Longland offered to give his bond in 10,000 dollars as surety that, if they were set at liberty, they would go to Holland and remain

there on parole until they were exchanged, or, if
that could not be allowed, to secure their return to
the Dutch fleet at night, if they might be permitted
to come on shore during the day. The Dutch commander replied that he could do nothing towards
the release of the prisoners without instructions from
home.[1] Appleton afterwards made it a grievance
that Longland did not visit him in person, forgetful
apparently of the fact that the English Resident
had nearly 400 sailors to care for on shore.

The three captains remained prisoners on board
the Dutch ships for about nine weeks. At the end
of that time, through the intervention of the Council
of State,[2] Longland was able to obtain their release.
Longland, together with two other English merchants, entered into a bond to secure that the prisoners would present themselves in Holland within
two months from the date of their discharge.[3] But
their troubles were not yet at an end. The Dutch
had recently captured a small ship from Tunis laden
with wool which was said to be infected, and they
had forfeited, in consequence, their right of free
entry into the port of Leghorn. When, therefore,

[1] Longland to Cromwell, Nov. 14, 1653, and deposition of
Jonathan Parker, same date. Cal. S.P.D., 1653–4, pp. 243–250.

[2] Deane and Monk to Admiralty Commissioners, April 9,
1653. Cal. S.P.D., 1652–3, p. 270. Longland to Admiralty
Committee, June 6, 1653. *Ib.*, p. 389.

[3] Bond of Charles Longland, Geo. Northleigh, and Hen.
Browne, English merchants in Leghorn, in 5,000 pieces of eight
for the appearance of Capt. Appleton; in 4,000 for Capt. Seaman; and in 3,000 for Marsh, in North Holland, within two
months. May 20, 1653. Cal. S.P.D., 1653–4, p. 249.

the three captains, on May 20, 1653, found themselves at liberty to quit the Dutch fleet, they were, on landing, immediately confined in the Lazaretto to undergo quarantine.

The next day Longland, with several other English merchants, went down to the Lazaretto to visit the captains and welcome them ashore. Longland, having risked a large sum to secure their release, no doubt expected some acknowledgment of his kindness, more especially because, only five days before, the three had addressed a joint letter to him, thanking him for his intervention in their behalf.[1] If he cherished any such expectation, he was speedily disabused. He sent Badiley the following account of his reception :—

"At the request of Capts. Appleton, Seaman, and Marsh, I entered into bond to the Dutch Vice-Admiral for 12,000 dollars, that in two months they should render themselves prisoners in Holland. The Dutch having lost their prattick (by taking a polatto which brought some wools from Tunis), our captains were necessitated to make purgo in the Lazaretto when they came thither. Two days since I went to see them and bid them welcome ashore, but I found such an encounter from Seaman that in all my lifetime I was never half so much abused. He called me all the base, scandalous names he could imagine, took up great stones and flung at me to have brained me, and I am confident, if he could have come at me, had done me some notable mischief, if

---

[1] Appleton, Seaman, and Marsh to Longland, May 10, 1653. Cal. S.P.D., 1653-4, p. 249.

not the loss of my life. If the State take not some
order to tame such men, it will not be in my power
to do them any service, nor fit to be a commissioned
servant of theirs when I shall be subject to the
abuse of such a scandalous fellow, whose extreme
malignancy and backwardness has been the ruin of
all our ships here. And now he has basely lost his
ship, he vents his venom to the full. There were
above forty witnesses of this abuse. Neither did
he leave you and Captain Cox unabused, but told
me, before all men, that cowardly, base fellow Badiley and that base rogue Cox were likewise confederates. In fine, if he could have mentioned any
man else that bore any affection to the State, or
served them with faithfulness, they had likewise
come under his abuse. I am certain I have not
injured him in the least, but contrarily, am engaged
for him in a great sum of money. If the State do
not make me some reparation upon this man for the
injury he has done me herein (and likewise to let
him know it), I shall be subject to all abuses from
such fellows, which, rather than I will be, I will
return the State's commission, and so much I pray
you let them know."[1]

Longland turned and fled before the abuse and
the missiles of the rough-tongued captain. This
episode makes it easier to understand why Captain

[1] Longland to Badiley, May 23, 1653. Badiley's Answer,
p. 72. See also Longland to Badiley, June 13, 1653. Cal.
S.P.D., 1652–3, p. 408, written when his anger had cooled somewhat; and Longland to Cromwell, *ubi sup*. It could not be
justly said that Seaman had "basely lost his ship." He made a
good fight of it at the battle off Leghorn.

Fisher dared not speak to Seaman when the English ships were preparing for their precipitate departure from Leghorn on the morning of March 4. It is improbable that Longland paid any more visits to the Lazaretto while the three captains remained in confinement, or that he felt much regret when, in the first week of June, having completed their quarantine, they started on their tedious journey overland to Holland.

The Grand Duke had thus rid himself of the last of the English who had disturbed the port of Leghorn for so many months. When he resolved to drive the English out of Leghorn, he supposed that the Dutch held command of the Channel, and that the Commonwealth was at their mercy. On February 21, Salvetti wrote a despatch to his master which told a very different tale.[1] The English dockyards had been feverishly active during the winter, and early in February Blake had been able to put to sea with a more powerful fleet than he had ever before commanded. On Friday, February 18—the very day on which the Grand Duke sent Montemagni with his ultimatum to Badiley—being off Portland, Blake sighted the Dutch fleet, under Van Tromp, running up Channel with a hundred and fifty merchantmen under convoy. The battle commenced at eight o'clock in the morning and lasted for three days, at the end of which Van Tromp, with the shattered remnants of his fleet, succeeded in reaching Holland. The George of England flew once more triumphant in the Narrow Seas.

[1] Salvetti: Despatches, O. 18–21.

Thus it fell out that while the Grand Duke was driving Badiley and Appleton out of his ports, under the impression that England was an "undone nation," England was in reality mistress of the situation, and the Dutch were smarting under the severest and most decisive defeat that they had suffered during the war. The preparations for sending a fleet to the Mediterranean Sea were speedily renewed.[1] "All hands and heads," wrote Blackborne to Badiley, "are now at work for sending you relief, which I trust will come furnished to your expectations, and a squadron was thought upon for that purpose. Meantime the Commissioners desire you will use all possible circumspection, and rest assured they are as mindful of your condition as if they were upon the place."[2]

Badiley was far upon his homeward voyage when this letter was written, and it never reached his hands. Not long after, the news of the defeat off Leghorn arrived in England.[3] "Your news of the 29th is bad," wrote Captain John Lawson to Blackborne, "because honest men have suffered and the cause of God will be reflected upon. But if our mercies were not mixed with some bitter pills, we

---

[1] Blackborne to Longland, March 14, 1652/3. Cal. S.P.D., 1652–3, p. 212.

[2] Blackborne to Badiley, March 14, 1652/3. Cal. S.P.D., p. 213.

[3] Whitelocke gives it as arriving at the end of March (Memorials, p. 553). Longland's letter of March 4th (o.s.) was before the Council of State on March 29, 1653. Cal. S.P.D., 1652–3, p. 239. This was fast travelling for those days. See also Salvetti: Despatches, 1/11 April, 1653, O. 39.

should be either lifted up or undervalue them. The enemy has gained no great victory, considering the great inequality between the ships engaged."[1] The knowledge of the defeat put a temporary stop to the fitting out of the fleet for the Mediterranean,[2] and eventually the Council of State decided that the ships were to be victualled as if they were to be employed in home waters.[3]

The news of the defeat of the Dutch off Portland had certainly reached Leghorn before April 18. At first the Italians and the Grand Duke declined to believe it, so convinced were they that England was undone.[4] But belief was at last forced upon them by Salvetti's confirmation of his earlier account of the battle. The Tuscan councillors of the Grand Duke were unwillingly driven to the conclusion that they had been somewhat precipitate in their dealings with the English ships at Leghorn. If, after all, the Commonwealth should prove finally victorious over the Dutch, it might be that an English fleet would appear off Leghorn to demand reparation. The Tuscan Court came to the conclusion that it had better endeavour to retrace, as far as possible, the false step which it had taken. Salvetti was instructed to congratulate the Council of State upon the victory

[1] Lawson to Blackborne, March 30, 1653. Cal. S.P.D., 1652–3, p. 243.

[2] Deane and Monk to Admiralty Committee, April 4, 1653. Cal. S.P.D., p. 254.

[3] Council of State : Day's Proceedings, April 13, 1653. Cal. S.P.D., 1652 3, p. 276.

[4] Longland to Blackborne, April 18, 1653. Cal. S.P.D., 1652–3, p. 285.

that they had obtained, and to express the Grand Duke's unswerving friendship for the English nation. Salvetti would have a hard task to explain away the somewhat peculiar manner in which Ferdinand had shown his friendship; but, nevertheless, the attempt had to be made. The times were not propitious for the undertaking. The Long Parliament was in its death-throes, and politicians had no time to spare for Salvetti's orations. The Council of State put off his application for an interview twice, the second time on the significant excuse that the day was set apart for a thanksgiving for the victory over the Dutch.[1] Before another appointment could be made, the Rump had been dissolved, its Council of State had disappeared with it, and Oliver Cromwell was the arbiter of the destinies of England. It was not until June 10 that Salvetti had audience with the new Council of State. They were frigidly polite, but they did not attempt to disguise their disgust at the conduct of the Grand Duke.[2]

Salvetti had put the best face upon the matter that he could, but the emergency demanded a scape-goat. It was essential to prove that Ferdinand had not forced the English ships to depart from Leghorn. No more hopeful plan could be adopted than that of laying the blame upon the "perverseness and obstinacy" of Captain Badiley. If the Council of State could be persuaded to take this view, the whole blame for the disaster might be shifted on to Badiley's shoulders. For this purpose,

[1] Salvetti: Despatches, O. 44, 47.
[2] *Ib.*, O. 80–83.

Appleton, Seaman, and March were fit instruments to hand. Appleton especially had reason to desire to exculpate himself at the expense of his commander-in-chief. It was notorious that the three captains had been loud in their accusations against Badiley during their sojourn at the Lazaretto. If they could be induced to assert that Badiley had ordered them to come out of port while the Grand Duke was willing that they should remain, the aim of the Tuscan Court would be secured. There is no evidence that Appleton was directly incited by the Tuscan officials to tell this story ; but the facts that he secured a written statement from Montemagni in support of this aspect of his case, and that, before publishing his charges, he had consultations with Salvetti, both point to such a conclusion.

Appleton, no less than Ferdinand, was in need of a scapegoat, and was doubtless eager to fall in with the views of the Tuscan Court. When he returned home, he would have to face the charges concerning the French sattee, and the assault upon the sentinel which had been lodged against him by the Grand Duke. He would also have to answer the accusation that he had caused the defeat of the English off Leghorn by coming out of the harbour too soon, which, he could hardly doubt, had already been formulated by Badiley. To secure Tuscan aid in his contest with Badiley, and at the same time to obtain a withdrawal of the complaints which the Grand Duke had preferred against him, was a rich compensation for such small perversions of fact as would be necessary to establish the Tuscan contention.  There can be little doubt that some such terms as these were proposed and accepted; and thus it happened that Appleton's offences at Leghorn were no longer remembered against him, and he returned to England no culprit, but the man who was to stand between Duke Ferdinand and the vengeance of the English nation.

# Chapter XVI

## HOMEWARD BOUND

AFTER the battle of Leghorn, Badiley steered his battered ships for England, quite unconscious of the net that was about to be spread for him. Longland had surmised that Badiley would sail southward and endeavour to join the squadron which was to come from Venice ; but the ships were in no condition for such an undertaking.[1] Their crews were on the verge of mutiny, and, indeed, considering the hardships which they had endured, it was not surprising that they should grumble. It was fifteen months since they had seen their homes,[2] and during that time they had received little pay, and had suffered great privations. The sailors who manned the *Phœnix* had, since her re-capture, been obliged to make shift with no more clothing than was upon their backs when they sailed away with her from the Road of Leghorn. The captains of the merchant ships had entered the State's service under compulsion. Their one

[1] Longland to Navy Committee, March 4 (o.s.), 1652/3. Cal. S.P.D., 1652–3, p. 214.

[2] The *Constant Warwick* had been at sea for two years. Badiley to the Admiralty Committee, May 13, 1653. Cal. S.P.D., 1652–3, p. 326.

desire was to escape from it, and, as their conduct has shown, they were little inclined to obey orders. The frigates were foul from long service, and had suffered great damage in the battle of Leghorn. In such circumstances, all that Badiley could hope to do was to make some port, where he could repair his vessels and enhearten his men with proper supplies.

He sailed straight for Cadiz, but not without molestation on the way. He fought with and took a Dutch man-of-war, which was convoying two merchantmen, and rumour attributed to him a still more heroic enterprise against a French privateer.[1]

While Badiley was repairing and revictualling his ships at Cadiz, he was also taking thought for the future. He hoped that, when he reached England, he would be despatched once more to the Mediterranean, in command of a powerful squadron, to avenge the injury that the nation had suffered. But it appeared to him that if meanwhile the Dutch were left unmolested in those waters, they would be at liberty to send back a large portion of their strength to reinforce their fleet in the Narrow Seas. Two good frigates, sailing hither and thither to attack Dutch commerce as opportunity offered, would compel them to spread abroad their squadrons in order to maintain for their traders the advantages which victory had bestowed upon them. He designed, therefore, to commission the *Elizabeth*

---

[1] May 3. "Letters that Captain Bodiley in the Straits . . . met and fought the great pirate Chevalier de Ferrier, and killed and sunk 6co of his men." Whitelocke : Memorials, p. 555.

and one other man-of-war for such service, and to return with the remainder of his squadron to the Downs. But when the crew of the *Elizabeth* heard their orders they broke out into a mutiny, and "no encouraging language, with a proffer of six months' pay, nor laying before them the advantage like to come to the nation thereby, nor the danger of refusal according to the tenor of the 11th article of war, would work upon them."[1] Badiley was, therefore, compelled to relinquish his design, and to return home with the whole of his fleet and his prizes.

Soon after leaving Cadiz the fleet captured a Dutch merchantman named the *Augustine* near Cape St. Vincent. Badiley's ships were so sorely under-manned that it was almost impossible to raise a crew to sail her. He proposed, therefore, to take two English sailors from each ship, and to replace them by two of his Dutch prisoners. But Fisher and Ell, the merchant captains of the *Mary* and the *Lewis*, when they received Badiley's warrant to that effect, stubbornly refused obedience. Badiley threatened to dismiss them from the State's service for insubordination, but with no result. As he could not spare a man from the fleet at that juncture, he was compelled to overlook the offence.[2] He trusted, however, that they would be called to

---

[1] Badiley to the Admiralty Committee, May 13, 1653. Cal. S.P.D., 1652-3, p. 326.

[2] Badiley's Answer, p. 10, and affidavit of John Plumpton, mate of the *Phœnix. Ib.*, p. 87, and of Geo. Hughes, commander of the *Thomas Bonadventure. Ib.*, p. 79.

account at home for their insubordination. " The
laws martial," he said, " were either made to be put
in execution, or to be like bug-bears which are to
scare children." He had not succeeded in asserting his authority, but he had made enemies of
Fisher and Ell, who were not slow, when they
found a chance of revenging themselves, to side
against him.

On May 8, 1653, Badiley's squadron cast
anchor in the Downs,[1] and the hearts of his toil-
worn crews were rejoiced by the sight of their
native land. At last, they imagined, they were to
find rest and pay after their manifold hardships.
Badiley also, no doubt, looked forward to a period
of repose after his labours, and to visiting his house
at Wapping and the wife from whom he had been
so long separated. But the Council of State had
other intentions. They were desirous of crushing
the Dutch in the Narrow Seas, and for this purpose
they had resolved to keep afloat every vessel in
their fleet. The Admiralty Committee despatched
a letter to Deal, complimenting Badiley upon his
services, and ordering him to make his squadron
ready for sea at once. Badiley knew that the command was unreasonable, but he was not the man
to shirk an unpleasant duty. " Being called on
shore to confer with Major Bourne and Captain
Limbery," he replied, " I saw yours of yesterday,
by which I find not only your remembrance of my

---

[1] Certificate by Badiley, May 8, 1653. Cal. S.P.D., 1652–3,
p. 313. Whitelocke gives the date as May 10. Memorials,
p. 556.

services, but your commands about the ships of my squadron. I will endeavour to execute your orders, but I fear the carrying on of our[1] service, as there is a wretched distemper of mutiny among my mariners to go in until they are paid off, or are sent for to the fleet near Lee Road to be called to account for their disobedience. It has made my trouble inexpressible, and tended much to the nation's loss."[2]

Badiley at once set about the attempt to persuade his wearied crews to go to sea once more, and on the following day he reported the result of his efforts. "I have conferred with the subordinate commanders," he wrote, "as to the necessity of our present going forth to lie in the Narrow [Seas],[3] and laboured to compose that disorder and boisterous spirit among the mariners in the frigates, and been from ship to ship to impress upon them the great damage the State has suffered, or is likely to suffer, by their disobedience, and what guilt they will bring on their body and soul by casting themselves on a trial for life, according to the 11th article of war ; and after much insinuating language, I could only prevail with them to take six weeks' victuals and go out with us, provided I went with this ship (the *Paragon*), and the rest related to us ; but I cannot at all prevail with those on board the *Phœnix* and the *Constant Warwick* to go forth upon any service

---

[1] "On " in the Calendar.

[2] Badiley (Deal) to Admiralty Committee, May 12, 1653. Cal. S.P.D., 1652–3, p. 324.

[3] Not in original.

before they have been in and are paid off, although I laboured to answer all their objections. The company of the former frigate have more reason than the other, being manned with men that belonged to several ships who went to regain her, with no more clothes than backs, and in that condition they say they have continued to this day, and the ship is foul. The sooner she is called in to be fitted, the better. Since their exploit they are very turbulent and disorderly.

" The main objection of those of the *Constant Warwick* is that she is leaky, and that the pump is never out of their hands at sea (whether they have the art to make her so, I cannot say), and, having been out twenty-five months, they want everything. This morning, ordering the fore-topsail to be loosed and otherwise fitting her to go out, the mutinous spirit broke out again. Nothing now but 'home, home!' and no reason will be heard among them; and to such a height have they got that a whole cluster of them have been heard to say this night that if I went out with this ship they would run down to the hold and suffer the enemy to batter her to pieces. So you see it is well that this ship is in England, with such a crew. I shall wait your orders as to coming up the river, since there is no trusting this ship abroad as she is. . . . [The *Paragon*] could not have stayed longer abroad without being completely spoiled with the worm, if nothing else. Although she will cost a great deal of money, as nearly all her timbers are cut to pieces with the shot, and not a mast in her but is shot through, yet as she is in the Channel, and in the midst of summer, I have been fitting, and always telling my officers and others that, until another dispute be over with the Dutch, we shall be kept abroad, so that one way or the other we may vindicate ourselves after so great a loss, and consequently be looked upon with cheerfulness when we come to the pay-table. But I see, when the evil spirit has entered in, no reason will rule this people." [1]

What man could do Badiley had done to encourage his men to fight the Dutch once more, and avenge the defeat at Leghorn. But he had been ordered to attempt the impossible, and it could not be denied that crews in such humour as he had described would prove worse than useless in battle. On May 24 the *Elizabeth* and the *Constant Warwick* were ordered to Chatham to be repaired. Badiley was instructed to bring the rest of his squadron into the Thames, and then to come to London and " report the state of all that was lately under his command." [2] The seamen went to Chatham and received their long-deferred pay. When they were freed from the control of their commander, they became an unmanageable rabble. Peter Pett, the Navy Commissioner, who saw to the business, reported upon them thus : " We are paying off the Straits' fleet, and I will secure all the men I can that are fit for service, but they are most disordered seamen. I hope to reduce them

[1] Badiley to the Admiralty Committee, May 13, 1653. Cal. S.P.D., 1652–3, p. 326.
[2] Minutes of the Council of State. Cal. S.P.D., 1652–3, p. 349.

to better temper, but an example ought to be made of the ringleaders of their many mutinies."[1]

While Badiley had been endeavouring to bring his demoralised crews into some semblance of discipline, Salvetti had been prosecuting the attempt to blast his reputation. The Grand Duke had sent a letter to the Council of State praising Appleton's conduct at Leghorn.[2]  Nathaniel Reading, who had been Appleton's mouthpiece in making the agreement that had tied the hands of the English commanders, was in London, eager to discredit his rival, Longland.  But Appleton, the main instrument in the conspiracy, had not yet reached England.  Without him all that could be done was to spread reports and insinuate suspicions.  It was dangerous work, and Salvetti was anxious for Appleton's arrival, so that all the conspirators might tell the same tale.  " I hope that [Appleton] will state the facts," Salvetti wrote, " in conformity with what I have said, which was by no means to the prejudice of him or of his valour in the fight, and that consequently he will prove that the Grand Duke did not compel the frigates to quit Leghorn harbour, as Admiral Badiley keeps saying."[3]

Badiley was not yet in disgrace, but men's tongues were beginning to wag about him.  Rumours that

---

[1] Pett to the Admiralty Committee, June 1, 1653.  Cal. S.P.D., 1652–3, p. 370.  See also Pett to the Navy Commissioners of the same date.  "We are paying off the Straits' Fleet, who are the worst people I ever saw.  I hope the ringleaders will be called to account."  *Ib.*

[2] Salvetti : Despatches, O. 84.

[3] *Ib.*, O. 88–89.

he had turned coward at Leghorn, springing from one knew not where, found ready currency. On June 10 "the whole account of Captain Badiley's transactions beyond seas, in several papers," was referred by the Council of State to the Committee of Foreign Affairs.[1]

Although Salvetti chafed at the delay caused by Appleton's prolonged absence, the three captains had, in fact, lost little time upon their journey homewards. They left Leghorn early in June, and before the first of July they were in Amsterdam.[2] Long before that date their wives had petitioned the Council of State to provide exchanges for them,[3] and at about the time of their arrival at Amsterdam the necessary order was made.[4] Not long after they landed in England.

---

[1] Minutes of the Council of State, June 10, 1653. Cal. S.P.D., 1652-3, p. 397.

[2] "Here are come to this town from Leghorn, overland, those unfortunate captains, Appleton, Seaman, and Marsh, who desire nothing more than to be in England to clear themselves of those aspersions by some cast upon them. Truly, according to what I have seen and heard, I believe they may." Letter of Intelligence from John Peterson, July 1, 1653. Thurloe: State Papers, i. 326. "There arrived at Amsterdam three lusty captains from the Straits, viz., Captain Appleton and two others; very proper men and full of courage them seem to be." A Letter of Intelligence from Holland, July 1, 1653. *Ib.*, p. 327.

[3] Petition of Jane Appleton, Isabella Seaman, and Helena Marsh, June 9, 1653. Cal. S.P.D., 1652-3, p. 394.

[4] Minutes of the Council of State, July 1, 1653. "A pass to be granted for Capts. Cornelius Arentse Cruyck, Jan Gedeonse Verburghs, and Cornelius Lourense to Holland, being ordered to be exchanged for Captains Appleton, Marsh, and Seaman, now prisoners with the Dutch." Cal. S.P.D., 1653-4, p. 2.

Appleton was eager to justify his conduct at Badiley's expense, and he knew that he would find in the Tuscan ambassador a friend ready to aid him in his endeavour. For some reason he appears to have objected to the Committee of Foreign Affairs as a tribunal to hear his cause, for on June 23 an order was made by the Council of State, upon his petition, referring the question to a specially appointed committee.[1] By this Committee Appleton was examined with some rigour. On August 5 he visited Salvetti and told him what had taken place. He said that he feared that Badiley had already half persuaded the Committee that if the Grand Duke had not ordered the English to quit Leghorn harbour within a limited time the catastrophe in the Road would not have taken place, and he said that Longland had written a letter confirming this opinion. He also said that he was soon to be examined again, when he would contradict Badiley's statements and tell the whole truth. "I did not think well to say more to him," the prudent ambassador wrote, "than that in telling the truth he would be doing something to merit the favour which his Highness had conferred upon him in writing a letter in his behalf to this Republic."

[1] Order on petition of Capt. Hen. Appleton that Sir Ant. Ashley Cooper, Mr. Howard, Mr. Strickland, and Col. Hewson be a committee to hear what he has to relate concerning the management of the business of the Straits, wherein he with others was engaged. Sir A. A. Cooper to take care thereof, and report what Appleton shall relate to them. Cal. S.P.D., 1653–4, p. 47.

Then Appleton departed, promising to come again and tell Salvetti how the case progressed.[1]

Soon after this Appleton was ordered to state his charges in writing, and he did so with the help of Nathaniel Reading. His statement was printed by the Parliament's printers, but before sending it in to the Committee, he brought it to Salvetti for his approval. As Salvetti had also made a statement in writing it was essential that there should be no manifest discrepancies between the two documents. "Appleton has presented a Remonstrance," wrote Salvetti to the Grand Duke, "in which he tells the story of his service from the time of his departure from England until his arrival at Leghorn. He tells it with sincerity, showing up the bad conduct of Badiley in the last fight off that port with the Dutch, together with the double dealing of Longland in that and other matters. Before presenting it he came to show it to me, and I, finding nothing in it to gainsay, did not think it wise to say more than that he ought to stand firm in asserting *vivâ voce* what he had stated in writing."[2] The latter counsel was not altogether superfluous. The wily old ambassador had probably, in his two interviews with Appleton, taken the measure of the man. Salvetti had considered the Remonstrance merely from the Tuscan point of view, to ascertain that it contained nothing that would weaken his contention that the Grand Duke had always endeavoured to befriend the English. When he had satisfied him-

---

[1] Salvetti: Despatches, O. 113.     [2] *Ib.*, O. 116.

self that Appleton had laid the blame for the departure of the English ships from Leghorn upon Badiley, his curiosity was satisfied, and he did not trouble
himself to find out whether Appleton's personal
defence was consistent, and in agreement with previous reports which that commander had sent home.
Had Salvetti been able to test the Remonstrance
thus, he might have seen cause to regret that the
Grand Duke's defence rested upon so untrustworthy
a support.

Appleton's statement was styled "A Remonstrance of the Fight in Leghorn Road between the
English and the Dutch," and it was addressed " To
His Excellency the Lord General Cromwell and the
Right Honourable the Council of State." [1]  Being
printed by the Parliament's printer, it received a kind
of official sanction.  Soon after its appearance the
venue was once more changed, and the cause was
transferred from the Committee especially appointed
to hear it to the Admiralty Committee,[2] and from
them, four days later, it was for some inscrutable
reason handed over to the Committee for Scotch
and Irish Affairs.[3]

The case which the Remonstrance presented
was superficially plausible.  Men began to say

[1] London.  Printed by John Field, printer to the Parliament
of England.  British Museum : Press Mark, E. 1068 (5).

[2] Council of State, Aug. 6, 1653.  " The Remonstrance of
Capt. Hen. Appleton referred to the Admiralty Committee to
hear both parties and report."  Cal. S.P.D., 1653-4, p. 76.

[3] Minutes of the Council of State.  "The Remonstrance of H.
Appleton referred to the Irish and Scotch Committee to report."
Aug. 10, 1653.  Cal. S.P.D., 1653-4, p. 85.

that the charges against Badiley looked black. This unfortunate man Appleton, it would appear, had been but scurvily treated by his commander-in-chief, who had deserted him in his sorest need, leaving him to fall into the hands of the State's enemies whom he had valiantly resisted until he could hold out no longer. The truth was coming to light at last, else why should the Council of State permit the Remonstrance to be printed officially, and why should Salvetti, who had lived so long in England that he was himself almost an Englishman, support Appleton's case so strenuously? His Excellency the Lord General and his Council of State would doubtless see the poor man righted, and Badiley might think himself fortunate if he escaped a visit to Execution Dock.

Such was the gossip of the sailors along the river-side, and of the merchants upon the Exchange. Badiley found himself a shunned man; even old friends avoided him, or looked askance as they passed. " It is more than three months," he wrote, " since I came home out of the Mediterranean Sea, and none, high or low, hath said it to my face, ' this or that hath been ill done by you whilst you were on the said voyage.' Yet about the time that Captain Appleton's Remonstrance was given in, as those that triumph before victory, news must needs be carried to my relations and [1] family (whilst I was absent) [that] a file of Musquetiers was provided for me to carry me to the Tower. Another friend coming to my house, said [that] the watermen on

<hr>

[1] " In " in original.

the Thames gave out I was gone to prison, and this report was raised about Chatham and the Exchange. But when I heard thereof, and that some were troubled at it, I answered, 'one that is accused of theft and never played the thief, either directly or indirectly, he knows not wherein he is guilty, so I know not any offence to the State that I can be made culpable of. Surely therefore, before they do such a thing, they will tell me for what, and wherefore it is.'"[1]

Badiley was not sent to the Tower, but he was, in a manner, placed upon his trial as a culprit before the Irish and Scotch Committee, and it was necessary that he should make his answer to the charges contained in the Remonstrance. It would appear that he was not at once furnished with a copy of the case against him. On September 2, nearly a month after it had been made public, he wrote thus to his friend Robert Blackborne, the Secretary to the Admiralty Committee: "Although innocency and a good conscience be a sufficient buckler against the tongues and pens of malignant spirits, yet considering that truth and the justness of a cause may be somewhat eclipsed for want of clear witnesses, as some now going to sea may be useful to me, pray procure me a copy of the allegations against me before the Irish and Scotch Committee, and my servant will call for it."[2]

There was just cause for this complaint. The

---

[1] Badiley's Answer, p. 1.

[2] Badiley to Blackborne, Sept. 2, 1653. (dated "Near London.") Cal. S.P.D., 1653–4, p. 125.

*Phœnix* and the *Constant Warwick* had already sailed to join the fleet,[1] and others of the ships which had been under Badiley's command in the Mediterranean were upon the point of departure. Unless he could produce the evidence of some of the seamen who had served under him, he could not hope to disprove the allegations that Appleton had made. For Appleton's charges did not rest upon his unsupported assertions. All the malcontents who had any ground of complaint against Badiley's discipline in the Mediterranean made common cause with the accuser. Seaman and Marsh came forward with statements more extravagant than those contained in the body of the Remonstrance. Fisher and Ell, who had behaved so mutinously upon the homeward voyage, avenged their supposed grievances by alleging cowardice against their former commander. Reading was forward with his help to press home the charge, and more serious than all was the statement of Montemagni, the Grand Duke's Secretary, that the English ships might have remained in the port of Leghorn had Badiley been so minded. Well might Badiley think, when he read this accumulation of evidence against him, "a three-fold cord is not easily broken, how much less that which may be compared to a seven-fold cord."[2]

Badiley resolved that, if he could not break the cord, he would unravel it. He must have spent

1 Minutes of Council of State, July 4, 1653. Cal. S.P.D., 1653–4, p. 5.
2 Badiley's Answer, p. 119.

many days on the Thames bank, at Chatham, and perhaps even at Portsmouth, searching for the men who could give evidence in his behalf, for they were scattered over the face of land and sea. He succeeded in securing a goodly number, whom he caused to swear affidavits of the facts within their knowledge, and then he sat down, with only his mother wit to help him, to write "Captain Badiley's Answer unto Captain Appleton's Remonstrance."

# Chapter XVII

## DISGRACE

APPLETON'S Remonstrance ended thus :—
"This is the sum of what hath happened
since my going out, the truth whereof, as in His
presence, who is the Searcher of all hearts, I do
aver. Nor hath my naming any particular [person]
in this narrative proceeded from spleen to him, but
love to truth, to the end your Honours might
be impartially informed how your affairs were
managed." [1]

These were solemn words. No man would believe that Appleton could make such an appeal
with a lie upon his lips unless the lie were conclusively proved. But the very first allegation in
the Remonstrance afforded evidence of this want
of veracity. Appleton commenced with an attack
upon Cox. No doubt he thought that Cox, who
was honest enough, although too much inclined to
independence of action, would be a witness in
Badiley's favour, so he sought at the outset to
discredit him. Cox was at sea, and his evidence
was not to be obtained ; but Appleton could not
have been assured of this when he was preparing

[1] Remonstrance, p. 11.

the Remonstrance. So he raked up the old story of the French sattee, which has already been told,[1] narrating it in its final form as an act of intentional disobedience to his orders. If Appleton's latest version of the affair was true, then Appleton was lying in November, 1651, when he took upon himself the responsibility for the capture of the sattee. If he represented the facts accurately then, the account given in the Remonstrance must have been false. There can be no reasonable doubt that the earlier account represented the facts, and that the story in the Remonstrance was a concoction to discredit a possible opponent. The man who could be guilty of such a perversion of the truth placed himself outside the category of credible witnesses, even though he had the hardihood to assert, as in the presence of the Almighty, that his naming of any particular person proceeded solely from the love of truth.

Having thus attempted to destroy Cox's reputation he continued the story of his voyage until his squadron arrived at Leghorn on its homeward journey, and he came into contact with the Dutch fleet. Then, to establish his reputation for courage, he told the marvellous story of his towing the *Leopard* through and through the Dutch fleet, which so much excited Badiley's derision.[2] The statement may be safely dismissed as a fabrication.

Appleton passed lightly over the question of his engagement to the Duke not to attack the Dutch

<hr>

[1] See *ante*, p. 60 *et seq.*　　　　[2] See *ante*, p. 84.

ships, because he knew that it would not be raised against him by the Tuscan Court, and without their aid it could not be effectually pressed home.[1]   But he enlarged upon Cox's supposed insubordination when he was appointed to the *Bonadventure*, in order more completely to discredit that captain in the event of his appearance against him.[2]   Then he told the story of the capture of the *Phœnix*, apparently for the purpose of bringing up for the first time an accusation that Cox appropriated money which was found on board her to his own use.   He said that several men were ready to make this good upon oath, but he failed to produce these witnesses.[3]

Then followed the story of the attack on the sentinel.   In this case also he was assured that

---

[1] But even his casual allusion to the affair was inaccurate.   He said that Reading undertook on his behalf that " I should not disturb his Highness' *port* except I were commanded to the contrary."   Remonstrance, p. 4.

[2] Remonstrance, p. 5.

[3] "The ship being under sail and the fight over, up comes Captain Cox, drives the men out of the cabin which had done the service, and, after, found the money, saying the cabin belonged to him ; and notwithstanding the promise made before the enterprise to share the booty equally, he kept it to his private use." *Ib.*, p. 5.   On June 3, 1653, Cox petitioned the Council of State for a reward for the seamen who had captured the *Phœnix*. He undertook to pay them £10 each if the undertaking prospered, and the mariners persecuted him for the performance of his promise, which he was unable to make good.   Cal. S.P.D., 1652-3, p. 376.   Cox would never have dared to appeal to the Council of State in such a matter if the investigation which would necessarily follow would have disclosed such a delinquency as Appleton alleged against him.

the representative of the Grand Duke would remain
silent, and that he could safely state the case to his
own advantage. Imagining that he had disposed
of Cox as a credible witness, he proceeded to deal
similarly with Longland, whose evidence might
press hard upon him. So he alleged that his
summons to Pisa and his subsequent imprisonment
were instigated by Longland, in order to screen
himself and Badiley from the Grand Duke's displeasure on account of the taking of the *Phœnix*.[1]
" Mr. Longland and Mr. Wood," he said, " publicly
triumphed that they had brought me into that condition. And, notwithstanding they pretended kindness in their going with me, it seemed it was only
to work their ends upon me, for, during my four
days' imprisonment in the castle, they not only
came not near me themselves, but none else were
suffered to come that would, denying to let my men
know what became of me, or where I was, that
they might find me clothes." Longland's contemporary account of the affair, written when he
could not have supposed that his action would be
brought up against him as an offence, sufficiently
disposes of this charge.[2]

In order to discredit Longland still further, Appleton alleged, although he could not know, except by
hearsay, that Longland had neglected the prisoners

[1] Appleton : Remonstrance, p. 6.

[2] See *ante*, p. 151. Moreover, Appleton at the time stated
that it was the Grand Duke's order that none should come near
him, and he attributed his imprisonment to the malice of the
French and the Dutch. Appleton to Council of State, Dec. 18,
1652. Cal. S.P.D., 1952–3, p. 40.

which the Dutch had sent ashore after the battle off Leghorn; that when he sent them to Venice and Messina he did not give them sufficient money, and that many of them died of starvation by the way, or sold their clothes for victuals.[1]

It was doubtless part of the pact between the Tuscan Court and Appleton that Longland should be thus assailed; and as he was at Leghorn, and had little chance of defending himself against these aspersions before the Irish and Scotch Committee had given its decision, the task was not difficult. Apart from Badiley, who was in the position of prisoner at the bar, Longland was the witness who could most conclusively prove the unfriendliness of the Grand Duke, and Salvetti, when he read the Remonstrance, was not ill-pleased to find the English Resident thus attacked.[2]

Having thus disposed, as he imagined, of the most dangerous witnesses against him, Appleton addressed himself to the main object of the Remonstrance—the attack on Badiley for his conduct at the battle of Leghorn. For this purpose he made three charges. The first was that Badiley had been under no obligation to take the English ships out of Leghorn harbour, because the Grand Duke had fixed no definite date for their departure. This was precisely what Salvetti desired to prove; for, if it could be made good, the Commonwealth would have no cause of complaint against Tuscany, and would have to content itself with blaming

---

[1] Remonstrance, p. 11.

[2] Salvetti: Despatches, Letter of Aug. 12 (o.s.), O. 116.

Badiley for rashness. Appleton's second charge was that he had acted in strict obedience to the orders of his commander-in-chief and with Longland's approval when he quitted Leghorn harbour. If this could be sustained, he could not justly be accused of precipitancy and held responsible for the consequent destruction of his squadron. His third charge was that, after his squadron had become engaged with the Dutch, Badiley, had he chosen to do so, might easily have come to its relief, and thus have averted the defeat.

In support of the first charge Appleton adduced the evidence of Montemagni, who gave a detailed account of the negotiations which he had conducted, in the name of the Grand Duke, with Badiley and Van Galen after the capture of the *Phœnix*. Montemagni's main object was to show that the Duke had acted to the last as the protector of the English against the Dutch, and the bulk of his statement was devoted to proving this. But his last paragraph gave Appleton the foothold that he needed. " The English," he said, " departed four days before their time expired, and might have had what longer time they would ; whence it is supposed that Captain Badiley, going out to fight by his own election, and not at all compelled, did think he had advantage over his enemy, and surely so he had, if the battle had been better managed." [1]

It was a fact that the English left Leghorn harbour four days before the expiration of the limit of time allowed them, but the Grand Duke's

[1] Remonstrance, p. 20.

letter to Badiley, dated February 28 (o.s.),[1] disposes of the allegation that they "might have had what longer time they would." "I . . . am content," he said, "to prolong your time for the departure of your ships . . . to the 8/18th day of this present month." The only extension of time permitted beyond that date was in the event of "wind and weather" preventing. His postscript hinted that the present time was favourable for departure. The clear interpretation of the letter is that the ships were to quit Leghorn harbour before March 8, unless continued contrary winds held them weather-bound until after that date, not that they were at liberty to neglect favourable opportunities for sailing which might previously offer.

The charge, therefore, which Salvetti was so anxious to prove, broke down. No reasonable man could doubt that Badiley had acted prudently in the endeavour to extricate the ships from the meshes in which they were entangled before the last day of grace accorded to them had expired. Appleton's second charge was that he was acting in obedience to Badiley's orders when he sailed out of Leghorn harbour with his squadron. To prove this he quoted Badiley's letter, written off Piombino on March 1,[2] and he quoted it incorrectly. "Captain Badiley departs for the fitting of his eight ships and

---

[1] See *ante*, p. 182.

[2] See *ante*, p. 186. This letter, being amongst the State Papers, must have been before the Admiralty Committee, but Appleton did not print it in the Remonstrance.

a fire-ship at Port Ferrajo," he wrote, " and, being under sail, sends me orders to haste to him so soon as the Dutch *weighed anchor to go towards him,* and that he might not be overpowered by the Dutch before I could assist, commands me for to haste upon my life, and that with all the sail that I could make."[1]  If that had been Badiley's order, Appleton's action would have been justified ; but there is no word about the Dutch weighing anchor in Badiley's letter.  Badiley wrote : " If the wind be off shore and you see them coming out to me, haste as for your life to follow with all the sail you can, that we may not be too much oppressed before you come."  The evident meaning of this order is that Appleton was to sail in time to prevent Badiley's squadron from being destroyed by the superior force of the Dutch.  And it was so understood by the captains who met in council with Longland on board the *Leopard* on the morning of March 4.[2]  But Appleton, in his folly, had sailed when he saw the Dutch weigh anchor.  He therefore endeavoured to persuade the Irish and Scotch Committee that he had been ordered to do so, and for this purpose he garbled his instructions.  To support the allegation he produced the evidence of Captain Seaman, of the *Sampson*, who must have proved a very Balaam to him.  For lack of careful editing, or from some other cause, Seaman's statement corroborated Badiley's contention.  " Captain Badiley sent his lieutenant to us [to say] that if in

<hr>

[1] Remonstrance, p. 8.
[2] Longland to Cromwell, Nov. 14, 1653, *u.s.*

case the wind should come off shore, we should come out upon our lives *before he was too much engaged*,[1] which he, for his part, as far as I could see, did never intend to do. And on Friday morning we received order to come out with all speed,[2] and that morning Mr. Longland, with the rest of the captains, resolved to go with one general consent, the Dutch being all weighed and stood to Captain Badiley, so that it was Mr. Longland's desire that we should make all haste that possibly[3] we could *before our admiral was too much engaged.*"[4] The contention of Longland and Badiley was therefore confirmed unintentionally by this hostile witness.

But Appleton felt that, even if his garbled version of his instructions found acceptance, some explanation was needed of his failure to come out, as he had himself proposed, on the night of March 3, when Hughes came on board the *Leopard* with the news that Badiley was at hand to receive and assist him. The following was his somewhat incoherent account of this episode : "Captain Badiley, plying near the Malora,[5] sends his lieutenant to me in the night to know our readiness and to advise

[1] Referring, no doubt, to the visit of Thomas Hughes, lieutenant of the *Paragon*, on the night of March 3. Seaman misstates the object of Hughes' visit. See *ante*, p. 193.

[2] March 4. No such order from Badiley can be traced, and it could hardly have been given. Badiley was then beyond the Malora. Seaman admits that he was "three leagues off."

[3] "Possible" in text.

[4] Declaration of Edward Seaman. Remonstrance, p. 15.

[5] Badiley was near the lighthouse, not the Malora.

that the *Warwick*[1] should be ready near the Mould-head by break of day to keep off the enemy's fire-ship which, with twenty-five more, lay ready with their topsails loose in the tops and their anchors a-peek, ready to wait our motion. I called a consultation upon his coming, and at that time there springing up a small gale, had some thoughts of getting out ;[2] but Mr. Longland not being there, without whom we durst not stir, Captain Badiley's order being to the contrary.[3] And during this consultation the gale ended and there was no wind stirring, it was agreed on not to stir till morning."[4]

The statement that he dared not stir without Longland's sanction is a good illustration of the way in which Appleton's trickiness overbore his sense of what was credible. He asked the Committee to believe that an order by Badiley to consult with Longland in certain events should be deemed to over-ride a particular order of his commander-in-chief upon the eve of action—an order which, in fact, was a compliance with Appleton's own proposal, although he refrained from mentioning that aspect of the incident. The assertion that the wind dropped while the midnight council of war was

[1] *i.e.* the *Constant Warwick.* This alleged part of Badiley's message is clearly false. Appleton's proposal was to come out under cover of the night.

[2] Yet he said that Badiley's message was that he was to come out at break of day.

[3] Probably relying on certain words in Badiley's letter off Piombino. See *ante*, p. 186. "Consult with Mr. Longland and the commanders whether it were not best to warp the ships without the Mould-head": or the letter of March 3rd. *Ante*, p. 190.     [4] Remonstrance, p. 8.

being held is false if Hughes' story of his mission is true, and there is no reason to suspect it. It will not be forgotten how, while Hughes was leaving the *Leopard* after the council of war had broken up, Wrightington, the master's mate, abused the commanders for refraining from taking advanvantage of the " gallant gale of wind" which was then blowing.[1]

The last charge which Appleton made against Badiley was by far the most serious. The two former affected his judgment only; the last touched his honour. Appleton alleged that while he was waging an unequal conflict with the Dutch in Leghorn Road, it would have been quite easy for Badiley, had he been so minded, to come to his relief, and thus have saved the squadron from destruction. In the body of the Remonstrance he only dared to hint at this charge. " All this while," he said, after describing the fight, " Captain Badiley lay aweather of us, making several shot, though at too great a distance, notwithstanding the wind was very good for his coming up"; and again, " Captain Badiley orders Captain Whyting in our fire-ship to board the Dutch Admiral, promising that himself would engage him till he made his graplings fast. Accordingly he (Whyting) makes towards him, but Captain Badiley, not coming up as he expected, by which means the Dutch Admiral played all his guns upon him, [the fire-ship] was sunk just at his stern."[2] Then he went on to allege that when Fisher and Ell were coming to his relief,

<hr>

[1] See *ante*, p. 195.    [2] Remonstrance, pp. 9, 10.

Captain Badiley called them off and fled with the whole of his squadron.

Appleton's charge, therefore, was that Badiley, when he saw that the engagement had begun, did not hurry to his relief, but he admitted that eventually Badiley did engage the Dutch, although in a half-hearted and ineffectual fashion. But he allowed Seaman to put in evidence which, if it had any foundation in fact, proved that Appleton's account of the affair was unreliable. "No sooner were we all clear of the Mould-head," Seaman said, "but Captain Badiley stood off.[1] The Dutch, seeing that, bore in upon us, and in less than half an hour after[2] we were come out, we were engaged. And, in the interim, of a sudden the wind shifted to the S.E. and S.E. by S. Captain Badiley and his fleet, if he had pleased, might have been as near the Dutch as we were. The *Bonadventure* in a short time blew up, and then, we looking for Captain Badiley and his fleet to have fallen on, could have no relief of him, but instead of coming to relieve us [he] chased one of the ships belonging to Livorna, though he saw the Duke's colours flying, and as soon as Captain Cox made him coming back, ran his frigate aground on the weather shore, so that we had but little relief all this time. . . . If Captain Badiley had been a pensioner to the States of Holland, he could not have done them better service."[3] So if Seaman were at all worthy of credit,

---

[1] Thus inverting the order of Badiley's manœuvres.
[2] "That" in orig.
[3] Seaman's Declaration. The Remonstrance, p. 15.

Badiley's squadron had never been engaged at all in the fight in the Leghorn Road, and the affair of the fire-ship was merely an unfounded imagination.

But the sting which was to give the greatest smart was yet to be inflicted. It was hinted that Badiley had goods on board one of the merchant-men in his own squadron, and that, to save himself from loss, he purposely left Appleton to his fate. The statement was partially true. Badiley had on board one of his ships a few parcels of currants; but no mention was made of the fact that he was part owner of the *Peregrine*, under Appleton's command, and that his loss by her capture was far greater than that which he would have suffered. if his currants had fallen into the hands of the Dutch. "My loss in the *Peregrine* for want of timely suc- cour," he asserted, "was more than I had in our part of the fleet that came away though the shirt on my back had been prized at the highest value."[1] But it had been pre-determined that no effort should be omitted to compass Badiley's ruin, and even the currants were not allowed to pass unnoticed.

Captains Fisher and Ell were found ready to declare their belief in the truth of Seaman's wild statements;[2] but the case against Badiley seemed incomplete, unless some testimony could be pro- duced that he had admitted his shortcomings. To obtain this desirable end, two seamen belonging to the *Paragon* were secured. Robert Daines and Samuel Wily bore witness as follows: "We whose

[1] Badiley's Answer, p. 26.
[2] Remonstrance, pp. 16–18.

names are hereunder written do testify that Captain
Peter Whyting, commander of the fire-ship, after
the sinking of the ship and his coming aboard
Captain Badiley, did, in our hearing, several times
say that Captain Badiley, having left Captain
Appleton in the middle of his enemies, two hours
after seeing from his poop that the *Leopard's* colours
were still in the foretop and the guns firing, fell,
as he had good reason, into passion, saying he was
an undone man for ever."[1]

It was a clever stroke to bring forward two of
Badiley's own seamen, who would not be suspected
of antagonism towards their old commander, to
testify against him. The reader of the Remonstrance, unversed in rules of evidence, would not
be likely to notice how unsatisfactory it was that,
while Daines and Wily reported what Whyting had
said about Badiley's self-condemnation, Whyting
himself should be silent. Even the Irish and
Scotch Committee, composed mainly of men with
no legal training, might fail to detect the futility
of this evidence. If Appleton had rested content
with the dramatic picture of Badiley's remorse,
which Daines and Wily had drawn, he would have
done well. But the two sailors had a further statement to volunteer in prejudice of their former
captain, and this was embodied in a second affidavit.
"We whose names are hereunder written," Daines
and Wily declared, "do testify that the Italians
and French in Leghorn, seeing how Captain
Appleton behaved himself towards the Dutch, and

[1] Remonstrance, p. 13.

how Captain Badiley behaved himself towards Captain Appleton and the other ships, protested they would tear Captain Badiley in pieces for a coward as he is, if ever he should come on shore."[1]

Such evidence must surely have been too startling for any Committee. Daines and Wily were on board the *Paragon* from the time of the engagement off Leghorn to the moment when she cast anchor in the Downs. They were never within a league of the port after the battle commenced. To put them forward as witnesses to the comments of the French and Italians in Leghorn showed either that the prosecution was conducted with conspicuous imbecility, or that its promoters were so confident of support from persons of influence that they deemed no charge too reckless or too extravagant to launch against their victim. Appleton appended to these affidavits of Daines and Wily the statement that he could produce much more of such testimony. For once, doubtless, he spoke the truth.

Of such stuff was the Remonstrance compounded : falsehoods that needed only to be examined to be exposed, and perversions of fact which were more specious but could not stand critical analysis, interlarded with mere idle rumour, gossip, and surmise, which could impose upon the credulity of no man. There can be little doubt that the plot against Badiley had deeper ramifications than the mere desire of Appleton and his associates for revenge,

---

[1] *Ib.* The "as he is" is a charming unconscious revelation of hostility.

or even the endeavour of Salvetti to justify his master's conduct in the eyes of the English Government; but it is impossible to trace all the details of it. The Royalists in England and Holland lost no opportunity of supporting any movement which tended to bring discredit upon the Commonwealth,[1] and they may well have thought that the overthrow and disgrace of a man, whose reputation for seamanship was rising, might indirectly benefit a cause which, at the close of the war with Holland, had sunk to its lowest ebb.

[1] Cf. Badiley's Answer, p. 37.

# Chapter XVIII

## ACQUITTAL

ALTHOUGH the evidence in support of the Remonstrance contained so many falsities and evasions, Appleton's part of the case, which was probably written by Nathaniel Reading, was as cleverly composed as the material from which it was prepared would permit. In tone it was moderate and forbearing, as if the writer performed regretfully the distasteful task which had been imposed upon him. Until the other side of the story could be told, its effect could not but be prejudicial to Badiley, and it is hardly surprising that, for a time, the feeling against him ran high. Even the Scotch and Irish Committee seem at first to have thought that a case was made out ; and, so late as October 7, 1653, at which time Badiley's Answer had just appeared, Salvetti wrote home triumphantly that " the universal opinion was that all the blame would light on Badiley." [1]

A week later Salvetti had read Badiley's Answer to the Remonstrance, which, he said, was " so malicious and far from the real truth that it had proved and confirmed his cowardice rather than excused it," [2] but he added that the proceedings

[1] Salvetti: Despatches, O. 141.  [2] *Ib.*, O. 144.

still hung fire. He suspected that Badiley had good friends at Court, otherwise he would not have had the audacity to cast upon Appleton the blame for the loss of the five ships outside Leghorn harbour. On October 21 his hopes had sunk low. He wrote that he had been promised an audience with the Council of State at four o'clock on the following day (a bad hour, he interjected, for a sickly old man), and he added that he should refrain from mentioning the affair of Leghorn unless the Council raised the subject, as it would be well if they could forget it.[1]

Salvetti received his audience in due course. He made an elaborate speech to the Council, congratulating them upon the stability of their Government, and expressing undying friendship on behalf of his master. He received but a curt reply. The Council, he was informed, would send a written answer to the Grand Duke. No mention was made of Leghorn, but Salvetti could see that the members of the Council were disgusted about it, and he did not desire further to stir troubled waters.[2]

In the middle of November his hopes rose slightly. He thought that the Committee,[3] without coming to any definite decision upon the merits of the issue, would nevertheless cashier Captain Badiley and declare him incapable of serving the

---

[1] Salvetti: Despatches, O. 149.

[2] *Ib.* Despatch of Oct. 28/Nov. 7, 1653, O. 151.

[3] On Nov. 1 a new Council of State was elected. C.J., vii. 343. Its Committees were consequently reconstructed. Cal. S.P.D., 1653–4, p. 237.

State in the future.[1]   After that, he made no mention of the case again.   Badiley's Answer had been received and considered, and the statements which were "so malicious and far from the real truth" had brought him who had made them triumphantly out of his difficulties.

Badiley's Answer to the Remonstrance forms quite a bulky pamphlet.   In arrangement it is perhaps the most remarkable document that ever came from the pen of man.   It is strung together in most disorderly fashion.   The old sea captain was unused to such work.   Whenever he saw a lie or an evasion he pounced upon and worried and rent it as a mastiff worries a cur.[2]   He commenced, quaintly enough, with "An Appendix, showing the chief heads and principal things in the ensuing Answer, for the right understanding of such as would be brief in ascertaining the truth."[3]   Then he proceeded to set down his Answer to the Remonstrance, "or at least that part which, he judgeth, concerns him in any kind to answer, as it was given

---

[1] Salvetti : Despatch of Nov. 18/28, 1653, O. 161.

[2] The full title is "Captain Badiley's Answer unto Captain Appleton's Remonstrance, given in to His Excellency the Lord General Cromwell and the Right Honourable the Council of State, as also his true relation of what past between the Great Duke of Tuscany and himself, with sundry letters, affidavits and certificates, discovering the fallaciousness of the said pamphlet called, 'A Remonstrance of the fight in Leghorn Road between the English and the Dutch,' with some other particulars not impertinent to the purpose of clearing the truth.   London.   Printed by M. Simmons in Aldersgate St., 1653."   British Museum : Press Mark, E. 1952 (9).

[3] Badiley's Answer, pp. [1–8].

in to the Committee of Scotch and Irish Affairs, with very little digression."[1]  When the Answer was completed, he added " A short breviate or abstract of what to my understanding appeareth to be the causes of that great disaster [which] befel the squadron near Leghorn the 4th of March last."[2]  Then followed a confused mass of correspondence and affidavits, strung together with little regard to date or subject.  The " Answer " is in many ways a most exasperating document, but in spite of its crudities and confusion, it holds attention spellbound, because it is instinct with the old seaman's thoughts as they rushed and tumbled through his brain in the autumn of 1653, when, standing at bay before his pursuers, he wrestled with the difficulty of expressing those thoughts in words.[3]

It is not necessary to struggle through this tangled web of evidence, because the story which it tells is, when it is unravelled, that which has already been narrated in its historical sequence.  The statements of Badiley and his witnesses have been accepted as authentic, not merely because the Council of State so accepted them, but because they do not contradict one another, and they are supported by evidence derived from independent sources.  Longland wrote from Leghorn a long and detailed reply to the Remonstrance, and in no particular does it fail to corroborate the assertions made in Badiley's Answer.[4]  If Appleton, in London, with all his

---

[1] Badiley's Answer, p. 1.      [2] *Ib.*, p. 40.

[3] Badiley also wrote a separate reply to the Declaration of Seaman, Fisher, and Ell.  British Museum, E. 1952 (8).

[4] Longland to Cromwell, Nov. 14, 1653, *u.s.*

witnesses about him, was unable to put together a story that did not contradict itself, and contradict also former accounts which he had written of the events which he professed to narrate, it was scarcely possible that Longland and Badiley, separated as they were by hundreds of miles, could have succeeded in telling a coherent story unless they were writing the truth.

But that portion of Badiley's defence which is his own composition is too characteristic of the man to be thus passed over in silence. The introductory "Appendix," which was really a short summary of his case, contained the expression of a wish that "if the Remonstrancer hath heft dirt in the face of the State's faithful servants most wrongfully, he may be made to know it,"[1] and ended with a protest against the printing of the Remonstrance by the printers to the Parliament, "as if they (the Parliament) had fathered it."[2]

He then proceeded to tell the story of his command in the Mediterranean from the battle of Monte Cristo to the battle of Leghorn, but he told it in no sort of sequence. He first laid bare Appleton's conduct at the time of the former fight, alleging that the illness which Appleton urged as his excuse for not sailing to support his comrades was "a feigned sickness."[3] Then he told of his endeavours to shield Appleton from the consequences of the Grand Duke's displeasure on account of the attack on the

---

[1] Badiley's Answer, p. [4].

[2] *Ib.*, p. [5]. The Parliament referred to is the "Little," or "Barebone's" Parliament.     [3] *Ib.*, p. 2.

sentinel, and how he had subsequently restored him to his command. " It would have been a good business for this man," he said, " who feared the questioning of his life at home, to have an opportunity given him that by his gallantry in service he might have done something to remove that fear, as also the disreputation, which otherwise he could not." [1] And the reward of Badiley's generosity was the " questioning " of his own life.

He next laid stress upon the many shortcomings and disobediences of Seaman, Marsh and Ell, who were the chief witnesses against him. They were, indeed, a disreputable crew, and it was not difficult to prove their untrustworthiness. " I have always tried to mix serenity with authority and to cover mistakes," he said, in explanation of the fact that he had borne so long with their ill-behaviour; " but," he added, " we see not only many proverbs fulfilled now and then, but old stories. Wash some creatures' ears with never so much water, and they will be no whiter. Heap coals of love upon some, and they will turn back coals of fire on you when it is in their power. Traitor or anything they will not baulk at." [2]

Next came the story of the capture of the *Phœnix* and of Appleton's attack on the sentinel. Badiley admitted that he had sanctioned the former, being ignorant of Appleton's agreement with the Duke. At first, he said, the Duke commended the exploit, and would never have taken notice of it, " had not that foolish childish act of Captain Appleton's, in

---

[1] Badiley's Answer, p. 4.    [2] *Ib.*, p. 11.

taking the Dutchman out of his sentinel's house (as if he had been Lord Paramount in that country), highly incensed him, as indeed it would any other prince."[1]   This led on to the narration of the negotiations between the Grand Duke and Badiley which ultimately resulted in the enforced departure of the English ships from Leghorn.

Badiley was now approaching the portion of the indictment which most stung and rankled, the allegation that he had played the coward in the battle of Leghorn.   " In answer to the charge of treachery or cowardice," he said, " I suppose the proofs that are herein included will acquit me of the former, and if those (who very well know I have complained of them as great failers in service) will not acquit me of the latter, let me lie under that indignity.   I ever counted it one of the unhandsomest things in the world to be speaking out anything tending to self-applause, yet I am in a manner constrained to write like such an one at this time, although my aim is that God alone may have honour by it."[2]

So, with great self-restraint, he told the story of the battle of Monte Cristo : how during a long August day, he with his four frigates had resisted the attack of ten Dutch men-of-war ; how he had refused to surrender, even when the merchant captains, of whom his adversary Ell was one, besought him to do so ; and how the ships had been preserved by the sudden stilling of the wind.   " Of which miraculous preservation," he added, " (if some merchants were rightly sensible) they would not

[1] Ib., p. 13.       [2] Ib., p. 24.

murmur and quarrel and be ready to speak all manner of evil, whether right or wrong, against the State's faithful servants." [1]

Then, with splendid disdain, he drew the veil down upon this enforced " self-applause," and shut out the picture. " But why talk of this fight ? " he said. The charge was that Badiley turned coward. When the evidence was weighed, there was not an honest man in England that would not admit that they might as well have cried, ' Badiley has turned Turk '; [2] the grossest insult which, in those days, could be levelled against an Englishman.

Thus he was led on to tell in great detail the story of the battle of Leghorn, and of the various communications between himself and Appleton which preceded it. He had no difficulty in exposing the evasive interpretation which Appleton attempted to put upon the letter from off Piombino, [3] which urged Appleton to " haste as for life," and in proving that the deliberate decision of all the officers of the Leghorn squadron was that the ships should not leave port until Badiley was engaged with the Dutch. [4] Then he showed, by an overwhelming mass of evidence, that he made desperate efforts to come to the relief of Appleton, when the latter had prematurely drawn upon the Leghorn ships the attack of the Dutch, which should have been directed against Badiley, and that he did not cease

---

[1] Badiley's Answer, p. 25.

[2] *Ib.*, p. 26.

[3] *Ante*, p. 186.

[4] Badiley's Answer, pp. 27–30.

from the endeavour until the salvation of the *Leopard* was manifestly hopeless, and a prolongation of the battle threatened the destruction of the whole fleet. "When I saw all hopes past," he said, "in human reason [I withdrew], not because the enemy had grown three to one, there being four of our best ships lost before I could come up, and one since, nor because many more were expected from the east and west every hour to their assistance, but none to ours, although I believe it's justifiable for a commander-in-chief to withdraw in such a case, or else old Van Tromp had been in a poor condition, whereas twice together, although the numbers were upon the matter equal, he let us take away so many ships and stayed not by it, but withdrew with the rest.[1] . . . Hence it was I set my mainsail and came away, and if he looks on that to be the sign of calling off the fleet, Captain Appleton is in the right; but if his meaning be according to the literal sense of his expressions, how that I called to Captain Ell and Captain Fisher to come away when they were going to relieve the *Leopard* by sufficient testimony, it will be proved a most false thing." The fact was, as Badiley conclusively showed, that Ell and Fisher, instead of attempting to relieve the *Leopard*, were sailing, out of call, "after their own inventions."

Then, after pointing out that the Italians who watched the battle from the shore were incompetent witnesses, as they had no means of judging the con-

---

[1] Badiley probably referred to the battles of Portland and the Gabbard.

duct of the fight, he made an appeal for justice, and he ended his answer with a text—" 2 Sam. xxiii. 3 : The God of Israel said and the Rock of Israel spake : He that ruleth over men must be just, ruling in the fear of God," etc.[1]

The mystic utterance from which these words were quoted is worth perusal. Bearing in mind the circumstances in which the Answer appeared, there can be little doubt that Badiley's intention was to make, through them, a direct appeal to the mind and heart of Cromwell. The Convention which is known as the " Little Parliament " was near the end of its brief and troubled existence,[2] and Oliver Cromwell was soon to become the uncrowned King of England, under the title of Lord Protector, " the man who was raised upon high." Cromwell, like Badiley, knew his Bible well, and at such a juncture the

---

[1] Badiley's Answer, pp. 31–39. The passage from which these words are taken runs thus : " Now these be the last words of David. David the son of Jesse said, and the man who was raised up on high, the anointed of the God of Jacob, and the sweet Psalmist of Israel, said : The Spirit of the Lord spake by me, and His word was in my tongue. *The God of Israel said, the Rock of Israel spake to me, He that ruleth over men must be just, ruling in the fear of God.* And he shall be as the light of the morning, when the sun riseth, even a morning without clouds ; as the tender grass springing out of the earth by clear shining after rain. Although my house be not so with God ; yet He hath made with me an everlasting covenant, ordered in all things, and sure : for this is all my salvation, and all my desire, although He make it not to grow. But the sons of Belial shall be all of them as thorns thrust away, because they cannot be taken with hands : but the man that shall touch them must be fenced with iron and the staff of a spear ; and they shall be utterly burned with fire in the same place."

[2] It surrendered its powers to Cromwell on Dec. 12, 1653.

solemn prophetic words of the Psalmist would appear fraught with a direct message from a Divine source.

At the end of the confused mass of evidence which was appended to the " Answer," Badiley took final leave of the subject. " To wind up all," he wrote, "when that fallacious Remonstrance of a fight near Leghorn came to my hand, seeing the Great Duke his secretary and I know not whom besides (among some of our captains' interest) all woven together, I thought of these words, ' A three-fold cord is not easily broken,' how much less that which may be compared to a seven-fold cord, to draw on mischief (if possible) upon the State's faithful servants. Yet a little skill, where there is honesty and integrity, may make it like unto rotten tow. Whether it hath or no, I shall not query.

" But in my proceeding in this short discovery of truth I shall only say thus much by expressing what is before denoted. I have been cautious that none might be offended except it be such whose contentious spirits have sufficiently discovered themselves. And although some may think Sir Walter Raleigh's words concerning those times are like to prove true in all ages, ' he that traceth truth too near at the heels may chance to have it kick out his teeth,' for my part, I am of another opinion and do yet hope better of the present season.

" But, as a gentleman expressed himself not long since, upon another occasion, ' I am in a land of miracles,' meaning in England, I was thinking whether it may not be added, 'Are we not in an age of miracles ?'

"That a commander of a force having been sent forth, should be so neglected, and as if he had been sent abroad for destruction (although I confess I had better hopes), and being in foreign parts, should there conflict with as many hazards and troubles as almost was possible for any man to undergo in the time, and yet when he shall come to his own country, hoping to find that as good harbour after a storm, shall *per contra* be made liable to contempt from such as have absolutely disobeyed commands and have been the causes of all the damage which hath befallen the nation in those parts in which he hath been, and few seem to take notice of it—to which I need add no more, being your servant as before, RI. BADILEY."[1]

There is pathos in this last unfinished sentence. The valiant old seaman, as he approached the end of his task, appears to have been overwhelmed with a sense of his friendlessness. He had told a plain unvarnished tale, but would any man believe it? The Salvettis and the Readings, with the merchants who had lost their goods, were all in league against him. His friends had all deserted him, and he was looked upon as a dishonoured man. It seemed useless to press his case further, and he left the sentence uncompleted, adding no more to a useless complaint against his fate.

Longland's spirited defence of himself in answer to the charges which Appleton had brought against him, arrived in England too late to affect the result

---

[1] Badiley's Answer, pp. 119, 120.

of Badiley's trial.[1]  It was a very long letter, and only a few of its closing sentences can be quoted.

"Men fallen into errors by their own ignorance or rashness often lay the blame on others," he wrote.  "Captain Appleton had shown more wisdom in submitting to the hand of Providence than in falling to beating his fellow-servants.  He has heaped abuses on Captain Badiley, whose integrity is so well known to you, as also his wisdom and courage in managing the late fight with the Dutch before Porto Longone,[2] and in preserving so many rich ships, and his endeavours were ten times more employed to save this unhappy squadron.  I have been eye-witness of his care therein, besides those many dangers which he escaped going to and fro between this place[3] and Porto Longone, being waylaid by the enemy, who were greedy of his destruction and sought all manner of ways to compass it, while Appleton never made a motion in six months to get out of the Mould."

Thus Longland spoke out for his friend ; for himself he added : " I could say much more, but less I could not say to clear myself of those foul aspersions, yet what is behind is more than all the rest. I have lived here a long time as a factor, and my fair and honest dealing, with the good repute I had among many worthy gentlemen and merchants in London, brought me employment and thereby my

---

[1] It was received on Dec. 7, 1653, the day on which Badiley was appointed a rear-admiral. Cal. S.P.D., 1653-4, p. 289.

[2] The battle of Monte Cristo.

[3] Leghorn.

livelihood. But now, while I lie in the condition this man (Appleton) has set me, printed and posted up for a villain and a traitor, who will acknowledge or own me ? This man has ruined me, and that by your umbrage[1] and patronage, for his Remonstrance is directed to your Excellency and the Council of State and printed by the Parliament's printer. . . . I therefore beseech you, that if it appear to you that I am innocent of those foul crimes, you will give reparation to my credit in such a way as shall seem fitting, which will encourage me to go on cheerfully in performing my duty in this place."[2]

It is probable that all the documents in Badiley's case were perused by his Excellency the Lord General, although more important questions of State were at the time absorbing his attention. Cromwell was a member of the Committee for Irish and Scotch affairs, which decided upon the truth or falsity of the Remonstrance; and his son, Colonel Henry Cromwell, was its chairman.[3] Cromwell had a keen eye for an honest man. If he attended the meetings of the Committee, he had an opportunity of seeing the two antagonists face to face. Appleton would fare but ill under the keen questioning of such a man as Oliver Cromwell.

The result of the inquiry can only be gathered incidentally. Some time in December, 1653, a

---

[1] *i.e.* protection.

[2] Longland to Cromwell, Nov. 14, 1653, Cal. S.P.D., 1653-4, pp. 243-8. Longland went on cheerfully performing his duty for many years.

[3] Council of State: Day's Proceedings, Nov. 8, 1653. Cal. S.P.D., 1653-4, p. 237.

certain Captain Marryott wrote thus to the Admiralty Committee: "I beg leave to defend myself before you. You know how Captain Rich. Badiley was accused, so that it was said he would be hanged; but when he came to plead his own cause, he came off with honour and his adversaries with shame."[1]

The acquittal took place early in December, and it must have been one of the last acts of the Council of State nominated by the Little Parliament. The date of the Council's decision cannot be exactly ascertained; but it must have been before December 7, for on that day Badiley was appointed a Rear-Admiral of the Fleet.[2] On the following day he was recommended by the Commissioners of the Sick and Wounded as one of the trustees for the money given by the State to the children of Captain Reeve.[3]

Badiley was traitor and coward no longer, but a man honoured and trusted by the Government which he served. Within a week after his appointment as Rear-Admiral, the Little Parliament quietly extinguished itself, and four days later Cromwell became Lord Protector of England. There was work yet to be done by both these men before they should rest from their labours.

Appleton and his confederates, Seaman and Marsh, Fisher and Ell, were "as thorns thrust away." They were afforded no further opportunity

---

[1] Marryott to the Admiralty Committee. Undated. Cal. S.P.D., 1653–4, p. 335.

[2] *Ib.*, p. 289.

[3] *Ib.*, p. 528. Trustees' Bond, p. 532.

to exercise their malignancy in the service of the
State.  Divers glimpses of Appleton may be caught
occasionally, in subsequent years, praying for money
alleged to be due from him, complaining of its non-
payment, or recommending candidates for employment by the Government—recommendations which,
it may be surmised, carried no very great weight.[1]
What became of him, how he lived and when he
died, no man knows and none need greatly care.

[1] *e.g.* Appleton to the Admiralty Committee, Feb. 17,
1653/4.  "Petition for an order to the Navy Commissioners to
hasten the passing of his accounts and praying his arrears for
service in the Straits, as Captain Badiley's have been passed, and
he has been waiting seven months." Cal. S.P.D., 1653–4, p. 576.
See also *Ib.*, pp. 522, 554; 1654, p. 469.

# Chapter XIX

## ENGLAND TRIUMPHANT

WITH Badiley's acquittal, the story of the sufferings of the English in the Mediterranean Sea was ended, and the main incident of Badiley's life was closed. The remainder of his sea service was performed under Blake, and it is overshadowed by the renown of the greater captain. The events of his closing years may therefore be told with less detail.

It must have been a cause of no little regret to Badiley that, while his trial was dragging its slow length along, notable deeds were being done in the Narrow Seas, in which he was disabled from taking a part. The Dutch had been actively employed, since their defeat in the three days' engagement which commenced off Portland, in preparing to renew the contest. When Badiley arrived in England, both sides were expecting to bring the contest to an issue. The English were eager, by a second victory, to confirm the supremacy which they had gained in the battle of Portland, and the Dutch were burning to recover their lost superiority. On June 2, 1653, Van Tromp, with a hundred and twenty ships, sighted the English fleet, which had been hovering off the coast of Holland, but which then lay nearer home. The two fleets were about equal in numbers, but the Dutch were disorganized and divided by political intrigue. Some of the commanders were adherents of the House of Orange, others were Republicans, and it was alleged that many of them failed in their duty on that account. The engagement took place off a shoal called " The Gabbard," which lies some miles east of Harwich, and it lasted all day, to the disadvantage of the Dutch ; but the English lost General Deane, who commanded in conjunction with Monk. Blake was on shore ill; but when the news was brought to him that a battle was impending, he went to sea at once with fourteen sail to assist the English. He arrived on the following day in time to take part in the final defeat and chase of the enemy, who were driven to seek refuge in Dutch ports, having lost twenty of their ships.

Never before had the Dutch suffered so great a disaster. The English fleet was able to blockade their ports and to paralyse their commerce. The condition of the people, thus impoverished, was pitiable, and a loud cry went up for peace. Before the month of June was ended, ambassadors had been despatched to London to propose a treaty. But the Dutch did not on that account slacken their efforts to prosecute the campaign. They believed that by showing a bold front they might induce the victorious foe to moderate the hard conditions which otherwise he might be inclined to impose. They therefore continued vigorously the preparation of another fleet with which they might, in the worst event, strike one more blow for victory. And this was the fate which was in store for them. In the middle of July, when the negotiations for peace were slowly proceeding, the English fleet, which had returned home to re-victual, sailed again for the Dutch coast, under the command of Monk, Penn, and Lawson. Blake, who had been quite unfit for service when he went forth to the battle of the Gabbard, was lying dangerously ill at home.

On July 29, 1653, Van Tromp sailed forth to the last sea-fight in which he was to engage and also the last in the war against England. He commanded eighty ships, and the afternoon was spent in a desultory cannonade between the two fleets. On the following day he was joined by forty more vessels, but a great gale prevented any further engagement. On the next day, Sunday, July 31, the main battle was fought. The English commanders had resolved that they would, if possible, put an end to the war by a final and crushing victory. After some manœuvring, they bore down upon the Dutch fleet and broke through it, reserving their broadsides until they came to close quarters with the enemy. Then, putting about, they repeated these tactics again and yet again, until the Dutch fleet, overwhelmed and shattered, hoisted sail and fled. Van Tromp did not live to witness the final disaster. He was shot through the heart at the commencement of the action, and he fell with a prayer for his country upon his lips.

The aim of the English commanders being to break the sea power of the Dutch, they did not attempt to take prizes; they concentrated their efforts upon sinking and burning. The consequence was that this last battle was the most bloody and desperate that had been fought during the war. Twenty-six Dutch ships were destroyed, while the English lost only two.

Captain Cox commanded the *Phœnix* in this engagement, and after the fight was over he sent a short account of it to Cromwell. "Being near Texel on the 29th ult.," he wrote, "we discovered Tromp and his fleet of eighty sail who had come from Flushing, and who came within two leagues of us; but when he saw that we also came on with undaunted spirits, their hearts failed them so much that they tacked about, but we ultimately forced them into a defenceable position, and our dispute continued until 8 p.m., when, on account of the darkness, we left him (*sic*), intending to give him a breakfast next morning, but the wind and sea prevented our coming together. The day after, being Sunday, we began the dispute about 6 a.m. until 3 p.m., they having the advantage of the wind. At the first encounter we destroyed divers of their ships, amongst which was the *Garland*, which they took from us in a former engagement.[1] As she had all her masts shot by the board and was incapable of being brought home, we set her on fire, with some others of their ships. I judge they never received such a blow since they wrote themselves

[1] In the battle off Dungeness.

' High and Mighty,'[1] and we desire that God may have the glory."[2]

This appears to have been Cox's last naval exploit. He had received a sum of £500 as a reward for re-capturing the *Phœnix* at Leghorn.[3] But the money seems hardly to have compensated him for his losses in the service of the State. On January 1, 1655–6, he petitioned for further relief or employment,[4] and after that date nothing is to be discovered concerning him.

After this last defeat the Dutch gave up the hopeless struggle; but peace was not concluded until many months later, in April, 1654. When Badiley had been acquitted of the charges brought against him and raised to the rank of Rear-Admiral, in December, 1653, he soon found active employment once more, although it was evident that there would be no further fighting with the Dutch. Cromwell was still intent upon strengthening the fleet, for what purpose no man knew. He had resolved upon a policy for the assertion of England's supremacy at sea, but for the time he kept his secret locked within his breast. Only vague rumours floated about concerning the destination of the ships which were being so rapidly collected in the Downs.

---

[1] The official style of the Dutch Government was " The High and Mighty Lords the States-General of the United Provinces."

[2] Cox to Cromwell, Aug. 2, 1653. Cal. S.P.D., 1653–4, p. 68.

[3] *Ib.*, p. 457.

[4] He said that he lost £400 in the *Bonadventure* and was wounded on the *Constant Warwick*. The £500 granted hardly countervailed his losses and charge of cure. He had six children and no employment. Cal. S.P.D., 1655–6, p. 98.

In April, 1654, Rear-Admiral Badiley was on board his flag-ship, the *Vanguard*, sailing the Narrow Seas, under the command of Lawson.[1] The fleet, of which the *Vanguard* formed a part, was employed in enforcing the provisions of the Navigation Act, until such time as the ships which were mustering in the Downs should be ready to sail upon more important service. Salvetti, alarmed at the result of Badiley's trial, watched these vigorous naval preparations with great anxiety. Kind friends were not lacking who hinted that part of the fleet would sail for the Mediterranean and visit Leghorn, with results that might prove disastrous to Tuscany. He was informed that Cromwell had become possessed of certain letters, written by Van Galen, in which that commander boasted of the favour which the Grand Duke had shown him at the expense of the English.[2] Cromwell doubtless kept the intended movements of the fleet secret, in order thus to inspire dismay in the hearts of all Princes who, in England's hour of danger, had shown themselves unfriendly. Salvetti became still more anxious when the rumour reached him that Badiley, "the author of all this mischief," was to sail with the Mediterranean fleet.[3] It boded ill for Tuscany, if this man were to be allowed to have a hand in wreaking vengeance for affronts which he, at any rate, did not deem to be imaginary.

[1] Sacheverell to the Admiralty Committee, April 14, 1654. Cal. S.P.D., 1654 p. 101.

[2] Despatch dated April 3, 1654, O. 222.

[3] Despatch dated April 10, 1654, O. 226

Salvetti could hardly believe that the Protector was harbouring resentment against the Grand Duke on account of the treatment of the English ships at Leghorn, but the aspect of affairs was decidedly unpleasant. He had been endeavouring day after day to obtain an audience with Cromwell, to present a letter of congratulation from the Grand Duke upon his accession to the Protectorate, but he found himself constantly put off with one excuse or another. When Cromwell considered that he had sufficiently frightened the old diplomatist, the interview was granted. Salvetti was somewhat relieved by the manner of his reception. Cromwell was in a cheerful mood: he received the ambassador with great courtesy,[1] and he listened intently to Salvetti's speech, setting forth the undying affection which the Grand Duke cherished for the English nation. When Salvetti had finished, he presented Ferdinand's letter. Cromwell took it, "with a laughing face," replying that he was deeply indebted to the Grand Duke for such noble expressions of friendship, and he flattered Salvetti for the able manner in which he had conducted the business of Tuscany in England.[2]

All this at first seemed most consoling; but Salvetti doubtless knew that Cromwell was most dangerous when he was most merry. When he came to meditate upon the interview, he perceived that it had consisted merely of fine speeches, which

[1] " Molto benigna e courtese, ascoltandomi sempre con faccia molto gioviale."

[2] Despatch dated April 17, 1654, O. 230.

meant nothing. He was still kept in ignorance of the ultimate destination of the Mediterranean fleet. " However it may be," he wrote in his next letter, " the Princes of Italy ought to note it, and stand prepared for it by good government. And that Badiley will be one of the commanders of the Mediterranean fleet makes me fear lest our avowed enemy should do us all the possible harm he can." He added in cypher his opinion that Cromwell's friendliness at the last interview was put on to conceal his real designs.[1]

For more than a month Salvetti remained in anxious suspense as to the ultimate destination of the fleet. He attached so much importance to the question whether Badiley was to return to the Mediterranean that his communications to the Tuscan Government on this point were almost invariably written in cypher. He did not doubt that if Badiley came to Leghorn, severe reprisals would be taken by the English.[2] At last the purposes for which the great fleet had been assembled leaked out. Blake and Badiley were to sail with one portion of it for the Mediterranean, to restore English prestige in those waters, and the remainder was to go, under Penn and Venables, to the West Indies, with instructions that were not disclosed. Although England was technically at war with France, and at peace with Spain, Crom-

---

[1] Despatch dated May 1, 1654, O. 238; see also Despatch dated May 15, 1654, O. 247.

[2] Despatches dated June 26, July 17, and July 24, 1654, O. 269–281.

well was, at that time, developing the new policy, which a little later was to result in an alliance with France against her ancient enemy. The West Indian fleet was destined to attack the possessions of Spain in the Caribbean Sea. It failed in its main object, which was the capture of San Domingo, or, as it was then called, "Hispaniola," but it took Jamaica, which has ever since remained a British possession.

It was intended that Badiley should sail in the *Vanguard* upon the Mediterranean expedition; but in June, when that ship was coming out of Chatham Dockyard, she ran upon a shoal,[1] and was so damaged that he had to transfer his flag to the *Andrew*.[2] It was not until September 24 that the Mediterranean fleet set sail from Plymouth.

There can be little doubt that the service which this fleet was intended to perform was an attack upon Spain in Europe, but Cromwell did not desire to engage in open warfare with that kingdom before the West Indian fleet had struck some decisive blow against her colonies. Until such an event had happened, Blake was instructed to employ his fleet in making the power of England felt amongst the States which bordered the Mediterranean Sea, and to punish the "Turks" of Africa for their depredations upon English commerce. But it was no part of Cromwell's policy to embroil himself

[1] Badiley to Navy Commissioners, June 22, 1654. Addl. MSS. 18,986, f. 140.
[2] Badiley to the Admiralty Committee, Aug. 25, 1654 Cal. S.P.D., 1654, p. 336.

needlessly with any other European Power. He merely wished to show the States of the Mediterranean sea-board that England, not Holland, was supreme upon the ocean, and that treatment such as that which the English had received at Leghorn and other places in the previous year could not be repeated with impunity.

For this purpose Blake divided his fleet into two squadrons when he entered the Mediterranean Sea. One squadron sailed for Naples, and it arrived before that port the day after the Duke of Guise, who had made a hostile demonstration against that part of the Spanish dominions, had taken his departure. The English had no orders to attack Naples. Their presence was only needed to show that England was able, if she were so inclined, to avenge the unjustifiable action of the Viceroy in imprisoning Cox and Reeves. The other squadron, under the command of Blake, in which was the *Andrew*, sailed for Leghorn, and in December, 1654, Badiley was once more riding in the Road which had been the scene of his many adventures and hair-breadth escapes.

Salvetti suffered grievous anxieties while the fleet was making its slow way from Plymouth to Leghorn, for Cromwell, with grim humour, never suffered him to know that Blake's mission was not one of war and reprisals. Moreover, he was troubled on another score. The Genoese, eager to profit by the disfavour into which they supposed that Tuscany had fallen, had sent ambassadors to Cromwell, urging him to divert the trade between

England and Leghorn which, before the recent troubles, had proved so remunerative to the port of Genoa. Salvetti feared that they would be successful, and that Badiley and Longland would do all in their power to promote the change.[1] But in this respect he alarmed himself without cause. He. soon discovered that English merchants were averse from any attempt on the part of the Government to prescribe where and how they should trade, and the Genoese ambassadors received nothing but fair promises.

The rumour had spread abroad that Blake had boasted that he would not leave Leghorn until the Grand Duke had paid 150,000 scudi as damages for his maltreatment of the English ships; but before the end of January, 1654–5, Salvetti had learned, greatly to his satisfaction, that no such hostile action was to be attempted. Blake was reported to be behaving himself with great civility and friendliness.[3] He saluted the port with his cannon, and the courtesy was returned by the guns of the castle. He wrote "a well-penned letter" to the Grand Duke, asking that the English merchants at Leghorn might be allowed free exercise of the Protestant faith; a favour which Ferdinand deemed it safe, in the altered circumstances, to refuse.[4] The English fleet obtained

---

[1] Despatch dated Dec. 25, 1654, O. 356.
[2] Despatches dated Feb. 12, and Feb. 19, 1654/5, O. 380, 386.
[3] Despatch dated Jan. 29, 1654/5, O. 374.
[4] Longland to Thurloe, Oct. 29, 1655. Thurloe: State Papers, iv. 92.

supplies from the town, and the Grand Duke honoured Blake with a present of some very choice wine from his own cellar. Blake expressed approval of the vintage, and consequently, some cases of the same wine were despatched to England for Cromwell's acceptance.[1]

Thus Badiley visited Leghorn once more in circumstances far different from those in which he quitted it. No hostile Dutch ships anchored in the Road : the English George floated proudly over an invincible English fleet, the first that had ever sailed those waters to proclaim the might of England to Princes who, a year before, had looked upon her as "an undone nation," and the pioneer of many others which were to confirm and augment her supremacy.

The English fleet was detained at Leghorn longer than the necessary exchange of courtesies demanded, partly on account of Blake's bad health, partly because, in spite of the pending alliance with France, the English had captured two French merchantmen which had sailed from infected ports, and the quarantine regulations prevented them from revictualling for a voyage.[2] When these hindrances had been overcome, the fleet set sail on January 15, 1654/5, intending to effect a junction with the squadron which had been

---

[1] The vessel which carried the wine was greatly delayed in its voyage, and Salvetti was much agitated by its non-arrival, for he feared that the delicate flavour of the wine would be injured.

[2] Blake to the Admiralty Committee, Jan. 12, 1654/5. Addl. MSS., 9304, f. 99.

sent to Naples, and then to make for Trapani in Sicily to display England's power to the governor, who had permitted the Dutch to capture the *Harry Bonadventure* and her prize within that harbour. But this plan was frustrated by the weather. "It hath pleased God," Blake reported, "to exercise us with a variety of wind and weather, and with divers mixed providences and strange dispensations, never to be forgotten by us, especially in regard that He hath been likewise pleased in them all to cause His compassions to prevail against His threatenings, and His mercy to triumph over His judgment." [1] The wind, which had been in Blake's favour when he left Leghorn, suddenly dropped, and several of the ships, including the *George*, Blake's flagship, and the *Andrew*, were in danger of drifting upon the rock-bound island of Capraia. "It pleased God to spring up a fresh gale in the very nick"; but it blew so dead in the teeth of the ships that, after much beating up and down, they were forced to return to Leghorn. [2]

As soon as the weather served, Blake set sail once more, and made for Tunis. His instructions bade him show himself more sternly to the Turk than to European Princes. He had heard that a Turkish fleet had been ordered to assemble at Porto Farina, hard by Tunis, early in the year. On February 8, he cast anchor in the great gulf, at the

---

[1] This is certainly the word in the letter. Blake probably intended to write "judgments."

[2] Blake to ——, Jan. 19, 1654/5. Addl. MSS., 9,304, f. 101.

head of which the city of Tunis stands, and he at once summoned the Dey to make restitution for the damage which his corsairs had inflicted upon English shipping. A conference was held on board the *George*, in which the Turks, while expressing a keen desire for future amity with England, demurred to the demand that they should make satisfaction for past injuries. This was by no means Cromwell's aim. He sought no friendship with the Turks, but he was resolved that English traders should no longer suffer from their thievish habits, as Badiley had suffered in those early days when he commanded the *Advance*. So Blake broke up the conference and sailed close up to Porto Farina, where he found nine Turkish galleys drawn into the harbour, close under the protection of a newly-erected fort. The position of the enemy was so strong that Blake hesitated to attack it. His fleet was in great straits for provisions, so, leaving a squadron to blockade Porto Farina, he sailed for Sardinia, where he revictualled. Then, after making a display of his strength off Trapani, he returned to Porto Farina in March, to find that the blockading squadron still held the Turkish galleys confined in the harbour.[1]

The Dey of Tunis had imagined that Blake's hesitation to attack the galleys had been due to fear of the prowess of the Turks, and he treated

---

[1] Blake to —— (? Admiralty Committee), March 14, 1654/5. Addl. MSS., 9,304, f. 103, and to similar effect, Thurloe : State Papers, iii. 232. Blake was also uncertain whether he was authorized to destroy the Tunisian fleet.

the English with contempt and contumely. "These barbarous provocations," Blake reported, "did so far work upon our spirits, that we judged it necessary for the honour of our fleet, our nation, and religion, seeing they would not deal with us as friends, to make them feel us as enemies; and it was thereupon resolved, at a council of war, to endeavour the firing of their ships in Porto Farina." Early on the morning of April 4, 1655, the English fleet sailed into Porto Farina before a favouring breeze, and cast anchor close to the forts and the galleys. It was an audacious enterprise, for in those days it was deemed impossible for ships successfully to measure themselves against coast defences. Blake taught his fellow-countrymen otherwise. The wind that had brought the ships into the harbour blew the smoke of their cannon across the enemy's works, and hindered them in the service of their artillery. After several hours' fighting, all the nine Turkish galleys were set on fire and destroyed. The English retired without losing a ship, and with only twenty-five men slain and forty wounded.[1] "The Turks seldom or ever heard such a peal before,"[2] wrote one of the captains who took part in this brilliant exploit. They had received a lesson that they would not easily forget for a long time to come.

[1] Blake to Thurloe, April 13/23, 1655. Thurloe: State Papers, iii. 390.
[2] Capt. Geo. Crapnell to Thos. Smith, April 17, 1655. Cal. S.P.D., 1655, p. 129.

Having thus scourged Tunis, Blake sailed for Algiers to bring the Turks of that region to their senses, but the fame of his valour sped before him and he found the Algerines in a very submissive mood. They surrendered their English captives without a murmur, and thus escaped the fate of the Tunisians. While the fleet lay off Algiers, a strange sight was to be seen day after day. There were Dutchmen among the miserable captives taken by the Algerines, and, whenever the chance offered, these unfortunate men plunged into the sea and swam towards the English ships, choosing rather the chance of death by drowning than the certainty of lifelong captivity amongst the infidels. Seeing the sad plight of these Dutch prisoners, the English sailors were moved to a spontaneous act of generosity. Less than two years before the English and Dutch had been cutting one another's throats, and even then there was still a soreness between the two nations. But Dutchmen were Christians after all; and the Turk—well, he was the "Turk"; worse could hardly be said of him. So the rough, kindly sailors agreed among themselves that they would subscribe a dollar a head, to be deducted from their pay when they reached home, to purchase the freedom of those Dutch prisoners who had not the hardihood, or the opportunity, to regain it by swimming.[1]

The remainder of the summer was spent in cruising off the Spanish coast in anticipation of the

---

[1] Blake to the Navy Commissioners, Oct. 9, 1655. Cal. S.P.D., 1655, p. 374.

war with Spain, which, for reasons of policy, was still delayed. The expedition to the West Indies had not fulfilled the hopes of its projectors, and Penn and Venables were in disgrace. Cromwell hesitated to risk war with Spain in Europe until his alliance with France was assured, and Spain did not feel strong enough to declare war on account of the capture of Jamaica. So after months of useless cruising, the fleet returned home in the autumn. Badiley, on board the *Andrew*, with two other ships, arrived in the Downs on October 6, 1655, having parted company with Blake in a fog.[1] Blake came in on the day following. The ships were in a very crazy condition after their year of service at sea. They were at once sent into dock for repairs. Their crews were paid off, and Badiley was appointed a Vice-Admiral of the fleet.[2]

[1] Badiley to Blackborne, Oct. 6, 1655. Cal. S.P.D., 1655, p. 551.
[2] *Ib.*, p. 572.

# Chapter XX

## LAST DAYS

IT is probable that, when the *Andrew* was paid off, Badiley had resolved to quit the service, and to spend the remainder of his life in retirement. He had seen long and arduous service, and he was growing old. His handwriting, which had been firm and clear in his letters from Leghorn, became shaky and almost illegible in his later correspondence, indicating the approach of old age. He may well have wished to leave the work of the future to younger men, and to seek, in his home at Wapping, the repose which he had so well earned. But the call of duty was to come to him once more, and he was not the man to fail to answer it.

Before the year 1655 had ended, Cromwell's treaty of alliance with France had been signed, and war with Spain had become inevitable.[1] In the negotiations with Spain which had preceded this result, Cromwell had demanded, as the terms of his friendship, that England should enjoy freedom of trade with the Spanish Indies and liberty to exercise the

---

[1] Peace with France was proclaimed on Nov. 20, 1655. Cal. S.P.D., 1655–6, p. 28. War was virtually declared against Spain on Nov. 29. *Ib.*, p. 40.

Protestant religion in all parts of the Spanish dominions, without molestation from the Inquisition. "My master has but two eyes," the Spanish ambassador is reported to have replied, "and you ask him for both." The King of Spain was resolute in the determination to fight for his eyes, and Cromwell's alliance with France was the result. Great preparations were made during the winter to fit out an adequate fleet to attack the power of Spain.

Blake was once more appointed to command the English fleet, but in consequence of his failing health, he asked that some younger man should be joined with him in the commission. Cromwell's choice fell upon Edward Montagu, who was, at the time of his appointment, only about thirty years old. Montagu was a great favourite with the Lord Protector. When little more than a boy, he had distinguished himself in the Civil War, and had shown great courage at the battle of Naseby, and at the storming of Bristol. He had never before commanded a ship, but he was about to serve an apprenticeship under one of the greatest sea-captains of his age, which was to lead him to a brilliant career and the highest naval honours. When the Monarchy was restored Montagu became Earl of Sandwich, and, later on, the commander-in-chief of the English fleet. He died at the battle of Southwold Bay, on May 28, 1672, when his flagship, the *Royal James*, was blown up. Little did young Montagu dream, as he paced with Blake the deck of the *Naseby*, that in about five years' time he would conduct that ship to Holland, rechristened the *Royal Charles*, to bring back England's king to the shores from which he had so long been an exile.

Early in January, 1655–6, when the fleet was ready to sail against Spain, Vice-Admiral Lawson was appointed to the *Resolution*, and Rear-Admiral Bourne to the *Swiftsure*.[1] All seemed to be in readiness, when an unexpected difficulty occurred. It was rumoured that Lawson had refused to sail under sealed orders, and had been cashiered in consequence. Such was the story of Royalist gossips, but it is more probable that Lawson was suspected of complicity in a plot which a year later threatened to break out into insurrection.[2] In July, 1657, Lawson was imprisoned for his suspected connection with the designs of the Fifth Monarchy men, a sect of wild enthusiasts, who believed that Christ was about to descend from heaven to reign over England, and that it was their duty to prepare the way for His advent by overthrowing the Commonwealth. The flame of this madness was fanned by the Royalist party, with whom there can be little doubt that Lawson was in sympathy. They saw advantages in the immediate design of the Fifth Monarchy men, however little they might have relished the consequence which their allies hoped would flow from it. Whatever the truth may have been about Lawson's dismissal, the sudden loss of his services dislocated the arrangements of

---

[1] Cal. S.P.D., 1655–6, p. 138.
[2] Thurloe, vi. 184–5.

the naval authorities. In this difficulty they appealed to Badiley, and he at once came forward to fill Lawson's place.[1] Thus Badiley once more found himself in active service as a Vice-Admiral, with the *Resolution* for his flag-ship. Concerning these events Nicholas, the secretary and councillor of Charles II., wrote as follows: "The fleet in the Downs is very mutinous. Blake and Montagu were sent by Cromwell to pacify the seamen, who are angry because Lawson is not Vice-Admiral. Cromwell took his commission from him, suspecting him to have had a hand in last year's mutiny.[2] Badiley takes his place, but is not so well beloved as the other."[3]

It is probable enough that the crew of the *Resolution* were attached to Lawson, and murmured loudly at the change; but there is no evidence of any more widely spread disaffection apart from the rumours circulated by Royalists, who persistently magnified every small indication of insubordination into a demonstration in favour of the Stuarts.

That Badiley's unexpected appearance upon the

---

[1] D. Francis (Dick Pile) to Col. Whiteley, Feb. 21, 1655/6. Cal. S.P.D., 1655–6, p. 197.

[2] The reason alleged appears improbable. Had it been the case, Lawson would never have been appointed.

[3] Nicholas to Jane, March 4/14, 1655/6. Cal. S.P.D., 1655–6, p. 209. Nicholas goes on to say: "The discontent among seamen is so general, that if they had known they would have security in the King of Spain's ports, by his having made a fast conjunction with our king, many, nay most of the fleet, would have abandoned Cromwell, who is said to be most odious among the seamen."

scene caused bitter disappointment, either to Royalist intriguers or to Lawson's personal friends, is evident from a somewhat obscure transaction, which took place shortly after his appointment to the *Resolution*. When he was about to leave London to take up his command, he was arrested and cast into prison for debt, at the suit of one Robert Hammond. It would appear that there had been litigation between Badiley and Hammond, probably about money paid as compensation for ships or goods taken by the Dutch in the late war. The difference had been referred to an arbitrator named Andrew Pope, who had given his award in Badiley's favour, and had ordered Hammond to enter into a bond to pay the money. Nevertheless, Hammond, upon some pretext, and urged thereto, no doubt, by persons of more consequence than himself, obtained Badiley's arrest. The matter was reported to the Council of State on March 6, who deemed it "a great affront of the public service," and they appointed a special Committee to inquire into the matter that afternoon.[1] As Badiley was, not many days later, on board the *Resolution*,[2] it is evident that the Committee of the Council of State made short work with Hammond, and his fellow-conspirators if any such there were.

Soon after this event the fleet set sail from the Downs, and early in April, 1656, it was riding off

---

[1] Cal. S.P.D., 1655–6, p. 211.

[2] He left London on March 9th, Niewpoort to the States-General, March 10, 1655/6. Thurloe: State Papers, iv. 567.

the coast of Spain once more, anxious to try con-
clusions with any Spanish ships that might fall in
its way. But the Spaniards showed no alacrity to
engage, and their ships lay secure in Cadiz harbour,
where it was impossible for the English to attack
them, and whence they refused to be enticed. In
May, there was an inconclusive skirmish with a few
Spanish galleys at Porto Santa Maria,[1] but nothing
was done that redounded to the honour of the
English fleet, or inflicted a blow at the power of
Spain. Days and months passed in the enforced
weariness of blockade work, and it seemed as if
Blake, whose health was fast breaking down, was
not destined to earn further laurels in naval warfare.

At one time, indeed, it appeared as if the fleet
would be compelled to divert its attention from
Spain to Portugal. Ever since King John had
incurred the enmity of England by the assistance
and protection which he had afforded to Prince
Rupert and the revolted ships, he had been endeavouring to appease Cromwell's wrath, without,
at the same time, incurring any considerable inconvenience as the result of his partiality. He had
been understood to promise, through his ambassador, that he would pay compensation to the English merchants whom he had cast into prison,[2] and
also that he would permit to Protestants the free
exercise of their religion within his dominions.
When however, after a prolonged delay, the text

---

[1] Thurloe: State Papers, iv. p. 762.

[2] See *ante*, p. 43.

of the treaty was received in England, it was found that it had been framed in evasive language. The clause relating to freedom of Protestant worship had been drawn so that its validity was made subject to the consent of the Pope, "whereby," Cromwell wrote to Blake and Montagu, "he (the king) would bring us to an owning of the Pope, which, we hope, whatever befall us, we shall not, by the grace of God, be brought unto." Cromwell therefore became peremptory. He instructed the Admirals to give King John five days' grace for the ratification of the original terms of the treaty. In default, they were to attack Portuguese ships, and particularly the Brazil fleet, when and where they could get at them.[1] This threat brought the king to reason. The treaty was concluded by May 18, and in June some of Blake's frigates returned home with the £50,000 which had been paid on account of the indemnity.

Blake and Montagu were thus set at liberty to turn their attention entirely to Spain, but as her men-of-war still sulked in harbour, nothing could be done against her until the return of her rich merchant fleet from the West Indies, which was not due until the autumn. To pass the intervening time the two Admirals planned an expedition against the Turks of Tripoli, who had received no such salutary lesson as that which Blake had inflicted upon their brethren of Tunis and Algiers in the previous year. But the proposal was frustrated by an accident. On

---

[1] Cromwell to Blake and Montagu, May 6, 1656. Thurloe: State Papers, iv. 768.

the night of July 2 the fleet was overtaken and well-nigh overwhelmed by a furious gale. The night was pitch dark, and the sea "ran mountains high." Several of the ships, amongst which was the *Taunton*, broke cable. The *Taunton* was driven helplessly towards the *Naseby*, and it seemed to be only by miracle that she did not run down and destroy her. It would have been a strange fate if a vessel which had been named in honour of Blake's greatest military triumph had cut short his career as a Naval Commander. "Thus," Blake and Montagu wrote, " Providence hath occasioned our laying aside all thought of Tripoli during this summer." [1] The fleet was so damaged that after the necessary repairs had been effected, no time was left for such an expedition if it were to make sure of the West Indian merchantmen and their rich cargoes. So the seemingly endless task of cruising between Cadiz and the coast of Africa was resumed while the fleet waited the coming of that great prize. Cromwell had grown so hopeless of any substantial result from the expedition that towards the end of August he ordered Montagu to return home with the larger frigates, leaving Blake, with the remainder of the fleet, to watch for the West Indiamen.[2] But before this order could be delivered the long-coveted prey was in the grasp of the English. While Blake and Montagu, with the greater part of the fleet, were

[1] Blake and Montagu to Cromwell, July 3, 1656. Thurloe v. 178.

[2] Cromwell to Blake and Montagu, Aug. 28, 1656. *Ib.*, p. 363.

cruising about Gibraltar, Captain Stayner, with three vessels, sighted the West Indian fleet, consisting of eight ships, nearing the coast of Spain. Stayner at once attacked them, and after a desperate struggle, he captured two and sunk or burnt four. One ran ashore and one succeeded in escaping, and made for Cadiz.[1] Of the captured ships one was laden with hides and sugar, and the other with silver, to the value, it was said, of £2,000,000.

On board the Spanish Vice-Admiral were the Marquis of Badajoz and his family, who were returning to Spain after a prolonged absence. The marquis was a poor, proud Spanish nobleman, who had been governor of Chili, and afterwards of Peru. During many years of office he had amassed a great fortune, and he was returning to enjoy his gains in his native land. The ship upon which he sailed, the *Capitana*, was attacked by Captain Stayner's ship, the *Speaker*. Both fought stoutly—the one for plunder, the other for life. After the duel had raged for a while, it was discovered that the *Capitana* had been set on fire. The English did what they could to save, not only the wealth, but also the lives on board her. But " in the fire the Marquess' lady and one of his daughters fell down in a swoon, and were burnt. The Marquess himself had opportunity to have escaped, but seeing his lady and his daughter, whom he loved exceedingly, in that case, said he would die where they died, and embracing his lady was burnt also with them." Only the eldest son es-

---

[1] Stayner to the Generals of the Fleet, Sept. 9, 1656. Thurloe : State Papers, v. 399.

caped of all the family, "a most pregnant ingenious learned youth," of about sixteen years of age.[1]

Among the ships which soon after returned to England, escorting the booty which had been taken from the Spaniards, was the *Resolution*. Vice-Admiral Badiley had sailed his last voyage, and on November 7 he obtained his final discharge.[2] He retired to Wapping to spend the few remaining months of his life. He had served his country faithfully, but he had not, like many another bold seaman, made a fortune by so doing. It seems probable that his last days were spent in poverty, for beyond the sum legally due to him on his retirement, he only received £300 for his service in discovering two parcels of plate which had apparently been concealed by thievish seamen.[3] Many politicians had received lavish grants of lands and money for their services, but this generosity was not extended to those who had borne the brunt and turmoil of sea-warfare. The expenses of his trial, and of the publication of his "Answer," had probably exhausted the savings of his lifetime, and these were never made good to him. He recovered a small sum on account of his share in the *Peregrine*, which had been lost in the battle of Leghorn. The honesty of the man is shown even in this trifling transaction. He claimed £140, and he received £142 7s. 8d.[4]

After his retirement he endeavoured to add to

---

[1] Montagu to Thurloe, Sept. 19, 1656.  *Ib.*, pp. 433, 434.

[2] Cal. S.P.D., 1656–7, p. 463.

[3] *Ib.*, pp. 173, 517.

[4] *Ib.*, 1655–6, p. 493.

his income by contracting with the Navy Commissioners for the supply of wine to the ships which remained at sea with Blake. In this undertaking he was helped by his old friend Longland, who still represented England at Leghorn. Longland, at Badiley's order, shipped two hundred butts of wine for the use of the fleet; but he was evidently uneasy about the contract. "If the fleet should return home," he wrote to Badiley, "the beverage wine would be cast on our hands and lost, as the Customs would eat it up,"[1] and to Blackborne he wrote: "The Commissioners should not leave any purchased wines on our hands if the fleet is recalled, or they would ruin their servants."[2] But these protests arrived too late. The contract with Badiley had already been rescinded, and it is to be feared that the old Vice-Admiral was a considerable loser by the transaction.[3]

But although the naval authorities treated Badiley so shabbily, they constantly consulted him on questions upon which he was able to give them sound advice, more especially concerning the affairs of the Mediterranean Sea, and he was occasionally summoned to London to attend their meetings. Early in the year 1657 his health began to break

---

[1] Longland to Badiley, Mar. 9, 1656/7. Cal. S.P.D., 1656–7, p. 307.

[2] Longland to Blackborne, April 13, 1657. *Ib.*, p. 339.

[3] Blackborne to Navy Commissioners, Jan. 8, 1656/7. Returning Commissioners' order for a contract with Vice-Admiral Badiley for supplying the fleet with 200 or 300 tuns of wine from Leghorn, they since judging it more proper to leave that affair to the Victualler. *Ib.*, p. 507.

down.  On April 15, he wrote to the Admiralty Committee that he was not well enough to attend them, so he sent his thoughts in writing.[1]

He lived long enough to hear of his great commander's last and most brilliant victory, and his heart no doubt beat faster with pride and exultation when he learnt how Blake had dashed into the harbour of Santa Cruz de Teneriffe, and had destroyed the Spanish fleet.  But the end of both these brave seamen was not far off.  On August 7, 1657, when Blake lay dying on board the *George* as she entered Plymouth harbour, Richard Badiley was breathing his last at Wapping.[2]

[1] *Ib.* p. 541.
[2] Whitelocke says that Badiley died on Aug. 11.  Memorials, p. 665.  Giovanni Salvetti is a much more reliable authority. Whitelocke probably heard of the death of Badiley on Aug. 11.

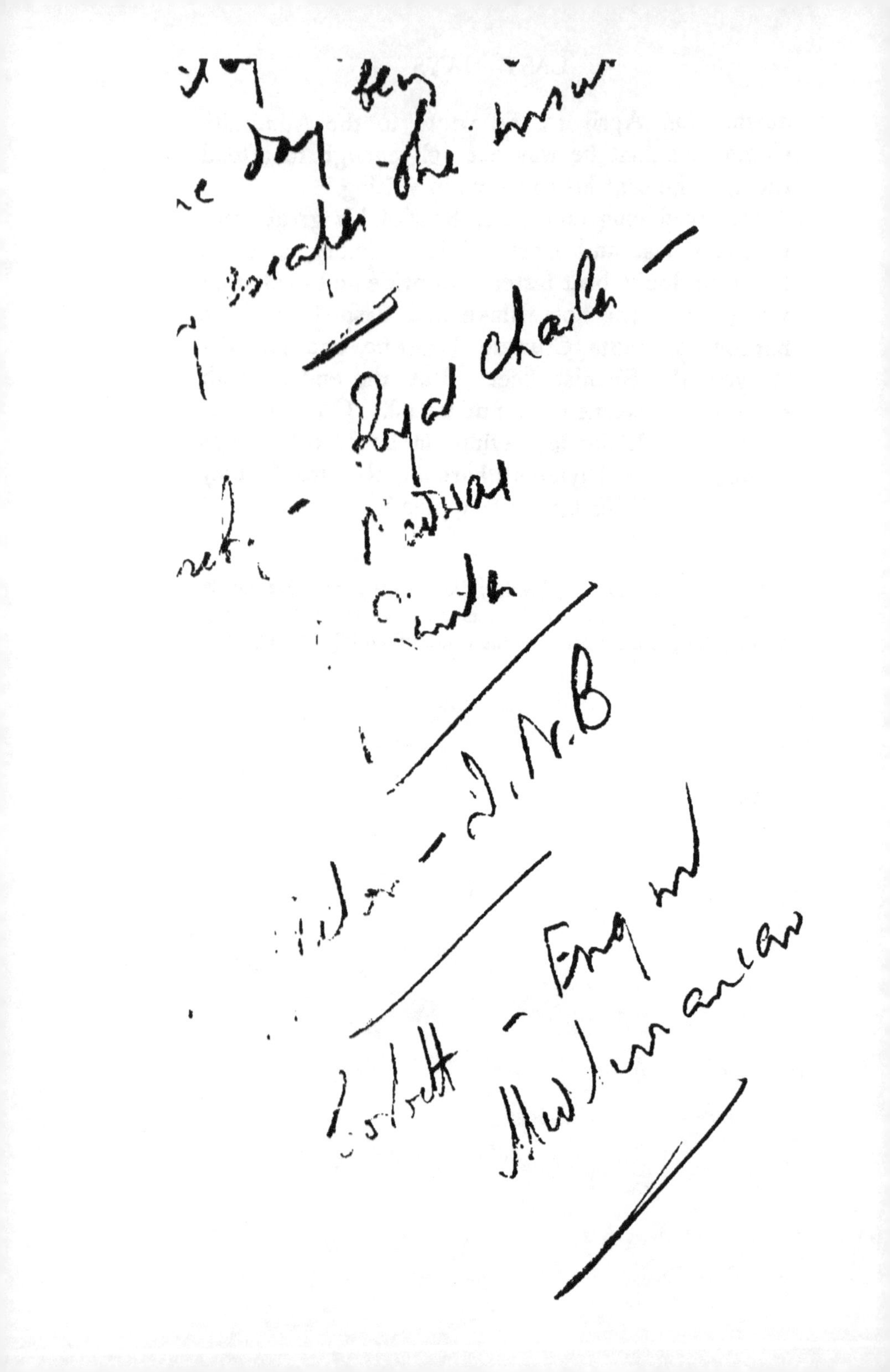

[illegible] fly
[illegible] day fly - the known
[illegible] israel [illegible]

ret. - Lloyd Charles -
[illegible] actual
Surah

[illegible] - D.N.B

[illegible] - England
[illegible] Mediterranean

Mediterranean

his letters to/from Cromwell

Any letters by Cromwell

Ireland

Rossetti

Scotland

# RUPERT, Prince Palatine

By EVA SCOTT

Late Scholar of Somerville College, Oxford.

With Twelve Illustrations from Contemporary Portraits and Engravings.

Demy 8vo.  15*s.* net.

" An uncommonly clever and erudite biography, ' Rupert, Prince Palatine,' in which she gives a most interesting sketch of the adventurous career of this remarkable man, and incidentally casts new light upon the history of the Civil War."—*Daily Mail.*

# A Russian Province of the North

By ALEXANDER PLATONOVICH ENGELHARDT

Governor of the Province of Archangel.

Translated from the Russian by HENRY COOKE.

With 90 Illustrations after Photographs and Three Maps.
Royal 8vo.  18*s.*

The aim of the writer of this work, a nobleman of infinite resource and energy, and a man whose ideas are essentially progressive, is to place before the public information concerning the little-known Russian Province of Archangel, which is likely at no distant date to become of first-rate commercial and naval importance.

"Abundantly illustrated with photographs of judiciously-selected landscapes, types of the people, cities, villages, monasteries, interiors and exteriors, and animals. This volume contains a mass of valuable statistical and geographical information, with Maps, Plans, and Tables. It is, on the whole, the most instructive account of a little-known European region that has been produced for some considerable time past."—*Morning Post.*

# The Second Afghan War

## 1878-79-80

Its Causes, its Conduct, and its Consequences

By COLONEL H. B. HANNA

Formerly belonging to the Punjab Frontier Force, and late commanding at Delhi.

In this book the author presents a faithful picture of the war itself, and draws attention to the right military lessons from its experiences.

Volume I. Now Ready. Demy 8vo.  10*s.* net.

" His knowledge is great, and his industry almost excessive. The ability with which his case is presented is considerable, and it is probable that in his main line his view is a well-founded one."—*Athenæum.*

ARCHIBALD CONSTABLE AND CO. WESTMINSTER

1

CONSTABLE'S
# Hand Atlas of India

A New Series of Sixty Maps and Plans prepared from Ordnance
and other Surveys under the direction of

## J. G. BARTHOLOMEW, F.R.G.S., F.R.S.E., etc.

This Atlas will be found of great use not only to tourists and travellers but also to readers of Indian history, as it contains twenty-two plans of the principal towns of our Indian Empire, based on the most recent surveys and officially revised to date in India.

The Topographical Section Maps are an accurate reduction of the Survey of India, and contain all the places described in Sir W. W. Hunter's "Gazetteer of India," according to his spelling.

The Military, Railway, Telegraph, and Mission Station Maps are designed to meet the requirements of the Military and Civil Service, also missionaries and business men who at present have no means of obtaining the information they require in a handy form.

The Index contains upwards of ten thousand names, and will be found more complete than any yet attempted on a similar scale.

Further to increase the utility of the work as a reference volume, an abstract of the 1891 Census has been added.

## Crown 8vo. Strongly bound in Half-Morocco. Price 14*s*.

UNIFORM WITH THE ABOVE
CONSTABLE'S
# Hand Gazetteer of India

Compiled under the direction of J. G. BARTHOLOMEW,
F.R.G.S.

And Edited with Additions by JAS. BURGESS, C.I.E., LL.D., etc.

The Hand Gazetteer of India is based on the Index to Constable's Hand Atlas of India, which contains nearly 12,000 place-names. To these have been added very largely from various sources, bringing the number of entries to close upon 20,000. The populations of districts, towns and villages, and the position of each place are clearly indicated, thus forming within a small compass a general reference book to the topography of India, and a companion volume to the Hand Atlas of India.

## Crown 8vo. Half-Morocco. Price 10*s*. 6*d*.

# The Chronology of India

## FROM THE EARLIEST TIMES TO THE BEGINNING OF THE SIXTEENTH CENTURY

### By C. MABEL DUFF (Mrs. W. R. RICKMERS)

Demy 8vo. Cloth. 15*s*. net.

"Mrs. Rickmers has arranged the volume as a table of events in chronological order. The marginal date represents the year B.C. or A.D. If only approximate, it is printed in italics. For the benefit of students engaged in epigraphical research, references to inscriptions have been specially noted. By way of supplementing the chronological tables a brief revised list of Indian dynasties is appended. The book is also provided with a copious and carefully arranged index. The work has been compiled with great care, and contains in a condensed form a vast mass of information and erudition."—*Daily News.*

ARCHIBALD CONSTABLE AND CO. WESTMINSTER

# A Northern Highway of the Tsar

### By AUBYN TREVOR-BATTYE, F.R.G.S.

Author of "Ice-bound on Kolguev," etc.

With numerous Illustrations.

#### Crown 8vo. 6s.

The Tsar of Russia has accepted the Dedication of this book, which treats of adventure in a wild, remote part of His Imperial Majesty's Dominions.

"Such a journey may therefore be regarded as quite exceptional and almost unique, and on that account alone it is well worthy of permanent record. Though Mr. Trevor-Battye tells his story with a light heart and unflagging spirit, it is an unbroken record of hardship, difficulty, exposure, privation, discomfort and incessant peril."—*Times*.

"A vivid and entertaining account of his journey."—*Literature*.

# On Plain and Peak: SPORT IN BOHEMIA AND TYROL

### By R. LLEWELLYN HODGSON

Illustrated by HER SERENE HIGHNESS PRINCESS MARY OF THURN AND TAXIS, and from Photographs.

#### Demy 8vo. 7s. 6d.

"An excellent idea of this lively volume may be obtained by glancing through the numerous illustrations. The drawings of Princess Mary of Thurn and Taxis are always admirable. The instantaneous Photographs of animals are equally good and, of course, thoroughly life-like."—*The Times*.

# The Sportswoman's Library

### 2 Vols. Edited by FRANCES E. SLAUGHTER

Dedicated by permission to the Marchioness of Worcester.

Fully Illustrated, cloth gilt, 12s. 6d. per vol.; half-leather, 15s. per vol.

The volumes may be purchased singly.

## CONTENTS OF THE TWO VOLUMES

### VOLUME I

1. English Women and Sport — The Editor.
2. Foxhunting — Mrs. Burn.
3. Hare Hunting — The Editor.
4. Shooting — The Hon. Mrs. Lancelot Lowther.
5. Fishing for Tarpon — Mrs. Murphy-Grimshaw.
6. Archery — Mrs. Berens and Miss Walrond.
7. Skating — Miss May Balfour.
8. Golf — Miss Starkie-Bence.
9. Croquet — Miss Spong.
   Appendix A. Golf Rules and Glossary.
   Appendix B. Croquet Rules.

### VOLUME II

1. Cruising and Small Yacht Racing on the Solent — Miss Barbara Hughes.
2. Punt Racing — Mrs. W. L. Wyllie.
3. In Red Deer Land — Mrs. Penn-Curzon.
4. Chase of the Carted Deer — The Editor.
5. Women's Hunters — The Editor.
6. Otter Hunting — Mrs. Wardell.
7. Salmon Fishing, with Notes on Trout and Coarse Fishing — Susan, Countess of Malmesbury.
8. Fly Fishing — The Editor.
9. Driving — Miss Massey-Mainwaring.
10. Cycling — Miss A. C. Hills.
11. Fancy Figures and Musical Rides — Miss Van Wart.
12. Tennis — Miss Maud Marshall.
    Appendix A. Glossary of Nautical Terms.
    Appendix B. Rules of Lawn Tennis.

"A book which, so far as my familiar knowledge of some branches of sport enables me to test it, is eminently practical and valuable."—*Country Life Illustrated*.

# The History of the Belvoir Hunt

### By T. F. DALE

With Five Photogravure Plates and numerous other Illustrations. Also a Hunting Map showing Historic Runs, and a Map of the Country hunted in the middle of this Century.

#### Demy 8vo. 21s. net

Also a Large Paper Edition limited to 75 copies. Price on application to the Booksellers.

# The Game of Polo

### By T. F. DALE ("Stoneclink" of *The Field*)

Containing a large number of full-page sepia plates illustrative of celebrated ponies, many text illustrations, and a photogravure portrait of Mr. JOHN WATSON.

### Demy 8vo. £1 1*s.* net.

"Mr. Dale goes over the whole ground, treating of the rise and development of polo in India and England, with much excellent advice on the training both of player and pony. The author writes in a pleasant, spirited style, and may be taken as an admirable guide for those who intend to practice polo either at home or abroad."—*The Globe.*

"A book which is likely to rank as the standard work on the subject."—*Morning Post.*

---

## TWO HANDY REFERENCE BOOKS ON INDIA

### Constable's
# Hand Atlas of India

A new series of Sixty Maps and Plans prepared from Ordnance and other Surveys under the direction of

### J. G. BARTHOLOMEW, F.R.G.S., F.R.S.E., etc.

This Atlas will be found of great use not only to tourists and travellers but also to readers of Indian history, as it contains twenty-two plans of the principal towns of our Indian Empire, based on the most recent surveys and officially revised to date in India.

The Topographical Section Maps are an accurate reduction of the Survey of India, and contain all the places described in Sir W. W. Hunter's "Gazetteer of India," according to his spelling.

The Military, Railway, Telegraph, and Mission Station Maps are designed to meet the requirements of the Military and Civil Service, also missionaries and business men who at present have no means of obtaining the information they require in a handy form.

The Index contains upwards of ten thousand names, and will be found more complete than any yet attempted on a similar scale.

Further to increase the utility of the work as a reference volume, an abstract of the 1891 Census has been added.

### Crown 8vo. Strongly bound in Half Morocco, 14*s.*

---

### UNIFORM WITH THE ABOVE

### Constable's
# Hand Gazetteer of India

Compiled under the direction of

### J. G. BARTHOLOMEW, F.R.G.S.

And Edited with Additions by JAS. BURGESS, C.I.E., LL.D., etc.

The Hand Gazetteer of India is based on the Index to Constable's Hand Atlas of India, which contains nearly 12,000 place-names. To these have been added very largely from various sources, bringing the number of entries to close upon 20,000. The populations of districts, towns and villages, and the position of each place are clearly indicated, thus forming within a small compass a general reference book to the topography of India, and a companion volume to the Hand Atlas of India.

### Crown 8vo. Half Morocco, 10*s.* 6*d.*

# Biography, Reminiscence and History

## Rupert, Prince Palatine

By EVA SCOTT

With Photogravure Frontispiece and many full-page Illustrations.

Demy 8vo. 15*s.* net.

"She has written a book which is alike delightful to read and valuable for purposes of historical study."—*Daily Telegraph.*

"It is altogether an excellent piece of historical writing; but the most notable feature of the book is the promise which it gives of the advent of a new historian in Miss Scott."—*Daily Mail.*

"It is a very interesting and welcome work—a permanent contribution to the literature of biography. It includes some attractive portraits."—*The Globe.*

## The Second Afghan War

1878-79-80.

### Its Causes, its Conduct, and its Consequences

By COLONEL H. B. HANNA

Formerly belonging to the Punjab Frontier Force, and late commanding at Delhi.

In this book the author presents a faithful picture of the war itself, and draws attention to the right military lessons from its experiences.

Volume I. now ready. Demy 8vo. 10*s.* net.

"The author writes with a very thorough knowledge of the subject; his facts are marshalled with remarkable skill, and his argumentation is exceptionally vigorous. These qualities mark his book as a valuable contribution towards the adequate understanding of a question which has not yet lost its importance."—*Glasgow Herald.*

## The Rise of Portuguese Power in India 1497-1550

By R. S. WHITEWAY

Bengal Civil Service (retired).

Demy 8vo. With Bibliography and Index, 15*s.* net.

"Mr. Whiteway has many of the best qualities of a historian. He has gone for his material to original documents, of which he gives an excellent bibliography, and he has resisted the temptation—which besets the historian of heroic feats of arms—to spend himself in picturesque anecdote. Yet though he has reduced his materials to convenient bulk, he has continued to draw the character of the Portuguese leaders so vividly, that his story has the human interest of the most exciting romance."—*Pall Mall Gazette.*

## Our Troubles in Poona and the Deccan

By ARTHUR TRAVERS CRAWFORD, C.M.G.

Late Commissioner at Poona.

Illustrated by HORACE VAN RUITH.

Demy 8vo. 14*s.*

"We have rarely come across a book which in all respects brings us closer to the realities of Indian life."—*St. James's Budget.*

# Life of Richard Badiley, Admiral

By THOMAS ALFRED SPALDING

Demy 8vo.

# The Life of Sir Charles Tilston Bright, C.E., M.P.

By EDWARD BRAILSFORD BRIGHT, C.E., and CHARLES BRIGHT, C.E., F.R.S.E.

With many Illustrations, Portraits, and Maps.

2 Vols. Demy 8vo. £3 3s. net.

### ABBREVIATED LIST OF CONTENTS

First Land and Underground Telegraphs — Engineership to the Magnetic Telegraph Company — Laying of the first effective Cable to Ireland.

The Atlantic Cable : Sir Charles Bright one the three original projectors, and engineer-in-chief.

Mediterranean Cables laid by Sir Charles Bright.

First Cable to India laid by Sir Charles Bright along the Persian Gulf—Board of Trade Commission on the Construction of Submarine Cables—Government Telegraph Bills —House of Commons Committees—Railway Telegraph Arbitrations.

Telegraphic Communication with our Colonies—Sir Charles Bright lays a line telegraphically uniting the West Indian Islands with the American Continent by over 5,000 miles of Cable.

"Reform," "Garrick," and "Royal Thames Yacht" Club Reminiscences.

Mining—Silver and Lead Mines in Servia—Electric Light Work : British Electric Light Company—Telephony : Government Telephone Case—Greek Railway.

Inventions—Scientific Papers and Speeches at the Institution of Civil Engineers, British Association, Geographical, Geological, and Astronomical Societies, and elsewhere.

Commissioner for H.M. Government at the Paris Electrical Exhibition : Reminiscences.

Presidency of the Institution of Electrical Engineers—Jubilee Year.

Etc.    Etc.    Etc.

# Emin Pasha : His Life and Work

By GEORGE SCHWEITZER

Compiled from his Journals, Letters, Scientific Notes, and from Official Documents. With an Introduction by R. W. FELKIN, M.D., F.R.S.E.

With a Portrait and Map.

2 Vols. Demy 8vo. 32s.

"The interesting collection of documents contained in these two volumes fills up an important gap in the chequered history of the Soudan and Central Africa during the last twenty-five years, and enables us better to understand the strange personality of Emin Pasha. All who are interested in this part of Africa—and who is not at present?—where the competition among the European powers is keenest, and where the forces of darkness are making their last stand, will welcome this English translation. . . . It is a piece of rare good fortune that Emin's carefully written and copious diaries have been so completely recovered from the hands into which they fell after his wanton murder by the Arab slavers in Central Africa. These diaries and letters shed light on several matters which were previously obscure."—*The Times.*

"His diaries give a graphic account of the difficulties he had to face during these trying years, of the worthlessness of the gang of officials whom he had with him, and the treacherous character of the native chiefs by whom he was surrounded."—*Daily Telegraph.*

### BY THE VICEROY OF INDIA

# Problems of the Far East—Japan, China, Korea

By the Right Hon. GEORGE N. CURZON, M.P.

New and revised edition. With numerous Illustrations and Maps.

Extra crown 8vo, 7s. 6d.

"We dealt so fully with the other contents of Mr. Curzon's volume at the time of first publication that it is only necessary to say that the extreme interest and importance of them is enhanced by recent events, in the light of which they are revised."—*Glasgow Herald.*

# Constable's Edition of " Boswell "

## COMPLETE IN 8 VOLUMES

# Boswell's Life of Johnson

### Edited by AUGUSTINE BIRRELL, Q.C., M.P.

With Portrait and Frontispieces in Photogravure by ALEXANDER ANSTED.

6 vols., fcap. 8vo, paper label, or cloth gilt, 12*s*. net the set.

Also in half leather, 18*s*. net the set.

Also in half vellum, price on application at the booksellers.

# Boswell's Tour to the Hebrides

# with Samuel Johnson, LL.D

### WITH NOTES BY SCOTT, CROKER, CHAMBERS, AND OTHERS.

In 2 vols., fcap. 8vo, paper label, or cloth gilt, gilt top, 4*s*. net the set.
Also bound in half leather, 6*s*. net the set.
Also in half-vellum, price on application at the booksellers.

The eight volumes, comprising " The Life " and " The Tour," in a
box, price 16*s*. net; or in half leather, £1 4*s*. net

# Fine Art

## English Contemporary Art

Translated from the French of ROBERT DE LA SIZERANNE by H. M.
POYNTER. With numerous Illustrations after G. F. WATTS, PROF.
HERKOMER, SIR JOHN MILLAIS, LORD LEIGHTON,
SIR E. BURNE-JONES, etc.

Demy 8vo. 12s.

"A most readable and well-written volume of criticism. . . . The book is well worth reading
for the virility and excellence of its author's style."—*Pall Mall Gazette.*

## London Impressions

Pictured by WILLIAM HYDE, with Notes by ALICE MEYNELL,
containing numerous photogravure plates and etchings printed on
hand-made paper.

Imperial 4to. 8 guineas net. Edition limited to 250 copies, on hand-
made paper. Also 12 copies on Japanese vellum, with duplicate set of
signed plates. 15 guineas net.

## English Illustration

### "The Sixties": 1855–70

### By GLEESON WHITE

With numerous Illustrations by—

| | | |
|---|---|---|
| H. H. ARMSTEAD, R.A. | GEORGE DU MAURIER | M. J. LAWLESS |
| FREDERICK SANDYS | FREDERICK WALKER, A.R.A. | ARTHUR HUGHES |
| SIR J. E. MILLAIS, P.R.A. | SIR JOHN TENNIEL | FORD MADOX BROWN |
| J. McNEILL WHISTLER | SIMEON SOLOMON | J. W. NORTH, A.R.A. |
| LORD LEIGHTON, P.R.A. | SIR E. J. POYNTER, P.R.A. | SIR E. BURNE-JONES |

Price £2 2s. net.

The object of this work is to give a record of the more important English illustrations that were published between 1855–70. That is to say, the period which saw
the rise of the pre-Raphaelite school, and the naturalistic movement which followed
so closely upon it.

"Contains a wealth of information concerning the English illustrated publications of 1860, now as
a whole for the first time collected."—*Daily Chronicle.*

## Medals and Decorations of the British Army and Navy

By JOHN HORSLEY MAYO. With many coloured plates. Fully
Illustrated. 2 vols. Super-royal 8vo. £3 3s. net.

"Of the manner in which the work has been carried out it is impossible to speak except in terms
of warm praise. We can scarcely imagine a barracks or a queen's ship that will be long without it."—
*Pall Mall Gazette.*

# Highland Dress, Arms, and Ornament

By LORD ARCHIBALD CAMPBELL

With 74 Illustrations, many of them by the collotype process, and a Coloured Plate.
Printed on hand-made paper.

Demy 8vo.   25*s.* net.

The edition is strictly limited to 250 copies.

# Ornament in European Silks

By ALAN S. COLE

With One Hundred and Sixty-nine Illustrations.

Crown 4to.   Bound in half vellum, gilt.   32*s.* net.

" His many illustrations, with the sometimes very ample descriptions printed under them, afford at a glance a most comprehensive survey of the course of woven pattern. . . . They are chosen with knowledge and judgment."—*Manchester Guardian.*

# London  Riverside  Churches

By A. E. DANIELL.     Illustrated by ALEXANDER ANSTED
Imperial 16mo.   6*s.*

" A little time ago Mr. Daniell gave us a book on the churches of the City of London.  He has now turned his attention to ' London Riverside Churches.'   He takes the Thames from Greenwich to Kingston, and tells the stories of the various notable churches touched by this line.  The book is fully illustrated from sketches by Alexander Ansted."—*Daily Chronicle.*

# London  City  Churches

By A. E. DANIELL.   With numerous Illustrations by LEONARD MARTIN, and a Map.

Imperial 16mo.   6*s.*   Second Edition, with Map.

" The author of this book knows the City churches one and all, and has studied their monuments and archives with the patient reverence of the true antiquarian, and, armed with the pen instead of the chisel, he has done his best to give permanent record to their claims on the nation as well as on the man in the street."—*Leeds Mercury.*

# The  Artist

An Illustrated Monthly Record of Arts, Crafts and Industries.
Conducted by A. TREVOR-BATTYE

Published Monthly, 1*s.*   Annual Subscription, 15*s.*, post free.

# Criticism, etc

## Commune of London, and other Studies

By J. HORACE ROUND, M.A.
Demy 8vo.   12s. net.   Edition limited to 750 copies.

## The Principles of Local Government

By G. LAURENCE GOMME
Statistical Officer to the London County Council.
Demy 8vo.   12s.

" His criticisms on the existing system show a thorough mastery of a complicated subject."—*Daily Chronicle.*
" The Statistical Office of the County Council has produced a work of great value on the Principles of Local Government."—*London.*
" There is much to be learned from Mr. Laurence Gomme's historical and analytical lectures."—*Daily Mail.*

## The Nation's Awakening

By SPENSER WILKINSON
Crown 8vo.   3s. 6d.
### CONTENTS

| | |
|---|---|
| Our Past Apathy. | The Organization of Government for |
| The Aims of the Great Powers. | the Defence of British Interests. |
| The Defence of British Interests. | The Idea of the Nation. |

" It will be seen that Mr. Wilkinson's programme is not lacking in ambition, . . . his pages contain many pregnant suggestions, and much food for reflection."—*The Times.*
" Of the highest value towards the formation of a national policy, of which we never stood in greater need."—*Athenæum.*

## The Rival Powers in Central Asia

Translated from the German of JOSEPH POPOWSKI by ARTHUR BARING BRABANT, and edited by CHAS. E. D. BLACK.   With a large map of the Pamir Region.
Demy 8vo.   12s. 6d.

" The historical sketch of Russia's advance into Asia is unique in its clearness and accuracy, . . . the book deserved to be translated.   It contains the most open avowal extant of an important school of European statesmen."—*The Statesman* (Calcutta).

## Human Immortality

TWO SUPPOSED OBJECTIONS TO THE DOCTRINE
By WILLIAM JAMES
Professor of Philosophy at Harvard University.
16mo.   2s. 6d.

" Professor James is well known as one of the most suggestive and original writers, and as certainly the most brilliant psychologist living.   Whatever, therefore, he has to say on this subject is worth listening to ; for he thinks freely, and he knows all that the scientist knows, and more too."—*The Spectator.*
" Deserves the attention of every one interested in the subject."—*Scotsman.*

# Fiction

CONSTABLE'S EDITIONS DE LUXE OF STANDARD NOVELS.

## THE WORKS OF

# Tobias Smollett

In 12 vols., demy 8vo. Limited to 750 copies for England and America.
Mr. W. E. HENLEY has written a critical essay specially for this edition.
Each volume contains an engraved Frontispiece.

Price 7s. 6d. net per volume.   Sold in sets only.

The following is the order of the volumes—

RODERICK RANDOM.  In 2 vols.

HUMPHRY CLINKER.  In 2 vols.

PEREGRINE PICKLE.  In 3 vols.

COUNT FATHOM.  In 2 vols.

SIR LAUNCELOT GREAVES.  In 1 vol.

HISTORY OF AN ATOM.  In 1 vol.

MISCELLANIES.  In 1 vol.

UNIFORM WITH THE ABOVE EDITION OF THE WORKS OF
SMOLLETT

## THE WORKS OF

# Henry Fielding

In 12 vols., demy 8vo. Limited to 750 copies for England and America.
Mr. EDMUND GOSSE has written a critical essay specially for this edition.
Each volume contains an etched Frontispiece.

Price 7s. 6d. net per volume.   Sold in sets only.

The following is the order of the volumes—

JOSEPH ANDREWS.  In 2 vols.

TOM JONES.  In 4 vols.

AMELIA.  In 3 vols.

JONATHAM WILD.  In 1 vol.

MISCELLANIES.  In 2 vols.

"It is an encouraging sign that publishers should find it profitable to include amid the flood of mediocre fiction (perhaps mediocre is too favourable) so many reprints of work that has stood the test of time.  It would be difficult, for instance, to recommend an antidote to the effeminate nastiness of the novel of sex more salutary than 'Tom Jones' or 'Joseph Andrews,' and here we have the first of a handsome edition of the Works of Henry Fielding (Constable)."—*The Times.*

"The first two volumes are to hand of the handsome 8vo edition of the Works of Henry Fielding, which Messrs. A. Constable & Co. are bringing out.  They are printed in a very bold type, on good paper, and are exceedingly pleasant to the eye."—*Athenæum.*

# The Works
of
# George Meredith

The first Uniform and Complete Edition of this Author's Works. The issue contains, in addition to all the Novels and Poems which are in print at the present time, some work which has not been accessible for many years.

Mr. Meredith has revised his Works for this edition, which he wishes to be regarded as textually final.

The first volume contains a Photogravure Portrait of Mr. Meredith, reproduced from a drawing made specially for this edition by Mr. J. S. Sargent, R.A.

The issue is limited to ONE THOUSAND COPIES for sale.

The edition consists of 32 volumes, price £16 16s. net.

" The form is stately, the type of new, clear, and beautiful design, worthy of the matter ; neither does the outside with its square backing of canvas and its red-brown cloth fall behind in comeliness."—*Manchester Guardian*.

"The size is convenient, the cover simple and good, the paper of the best, and the printing so brilliant that you might suppose it to come straight from a hand press."—*Westminster Gazette*.

". . . He can give you the most poignant, heart-rending tragedy in a ' Rhoda Fleming,' the most generous, Molièresque comedy in ' Evan Harrington.' Is there a more exquisite love-idyll in the language than that of ' Richard Feverel ' ?  A more terrible exposure of human weakness—all Swift's irony without his savagery—than ' The Egoist ' ? In ' Shagpat' has he not beaten the ' Arabian Nights' on their own ground ?  Is there a more brilliant exploit in the grotesque-pathetic than ' Harry Richmond' ?  His books are studies of the will-to-live in all its various incarnations—young women and old men, ' roaring human boys' and cranky sea-dogs, pedants, men-about-town, ' fine old English gentlemen,' tailors, rustics, demagogues, adventurers, and even wet-nurses. And he paints them all, not in the dull photographer's monochrome that the mere realist affects, but in rich warm colours, from a full palette."—*Daily Chronicle*.

THE CENTENARY EDITION OF

# The Stories of Samuel Lover

A complete uniform edition of the Stories of Samuel Lover.
Edited, with an Introduction and Notes, by J. T. O'DONOGHUE.

Large crown 8vo, bound in half linen, flat backs, 6s. per volume.

Order of volumes—                    Sold separately or in sets.

Vol. 1.  HANDY ANDY

„  2.  RORY O'MORE

„  3.  TREASURE TROVE; OR, "HE WOULD
           BE A GENTLEMAN"

„  4.  LEGENDS AND STORIES OF IRELAND
           FIRST SERIES

„  5.  LEGENDS AND STORIES OF IRELAND
           SECOND SERIES

„  6.  FURTHER STORIES OF IRELAND

The last volume includes Stories which have never been
previously collected.

"A capital reprint, in most artistically designed covers, and beautifully printed on special paper,
—at six shillings this is incontestably one of the cheapest and best editions on the market."—*Whitehall Review.*
"We congratulate the publishers on producing so fine a volume."—*The Outlook.*

In 12 volumes.  Imperial 16mo.

# The "Whitehall Edition"

OF THE WORKS OF

# William

# Shakespeare

Edited from the Original Texts by H. ARTHUR DOUBLEDAY,
with the assistance of T. GREGORY FOSTER and
ROBERT ELSON.

The Edition is issued in three forms—

Red Buckram,  price 5s. per volume, or £3  0s. the set of 12 vols.
Green Cloth,      „    5s.   „    „    £3 0s.         „      „
Half Parchment, „   6s.   „    „    £3 12s.        „      „

"The print is clear, the paper good, the margin sufficient, and the volume not too cumbersome."
—*The Times.*
"It combines, as far as possible, the requirements of a library and popular edition."—*The
Literary World.*

14

15

16